THE

Thomas Bustle was blessed when he entered the world, a bright and happy blue eyed boy. His brother Joseph followed two years later and he, too, was born under a star that sparkled and gave great light. An old Yankee cradle welcomed each of them and two loving parents faithfully rocked that cradle until the boys found their legs and the world beyond.

Tom and Joe were lucky because their parents, Cal and Esther, were attentive parents, who focused entirely on their children. The kids were amply fed and properly schooled. They were taught to be honest and respectful, too. Quite simply, they did everything in their power to equip the boys for the future that lay ahead. The boys would have difficulties along the way as we all do, but their challenges were greater than normal because of an accident at birth. Instead of growing up on a farm or in Times Square like everyone else in America, they grew to full maturity on a tiny island, a little fragment, a sun splashed phenomenon.

Many years ago, the island of Nantucket had become detached from a continent in much the same way as an iceberg is calved from its parental polar mass. It floated offshore for some time, finally coming to rest on a sand bar some thirty miles south of dry land. It may never have wished to leave but the rolling and bumping of tectonic plates dictated its departure and it simply went along for the ride.

So, too, did Tom and Joe. Once they were born and their heads stopped reeling from all that chaos in the birth canal they were very much at sea. As they grew into their teens, they learned that they would have to find a direction for themselves. They'd have to eke out a living much as their parents had done. Their family had lived on the island for several generations and had prospered modestly but after the depression and WW2, times were hard. It wouldn't be easy. The boys would have to make their own way. As we shall see, they tried and failed but they learned from each failure and advanced a bit until the next setback eroded the ground beneath them.

Opportunities are not as liberally sprinkled among islanders as they are among folks who live on mother earth. God may have provided a stunningly beautiful home for them but he failed to throw in any jobs. At least, the boys found themselves ill suited for the jobs that were thrown their way. The North Atlantic is harsh and unforgiving and as Tom always said with a shiver, "cold as hell". It was tough to stay on your feet. Both boys managed to avoid a proper Christian education, too, so neither would ever occupy the vicar's chair at St. Paul's. This meant that the island's two main sources of honest work--fishin' and preachin'--were closed to them. They'd have to find other ways to prosper, other ways to thrive.

Tom and Joe were men of vision, though. They thought beyond the confines of mere geographical accident. They thought internationally. They thought globally. They thought big, too big for the island that they were reluctant to leave. As island folk across the world will tell you, there is a gravitational pull back to it every time you leave that is more powerful than you can ever know.

The boys had been to the mainland a couple of times and seen things they never imagined from their perch on a sand bar way out there. They had grown tall and straight during the Eisenhower years and now were enjoying one of the most enthralling decades of the century. It was 1962 and as crazy as it seemed, a Bay Stater in the form of John Fitzgerald Kennedy ("JFK" to them) was the President of these United States.

A hometown boy was President and the boys would rise in the world, as well. Tom had worked at the general store for Doc Matthew so he knew something about hams and squash and tomatoes, too, so he got a seed catalogue and studied up. He found that sandy soil is good for carrots, strawberries and Swiss chard so he dug into his pocket and bought three cases of seeds. Doc signed up, so he had an outlet for his produce, too. No middle man.

He did have middle rodents, though. He had forgotten about the bunnies that inhabit every corner of the island, so he was sadly disappointed at the end of a beautiful summer when his crops reached the perfect shades of green, orange and red. Instead of enjoying a bountiful harvest and the proceeds therefrom, his gorgeous and succulent plants were plucked, pulled up and deflowered by those unholy varmints until nothing remained but piles of little round turds, nothing you could sell.

At the same time Tom was failing and learning about agriculture, Joe had turned his hand to goats. Goat milk was all the rage. "Just look at the papers!" he would tell himself as he walked out to the yard and the little pens where they slept at night. They were friendly, smelled better than hogs and gave fantastic, delicious milk.

Goats were proof against rodents, too. Goats are tough. Bunnies would not chew up his profits; that's for sure. That particular job fell to the Board of Health. When the town fathers learned about the goats, they went to the books. They seemed to fear goat husbandry as something different and as any islander will grudgingly admit, different is threatening.

To frustrate Joe's aspirations, the Board dug deep and were rewarded with a treasure trove of rules and regulations specially designed for the sole purpose of keeping the public safe and the breeder out of business. Mrs. Gordian Truscott, Chairperson of the Board—she of the Nantucket Truscotts—proudly quoted him chapter and verse from the municipal code that provided for "sanitary conditions" and proper pasteurization.

Joe had boiled the stuff in the kitchen in a big steel pot left over from the war and wasn't prepared to comply so that was that. He had bootlegged barrels of it all around town and created a terrific demand but they closed him down anyway. He could keep a she goat for "personal use" but that suggested a certain intimacy with little Helen that made him uncomfortable so he let her go, too.

For a long time, Tom and Joe went separate ways. They were always there for each other, willing to help and to accommodate but each had an identity and each wanted to express himself. Much like artists or people with wealth. Island people are like that. They're natural entrepeneurs not because they're inclined toward invention but because they're forced to adapt. They have to think their way through each day because scratching together a living is hard work. It usually means trying out a lot of ideas before settling on something that works.

Occasionally, the boys tried things together. They set up a lemonade stand near the ferry and smiled as each wave of happy visitors came and went but it left them with a lot of idle time between boats and little but sunburn to show at the end of the day. Tom quickly tired of it and Joe got sick of it too. Before long, they moved on.

They tried fiddlin'. Joe went one day to the St. Mary's rummage sale and came home with a small violin from a program some kid had quit. His long, muscular fingers were a squeeze but after a year or so he could bring out a dozen old favorites. Stephen Foster tunes. Camptown Races. That sort of thing. When Tom tried it, he was a natural. A God given talent. He would blush and then do you a bit from The Four Seasons if encouraged to do so.

They cultivated their musical tastes on those long, cold winter nights. Tom's were more traditional than Joe's who was the more exotic of the two. Tom loved DooWop and couldn't stand anything after the Beatles, not even the Rolling Stones. Joe found Flamenco and strains of Carlos Montoya's fevered strumming echoed continually through his little home. It often upset the dog, the stamping and the strumming and the castanets.

Over time, they grew distinct personalities and were no longer simply "the boys". Single men often do. No, single men invariably do. They settle into the embrace of such questionable lovers as the flat earth society or Catholicism and never look back. They talk to themselves and listen hard. If you looked closely, you could see Tom stomping his foot at a perceived outrage or personal bete noir. He could get indignant at almost anything but developers or self-promoters were the worst. He'd tuck in his chin, give you that bulldog look and you had to step away.

Joe became the more philosophical, the more relaxed of the two. He always felt he could drift along pretty well. That didn't mean he avoided the deep end; it just meant that he didn't drown. He could still keep his narrow chin out of the depths.

Weed helped. He smoked a bit every day and occasionally popped some into his oatmeal cookies. It added a subtle tone to the flavor, much like the sympathetic strings on a big guitar. Tom didn't care for it. Just like his taste in music, his taste in stimulants hadn't changed since he was twelve. Iced tea, made on the window every day, was all he drank. It added just enough caffeine to his system to keep him moving and convinced him that he was more clear thinking, more hard headed than the younger Joe. And, as older brothers do, he felt a bit superior. He just knew better; that's all. He knew better.

JOINT ENTERPRISE

At first, the boys followed much the same path. Indeed, they were often forced to follow the same path. Joe inherited Tom's crappy jobs just as he got his hand-me-down overalls and polo shirts. Tom delivered papers and passed his route on to Joe just after raking in his Christmas tips. He also mucked out the stable for their neighbor, a French Canadian whose daughter suffered from a cruel lisp that made her name, "Celeste", a torture each time she responded in class. Joe hated both jobs. He couldn't sleep all night, fearing as he did the ungodly ring of the alarm clock so he quit the paper route and forgot about the tips. As to the stables, they were too earthy, even for him.

All the kids wanted to work at White's, though. It was a general store but, as they joked, it had no generals for sale. Instead, it sold everything else. Its owner was an African American whose forebears had shipped out on whalers a hundred fifty years before, Owen "Doc" Mathew. As a young man, he had felt a justifiable pride in his ability to part the ocean seas. He could outswim every other living thing on the island and half of the fish. Now, he showed his pride by smiling broadly whenever his eyes rolled over the penny candy, ice cream, soda, seeds, tools, overalls, saddles, bridles, tractors, hay and gasoline. People flocked to White's from all over the island and often stood two deep at the counter.

Tom got the job on looks. He was tall even at a young age and although he and brother Joe maintained profiles all their lives that were like two pickets off an old wooden fence, he was really skinny as a kid, as thin as a rich man's smile. Whenever it came time to call on "volunteers", though, he always stood out. When they invited kids to work for the summer at White's, he stood out, too. It got him the job.

"Now, go stick that box of cabbages over there," Doc would say, gesturing vaguely in the direction of the barn. And Tom would do as he was told. He would always place the box of cabbages or crate of eggs in the wrong place but Doc was a kind and forgiving soul and patiently rearranged them himself. It wasn't important that Tom get it right; it was just important that he tried. This, of course, was a dangerous lesson for a young lad of fourteen as we shall see.

Tom gofered at White's for over two years, a long career for a teenaged boy. When he moved on to real industry, he banked all he learned and drew on those deposits whenever he felt tested or confused.

Joe was ready when Tom finished up at White's. Just like an Olympic sprinter, he ran alongside Tom until the perfect moment and seized the baton with all his might. He knew Tom was leaving, so he started hanging around at White's, helping old ladies with groceries and patting Doc's little Yorkie, Matilda. Soon, he became a fixture and his hire a foregone conclusion. It had to be.

He brought a little something else to the table, too. While Tom was conscientious, Joe was more of a people person. He could tell a joke and make people smile. He could carry out your seed, throw it in the back of your truck and wipe his brow, taking just long enough with that wipe to show the effort he had taken and just long enough for you to take that quarter out of your purse. You'd give it to him and he'd smile again, genuinely amazed at your munificence.

The boys hadn't benefitted from a vast inheritance. Unlike many of the city folk who visited the island each summer, they weren't going to surf through life on their offshore accounts. Their parents had been in the same fix as they were and would never pass fortunes down to them from tightly controlled LLCs or family trusts. They were lucky to survive much less pile up stock portfolios or municipal bonds. What were those, anyway?

When Tom graduated from high school Cal and Esther were so happy they went right out and bought him a half gallon of ice cream. They went right out and bought another one when Joe graduated, too. Neapolitan with vanilla, strawberry and chocolate. All three!

Those were happy days but they weren't the "stepping off point" kids enjoy today. It was, instead, time to "fish or cut bait". Neither boy could glide effortlessly through the world of White's or paper routes or lemonade stands any more. Come graduation day, they had to find work and that was a very difficult thing to do. They say Barcelona turned its back on the sea which means, apparently, that its people found other things to do. Tom did, too. A life on the ocean with all its bumps and tropical depressions was not for him so he tried his hand at manufacturing. He wasn't going to go to the VocTech or college to learn about it, either; he'd get paid from day one doing "OJT"--on the job training--and he knew just where to start.

About thirty years earlier, Parker Brothers had set out to make a fortune with their thrilling and exciting board game, Monopoly. It was a terrific success but they were the idea guys and manufacturing was not their natural milieu. They needed parts so they put out bids. A guy from the island, "Whiskey Bob" Truscott, got the contract. Like most small islanders, Bob thought big but humbly.

"We Truscotts are small thinkers," he used to say way too much. And when he won the bidding war, his business got big simply by building small. He took the originator's designs and refined them, finally turning out millions of little metal tokens, the teeny, tiny pieces we would all parade excitedly around the board. Hats. Thimbles. Boots. Thousands of them. Even little battleships for those still fond of war.

Tom went down and signed up. He didn't care if they put him in charge of the broom closet on the second floor. He wanted in. He wanted to be in the belly of the beast. He would learn manufacturing from the inside out. No need for school, just for a chance to learn. Maybe from the ubiquitous Truscotts.

They saw him coming and they picked him right up. He was too tall and too skinny to avoid. His stride was long, too, so he got up to you pretty quick. When he walked in the front door at Feldstein's— the name left over for good luck by Whiskey Bob—they greeted him with a smile. He quickly made out the application and skipped happily through their initial tour.

Cindy Truscott rolled her fat bottom and short legs through the manufacturing facility with surprising speed but Tom kept right up. As he followed her khaki covered behind up one aisle and down another, he tried to concentrate on her directions but just couldn't do it. He kept thinking about all those times he had mucked out stables and how much her haunches resembled those of a palomino there, Fred.

"Right here's where we make the boots," she announced proudly and pointed to something that might have been a drop forge. The guy with his handle on the wheel pulled the Camel out of his mouth, smiled back a toothless, greasy smile and then hauled on the crank. Smoke came out of the bottom and steam hissed out of the top. Tom was impressed. This could be fun!

The guys who made the thimbles seemed a cut above. They seemed to look at their job like a bunch of Bavarians. The press had to be made according to certain specifications and those specs had to be carefully checked at each and every point of the manufacturing process. This attitude accorded nicely with Tom's own sense of propriety so he was particularly attentive when they paused for a moment to explain things to him.

Each guy wore safety goggles and proper gloves, too. Each had on grey overalls with a pencil in the front and each guy resented the interruption. They knew they had to show Tom the process but it meant a drop in piece work, a cut in pay. Tom did not know about piece work but respected them and their time so he asked no questions and they quickly returned to their work.

"Thimbles!" Tom thought. "Who would have thought that so much could go into a thimble?" And not a real thimble, either, but a miniature thimble, a really small one good only for an infant or a six-toed cat. It was love at first sight. Tom would dedicate himself to thimbles, that and making his way in the world.

"We've got to haul ass if we want to see the hats," Cindy announced, thrusting her chubby little chin in the direction of Sector "C".

"Yes, ma'ame," Tom said with a nod, never taking his eyes off the Bavarians as they methodically banged out thimble after thimble, whole baskets of them. Wow!

That night, Tom reflected on his good fortune. He had scored his first real job on the first day of his quest. He had to chuckle about that. That was some righteous good luck. It would take a while, of course, but he would take apart that process bit by bit until he could put it back together in his sleep. He was on his way. Soon he could be making thimbles and hats and little toy trains himself. Why not?

Joe followed Tom's ascendancy like a bulldozer in low gear, grumbling at the restraints imposed by his youth. He had to endure the last two years of high school so he wasn't able to follow his brother into the world of heavy commerce. Instead, he watched and learned. And while Tom crept ever upward in the business world, learning how it worked, Joe took a more objective view. Tom learned the basics but Joe skipped right over them to the grander lessons at hand. One thing he learned was not a lesson coaxed on by Cindy Truscott: "You can make a whole lot of ridiculous crap but if somebody buys it, you'll end up rich."

Again, the boys were learning and learning curves are spectacularly unique to each and every one of us. Sometimes life is a slow plod and sometimes it's a steep and rapid climb. Sometimes it's a mess and sometimes, as in the case of the Bustles, it is transmuted by magical thinking into something mysterious and magnificent all at once. Tom had learned that it made no difference if you succeeded or failed, just so long as you tried. And Joe learned that people will buy the most foolish and silly things but if they buy enough of them you will become a very wealthy man, indeed. Both lessons stuck to them as tightly as fuzz on a peach. Small wonder they turned out as they did.

TOM AND CINDY

It took a while but eventually Tom realized that Cindy was paying a lot of attention to him. His job was still lifting and carrying but she checked up on him with alarming frequency. Guys who had risen much higher on the corporate ladder than "stocking clerk" got short shrift but Tom got a lot of attention from his boss. She was his "overseer" as they used to say when slavery still bestowed its benefits upon the land. She had a lot of say and she said it all. Whiskey Bob's sole daughter, next of kin and heir apparent, Cindy ruled as if born to it. Like royalty.

She got up early and met the trucks. She worked hard and didn't take time off. She'd pack boxes if she had to and chewed out her foremen if they lagged behind. Her job was her life and like workaholics across the globe, she looked down the corporate ladder for a suitable mate. She could see their shining faces, all upturned to meet her gaze and even though she knew they didn't adore her as much as it seemed, she chose to ignore that fact. When she saw Tom's smile and how happy she made him, she knew she was adored. She knew it.

Soon, Tom found himself promoted. He'd only been around a few months when he learned that the scrap heap was no longer his purview. They took him off nights, too. That fell to subordinates, something he'd never had before. He could sit once in a while. He even got a clipboard though he had nothing to mark but time.

At about six months, Whiskey Bob called him into the office. He needed the ledgers on top of the file cabinets and he no longer did anything that required physical exertion, not even climbing a ladder. As Tom shuffled the ladder into place, he could hear Bob muttering about something. As Cindy sat by, he made it clear: he had an axe to grind. "I'm sick and tired of dealing with these weiners!" he shouted. Tom froze in his tracks. He didn't even breathe. He had never heard the boss use such strong language and never seen him flushed and red in the face like this before. WB was always calm and cool, as cool as custard pie.

"These darned foxholes (You can imagine what he really meant!) can't seem to get out of bed in the morning!" He mopped his cheeks and looked mad enough to spit. In his right hand he held a stack of 3 by 6 punch cards and he slammed them down loudly on the desk.

"What do I have to do to get eight flappin' hours out of these guys!?!" Tom knew he didn't really mean "flappin", either. He meant something really bad that you only heard when someone was almost too mad to think. An uncomfortable quiet settled over the room. Cindy sat in the corner, chewing on the inside of her lip.

"Dock'em," was all she said. And when Bob turned in her direction, she repeated it. "Dock'em. Take it out of their pay," she said and meant it.

"I can't do that," Bob replied, "They're like family." He placed both hands down on the desk as if to pray, then shot back defiantly, "No! I'm not docking their pay. There has to be a better way."

"They're family that's eatin' your lunch," she said quietly but there was no mistaking the firmness in her tone. "You gotta dock'em."

WB just shook his head. Large droplets of perspiration streamed down on the desk from his fevered brow. His chubby features seemed to swell and his cheeks took on the color of a raspberry onestick. Again, the air stood still as if they were standing in a vacuum of some kind.

"Maybe I should just camp out down there where they punch in," he added. "I could just stand there and smile when they enter the building. Stand there right next to the punch clock. Maybe that would do it."

"Nope. I got it," Cindy said with a shake of the head. "I got it."

Pausing, she tapped her pencil on the top of her head and calculated.

"How d'they get paid?" she asked.

"Well, there's hourly and then they got a quota," replied her father. "They gotta put in eight hours and they gotta knock out so many doodads during each hour. At the end of the day if they're over, they get a bonus."

"Right. Right. We're not gonna do that any more," she said firmly. "We're gonna switch out. The heck with the darned punch cards."

"Whattaya mean?" Bob asked. "I gotta keep track of my guys, right?"

"Nope. You don't," she said, almost with a smirk. "You just gotta keep track of the doohickeys."

Bob had had it by this time. Even his beloved daughter couldn't tell him his own business. "That's horsefeathers!" he blurted angrily. "How will I keep track of their hours?"

Cindy knew better than to take him head on, so she ditched the eye roll and patiently explained the essence of manufacturing to him. "We can make these guys 'partners' or 'associates' or something by simply leaving them alone. They'd be like sharecroppers. They can come and go as they please. All they gotta do is crank out the gizmos." She let that thought sink in and then added, "Put Thomas in charge."

Bob shot Tom a worried glance out of the side of his eye. He wasn't buyin' but he wasn't walkin' away, either. A little air seemed to squeeze back into the room. When it looked as though they all could breathe again, she put in the clincher. "You can play nine holes before work, get here by ten and then just deal with the vendors."

Suddenly, Tom's clipboard made sense. He started thinking about graphs and spread sheets and how cool they looked on TV. Until then, he hadn't said a word but both Cindy and Bob looked at him now, sizing him up. Could he do it?

Bob spoke first. "By golly, that could work." He didn't want to give her a swelled head but he added, "That's not a bad idea." They all knew, though, that this was his ultimate compliment. This was the red-stockinged, blue ribboned seal of approval.

"Where would we start?" he asked. But that was right where Tom had the chops to step in. All those crates of stinky turnips and leaky boxes of PennZoil had left him with a healthy regard for numbers.

Moving them from one side of the barn to the other at White's had given him a genuine feel for basic math. A dread.

"Well, if you decided to do something like that," he started, showing proper deference, "…..you could take the quotas they're doing now and just divide them out. That would give you their average daily…..." and his voice trailed off.

But Bob picked it right up. "Yeah. And they'd just crank out the widgets all day…… Perfect." He smiled for the first time in a long, long time. He almost wept but kept his head down so they couldn't see. "This might work," he thought. And his troubles were over. More air came into the room and they all relaxed. He felt at peace and a deep love for his fellow man.

After a bit, Cindy whacked her palms down on her beefy thighs and stood up. "Look, I'll take Thomas down to the floor and start crunching the numbers. You've got nothing to lose," she said with a shrug, almost as though Whiskey Bob had thought it all up. "Try out the numbers and if they work, fine. If not, there's no harm done."

They all smiled anxious smiles to one another that clearly showed how relieved they were. Bob slumped back into his chair and Tom squeezed silently out the door in Cindy's wake. His mind was spinning. He'd just gotten a gigantic promotion and he hadn't even asked for it.

Right place, right time? What? But he didn't want to think about it too much; he just wanted to enjoy the moment and the thrill of going big time. No one mentioned moving the ledgers again, either. Nobody cared. Richie from shipping got the job instead and needed the next day off to see to the spasm between L-3 and L-4 that was the natural consequence therof.

ASPIRATIONS

All this time, while Tom was making his mark, Joe was biding his time, slowly checking off the boxes. Algebra (check), operating a motor vehicle that wasn't a tractor (check), masturbation (Check) and boat haulin' (again, check). He still hadn't had his hand on a breast but he had thought about it a lot. He thought about it so much that it often detracted from the time he spent plotting his way in life. It intruded; it snuck right in. It dominated. And it held him back.

Clouded as his mind was, though, Joe still thought as much as he could about his future. Tom had been lucky--no question--but Joe wasn't going to trust to luck. Tom fell into it but Joe was going to work out a job search for himself. He'd do it systematically.

Unlike Tom, Joe sought the advice of experts. He went directly to the guidance office and smiled up Mrs. Crisp until she stopped what she was doing and gave him her full attention. Forty, at least, and as stiff as rebar, she was an odd choice for one of the caring professions. She looked more like a prison guard or the lady who gives dominatrix lessons on Imperial cruises. Squinting through her little tortoise shell glasses, she primped up her hair and folded her hands on the desk.

"What do you have in mind?" she asked.

"Well, I want to make a lot of money," he said with admirable clarity.

"Oh, that's nice but how?" she persisted.

"I don't know," he replied, smiling again a little less confidently.

Mrs. Crisp paused for a moment, threw back her shoulders and quite by accident, heaved her formidable breasts in his face. The sight of those beauties shattered not only his confidence but his resolve, as well.

He sank a little in his chair and felt a stirring in his pants.

Unaware of Joe's discomfiture, she picked up his file and thumbed through it for a pattern of some kind. Perhaps she'd find the inner man.

"Well, it says here that you did well at ceramics and made some very fine ash trays."

This little bit of praise, modest though it was, gave Joe just the boost he needed to continue with his plan. Summoning all his strength, he forced himself to look her straight in the eye, avoiding the magnificent breasts that cried out so strongly for his gaze. Just enough of his savoir faire returned to allow him to confess, "Yes, I did." Clearing his throat, he strained to recover his self command.

"I really liked the class, almost as much as gym," he said enthusiastically.

This left Mrs. Crisp in a bind. She wanted to say something that would encourage the boy but there was little upon which she could build. She blinked at him instead and forced a smile.

"Mostly, I've worked," he said, regaining his stride. "I've had a bunch of jobs ever since I got my first paper route and I'm a real fast learner."

Mrs. Crisp doubted this last statement as her eyes slid over the parade of "C"'s on his record but let it go. He seemed earnest, certainly. Naive, but earnest. Perhaps he really did want to make something of himself.

"I have an idea," she said, closing the folder. "What if you help me this afternoon?" She paused for politeness sake and then continued the thought. "I've got to make room in my office for another body, a 'health' professional. We can talk more about it then."

Joe was delighted. He shot out of his chair, thinking of the opportunity. "I'd be happy to help," he said graciously. "Sure enough. What time?"

"You come back at three and we'll move this stuff around. Make room for my new assistant." She smiled, too, to show that it wasn't all going to be work. She didn't want him to think she was taking advantage of him which, of course, she was. He gave her a faux salute and ducked out of the room.

Joe didn't know it at the time but the two great passions of his life had just conjoined. Riches and red hot mamas. He did know that he was in for a long day. By the time he returned to his history class he had lost all interest in the Gadsden Purchase. Instead, he found himself in the grip of two very powerful forces: sex and the denial of sex. He was aching for a look at Mrs. Crisp in the buff but was heartily ashamed of himself for lusting after a woman two or three times his age. Or so. He wasn't sure until he slowly did the division, carrying the six.

Lunch was a trial. He couldn't eat a thing, a sensation that neither he nor his brother had ever felt before. He picked up an apple, took a sour-faced bite out of it and then threw it away. All he could think about was helping Mrs. Crisp and seeing her emerge naked from beneath a shimmering waterfall.

He struggled to figure it out. He had seen lots of girls in their bathing suits and it always gave him a little tingle but this was different. Mrs. Crisp had been wearing a skirt and blouse, the same navy skirt and white blouse he had seen her wear a hundred times, a sort of uniform. But today, when she stretched back and hiked up her shoulders, his eyeballs had nearly bounced out of his head. This was an older woman, a woman with experience, a woman at the peak of her beauty. Three o'clock would never come and when it did, what then? He was more anxious by the minute, as jacked up as a spider on a frying pan.

Mr. Finney called on him in Geometry. He knew angles from the pool table in the back of Bartlett's Garage, too, but his mouth went dry and he simply coughed a quiet, "Mmmmunh?" That earned him a sharp reproach from the teacher and the whispered, "Jesus, Joe!" from his buddy, Solly Higgins. "Wake the fuck up!"

When the bell sounded, the reality of his appointment with Mrs. Crisp hit him like a belt in the chops. The fifteen minutes until their meeting was the longest fifteen minutes of his short life. When his friends called out to him and Solly tried to sympathize about trapezoids, he had nothing to say. His face flushed and he could still feel that aching in his groin. He was too frightened to go and too frightened not to go. His shaky legs got him to her room, but just.

Mrs. Crisp took no notice of his blushes. She was all business. "It's very kind of you to help," she started, almost as if he'd volunteered. She smiled a tight smile to him and started to explain.

"We've got to make space for two in here without making the place feel cramped," she said, adjusting her specs. Pointing in the direction of an old oak desk, she added, "I think we'll start with that desk right there."

It weighed a ton. Two tons. But somehow, Joe managed to slide it a few feet closer to the wall. This allowed room to shift a file cabinet. She had already had a hand truck delivered, one Joe had used before and knew how to handle. She pointed where she wanted the file cabinet to go and he easily managed the job. Slowly, he felt more self-assured. He had accomplished two small tasks with no difficulty and took a minute to mop his brow and gaze at his handiwork.

"No time for resting on our laurels," she declared, almost smiling again. "We've got to move this other desk and cabinets and then tidy the place up. All of this stuff….," pointing to stacks of calendars and books and charts, "….has to be organized, too."

He simply followed her direction. Slowly, the ache in his trousers subsided and he started to feel okay. He actively tried to avoid peeks at her chest but still snuck a little look whenever given the chance. He no longer avoided her eye, though. He wasn't nearly as afraid of her as he had been one short hour before.

They were becoming a "team" but not a team as in a mule team or a team of oxen. She was the decider and director and he was the mule team but "team" in the sense that they were acting together. Working together. He started to like it. He certainly liked the relief he felt and began to think of himself as conscientious, almost like Tom. A guy who could do stuff.

Soon, the room started to make sense. The two desks were aligned but there was space enough between them for a waste paper basket and a rack for paper and pens. The large file cabinets had been lined up along the wall, thereby taking up as little floor space as possible. There was a certain harmony. It looked good.

When they finished, Mrs. Crisp said, "Well, you're a pretty good worker." He knew that was high praise coming from her. "I always thought your brother was the worker and you were the dreamer."

"Well, I….," but she held up her hand.

"Nope. That was a good job. Thank you." Again, he almost thought she was showing real approval.

"A'course," he muttered, although he would carefully avoid any and all risk of being dragooned a second time. He couldn't face those breasts again, not for love or money. It was all too confusing. What was he thinking? Was he queer in some way? Why was he lusting like a ferret after a big, scary middle-aged woman? Was he crazy or something? All these thoughts came rushing back and all he could do was slink out of the room. He got out quickly before she could bring up his future again. He couldn't take that, for sure.

In fourth grade he had been teacher's pet for about two weeks. It felt great. Was it that? No! This was more than that. That was kid stuff. This was the real thing. He was so churned up by his inner conflicts that he upchucked into the back of his throat and had to rush for the bath room to rinse out his mouth.

His mind raced frantically back and forth between two diametrically opposed thoughts: She wanted him; he could tell. She wanted to take advantage of him. He could tell that, too. He wasn't a complete stooge.

But why him? Why did she pick him? Surely, there was something there. Instinctively, he knew he needed more information. Just who and what was Mrs. Crisp? Where, when and how? Setting his jaw so hard the muscles bulged in his cheeks, he resolved to find out. He wanted in.

THE BEGINNING OF TIME

But before we venture further into the boys' first tentative grasps on the line that brought forth their future, it's necessary to return to the past, to the time before they were born, before the roundeyes ruled the world.

We've all enjoyed those wonderful tales of peace and harmony that the first Americans passed down to us. We know they're romanticized versions of the real story, one of sickness, privation and betrayal but we love the stories and feel better each time we repeat them to ourselves. We make hand turkeys from the time we're four; we love them so much.

That's not how it happened, though. We are the first Americans, that's true, but the people who inhabited this land before we arrived tell a different story. They enjoyed the bounty of our shores before the arrival of the Mayflower and didn't have as happy an experience. Truth be told, they'd probably like it back the way it used to be with a beaver in every pond and so many deer that you slept next to them at night.

New Englanders and those who still cling to the rocks and the sand on out islands like Nantucket know the truth but unlike those of us who have forgotten, they feel it in their bones. They know they kicked the native people out; they still fish their shores and scavenge their forests, just like the native Naumkeags and the Wampanoag. They can hear them in the woods and they can see them in the waters; they're that close. They feel a bit of shame each time they haul a striper out of the depths or put up a pheasant in the bush. We're all immigrants, intruders on a land meant solely for those ancient tribes.

As youngsters, ranging in the wild, the boys often thought that they might just be the first Americans to set foot on *that* particular stone. Prehistoric men, Native Americans had certainly stepped on that stone but not us. Not the roundeyes. Accordingly, both Tom and Joe felt a deep and genuine humility from the time they took their first steps. They were simply not good enough to live where they lived and nowhere near good enough to profit by it. Stuck here, at this time and place and at this point in our history, they just wanted to get by. They didn't want to take advantage of the land, just earn enough to sit back and relax at the end of the day.

We need to remember this because it's easy to be critical of the boys as they made their slow, slow way in the world. Most of us would have done better than they did but we must remember the limitations imposed by humility. It haunts our thoughts and it prevents us from reaching higher and higher and higher still.

At some point, Tom and Joe were going to realize that they were very lucky, indeed, to have attained the modest heights they reached. At some point, they would reflect and as any entrepeneur or real gambler will tell you, reflection is the sworn enemy of mindless greed. At best, it slows you down and at the worst, it makes you afraid to take more.

FELDSTEIN'S

At first, Cindy and Tom just poked around on the floor. They saw a varied work force that ran the gamut from the guys who were highly skilled to the guys who were highly lucky to have a job. They then went to the performance charts and saw that the highly skilled guys earned more than the highly lucky guys but not a lot more. Cindy's new system of piece work would reward the skilled guys and motivate the rest. Genius.

They started to work closely now. Tom was curious and, after all, had just been elevated in the world. But Cindy knew her onions and if not personable, she was focused and fair. He started to admire her and began to relax because he sensed that she wanted him to succeed. He even caught her eyeing him sometimes, the way you'd size up one of those Thanksgiving turkeys.

A week later, they got the guys together. They all groaned when they found out about the "short 15 minute meeting after work on Thursday" but Cindy calmed them all down with this assurance: "You're all going to start making more money." That fast (!!), they were already spending it.

"Right here we've got the best work force in the state," she started, crossing the line into bullpuckie. "You guys are the best," she continued, crossing the line again but in a way that they understood. This was gonna be a shmooze.

"We've all been doing great here," she smiled, waving her hand across a an ocean of thoroughly blank stares. "We've all made a buck and will continue to make a buck." She paused and added, "...a good buck." That got their interest.

"Up until now, we've turned out widgets and whatnots and refined our manufacturing process to the point where we can equal any company on the mainland." The guys all nodded at that. They were a good team and worked hard and got the job done. As she knew, guys are always way too susceptible to flattery and when technical language like "process" is thrown in, they positively glow.

"...So Bob and I have decided to give something a try." She paused just a millisecond to see that they were listening and then went on. "We've always had a split system here, a system split between piece work and hourly rates........." That got their attention. Frowns and squints started to appear. Was she gonna change somethin'?

".....But after thinking about it a bit and studying the charts, we've decided to try something a little different."

How different, they wondered? She saw a couple guys clench their teeth. One guy pawed his crotch.

"We're going to scrap the time cards. We're going to keep them punched out every day so we know who's here and who isn't, but we're gonna let you guys make your own schedules. Within reason, of course."

They loved that idea. She even got a couple of eager smiles. They were thinking about it, though, still worried. Change is scary.

"We want to make every guy his own boss." They liked that, too, she could tell.

"We're going to put you strictly on piece work so if you want to stay late and crank out more stuff, you get paid for it. If you want to take a few hours off, that's okay, too. So long as at the end of the week you continue to meet quotas." Mostly they looked puzzled, now. But not hostile, at least not real hostile.

"We're gonna try this system for a couple of months and see how it works. We think you guys are gonna make a lot more money and that means we can ship more stuff. It's good for everyone."

This was quite a lengthy speech for her. She'd only addressed the guys a few times before and those were announcements about the new Coke machine and the time they left the lunch room an ungodly disaster.

Tom just looked on. Some of the guys couldn't have looked more puzzled if crawdads crawled out of their ears. The sharp ones, though, the Bavarians and the guys who stamped out the wheelbarrows, could see it right away. They could continue to spin out their widgets but they didn't have to take an hour for lunch or their mandatory fifteen minute breaks at 10 and 2. That time, or a part of that time, could be spent making moolah. Glorious, splendiferous Monet! Hootchie Mama!

Well, they didn't exactly applaud but when there were questions, they were not negative. No bad juju developed and the men seemed to be taking it pretty well. They were assured that this was just a trial period and that they'd see how it all worked in a month or two. The new program wouldn't even start for two weeks so they could think about it and check back with Cindy any time. Or Tom.

She snuck that in. Tom had always been the gofer, little more than lobby boy for the whole plant. Anybody could boss him around. Now, he was (apparently) part of the office staff. If it wasn't for the danger of strangling in one of the ever-spinning, hyperactive machines, he might have worn a tie.

Most of the guys had only half heard the part about Tom and nobody paid much attention anyway. They knew who was in charge. The kid was now the office boy. They'd seen them come and go before. Their only thought was that weekly check. They were all about to earn a lot more money. A lot more.

THE FIRST KISS

Joe had had a crush on Patty DeSimone for over a month. He sat two rows behind her and one row to the left so basically, his vantage point had been from the Southwest. From Seven O'Clock, if you sailed.

Miss Alberico had been a great teacher and he had done alright, right through fourth grade so when he cruised into fifth he did so with a jaunty stride. He had mowed lawns and delivered papers that summer and spent his evenings playing second base for the Mustard Seeds, a team of heavy hitters sponsored by St. Anthony's.

Patty had never been to a game nor had she been one of his customers. She lived more toward S'conset in one of the old grey cottages. But she had seen him in class and had been smiling to him recently in the hall. Her hook was opposite his and every day when she hung up her jacket she would sneak a little peek at him. He knew it because she always seemed to catch him when he snuck a peek at her.

Patty was Italian and exotic. Her breasts had already started pushing against her sweater by the time she was twelve. Joe's ardor was beyond any affection he had felt for anything in his life, even Mickey Mantle. Her allure was exquisitely powerful, almost painful. He wasn't going to admit it, though. It was cruel, that terrible longing….. Better to stick to nature magazines and bathroom tissue. At least, then he could sleep.

One day, just before boarding the bus, they stood nervously next to each other. The other kids edged forward to board but he and Patty hung back underneath the iron fire escape that led to the second floor. Suddenly, inexplicably, he was overcome with passion. His face got hot and his ears burned like a flounder tossed face down on the griddle.

Joe could have been in Phoenix; he could have been in Gay Paree. He was definitely out of his mind, though. But, nature being nature, he leaned in her direction and puckered up his lips. Amazingly, she did the same. They held their lips together for less than a second and when they parted, opened their eyes. She was already smiling and for one brief second, he felt like smiling, too. Then, he heard all the kids on the bus. They were screaming and shouting and stomping and laughing and continued to do so for the rest of his life, or so it seemed. Later, he remembered thinking, "I sure as shit won't do that again."

In many ways, Joe had been lucky. According to Gray's anatomy, when you're ten or twelve, all your glands are unsecured and therefore floating around untethered in your body. Full maturity is a long way off and if you're a boy and you're still singing soprano in the choir, so is your pubic hair.

Joe hadn't yet felt the shame and degradation of the fully grown male. He had only been stung. His little heart hadn't been broken but he knew he'd never be able to handle that pain again. It would be too much for him. He had all the pride of a full grown man but unlike a fully grown man, he had not yet become accustomed to humiliation. He had learned a valuable lesson: Some pain can be avoided. He'd be more careful next time. When he saw her the next day at school, he was guided by his instincts and ran away. He also started to feel sorry for himself with real conviction as only a fully grown man can.

Your subconscious is a funny thing, though. Once you reach sixteen and your glands have found their moorings, your subconscious is still working on your sex career. You don't have to worry about it; ninety percent of your energy, whether you know it or not, is directed toward that moment when you glide gracefully to the top of the waterfall and take that magnificent plunge. It's built into you as much as your need to breathe; maybe more so. Nobody knows for sure.

Joe had stepped back after that first time when he put his toe into the deep, deep pool of sexual delights but he hadn't taken his eyes off the great sweep of God's blue horizon. As time passed and he got further and further from the moment of his disgrace, he figured out that he could have a lot of fun and a lot of sex. He just wouldn't make a spectacle of himself or become the object of ridicule, the foolboy for everyone else. He'd keep his focus and wait until the proper opportunity came his way.

Joe's moment was exactly like all of our moments, unexpected. Much as he wanted to think of himself as clever, he fell into it just like the rest of us. It wasn't a moment that he built toward like the time his bank book read "$100.02". It wasn't an assault on Everest; it was harder, way harder. And no plans have ever been known to work. It just happens.

By the time he was seeking Mrs. Crisp's good counsel, he had already logged some thirteen first kisses. They had mainly been at parties where the cool kids played Spin the Bottle or Closet Cuddle. Each kiss had, if anything, been even more perfunctory than Patty's but he had learned to make that little smooch sound with his lips: "TSSK". He had traveled a long way from the silent kiss he had shared with Patty. He was goin' downtown. No doubt about it!

Mrs. Crisp made him want to venture further into the waters, if not to the point of full immersion, then at least waist deep. The blood rushed in his temples when he thought of that, the next step into the depths. It started to possess him, erasing every other productive thought but his sensate self reminded him of the odds of advancing further. It helped to calm him down. He would bide his time, look for an opportunity and then...... see what happened.

THE FLOOR

Friday morning the floor was buzzing. The guys were wary but as they talked it out, this new piece work thing sounded good. Most had spoken to their wives, too, and had found them pretty receptive. "Why not?" was more the response than, "Sonsabitches!" Whiskey Bob had always treated them fair and square. Even his name was a joke. He never drank anything stronger than buttermilk and never to excess. He was always a good boss. If he thought it was a good idea, then it probably was a good idea.

Even then, it was just a trial. If it worked out, fine. If it didn't, they could go back to the old ways where their weekly income was split between the hourly rate and the number of pieces they'd racked up. It sounded okay. Grumbles started to fade away.

When Tom and Cindy appeared, the guys assembled without much fuss. A couple guys lit up. The others wiped their hands on oil rags or looked back over their shoulders at the machines. One or two guys smiled a bit, something they never did while they were watching the machinery. It was a good sign.

Cindy went first to the Bavarians. They looked to a man like guys on a Mercedes Benz assembly line: Stiff. Cocky. Conservative. When she asked Ollie Blumberg, the sole Swede on the crew, what he thought, he said as he always did, "Yah, sure." His English wasn't too good and that was his response to most things, be it an extra doughnut or an admission of guilt at traffic court.

That little assurance gave her the confidence to tackle one or two of the real Bavarians and they responded positively, as well.

"Do you think you'll make more money?" she asked.

"Yah, sure," said Rudy, mimicking Ollie and getting smiles from all the boys.

"No, really," she went on, "What do you think?"

"I think it's good," he said stiffly. He didn't want to say more but as she waited for him to continue, he forced himself to add, "I think we'll make a little more."

"Twenty bucks a week can make a difference," Cindy said firmly, as if she knew what that meant to them. They nodded grimly, knowing exactly what that meant to them. A bike for little Teddy. A roast on Sunday now and then.

"So we're going to look at your quotas and leave the rest to you. We're going to be as fair as possible and put you in charge of the work," she said finally, giving them a glimpse of her bright white teeth. As they walked away, Tom remained silent and clutched his clipboard as if it was an anchor in a storm. Cindy shot them a glance and gave them all a chubby thumbs up.

Bob and Cindy had been massaging the numbers, too. They argued about the quotas with Cindy leaning toward stricter guidelines and Bob showing his characteristic timidity. They talked about the thimbles first.

"I see them at 40 per hour, about 320 a day," Cindy said.

"That's way too much," Bob replied, "I gotta say maybe 35 per hour and around 280 would be fair." Cindy waved her finger at him and shook her head but remained silent. Eventually, they settled on 300. They did the same for most of the others, only reducing the number on battleships which required a bit more finishing what with the ordinance and all.

By week's end they had their numbers and they brought them down to the floor. Tom hadn't contributed much; he had shuffled a lot from foot to foot but he took it all in. When Cindy and Bob assembled the guys again, Tom stood to one side until the end of the meeting when they were told that he would be the one keeping track. He learned about it at the same time as the floor guys. Cindy must have thought of that, he figured. She's the numbers guy, for sure.

They all looked at the calendar. The new program would swing into effect on September first so the guys prepared themselves mentally for what they mainly saw as a foot race to riches. "May the best man win!" they all thought, whether they admitted it or not.

"Those idiots on wheelbarrows are so screwed," Mike said to Ollie, hauling out a Camel and lighting it with an old Zippo from Uncle Sam.

Mike's hats would pop out of the press like whole wheat out of the toaster and he'd be knocking down some really good bucks.

"Sure, sure," replied Ollie. "Yah, sure." His job was secure, he thought because although thimbles needed a little polishing, they came out of a straightforward mold, dimples and all. He could churn them out at speed. He was sure of it. He'd be the one laughing on Friday night, yah sure. Yah sure!

It all worked just like that, too, for the first week. The guys showed up early and stayed late. Time cards were punched but not even Bob looked at them after the first couple of days. The guys were whalin'!

The whole place was swingin' and swayin' like a ship at sea. They turned out so many whizbangs that they had to call UHAULIT for an extra truck on Wednesday night. Morale soared like a party balloon and even those challenged by basic math were totting up their sums. They all made their quotas but then kept on banging out those wheelbarrows and thimbles, battleships and hats. What a week!

It felt strange to Tom. He walked the floor and watched the guys as they churned through one ingot of base metal after another, the cheap, shiny junk that went into the molds. The guys were chowin' on that stuff, he thought. They're killin' it!

Then Ollie's buddy knocked off the end of his toe. He had been outperforming every other guy in Sector C until his foot missed the pedal and 1,700 pounds of punch press came down and hit his right foot, clipping off the pinkie. Later on, he reckoned that it hadn't been much use to him anyway, but it sure hurt that day. It hurt a lot. It also took him off piece work for a week so his pay check looked pretty small that Friday: Nothin'.

The guys started to bicker, too. They abandoned their leisurely island pace and went Hell for Leather at maxing out production. If one guy did one thing to slow things down he drew the unmitigated ire of all his friends. You had to concentrate and you had to grit your teeth to whack out those doodads and if you didn't you ran the risk of isolation or worse: real rage.

The guys had always gotten along real well. That, or they ignored each other. But if your team slid just a little, it affected the bottom line. Seen one way, if you fouled up you were taking money away from your buddies and they called you on it. Don't forget: The trucks were waiting and you had to deliver.

Worse yet, after two or three weeks, the guys were tired. They had reacted to the piecework scheme like hogs at the slops trough. They gorged themselves ignoring their families, their hobbies, their social life—such as it was—and just kept pumping out widgets. They made a ton of them and they backslapped each other when they collected their pay at the end of the week. But yeah: Eventually, they exhausted themselves.

Their spirits sagged and their lives started to fall apart. They couldn't make their wives happy on Saturday nights, either. They were too pooped.

When they got the news that some of the hats were being rejected by their customers, they were embarrassed and mad. When it looked as though they would have to rework the thimbles, the bottom fell out.

There were chargebacks and delays. Threats to discontinue. Clearly, they had been rushing the job and no longer gave a hoot for quality control. Hats came back with a sort of horn sticking out of the top and some of the wheelbarrows had folded up tightly, making them look more like busted zippers. Finger pointing ensued followed by a lot of finger wagging, head shaking and language not heard on the floor for years.

It took a while for word of this disaster to reach the office. Tom had kept track of the numbers and reported shipping quotas on a daily basis but his nose was too close to the ground. He overlooked a lot of the grumbling and general consternation. Soon, though, Bob had to ask, "What the flower is goin' on down there?"

Tom had to think. He'd seen the guys cut their breaks and he'd seen them work more hours. He'd reported the dramatic uptick in production and he'd seen the smiling faces each Friday afternoon. He really hadn't read the crowd, though. The last two weeks had seen returns, fatigue, sagging morale and two occasions when guys had to be pulled apart: They were that hot.

Something had to be done. Tom went home and thought it through. He thought about his job and the role he had played in the decision to switch down to piece work. None. But he was the face of the company in a way and the men were upset with him. He was the one who had accepted all their praise when they got their pay and he now he was the one they wanted to massacre. What now?

When he got to the building the next morning, Cindy was waiting for him. They were going to have to see Bob ahora! Now! She didn't say much, just nodded her head in the direction of the stairs and led him up.

Bob was short and to the point. "Well, our little experiment didn't turn out so good." Cindy started to say something but then clammed up.

"It looked like a good idea but it didn't work." He frowned and frowned and Tom could feel how terribly sad and disappointed he was. "It just didn't work." Bob turned and stared out the window as if for some answer, some divine insight into this catastrophe.

Cindy tried to ease his pain. "It was a good idea. You did your best but you just couldn't foresee all those problems. Who would have guessed that it'd turn out like this?"

"I shoulda seen it comin'," Bob whined. Tom thought he was looking at one of the most beaten men he had ever seen. Worse than the time when the crew of the BARBRY DOLL tried to fix a leak in her stern and set the whole thing on fire.

"You couldn't have seen it comin'", Cindy repeated.

"I don't give a Hell!" he exclaimed. "I don't give a Hell!" That did it. No one, not even his wife, had ever heard WB use profanity before.

Tom couldn't move. Cindy sat there with her mouth open, unable to say another word. Both wished earnestly to be in Tahiti instead of the deck of this rapidly sinking ship. The hurt!

"Well, we have no choice," Bob said finally. "We're gonna have to go back to the old ways and scrap this whole piece work thing." The entire experiment had been an unmitigated disaster. A mess. And now the only way to fix it was to restore the old production line from top to bottom.

Bob held up one finger and it meant this: "Be quiet and listen to me." For ten solid minutes he outlined the transition back to their original production scheme. They would reward the guys for trying and make sure they were treated right. If there was any question about the switchback the guys would be given the benefit of the doubt. The cost would not fall on the men; it would fall on Feldstein's. It would sting but it would be worth it in the long run. Peace would reign and a happy crew would once again occupy the stools down there on the floor.

The next morning, WB himself assembled the men. Each guy seemed to be calling for his attention but he smiled a cherubic smile to them and announced a return to the old hours and piece work plan. A few guys mumbled a little but it quickly became apparent that they were still mad about the stupidass piece work idea and hadn't had a chance to blow off steam. They had no beef with going back to the old ways. They couldn't do it fast enough.

At the end of the meeting, Cindy stepped up and said, "Now, I don't want you blaming Tom for this." A few guys shook their heads but some of them looked toward Tom and thought dark thoughts. Most of them hadn't even thought of Tom but they thought of him now. "He was just doing his job, overseeing you guys."

Tom didn't know what to think. Of course it wasn't his idea. He wasn't to blame. He was just doing his job. The seed had been planted, though. He could see a dozen red hot eyeballs squinting in his direction.

"So, now you won't have to report to Tom any more," Cindy went on. "You can just put in your time cards and production totals at the office the way you always did." And just like that, Tom learned that he was fired. Both Cindy and WB smiled to him when they asked him to step into the office and they both looked very sympathetic when they told him he was out.

"There's nothing for you to do," Bob said with a shrug. "You've done a bangup job but this whole piece work thing was a disaster. It cost us.....a lot!" He shook his head so sadly that Tom thought again that he might weep. "It's gonna take us a month to get back to where we were at before."

"Well, it won't be too bad," Cindy said as she scanned the ledger. "We shipped a lot of doohickeys....." But she stopped when she saw Bob's little frown.

Tom left the building an hour or so later. He carried with him three things: He got an extra fifty dollars as severance. He got a pat on the back from Bob along with a heartfelt, "Thank you" as he walked him out the door.

"Don't take any rubber chickens!" Bob joked, happy to cheer the poor kid up.

But Tom's most valuable lesson was a simple one that we all must learn: Always make sure you've got someone else to blame when things go bad or you're the one out on the street, starting all over again.

Failing and learning. Failing and learning. A certain rhythm was developing. As simple and syncopated as his favorite song from Frankie Lymon and the Teenagers, "Why do fools fall in love?" Tom's sun was setting on the world of manufacturing but other worlds would open up for him, even other suns.

HIGHER EDUCATION

Like Tom, Joe knew there was little to be gained from high school let alone college but unlike Tom, Joe had a shrewd streak in him. He could still benefit from an education if he made the most of it. He could learn; he just didn't want to learn too long. Like Tom, he was eager to get out and meet the world. He had a vision of his adult self, too, something so secret that he wouldn't even admit it to himself. He would always be a gypsy at heart, guided solely by a different star, perhaps the Southern Cross, invisible to those of us who live up North.

Maybe it was all that flamenco that rattled around his head. Gypsies played it, right? At least, that's what he thought. He never actually looked it up but those guys sure looked like gypsies. An island like Nantucket plays host to people from all over the world so he was never burdened with prejudice. Every sort of man went there during whaling days and they stayed, often living much more free and unfettered lives than their counterparts in America. He might have even met a gypsy; it was pretty likely that he had. They were, after all, everywhere. You just didn't know who, what, when, where or how; they were so mysterious.

He loved their music but more importantly, he loved their culture. He loved that they were "opportunists". They lived off the land and, if necessary, off the people of the land. He loved their swagger.

He had once seen a gigantic black Cadillac pull into the parking lot at the A&P in Hyannis. It took up a full parking space and half of another, along with three feet of a third space at the rear of the car. It was enormous. And from each window hung a hard black curtain to shut out the world. When that Caddy rolled into the A&P, the curtains were all clapped down hard, just like a hearse.

Joe couldn't take his eyes off the car so he was watching intently when the driver popped the door and set his black boot on the pavement.

Johnny Ice. That's what the sticker said on the back bumper and that's what the guy looked like as he stepped out on the pavement, all six foot three of him. He was skinny, as thin as a hundred dollar bill and draped in black silk with amulets and cufflinks and a necklace of silver and gold. His eyes scanned the parking lot through flint black aviators and his jaw never moved except to shift the toothpick from one side of his mouth to the other. When he reached into the car and brought out a tall black Stetson, Joe's eyes popped out of his head. Was that a feather on the side?

Joe thought, "I want to be like that. I want to be cool," and he kept that image in his mind whenever called upon to act grown up. It was not a nuanced view; it was that of a kid. He had discovered one band width of cool out of the whole spectrum that ranged from John McCain all the way up to Miles Davis and beyond. But again, he was a kid and the cool he saw that day at the A&P informed much of his view of the world for the rest of his life. It overwhelmed his adolescence. If he didn't go to school in black it was because he couldn't afford it. He knew to wait but underneath, he was Johnny Ice, too.

Mrs. Crisp forced Joe to inhabit an adult world and he slipped easily into the persona of the gypsy he had seen that day. He thought he would create his best impression by showing just how much more sophisticated he was than his peers. He was someone she should take seriously. He was cool, or if not actually cool, he had a better idea of what that meant than all his friends. He was gonna be cool some day, he thought. He just had to add experience to vision. Mrs. Crisp was just the one to provide those missing experiences.

Accordingly, when she asked him to stop and see her after school the following Tuesday, "...because we never really got down to careers....", he feigned annoyance but jumped at the chance. All weekend, he plotted the assault that would conquer those magnificent yum yums.

All weekend, he imagined that soft white skin and those two sweet pink areolar discs. He glowed confidently until just one minute before their meeting when he went as cold as ice but definitely not cool like Johnny Ice. He was scared stiff.

⌒

A brief dissertation on courage now: It's easy to make fun of people who are afraid of elevators or door mats or chocolate. They seem pretty silly and after all, what is there to be afraid of? Elevators are proven safe for over 93%** of their passengers and door mats don't really seize you by the ankle and throw you to the floor. Chocolate, too, is actually a treat and not something that should instill a feeling of dread.

That said, people who have these phobias show a tremendous amount of courage when they bravely push the fourth floor button and step to the back of the car or stride across a forbidding threshold. They deserve a lot of credit as they meet their fears head on. They may flinch; they may bite their lips but they still manage to kick themselves along and get where they want to go. Chocolate won't always soil your dress or drip all over your shirt, either. Stop being afraid!

So it is with sex. At some point, over 82% ** of us try it and over half that number come to think of it as something pleasant, desirable even. Of course, it's scary but it can also be enjoyable. It can be fun. You don't have to shy away from it all your life. You can try it out, too, like glass blowing and if you don't like it you can move on to something better. Home repairs. Gardening. Berating the neighbors. Golf.

(**U.S. Department of Labor Statistics, Division of Farms and Horses)

Most would agree: You should try sex maybe even a couple of times. For many, it becomes a lifelong interest, an interest that survives long after we've begun soiling our pants again in an old folks home.

Of course, it's easy to see the long view of anything, sex included, when you're a hundred years old. When you're only 17, like Joe, it's intimidating. When you kiss your teammate from Biology Lab it's scary enough but to kiss a woman? Anyone would be nervous. Any reasonable person would lose his resolve and just plain run away.

The thing about courage is that it can appear sometimes at the most unexpected of moments. You must never challenge a little guy in front of his friends or he may fly at you like a Banshee from beyond. He's more afraid of his friends calling him a coward than he is of taking a beating so he shuts off his Think Tank and just throws himself at you.

If he's got a knife you can be in real trouble.

Again, we're talking about sex here. Some dive forward with a kiss simply because they're afraid not to. They dare themselves to make that leap and then they do it. They would rather be rejected then have to go home and see that cowardice in the mirror. This is often taken for impulse but it's really not an impulse. It's an imperative and it can not be denied.

⁓

Joe knew instinctively that he would dare himself to do it. He also knew that it was a bad idea and that he'd probably get in trouble. Even so, and even though he never thought through the tension in the situation, he knew he would make the leap. He wanted to see those breasts that bad. Really, really bad.

That weekend he hauled boats with some of the other kids down at the town landing. The numbskulls who kept small craft out all season always had times when they had to haul either for a cleaning or for the town's famously cranky weather. A disastrously old and rusty crane there bore the humorous legend, "Bottoms washed: Fifty Cents a Foot" but rates had gone up considerably since it was first installed. The kids could all make a good buck if they hung out and helped with the hauling. It beat caddying and paper routes; that's for sure.

Monday arrived and before he knew it, it was Tuesday noon. He'd seen Mrs. Crisp in the hot lunch line but he'd slid away and avoided eye contact. He was scared stiff but he didn't want her to cancel, either.

Sports were always a joke to him but this was Game Day and he knew it. Time to drop the puck.

Someone had told him that smoking calmed your nerves so he snuck behind the bleachers after the bell and lit up a Chesterfield. His lips were too moist, though, so the end of it shredded and fell apart. He tried a few puffs anyway and found himself choking first on the smoke and then on the tobacco that stuck in his throat. His nose stung and his breath, he knew, was acrid and reptilian. He'd have to wash up and find a mint before he met Mrs. Crisp.

Right at three he opened her door and was pleasantly surprised. She smiled up at him from her desk and removed her glasses, an encouraging sign. He walked slowly up to her desk, trying not to look too jaunty, and placed his books on the floor.

"Well, here we are....", she said as if she, too, had looked forward to their meeting. He played he was fussing with his books but cast her a quick sidelong glance. She was wearing her "uniform" again, her blue skirt and white top but the top seemed a little more blousy than he remembered. It might have been silk and was just roomy enough to allow her to move freely when she shifted her weight, almost like lingerie. Joe was deeply aroused. He would have gulped if he'd had the nerve but instead looked at his shoes, as one does.

"Yup.....yeah," was all he could manage. His gypsy self had evaporated just like that.

"Well, let's take a look at the career book here," she said, reaching for a thick blue three ring binder on her desk. Joe was afraid to look at her so he was relieved when she plopped it on the desk and opened it up. It was upside down for him but he didn't mind. Just so long as he could look at something.....

"Let's try to think of the type of work you want to do....," she said, smiling a more youthful and encouraging smile than she had ever shown him before. She was in career mode now and not acting as the hall monitor or assembly person he saw each day. She looked good.

"You can break it down into simple categories." She paused to see if he understood and he nodded half-heartedly. He continued to look at the book and his gaze was so riveted to the upturned pages that she wondered if he was illiterate or if he had learned to read upside down.

"I try to think in big categories…," she went on but the word "big" made him think of her breasts again so his eyes involuntarily lurched in that direction.

"You can think outdoors/indoors, if you like. Or you can think office/shop, too." When he gave no sign of comprehension, she tried a different approach. "You have to break down the whole employment problem into little pieces just as you must break any problem down into its component parts." This stated her approach pretty well and most kids would have shown some degree of comprehension but Joe continued to stare at the binder as if it was either chock full of snakes or the head of John the Baptist.

"Are you listening to me?" she asked finally, a bit more tartly than she intended.

"….Uh, oh yeah….," he mumbled. "Sure. Of course," he tried, brightly.

But both of them knew he was faking it. The whole thing had been a big mistake. She wasn't getting through to him and he wasn't getting any closer to those magnificent breasts. Time to give up.

"Come over here and take a look," she said, pointing to a chair next to hers. "I'll show you how it works."

Joe shuffled a little but got up and stood over her, sneaking a peek past the top button of her blouse and seeing there a diamond pendant, as clear as holy water and just as sweet. What joy to be that chain, he thought, imagining the scent of her soft, soft skin.

"Sit down," she said firmly and unconsciously tugged at her collar. He sat down and leaned over the desk to display the sharpness of his focus. Later on, he thought he might have cocked an eye thoughtfully in her direction, too, but he wasn't sure if that was the truth or embellishment. Eventually, it became part of the story.

"Now, look at these two panels," pointing at several people on one page who were strolling happily through an insurance office. On the opposite page stood another group of guys wearing hard hats with bulldozers and cranes that called out for direction and control. They were terrific photographs and the pages were slick and glossy to show how carefully they'd been prepared.

"How do you see yourself?" she asked. "….Outside, working with your hands or indoors working in an office?" He only gulped in response. When she turned in his direction, a little drop of drool was slipping out of the corner of his mouth. He pursed his lips and caught it just in time.

Mrs. Crisp had to rethink her approach. Perhaps the boy was slow.

"I have an idea," she said. "I think you should join our seminar on Saturday." That got his attention. This would be work, the very last thing he wanted. He let slip the last bit of his self control and reverted to his true self, his eight year old self.

"...Oh, no.....", he groaned. "Noooo…...I can't.…...". Not more talking! Jesus Christ! Fuck that!

This time her smile was completely professional carrying with it all the condescension that attends our encounters with specialists. She knew best. He would see his future clearly and know his life's work be it logroller, orange crater or man in the moon. He'd have his answer and with that, his future. His destiny.

She turned toward him again, a fully realized woman and he just sank back helplessly in his chair.

"Oh, come on," she said brightly, "It will be fun."

"Jesus! Fuck! Shit!" was all he thought. "Jesus!" He managed to get up, return to his seat and grab his books. He sat there silently, waiting to be dismissed. All hope of fulfillment was gone, replaced by the worst, most dreary educational experience of all: The Workshop. It was all such bullshit! What a waste of time!

Mrs. Crisp put her glasses back on and thumbed through her pocket diary. "I can do this Saturday morning at nine. Is that okay for you?

I've got a couple of other kids coming, too, so let's do it." She even flashed him a mouthful of shiny teeth to show just how lucky he was.

He tried to protest but all of the blood in his body had drifted suddenly from his waistline to his feet. His nerves, too, seemed to have been cauterized. He nodded dumbly, knowing he had chores Saturday and would have to do them on Sunday, the day he'd hoped to ditch church and fish. Fuck! Shit!

That night, just before sleeping, he rubbed his belly. It was still full of the shepherd's pie and broccoli his mother had dished out earlier that night. He was more relaxed than he'd been all day and in many ways, more philosophical. His despair had left him or at least come down a notch. He thought, as we all do, that unlike lessons at school or at work, lessons in our sex life can tumble along in vastly greater number. He had failed but he was smart enough to make some very keen insights. He started to tick them off.

1. You have to figure everything out yourself;
2. Don't talk to anyone. They'll just make fun of you;
3. Don't listen to anyone. They don't know anything, either. Most importantly, he had learned the single and most important lesson we all must learn:
4. You basically have to decide. Will I go or will I run away? He decided without hesitation that he would not be a runawayer. He'd face rejection time and again but he'd go for it when he had the chance. He had no choice. Such is nature's imperative and such was the arc of his life.

⤔

Mrs. Crisp thought about it, too, a lot more than Joe would ever know or suspect. Husband Don had sacked out early as he often did and she laid on her back in bed staring at the ceiling.

"Was that boy thinking what I think he was thinking?" she wondered.

"I'm sure I saw him looking at my chest." Just as quickly, she thought, "Can't be. Impossible. Stupid." Then she remembered him standing behind her. She knew he was looking at her breasts. She just knew it.

Her mind went on in this way for some time, first providing ample evidence of his attention and then discarding it out of hand. It was just too absurd. She did everything she could to cultivate a persona that spoke of authority and assurance. She wanted to help kids; she didn't want to draw the wrong kind of attention.

It stirred her up, though. She didn't roll over on her side and then quickly go off to sleep as she usually did. Her heart was beating differently. More powerfully. It was surging, sending massive waves of warm fluids through her chest. It kept her wide awake despite her wish to sleep.

Still….. It felt good in a way. She went back and forth again from raw evidence of the boy's disease—his furtive glances, flushed brow and stammering—and she couldn't help but be flattered. It had been a long time since she had aroused that much excitement in anyone. She and Don had enjoyed a pretty good sex life at first but over the last seven or eight years neither one of them had much interest. Sometimes on vacations but otherwise, no. She took it for granted. Don certainly did.

But now, something was awakening in her. She really had never lost interest; if anything, she felt more responsive now than she had as a young woman. There were too many distractions then and she had been both frightened and shy. The church and Yankee prudishness had informed her views and she only just learned how very foolish and harmful they were. She had even gotten a vibrator and kept it in a secret place. "If Don ever found it……," she laughed, just managing to suppress one of her famous nasal snorts.

Her hand slid down below the sheets and she gave herself a tickle. It felt great. She relaxed and continued to tickle herself, gently and quietly, afraid to lift the sheet. Her eyes were firmly closed but images of the day swam before them. She saw the boy and felt an instant sympathy for his discomfiture. "The poor boy," she thought and she thought it sincerely, almost with love. For perhaps the first time in her life, she saw sexuality from a completely different point of view. She remembered how hard it had been for her to enter the world of sensual pleasure. "How very difficult it must be for boys," she thought. "They're so excitable but they're so vulnerable, too."

The combination of warmth, sympathy and touch began to reach a special place at the base of her spine. Her body became rigid and her nipples pressed against the sheet. She felt as if she was floating, with her buttocks, shoulders and calves pressed against the deck. She was on a raft, heading downstream and it was picking up speed. Just when she thought the river couldn't possibly go any faster, she heard a roar and the penultimate wave lifted her up and shot her over the falls. She could see herself falling heavily into the waters below, kicking and splashing, her heels up over her head.

SEEING THE WORLD

While Joe was failing and learning, Tom was at sea. The discharge from Feldstein's had been a bad blow to his self esteem. He moped around the house and tried to think of a way to make his way. Like most of us, he was impatient and cranky but that was understandable. His motors were still running but he was rudderless and making no progress in any one direction.

Cal and Es were patient to a point but eventually Tom's chronic irritability got on their nerves. Cal took his son aside and with one hand on his shoulder, nudged him toward century's end.

"Yer gonna have to think of something to do, " he said quietly.

"I know, dad. I know," Tom answered, his teeth clenched.

They walked out toward the water and were able to see the Light's faint pulse out on the point. Neither spoke. Then, with the thoughtlessness and questionable judgement so natural to youth, Tom finally said, "I'm gonna enlist."

This took Cal completely by surprise. He was prepared to hear that Tom would leave the island but only to go to Massachusetts, the land of libraries and big schools and people with too high an opinion of themselves. He wasn't prepared for this!

"Yeah. I've thought about it...." (Cal wondered for how long) "... and I'm gonna enlist. Sign up." He shot a squint at Cal and saw only a look of saintly acceptance. He didn't understand Cal's true emotion, one of horror; he only saw the set teeth and furrowed brow that he mistakenly took for patriotism and parental pride.

"Well, that's a big step," Cal said stoically. He was trying not to choke.

"Yeah, I guess it is....," Tom swaggered, ".....but I think it's the right one for me." Cal had seen the last war, WWII, and had his doubts. But it was fairly safe now. Korea was over and no large conflicts loomed on the horizon. It was 1962 and his son was now over 19 years old. Almost 20. He was a good kid, too. He masturbated too much but we probably all do, he thought.

"Have you told your mother?" Cal didn't want the job.

"I thought I'd tell you first." So Cal was off the hook.

"Well, all right then. Let's go do it," he said. And they did. There was a bit of weeping and wailing but they actually felt proud of him. They believed in service for other boys but when they saw how determined he was they felt they had to go along. They'd support him and secretly hoped he'd get no closer to enemy fire than the doughnut tray in the Company PX.

Two weeks later, they were at the recruitment office in Hyannis. Four weeks later, Tom was on a troop train, a sealed steel box as it choo-chooed its way South. He had never even heard of Columbia, South Carolina and now he was going to see it! Fort Jackson, here we come!

꙳

Basic training is different. Civilian life is a life of freedom, of choices. The Army and particularly basic training is the complete end of all freedom. Every action, every move is dictated and each recruit must learn to obey. You dress alike, walk alike, eat alike and sleep alike. You must eat your meals in five minutes while sitting on no more than three inches of your chair, your back as rigid as the American flagpole that stands outside. You learn about coming to attention and you learn it damn quick. Or else.

You also learn cussin'. Boys use profanity, of course, to show their manliness but Army cussin' is special. It never stops. Everything is "fuckin'" this and "fuckin'" that. No one uses a new word, ever. If an adjective (or gerundive) is needed to complete a sentence, "fuckin'" did the job. "Fuckin' A!"

꙳

If Tom had been failing and learning at island speed, he was now learning at breakneck speed. He saw things he'd never seen before. At the range the Sergeant showed how little kick you got from an M16 by placing the butt against his groin and firing off a couple of rounds. Then he did the same thing with the butt against his chin. Was he crazy?

Tom learned to adjust the sights by "mayshing" them down with his thumb. The guy was a "good ol' boy" from Baton Rouge and moved as slow as rice'n beans. Tom was not just learning Army, he was learning a whole new language: Southrun. Giddiup!

He learned the most, though, from his bunkmate, Adrianus Culpepper, the slowest man he had ever seen. A.D., as he was called, was from Tennessee and moved even slower than the range sergeant. He moved slower than cement. Tom didn't think the guy blinked; he was that careful with energy. They got along great because A.D. and Tom were both preoccupied and never had much to say.

The whole platoon was surprised, then, when they went through MOS testing. Early one morning they were frogmarched across the base to sit at school desks in a real, live classroom. They had on clean fatigues and polished boots. It was their sixth week in training and they had to take a test that would tell the Army where to send them for their Military Occupational Specialty, the six months or so after basic. Some guys would go to Cleveland and some to Kalamazoo. It all depended on that test. Here we go!

The language portion took a while. There was a lot of reading and situational nonsense to go through. "What would you do if you suddenly encountered a turkey, a piano and a sweet potato pie?"

"Which box is bigger, the big box, the bigger box or the really big box?"

Tom worked his way through these dilemmas and managed to finish by the time they blew the whistle. They then took a break for fifteen minutes and resumed with the mathematics part. This part was hard. Tom did okay right through long division but when it got to trapezoids (the family nemesis) and the time space continuum, he just faked it. Even then, he didn't look up from his paper until the Sergeant once again shocked them back into reality with his infernal whistle.

Tom handed in his paper and was the first one out the door. A.D. was waiting just outside. "Quit early?" Tom asked.

"Yeah."

Okay. That was a lot from A.D. so Tom left it alone and they joined the others. They marched back to their barracks and resumed the day. More drillin'. More marchin'. Order arms!

About five days later, they got the results. Tom had clearly been touched by the hand of God when he first picked up his clipboard because it was, in fact, his future. He would be going to a branch of the quartermaster corps. The medical branch. He'd be off to Fort Sam in San Antone as soon as he graduated. He'd be counting and shipping and moving and shuffling just as he had at White's and again at Feldstein's. All his training and all his education had taken him to this point in life and he couldn't have been happier.

A.D. didn't say much but they finally got him to admit that he had aced everything and was going to "Intelligence". The fuckin' guy was going to "Intelligence"! Nobody had ever heard him say a smart thing; nobody had ever heard him say anything. And to top that, he had never been further from his home town of Rat Knob, Tennessee than the adjoining town of Buck Snort. And that, to see a man about a horse. Oh my!

Things were looking up for Tom. It turned out he got a week off and expenses to get to Texas. Three hundred and ten dollars! That meant he could squeeze in a trip back to see the folks. He would also try to see Louise Papodopoulos, a girl he knew from school. They had once gone bowling together and she seemed to like him. Like a man with real confidence, he pulled himself together and called her one night, long distance.

He got her on the first try. "Jesus Christ!," he thought when she picked up the phone. He explained about his enlistment and the triumphs he'd enjoyed at basic training and although she seemed busy, she made Ooohs and Aaahs as if genuinely interested. Gradually, he led up to the part about his leave and, "Do you think you'd like to see a show some night?"

"Why.....sure," she answered. She really was busy, he thought and decided to hang up.

"I've got to go but I'll call you when I get home. About ten days," he blurted.

"Great," she said, anxious to get off the phone. "That would be great."

The truth is that Tom had learned a terrible thing about boot camp. You are tired and you are sore. You are sick to death of your buddies and you've had a grueling, punishing time in a godforsaken shithole of a place but....... There was something worse: loneliness.

His heart had ached. His soul had ached. He was that lonely. His spirit had been crushed along with the rest of his young identity. He missed his folks. He missed his friends. He missed everything. He was homesick in a way that he could never have imagined. And he ached for the human touch. It wasn't even about sex; there was an ache there, too, of course, but he just wanted some peace and quiet. He wanted to be loved again, even if it was just a little bit and even if it was forced.

God, how he needed that!

INFORMATIONAL SESSIONS

"Nothin' much," Joe said. "….You?" His mother had put him on the phone and he had his own problems. Tom was okay, nothing to worry about.

"Me neither," Tom replied and the two of them went silent, knowing they'd have to stay on the phone until Es grew impatient and snatched it away again. Soon, she did.

"You two!" she exclaimed. Joe was relieved that she wanted to talk and watched as she pumped his brother for information.

"Well, how are they feeding you?" she asked and then followed up with, "I hope they're taking good care of you." To which she received every assurance. This man's Army was especially considerate of her son Tom because he was special.

"I'm gonna come home for a couple of days and then go to Fort Sam in Texas," he informed her, using as much slang as was fitting for someone of long experience and glowing prospects. Es was impressed. She didn't see into the calculating mind of the raw recruit, deprived of women to the point of madness. He wanted to cut his time at home to a minimum so he called ahead to be sure he could use the car. He didn't want to waste one single minute. He already had his time slots marked. He was goin' downtown!

"Well, we're gonna feed you good," she said, confident that her Sunday roast would be just the treat to inspire the kind of chest pounding confidence he would need at his new post.

When they rang off, she wiped away the inevitable parental tear and gave Cal a hug. Their boy was going to be okay. He was going to be a paper guy, a guy who dedicated himself to the tabulation of crates and barrels, bushels and boxes. Ace bandages would be his domain along with whole warehouses full of paper goods. TP and PT and Kleenex enough for entire brigades. Box cars full of them. Wow!

Joe forgot the call the minute he got upstairs. He was trying to cope with his obsession, the constant thought of Mrs. Crisp. He couldn't wipe the image of her shapely figure from his mind. And did he even want to? And how old was she anyway? And was there something wrong with him? And why couldn't he be Johnny Ice, not even for a minute? He couldn't concentrate and couldn't sleep. Es asked him why he wasn't eating and he bolted from the room.

He tried to think of the slide show he'd have to see on Saturday morning ("9 a.m. sharp!") and only relaxed when he remembered that other kids would be there, too. He could keep a low profile and pretend to be friendly to the other kids. He'd be attentive. He'd stay awake through the whole lesson with a hearty smile and get the Hell out of there.

But first, he would take a bike ride by her house. "That's a great idea," he thought, actually congratulating himself.

⇆

Sex is a great, if confusing, teacher. Fact succeeds fact until it seems like the perfect time to draw a conclusion and it isn't.

You go on a date.

Your date smiles and gives you a peck on the cheek.

You get back to the house.

And nothing happens.

This should teach the lesson of humility or at the very least the lesson of lowered expectations but it doesn't. Our innermost self is involved, worrying, scheming and hoping that this time it will work out our way.

⇆

Joe got out his old Schwinn Speedster equipped practically if not stylishly with a basket in the front and wheeled away. He knew her address because his friend Bingo Pratt lived just down the street. He never went past Bingo's house because of the Rottweiler that lived nearby but he knew her car and he knew the street. He didn't have to consult a phone book or any other living human being. No one would know the reason for his journey. Only him.

He knew, too, that Bingo lived on a more upscale part of the island than he did. It was closer to town in a more fashionable neighborhood. A lawyer lived there, he thought, even a doctor. Serious people.

The sky was bright, the sun was high and it was easy to assume that the solitary biker was just out for a ride. He hummed quietly to himself. "Why do foo-oools fall in love?" His top secret mission would be carried out without anyone being the wiser. He just wanted to see where she lived.

After crossing Main Street, he headed the short distance down Pinckney toward Bingo's house. He wheeled right by Bingo's, though, digging in as if he had forgotten where his buddy lived. When someone came out of the house and headed toward the family car, Joe pretended to look at something fascinating to his left. A bush, maybe.

Six or eight houses up on the right, he saw what looked like her car. Mrs. Crisp always had a new car, never a junker. This was a turquoise Chevy Impala with six round taillights and a low slung chrome stripe on the side. It looked fast just sitting there. He slowed as he approached it and his heart skipped a beat when he saw her house. He was struck immediately by the grandeur of the place with its stone wall, sweeping drive and tasteful plantings. But he was also struck by the reality of it all: This was a house owned by a grown up.

He could never compete in that world. He would never have a real house of his own, never mind a sweeping driveway and two chimneys and the rest. How could he? He was just a kid. He'd never even have a beautiful, magnificent car like hers, either. It was too much! "I'm just not in her league," he thought. And then he felt the pain.

The grey ghost, Rodney, had hit him from behind. He had probably galloped up, making a racket with his paws and heavy breath, his tongue swinging back and forth but Joe never heard him. He was too busy listening to the sobering words that poured into his ears from God above. The Almighty said, "You're just not in her league," and the next thing he knew, he was on the ground. He felt those teeth on his leg and bang! He was up to his neck in hydrangea. He tried not to fall but came down in the spongey turf with a sound oddly like the sound a water balloon makes when dropped onto a parking spot from the fourteenth floor. "Pop, Squish!" was all he heard.

Almost immediately, he heard, "Oh, I'm so sorry!" Joe was tangled up in the bike but fortunately had fallen to his right and on to the grass. He could have hit his head but didn't. The dog, a full-sized Rottweiler, big enough to take down a Buick, was standing nearby with his tongue hanging out, looking very, very pleased with himself.

"He doesn't bite people," the voice said, "....He only pinches them."

Joe wanted to know how many times he had pinched the postman but when he looked up he was looking straight into the face of the sweetest little granny he'd ever seen. A long wisp of gray hair fell across her face as she stared down at him. She brushed it aside, then opened her eyes wider for a better look. Her left eye was a walleye and was staring down the street at Bingo's house but her right eye had a fixed and pained expression of real regret. As he looked up at her, he thought of a photograph he had once seen of Jean Paul Sartre, the famous Frenchman and Existentialist.

Joe did not think of literature, though. He was thinking bitter thoughts about Rodney, as she called him. "Rodney, bad boy!" she said with feeling. "Bad boy!" And when the dog put his head down in shame, she stroked him and kissed him and called him "Roddie. Roddie my love. My dear, sweet, sweet Roddie."

Joe had been brought up right and didn't swear. Bad, bad language rushed to his tongue but he still didn't allow himself to let it out. Instead, he just lay there. She asked him where it hurt and he couldn't say so she pulled up his pants leg revealing a calf covered with lurid red marks but no sign of blood. His right elbow was skinned and his shoulder hurt but somehow he had gotten through the whole mess without any serious injury. The old lady seemed pleased. Relieved, even.

"I think you just got a good scare, young man," she said with a bright smile. "I think you're going to be just fine."

He felt like any victim, though. He felt punked, abused and dismissed. He had been riding along, minding his own business.....

"Mom!" someone screamed. "Mom!"

And up ran Mrs. Crisp. Just like that. It was her mother and her mother's friggin' dog. Jesus Christ!

"Omigosh! Joseph!", cried Mrs. Crisp. "My goodness me!" She bent down and lifted the bike off his leg, then asked him to pull his pants leg up again. This time, Joe moaned a little as she examined the wound. He also snuck a look at her front.

"Well, there aren't any tooth marks and I'm heartily glad of that," she said, glaring at her mother, "...but this must be seen to and the doctor called."

"Oh, my," frowned the old lady.

"You must come into the house," she said, following that order with a nonstop barrage of additional questions and protestations. When he told her that his shoulder hurt a little, a look of real pain flashed across her face. Mrs. Crisp was in charge now and he was her sublimely happy patient.

She first took him to the downstairs bathroom where she asked him to remove his shirt and roll up his pants again. She then went to the First Aid box in the closet and soaked some gauze with alcohol, pressing it to his leg. "Hold this here a minute," she said. It stung like hell but he managed to wince out a smile to show his thanks.

She then attended to his shoulder. He could feel her fingers on his back and arm and grimaced convincingly when she applied a wash cloth to the area. Soap and water trickled down his arm and belly but he didn't care. He could feel her grip on his arm and her fingers stroking his back. He felt important; he felt sexy and he felt as though he had somehow managed to skip through a very important portal to his future.

It turned out that Mrs. Crisp lived with her husband Don and her mother, Ida. Don didn't really work; he collected money somehow. A trust or something. They had a cat and they had this dog, Rodney that actually came with mother Ida when she moved in with them. She had no kids but she gardened obsessively. She loved roses especially, beach roses—the rosa rugosa so revered by visitors and island folk alike.

All this information was disclosed voluntarily during the awkward period while Joe rested on their porch. Mrs. Crisp ran back and forth between the porch and the kitchen, fussing over lemonade and cold packs and, "Would you like something to eat?" Mother Ida walked past the door a few times, each time casting a suspicious eye in his direction. Wondering what he had done to provoke the dog.

"Boys do, you know," she said to herself. "They throw things at them and taunt them with sticks." The fact that Joe had been seized by the leg and thrown violently to the ground had long been forgotten. Now, she wanted revenge. "Some people will blame the dog," she thought indignantly, "...and that's just not right." She went over to Rodney and gave him a little pat on the nose to show she understood.

Joe was awash in a sea of emotions. Waves of revulsion and fear formed strong crosscurrents with feelings of excitement and stimulation. He was now getting a full view of Mrs. Crisp and his heart was drumming with excitement. His mind began a grand debate which, he thought, was both dispassionate and very passionate, indeed.

"Boy, she's pretty," he declared, then leapt to her defense. "....and really fit. She's very fit." Each trip to the kitchen left him with another impression. "She must be really athletic. Look at those calves!" He made a rigorous evaluation of her bottom, too. "...Hmmmmm...," he purred. He might have been sizing up a spring heifer but, again, he had a lot to learn.

He even submitted to her ministrations with something like grace. He thanked her for the lemonade and even managed to turn down a cookie, saying, "I really shouldn't have one this close to dinner." Wow!

When she insisted on driving him home later, he was ecstatic. She dropped him off, gave him a little wave and left him to his fantasies. They were more comfortable with one another now, too. She wasn't as stiff and he felt more of an equal than he ever would have imagined. He would always be acting, of course, because he would have to guess what an adult would do before responding to her but he was learning. He even thought he could learn one day to act grown up.

He didn't recognize one lesson that he had just learned, though. Women are more than objects, even to devotees of hot magazines. As he got to know her, the one dimensional dragon he had known in school had evolved into a surprisingly interesting person. Almost in spite of himself and in spite of his lumbering sexuality, he was growing fond of her in a thoroughly unexpected way.

The Saturday seminar proved to be nothing more challenging than a dozy night in front of the evening news. She had a slide presentation that encouraged kids to "follow their dreams" and "reach for the stars" but all the other kids had been shanghaied, just like him. They all sat there with disgusted looks on their faces. Some slept. Joe sat up straight and made approving noises whenever she asked their opinion. He didn't raise his hand because that would have been too much but nodded and smiled on cue. The rest of the kids saw his enthusiasm for what it was: the product of a disordered mind. They all looked at him funny when they left.

THE DREAM DATE

Tom's future was secure. He would learn about supplies and he would learn about putting them on trucks. He had a good running start at White's and actually dealt with some of the drivers at Feldstein's but the U. S. Army was the real thing. He would be learning logistics. He had never even heard the word before and now he couldn't use a sentence without it. He was ready to roll.

But first, he had to take care of his basic imperatives. He graduated from Boot Camp and whooped it up with all his buddies. He would always be proud of getting through but had no romantic illusions about the place. He had been brutalized and deeply resented it. He didn't know what to make of the elaborate ceremony that attended the end of his basic training. Parents from the area came and saw off their boys. The ceremony, with marching and drilling and a display of platoon unity, was completely over the top. He half expected the sergeant to show up with a cake.

All that fun was quickly kicked aside, though, when he picked up his "transport" check, the gigantic bonus check that provided the money to get to Fort Sam. He had figured out the money, too. The train from Chicago to Fort Sam was $25 sitting up so he'd have cash to spare. Instead of heading directly off to his next assignment he would visit the folks and then, of course, see Louise Papodopoulos. Most of the money would be spent on that.

Cal and Es met him at the dock. He had taken the ferry from Woods Hole and hadn't even stopped to pick up salt water taffy at Janey's for them. His mind was that focused. The folks were ecstatic to see him and he looked great in uniform, all green and trim. The cold sea air didn't seem to faze him. He glowed and glowed, his sunken cheeks all pink and full of pride.

Cal remembered his own adolescence and asked if Tom would like to use the car that night. Es sputtered and fussed but after some clumsy discussion, Tom would have a nice dinner with them and then maybe (MAYBE!) head downtown. There was always a lot of activity on Main Street and it was good to be home again.

Pork chops were followed by applesauce and a baked potato that night, setting him up for an evening out. He made polite noises as he got up from the table but wasted no time getting to the car. Joe waved from the kitchen window, uninterested in either the thrill of seeing Tom or the thrill of going downtown. He went into the little TV room and tried to get the Sox.

Tom got there pretty quick, sticking the car behind Michael's Men's Wear to avoid putting all those quarters into a meter. He got out and started down the street, seeing the cobbles and the street lights that had always been a part of his life. Everything quickly started to seem strange, though. He had taken out a pair of khakis and a shirt he liked and checked himself in the mirror. Everyone on the street seemed to have done the same thing. He saw more plaid shirts than striped shirts, his choice, but everyone still wore khakis.

Somehow, though, he seemed out of step. He wanted to throw his arms around every person he saw but everyone was distracted, going about his business. He wasn't special to them; that's for sure. But more importantly, they seemed to speak a different language—American language.

For four months he had been subjected to a nonstop assault on his native tongue. Never mind the swearing, the Army had a language all its own and you had to speak it to survive. If you went through the chow line, you thanked the servers, buck privates just like you.

Now, when he ordered something, the clerk reached around back for it and simply said, "Fifty cents." That was it. He was then ignored almost as if a great steel door had slammed in his face. No one asked if he had been away or had been in a hell hole designed by the U. S. government to humiliate, degrade and dehumanize him. No one wanted to know.

Tom sat on a bench and watched his fellow man. They were passing him on a slow train while he watched from a window at the station. He had no connection to any of them and they had no connection to him. They were all caught up in complicated lives filled with families and jobs and hobbies and visits with friends. Tom had only been focused on the one thing: to get through basic training. It was almost as though he had been released from a time capsule and now had to catch up. He heard about guys who went to prison and he felt like that. He'd been out of society for too long and now had to start all over again.

"How do I order an ice cream?" he asked himself as he looked across the street at Norm's. Five or six tourists were clamoring for attention. "How do I do that?" In basic, everyone knew what you wanted. You held out your tray and they ladled, flipped or simply poured something into it. This was different. They were going to ask him whether he wanted a cone or a cup. Could he do it?

The next night when he saw Louise, he was a bundle of nerves. Everything seemed foreign to him. He struggled to change gears in the family car. Cal and Es loved their little Nash Rambler; its two tone, red over white exterior and corresponding upholstery were their pride and joy. They loved it! It was a big deal lending it to Tom so when he sat behind the wheel after all those months away he had to remember to insert the key, step on the clutch and shift into gear. Even the plastic seats seemed strange.

He bumped down the road to Louise's house and then sat out front, inhaling deeply. Did she really want to go out with me or did she feel sorry for me? His confidence, built up over all those triumphs at basic, simply melted away. He found himself completely unable to say a word.

This, of course, led to some difficulties because they were stuck together for fifteen minutes as they drove downtown and another ten minutes inside the theater before the movie started. Fortunately, women often misunderstand men and Louise took his silence for modesty, returning as he had from military service. She liked him for it. He wasn't like all of the other boys, the noisy boys who hung out downtown. He even asked her if she wanted salt in her popcorn. Very thoughtful and grown up.

He had also asked her preference and gone on Tuesday at the end of the run of VIVA LAS VEGAS instead of waiting until Wednesday's debut of ZULU, something he thought might be too martial for her sensibilities. The music helped to loosen him up, too. He was always an Elvis fan and Elvis was having so much fun that it was infectious. He relaxed, took a deep breath and put his arm around her seat being careful not to touch her shoulder until just the right moment. He waited and, as he learned later, she waited until that moment arrived with a special kind of thrill.

Attending the show took a lot of courage because not much happened on a weekday night in downtown Nantucket. They were too young for bars and had no money for a restaurant so whether they liked it or not, their choices were limited. All the other kids were there, too. They knew who was doing what to whom in the little theater; there were no secrets, just gossip. Louise and Tom were suddenly a couple, talked about as if they were already keeping house.

Tom did the best he could to follow the picture but he kept sneaking sidelong glances at her radiant black hair and lovely tan. She was wearing a scent of some kind and he noticed other things, too. Her glasses could have been more stylish but she was pretty good looking and above all, she seemed to like him. He decided finally to touch her shoulder, something that took more raw nerve than anything he had done at basic. When she didn't shrink back or object, he felt like a real man. Scared, but grown up.

Louise liked the way Tom nervously fussed over her. It was hugely flattering but more importantly, showed a side of him that she decided was "sweet". She hadn't really thought of him as being different from other boys—foolish and feckless—but now she saw something very different about him, indeed: She saw his fear.

Army life had changed Tom in ways neither one of them could ever fully appreciate. He walked differently, with better posture and he talked a lot less than the other boys who, after all, were still boys. They hadn't seen the greater world of boot camp or the sands and scrub pines of South Carolina. Most hadn't traveled any further than Providence, if that. Tom was more worldly and at least to Louise, more mature. When he dropped her off at the house, she still heard Elvis's voice in her ears. She even stopped for a moment, looked him in the eye and gave him a smart little goodnight kiss. He nearly crumpled up in joy right there on the front porch. When he asked if he could call her again, she smiled demurely and gave his hand a little pinch. "I'd like that."

The next day, neither of them could think of anything else. Fort Sam Houston was as far away as Tel Aviv. The monument of her virginity, so firmly erected by loving and fearful parents, was now standing on shaky ground. She could feel it slipping into the sand. Tom, too, could feel his muscles tightening involuntarily, unconsciously preparing to take a pick and shovel to the base.

Louise was busy Wednesday but wanted to encourage him so when he called she asked shyly if he'd like to go to a dance at her church on Thursday night. The two words "dance" and "church" clanked loudly in his ears. He avoided church whenever possible, happy to work or find another excuse including death to get out of it. And "dancing"? That was the next most undesirable activity on his list. His mind ranged back to basic and even the biscuits and gravy and live fire range looked better than that.

"Oh, come on," she said, "….It will be fun!"

"Uh…. I uhhh, don't know how….".

"Don't worry, It will be fun." And she closed the deal with the lie made by young women across the globe since the beginning of time. "I don't know how to dance either."

Basically, she outmaneuvered him. In the end, he had to say yes. His mind reverted to self-pity, the default mode of most young American men. He thought only of the agony he had suffered doing the shimmy at a "hop" two years earlier at school. He had walked away from that dance so badly damaged that he resolved never to dance again. He kept trying to decide whether he'd feel less pain being publicly hanged.

The long walk home after his high school dance had left him in a strangely relaxed frame of mind, a dangerous frame of mind. What would he do in the future to avoid that kind of embarrassment? Would he commit a crime? A misdemeanor? Or would he go full metal jacket and kill to avoid dancing again? He found his head involuntarily nodding, "Yes." No doubt about it: He would kill before ever setting foot on a dance floor again.

Tom had learned that lesson when he was young. He had failed at dancing and still felt the pain. The lessons he was about to learn would mitigate that pain and replace it with something very different. He just had to get himself to the church on Thursday night.

JEW DENZ GRIK?

Tom packed a lot into his six day leave. He had to go to White's with his mom for little things like a decent comb and a half way decent pair of jeans and then shrank back from the counter when his mother paid for it all. They fussed over him, though, and called him "Commander", a strictly naval term more appropriate to the island than just plain "General".

The time flew by. He thought about the "church" and the "dance" but he pushed them out of his mind. He couldn't allow them to weigh too heavily or he would ditch; he knew it. As he had many, many times before when faced with the inevitable, he kept himself busy and distracted. He even helped Tommy Stavola haul his boat, picking up a crisp new ten dollar bill for his troubles. It almost felt like normal.

Thursday night, he went through the motions. He got dressed, put on a tie--"Was this one too wide or too narrow?"-- and found a jacket in the back of the closet that looked all right. He would have preferred to be back in uniform but he knew that would only draw unwanted attention. It would have been a comfort to him but he would have had to answer a lot of questions. No: no uniform that night.

She was just inside the door when he arrived. She smiled and rather hastily directed him to the two very heavy middle-aged women who sat behind a folding table. They had a cash box and a roll of tickets and frowned exactly the same frown to Tom. Their hair had been frosted and stuck out in strange globes around their heads, bouffant style.

"They're twins," Louise whispered to him as they walked away from the table.

"Twin dragons," he thought. And then remembered his room back home where he could have been reading the Sports page or smoking out the window.

The pair was quickly forgotten, though, as Tom followed Louise. She took his hand and shuffled him through the hallway to the rear of the church. Dozens of older people were squeezed together talking ardently in the cramped hall full of coats and scarves, raingear and umbrellas. It was bedlam but the real bedlam was yet to come.

From inside the church he could hear music blasting, throbbing, squealing. He didn't know what to make of it. Louise tried to talk to him but nothing could be heard above the din. When they finally entered the room, he saw a dozen swarthy men all sweating and waving strange guitars, clarinets and concertinas at the crowd. They all had their white shirts open to the navel as if their real job was to provide sex to all the lucky attendees and not the music advertised outside.

Louise introduced him to an old man, an uncle named Nicholas John Matsikas. And to his son, John Nicholas Matsikas. He was holding his baby boy, Nicholas John Matsikas. Tom had entered a very strange world, indeed.

"Jew denz Grik?" Nick asked with a skeptical frown. His son John only smiled and tried to stop the squirming baby from toppling head first on to the floor. When Tom failed to respond, Nick repeated the question:

"Jew denz Grik?" Tom smiled back to him and nodded as if he'd been asked whether he preferred dollars to drachmas or filet to roasted goat.

Soon the break was over and as the cornets blew the spit out of their horns, Nick grabbed Tom by the upper arm and hauled him forward.

Tom was surprised by his strength. At 65 or so, Nick was heavily front loaded with a paunch that had been filled beyond capacity on many happy occasions. He had lost his shape but he'd lost none of his strength. Tom resisted but was dragged out to the dance floor without another word.

"Opa!" Nick stood in the middle of a large circle and continued to hold Tom's hand. When the music started, powerful strains from a balalaika filled the little hall. Nick held both arms out and dipped his right toe and then his left toe daintily in time with the slow cadence of the song. Tom stood flat-footed.

Nick then stepped to his left, pulling Tom to his left. Again, he dipped his right toe and then his left, turning toward Tom and forcing Tom to take two steps to his right. The pace quickened. And as it did, Tom tried to duplicate Nick's steps. Nick was astonishing. He was so light on his feet Tom thought he could kick the ceiling. After a minute or two, they were both bobbing up and down, repeating the dips and then returning back and forth from right to left. The crowd went wild.

Tom lost all self-consciousness. He was surrounded by a great blur of dark haired, totally crazed people and he was curious about each and every one of them. Who were they? And where did they come from? And what is this, anyway? It was nothing like anything he'd ever seen before. This wasn't dancing, surely. This was mayhem!

Soon others joined. Someone grabbed Tom's free hand and someone else took Nick's. Then others. They quickly formed a circle of a dozen people. They were laughing; they were shouting and they all seemed to know each other. They all seemed like cousins or something.

A long, long time passed and Tom, though fit, was getting winded. Sweat streamed from every pore. His shirt was soaked and his breath was fading but he kept going. He was possessed but then, so was everyone else. Rivers of sweat were pouring to the floor.

Just before he lost consciousness, he saw Louise facing him on the other side of the circle. She was laughing like the others but he could see a look in her eye that spoke volumes, a sympathetic look. It was caring and it was focused on him. His knees nearly buckled.

When the music stopped and everyone was still cheering, Nick turned to smile at Tom, his face a pool of mud. His nose and cheeks were swimming in perspiration, making his brown face look like the liquid clay from a pottery class. Tom could see the stubble of a beard trying to push to the surface but otherwise, his face was liquid, brown and undefined, with eyes, nose and mouth floating to the top.

"See now? Jew denz Grik!" Nick said, laughing and coughing until Tom thought his ghost would leave his body and he'd simply drop to the floor in a great brown puddle. "You dance Greek!" was what he'd been saying. "You dance Greek!"

What a people! What a night!

Louise squeezed her way through the exultant mob and patted him on the back. "You were great!" she said. "Really great."

Tom just mumbled something and tried to catch his breath. He couldn't think straight. Should he sit down? Surely, he wouldn't be called upon to do *that* again. No human being could...... and the band cranked it up a second time. Louise pulled him into the crowd and he watched as other men entered the circle and started to dance. Tall men, short men, pudgy and straight. It didn't matter. They all could dance and danced with a kind of abandon that Tom had never, ever seen or imagined before. Funny looking men. Tall, dark and handsome men. They all danced and they danced with elan, with poise and terrific athleticism. Tom was astonished. "Opa!" He even learned some Greek!

The noise was overwhelming. Louise had to signal to him or mouth words with exaggerated gestures like someone who had trained to be a mime. Tom was dumbfounded, though, thoroughly and completely out of his little world. Even the extended world of Fort Jackson and Columbia, S.C. didn't prepare him for this!

Two hours passed and all of it a rumble. It was a wonder they all survived but nobody even fell down, even with all of the ouzo and retsina that splashed from every glass. He got through to Louise now and then but it was frustrating. Everyone else was clamoring for her attention, too. Aunts, uncles, cousins, everyone. It was hard to communicate, just to enthuse.

Nick's son John grabbed Tom for one dance and they did pretty well.

John smiled and smiled and Tom just tried to catch his breath as they moved from right to left, tracing delicate steps on the floor. When others took their place, John took his arm again and dragged

him into the kitchen. Just minutes before the room had been filled with
a thousand women, all speaking at once. Grape leaves, moussaka and
pots of ovgolemino souppa stood ravaged on their trays.

"You did good," exclaimed John. At 35 or so, he had not as yet
developed his father's expansive belly but his enthusiasm was just as
high as Nick's. He smiled and smiled and again, clapped his hands on
Tom's shoulder. Tom fell in love, just like that.

"These people," he thought, "...these people are really cool!"

When the music slowed for a moment and Tom was able to hear
again, John said matter-of-factly, "You can't marry her, you know," .

Tom looked at John as if he had just stood up at Thanksgiving
dinner and, instead of carving the turkey, had bitten the head off a
squirrel. John laughed and clapped him on the back again. He smiled
broadly, still flush with endorphins and the pleasure of the dance. His
face looked as if he had just stepped out of the local pond. His white
shirt was transparent, showing the sleeveless tee shirt underneath.

Tom wanted more information but even more than that, hoped
he would be able to say something within the framework of normal
reason. He was on a "sort-of" date. He wasn't marrying anyone. Was
this guy crazy? Should he run away? Where would he start? He wanted
to explain that he and Louise barely knew each other but he was afraid
to use the word "bare". It might really set the guy off.

"She's great, huh?" John shouted, grabbing the infant Nicholas
from one of the aunties. The little one squirmed and burbled, his face
awash with the same salty perspiration as everyone else.

Now, Tom was really confused. Nicholas was a little boy. Why was
John calling him "she"?

"I thought Nicholas was a boy," he said.

John flashed him a look of anger. "Of course, he's a boy," and he
pulled out the diaper to show Tom his son's tiny little one ounce shrimp
of a penis.

"She's smart, too," he added. This time, though, he looked in
Louise's direction with the sharp eye of a pirate or profiteer.

"Oh...Oh!" Tom replied, finally catching on. But not catching on, not really. His mind was racing. "First the guy tells me I can't marry her and then he tells me how great she is. First he says 'No!' and then he says 'Go!'."

Confusion, if a definite condition of the mind, would have represented a base, a place from which to start the slow climb back to solid ground. He longed for confusion. He longed for puzzlement. Instead, he was totally disoriented with no compass, North or South. He could have been in Brazil or Tangiers with nothing but a tin drum and empty pockets, his world and now his future, were in such complete and utter disarray.

John was clearly a well-educated, worldly guy—a lawyer, maybe? He was already a parent, working with a real job and yet his words were not connected to any mental function. Things came out of his mouth like odd, stinky bits from a boulliabaise. What were they? What was he saying?

Tom reverted, as any thoroughly embarrassed person does, to smiling. His own deranged mind arrived at the usual conclusion: I'll fool them into thinking that I'm right at home here and understand every word. Many have come to grief through this kind of desperation and Tom was no exception. He nodded and smiled when John's sister approached, hoping for a change in the conversation. None came.

"She must marry Greek," she said flatly and didn't smile. She was doing business and that's all she was doing. No smiling, no preliminaries, no compliments on his horrendous dancing.

Tom stood there in a time warp. Everything had slowed down. He watched the sister as if from a great height, another planet, perhaps, or a satellite in Sector H. She was probably forty with that indescribably smooth skin of Greek women. Her unblinking eyes burned holes in the back of his head. It wasn't hatred, either, just the kind of resolve we see in golf nuts or bipolar folks on a manic high. He had never seen a "will" so strongly expressed or so clearly. His drill instructor began to look like the Faerie Queene.

He heard, "I don't want to marry her," coming out of his mouth. There! He had finally spit out a complete sentence.

Both John and his sister recoiled, their features twisted into expressions of shock and distaste. No greater insult, apparently, could have been hurled into their upturned faces. No cultural bias could have caused a greater affront. Did he just want to seduce her, take her precious thing and then dissolve into the sands?

"He don't want to marry her?" Uncle Nick grumbled nearby. "Why he no want to marry her?"

But Louise saved the day. She had caught a glimpse of them at the kitchen door, seen Tom's bewilderment and leaped to his defense.

"Thank you, thank you," she said over and over. "Thank you!" She slipped her hand through Tom's arm and nearly yanked him off his feet.

She was laughing heartily as she dragged him back through the hallway and out to the street. Tom clearly needed some instruction.

"Wave, smile and keep moving!" she said. "That's the only way to survive these kinds of situations, you know." He looked blankly back at her so she repeated herself. "Wave, smile and keep moving."

"Greek people are clannish, like most immigrant people. They keep going to church and they keep all their friends. Their children are the ones who start to assimilate," she explained. That made sense, he thought.

"So when you get into a tough situation, you have to get out of it and the way you get out of it is to 'Wave, smile and keep moving.'" This advice proved to be one of the most important lessons that Tom was ever to learn. As we shall see, it got him out of a lot of tight spots. He didn't even have to think about it. It became almost a reflex.

"What were they on about?" she asked, but Tom was afraid to answer.

"Was he trying to sell you a boat?"

"Nah, nothing like that."

"Well, it doesn't matter." She paused and asked, "You had fun, right?"

"Yeah, I did." He couldn't help himself. He leaned over and gave her a little kiss on the cheek. "It was fun." He wanted to say more but couldn't find the words that would adequately sum up the last two hours. "Wow!" was as close as he could get but that didn't nearly do the job.

"It's a lot of fun," she said, accepting the kiss.

"Well, it's a whole new world to me," he said, finally feeling a little more calm. His ears were no longer ringing and his shirt, damp with perspiration, now felt cold in the evening breeze. Time to go home.

Louise got into the car and Tom drove her home. It would take a while before he was able to figure it all out but he was now leaving for three or four months so the time line worked out pretty well. She gave him a rather nice kiss at the door and then a demure smile as she went inside.

Tom was still too young and too overwhelmed by the dance to say much more so he slunk away, happy to be on his own. He wanted to be with her and to sit down and see where the next kiss led but he was running on empty. Any energy he had, any resolve had drained away. He had had a hell of a time and had enjoyed Louise in a completely new way. She was a nice girl, something he'd always hated. Nice girls were bores, always happy to criticize but never any fun. They never laughed at his jokes and they always, always, always knew more about everything than he did.

But he was learning, he thought. He was learning.

THE THOUSAND MILE STARE

Joe had reached the time in high school when he was just shufflin' along. His future stretched endlessly in front of him and he was no longer able to focus on the here and now. This phenomenon usually happens to all Juniors after the holidays as they see Spring rapidly approaching, followed ever so quickly by a Summer of ruthless self-regard. Joe had glided right through the Spring. He was lost to the world, a slave to his preoccupations.

If he was asked about his "plans", Joe could answer truthfully that he had thought more about the funny looking nail on the big toe of his right foot, the one that he now had to clip *all the bloody time!* If asked about Mrs. Crisp, he would have hedged a bit. Yes, he had a crush on her but it was complicated. He was too young but....but.... he ached whenever she came to mind.

Most people would give up. Sensible people do give up but those addled by their imperatives struggle to fight on. They deny all of the obstacles and don't even consider logistics. If Mrs. Crisp took his hand and nodded a firm assent to his imprecations, what would he do?

If lovemaking is a fine art—and it is—then Joe had not yet advanced to fingerpainting. He didn't even know where to put his podgey little fingers or where to find the paint. Did he own a condom? And where would he get one? And how did they work? And most important of all, how do you do it, the thing?

Luckily, the fates chose to smile brightly down upon him. As he walked through town one day on his way to Jetties Beach, he saw his friend "Monkey" Phillips sweeping the steps of the Windsor place. "Windsor's" was a Bed and Breakfast midway between the town and Jetties Beach and was one of the few places where you could stay the night. Most tourists took the ferry out in the morning, walked around and then went home. If you didn't rent a house or find a berth at a B&B, you were stuck.

Monk whistled at Joe through the surprising gap in his two front teeth.

They called him "Monkey" because of his dental architecture, each tooth as far apart from its neighbor as a child's handful of Go Fish cards. It was rumored with all seriousness that he could chew through a coconut.

"'TChoo doin'?" he asked.

"Aw, I'm just going down the beach and hang out," Joe said forlornly.

"Ya got a job this summer?" asked Monk.

"Huh?"

"Ya doin' anythin' this summer?"

The thought struck Joe for the first time. "Naw," he answered. He hadn't really thought about it. He was too busy thinking about the imperative.

"Windsor's gonna be lookin' for somebody, you know," said Monk. "...And I'm leavin' in a coupla weeks."

Just like that, Joe was drafted into the wonderful and exciting world of hotel management. Just like that, a quiet young man, torn by love and consumed by passions, entered the ancient and thoroughly honorable profession of hostelry.

At first, he just followed his buddy around the place. The little cottage had been altered and reconfigured a dozen times and now contained nearly that number of small, inconvenient and unattractive rooms to let. Each room was provided with a sink and a washcloth and decorated with dingy flowered wallpaper. The dressers had been picked up at rummage sales and the lamps seldom worked. Four of the rooms had showers; the rest shared bathrooms down the hall. A large, lopsided "Knock Before Entering" sign hung on the door but it was dusty from neglect.

"He don't do much upkeep," his friend said quietly.

As he followed Monk through the rabbit warren of staircases and unexpected hallways, Joe tried to keep his bearings. Impossible. He tried but couldn't guess his location through the windows. Where was he? Which way was the street? And what was it that he was supposed to do?

"He's a porefikt bastid, ya know," Monk advised, sounding oddly Irish. Or was he? More questions for Joe. His curiosity was aroused, though. He had no plans and his father would soon be breathing down his neck. This job beat knocking on doors and facing a hundred rejections.

"What do you do?" he asked.

"Well, dare's da usual set up and clean up stuff. Dat's pretty much every day," said Monk. "Den dere's special stoff like when dere's a weddin' or a funeral or sumpin' loik da'." Again, Joe wondered why his friend was suddenly Irish. Had he simply never noticed?

"Are you Irish?" Joe asked finally.

"Naw, sure and I've just been practicin'," he replied happily. "Oy'm glad yer noticed. I'm goin' ta Dooblin to visit ma da'," he added, "...so I thought I'd better speak da language, ya know? Before I go."

Nonsense! But Joe had more important questions in mind: "Why was Windsor such a bastid? Did he know the guy?" He thought he might. "Was he that tall, slender guy with the hair sticking out? He has big ears, if I remember him right." He shrugged his shoulders without thinking about it.

"Oh, yeah," Monk said expansively. "Well, he's torrifically cheap, like all these rich blokes. Ya'll never get an extra dime out of th' guy and ya gotta make sure he don't short change ya or mess widjer hours."

Joe didn't care. He continued to hike up and down the stairways, feeling as though he had entered a sorcerer's labyrinth. Each twist and turn led him to unexpected stairwells and secret passages, the products of mischief and mystery but certainly not civil engineering.

"He's not here t'day, but I'll see him tomorrow and put in a good word for ye." Joe nodded enthusiastically and made a note of the time—

One O'clock sharp—when Windsor would be doing the bookings at his desk out front. He'd be there, for sure, and he'd be ready.

The proprietor, Helmut Windsor, saw him coming up the street and recognized him from the dock. He'd seen him clowning around with the other kids but that's all. He seemed like a good kid. He got right down to business when Joe had taken his seat. Joe had seen him before, too. He was always as perfectly manicured as a rich man's yard. Izod or Munsingwear, always. Stylish. He saw the tennis racket in the corner and the family pictures from Vail.

The guy had inherited the whole shebang from his father and hadn't worked a day in is life unless counting your money is work-- which it isn't.

"Can you haul boats?" Joe nodded that he could.

"Can you clean'em, too?" Joe nodded again and began to wonder what that had to do with the job.

"I want a kid who can do as he's told….," he said as Joe's head continued to bob up and down. Joe began to feel like a bobble doll as his head bounced back and forth and back again. He found himself agreeing to everything, no longer listening.

"Any kid can clean up and set up," he was instructed. "I need a kid who can swim—Can you swim?--and who can handle a boat, too." Joe's head dutifully bobbed up and down, finally developing a little stitch in his neck.

"So: You can swim, right?"

Joe had been in the local swim program, one sponsored by St. Anthony's, back when he was still a Mustard Seed serving up all those fast balls to the accursed Oystercatchers. The "black and whites", the bastids.

"Okay. You gotta fill out some papers and then we'll give you a little trial. Come to work with Maynard (Monk's real name?) tomorrow and he can show you the ropes. Pay is a buck fifty an hour. Izzat okay?"

Joe just kept nodding. "The guy isn't going to listen to me anyway so if I say something I'll just foul things up," he observed with admirable insight.

He had to laugh when he saw "Maynard" the next morning although he kept it to himself. He kept mostly to himself, in fact, as he followed him around and took in the scene. "Clean stuff is here and here and here," he was told, "….and dirty stuff goes dare!" A huge bin marked "LAUNDRY" stood to the side.

"Don't worry about Windsor, do'. He's just a rich guy and doesn't soil his hands with day to day. De guy ya need to watch is Mr. Parler. He's the real manager." Joe thought he knew the guy but wasn't sure.

"Is he the guy you see at Bartlett's all the time?"

"Yeah," said Monk with a nod. "He's okay, do'. Ya just gotta do yer job."

Parler's nickname was unbelievably "Billiards", "Billy" for short. He deserved the name for all the time he had a stick in his hand out back of Bartlett's. He could beat anybody. He ran table after table of straight pool, not sitting down until he got thirsty and needed a Coke. He could shoot behind his back. He could shoot from the left and he could shoot from the right. He could shoot anything. Joe had seen him do it.

"Just do your job and ya'll do fine," Monkey repeated, smiling. "Ya'll be fine."

As it turned out, he was right. It did take him two weeks to learn the routine but by the time his buddy shipped out to "Dooblin" he was a full fledged member of the team, the team being him and him alone. They had caterers and kitchen staff but he was the swing man which meant, of course, that he swung when something went wrong. He tried to see that it didn't.

Instead, things went remarkably well. Cal puffed his chest out proudly when Es congratulated him. "I never thought he'd find a job. His head is in the clouds, I swear," she said. "….Not like Tom, at all." They both nodded. "But you must have said something to light a fire under him because look at him now!" Joe would have a job not just for the summer but for all time, if he wanted it. He'd be irreplaceable. There was a lot going on at Windsor's and soon he'd be a proprietaire extraordinaire!

The school year wrapped up suddenly and summer banged along right after that. Joe found himself working a lot of hours not only on his regular shift but also on "events", special jobs like a prom, a "do" or a wedding. He'd even get tips. He was already packing it away by the time August hit and they were really slammed. He was learning what "full time" meant and he had no time for himself.

One day, for no reason at all, Billy took over the afternoon event and told Joe to go home. He was just about to do it when a thought popped into his head. Could he take one of the dinghies for a row?

Billy didn't mind. Why not? So Joe grabbed a pair of oars out of the shed, threw them over his shoulder and leisurely strolled down to the dock where they were all tied up. As he stood at the top of ramp, he heard a familiar voice.

"Joseph...... Joseph!" He turned to his left and saw the trim figure of Mrs. Crisp standing on the dock. He waved a nice wave and squinted into the sun. "How are you?" she asked.

"Gee, great," he said, thrilled down to his shoes. "Just great."

"What are you doing?"

"I'm working at Windsor's," he told her, "....helping with the day to day stuff and then managing the boats down here." He had given himself a promotion by describing himself as "manager" but close enough, he thought.

"Well, that's just great," she said and thought, "The boy may have a future after all."

"Yeah. A lot of it is pretty humdrum," he said modestly, "....but I'm learning a lot about hotels....." and his voice trailed off. Windsor's wasn't so much a "hotel" as it was a blight but she let it slide.

"That's great," she said.

"Yeah, it's fun," he concluded, turning his face toward the ramp and the little dinghies A, B, C and D that were secured below.

"I always wanted to row," she said suddenly, frowning slightly. She seemed to be thinking out loud.

"Well, why don't you come with me?" he said, proud of his expertise. "I can show you how".

"Oh, don't be ridiculous," she said. "I've got on this dress and a brand new sweater. I'm not going to get them all wet...".

"Oh, come on," he said, confident now. "I'll just potter around right over there," pointing to a little cove just beyond the dock. When she hesitated again, he said, "Come on! I need the practice."

So off they went. Mrs. Crisp had to fuss a bit, dropping her sweater and purse in the equipment chest labeled, "Windsor", and before she knew it he had untied A and was instructing her to "Keep your weight low and step into the middle of the boat or it'll tip and you'll take a header." He was thoroughly in control. Funny how a little authority can go to your head.

She settled into the middle of the stern of the boat, about an eleven footer, and he sat facing her with his feet wedged into the thwarts.

"Off we go," he said jauntily, and cast them off. Mrs. Crisp held the seat with both hands and tried to lean forward into each stroke but still found herself gasping as he made his slow way out to the cove. It was a hot day and the sun bore down on them but the breeze was cool and felt great on the skin. They were having a real adventure. Soon, they were laughing, first at her obvious fear and then at his rowing. He was a little out of practice and caught the occasional crab, throwing water back into the stern.

He looked back at her, horrified. "It's all right," she assured him. "I'm fine."

Twenty minutes or so went by when she remembered her errands and asked him to take her back to the dock. It was fun but duty was duty. She had to pick up her mother's meds or the old lady would suffer from the effects of that purgative so imprudently prescribed by Doctor Short the previous day.

"Any time," Joe said when she thanked him. He'd gotten a little buzz from their cruise to the cove and, as it turned out, she had, too.

"Thanks," she said, this time a little shyly. As she walked away, her head bowed as if she had troubles on her mind.

Now, Joe's focus had gone from the thousand mile stare to just two feet, the space between them in the boat. He thought about that two feet for the rest of the day and into the night. He really did have a crush on her; he knew it. Every move, everything she did was recorded on that thin little wire that runs directly from the eyeballs to the bottom of the spine. He kept picturing her over and over as she sat awkwardly in her seat, gazing out at the open ocean, the boats and then occasionally, at him. He was learning patience and was growing up. He wasn't failing this time, either; he simply wasn't moving as quickly as he'd like.

Neither Joe nor Mrs. Crisp had considered the most important lesson of all, though: The earlier a seed is planted, the deeper the root.

RETIRING THE CLIPBOARD

Somewhere along the way we learn that the boss is the man with the clipboard. And so it is. Tom learned quickly that being a medic was one thing but being a medic with a clipboard was the best. The absolute best. He easily mastered pointing with a pencil and chewing on the eraser and now added cautionary frowns and decisive spitting to his repertoire. He would be the guy pointing and giving orders and if he had to grab himself by the privates to underline the importance of an order, he'd do it and do it with panache.

His advance course at Fort Sam went smoothly and before he knew it he was headed to the wilds of upstate New York. Camp Drum on the Canadian border. He would be serving under a genuine warrant officer this time but he would be learning a lot about property management. He would be ordering supplies for all of Section 4 in these United States. He would be wearing his fingers to the bone writing stuff down, checking numbers and making damn sure that everything went where it was supposed to go.

There was a downside, of course, the weather. The place was really, really cold in the winter and dusty and hot in the summer. Hardy little pines grew on every inch of the place; pinecones were always under foot. And it was boring. After a few months or so, his routine droned on, day after endless day. First it was the unrelenting heat and then it was the unbelievable cold. Not to mention the friggin' snow!

Tom had seen very little snow back home but up by the border it just snowed and snowed and snowed. "Lake effect snow" they called it, from off Lake Erie. Monotony struck him down hard. He became a statistic, a mental casualty of all that snow. Worse yet, he started to think of Louise and couldn't do anything about it. He called her a couple of times and even wrote her a letter but then thought better of it and threw it away. He still hadn't figured out why they couldn't marry and he still hadn't figured out why he would want to get married in the first place. This confusion didn't add to either his pleasure or his peace of mind. His moods darkened to the point where he didn't care if he ever saw a box of Kleenex again for the rest of his life. Ever.

Late one afternoon, he saw a memo in the Stars and Stripes. An exciting career as a Pharmaceutical Tech awaited him if he should deign to apply. Before he knew it, he had not only applied but was accepted and ordered out. He was transferred to tech school, this time to a marginally more agreeable location, Fort Dix, not far from the City. He could get home easy on a three day pass. He was gonna get those passes.

Meanwhile, he was going to learn a new career. Yes, he would have to return to a stool much like the ones at Feldstein's. And yes, he would have to surrender his clipboard for a vest pocket pencil case. He would even run the risk of an expanding bottom but that was okay. He could handle it. He wouldn't have to worry about warehouses any more, just stick some pills in some little plastic bottles now and then. Easy stuff. Ten of these, twenty of those.

When he did get home, he was celebrated again for the hero he was. He was supporting the troops, slept dry at night and got home just like that! He even had a month off in the summer like a Frenchman or someone who worked in non-profits.

He quickly caught up with Louise and she was delighted at his good luck.

"We can do stuff," she said and she said it eagerly.

Soon, he wanted to do a lot of stuff with her. He could see the parents glowering out the window whenever they left her house but he chose to ignore it. "They just think I'm out for 'the thing'," he thought. And, of course, he was.

Island gossip is deadly. It's so fast that it truly may be the first manmade thing to exceed the speed of sound. They were a "couple" now, so hands off! It formed a part of a process, too. Sometimes it was a slow process and sometimes it went on and on and on, to everyone's delight.

First came the gossip, the news so eagerly awaited by island folk. Then came discussion of the gossip, the pros and cons. Then came the decision: Accept or reject. Ultimately, it didn't matter because in most cases they all had to accept the latest development, be it blasphemy or boon. Eventually, everyone just took it for granted. If they hated the news, they'd get a little buzz every time they condemned it to their friends. If they liked it, they'd get a little buzz from the story. The fun of it all!

Tom ducked John Nicholas because he just couldn't face him. He didn't see him much around town so that part was easy. He never saw John's sister, Christina. She was the one he feared, though, because of the Evil Eye and the will. My God, the will.

But he stayed the course because he really liked Louise. He'd never had a girlfriend before so he had to follow that process, too. His mother started giving him advice. So did Cal. Soon, his friends were telling him what to do even though they knew absolutely nothing about it—girls.

Louise was really special. She had a terrific sense of humor and laughed before the punch lines. She laughed at everything. He had never met anyone before with such a positive attitude. She was even more fun than his friends, something that jogged him a little. He was learning about girls, he thought, but he was really learning about Louise.

She liked fish, not surprisingly, given her ancestry. But not the fish you put in a pan, other kinds of fish. She seemed to like all kinds of wildlife. She wanted to, "...blah, blah, blah...," she said, something about study fish and the natural world. She had already spent two years at Woods Hole with the Oceanographic and she loved every minute of it.

He didn't care what she liked. Or rather, he liked her so much that he was just happy she was happy. He discovered she was reserved, dignified even, much of the time but when the ocean came up, she bubbled along non stop. She could talk and talk and that was something he learned, too. She hadn't had anyone to share her thrill. He was the first one. He was number one. Numero uno. And that attracted him, too.

After a few more months, they developed a rhythm. She could expect him on the 12th, say, as part of their routine. He would call on the 9th to confirm and she'd be home when he arrived. They would waste no time catching up and then, be it sandwiches or a splurge at Murphy's Pizza, they'd spend every minute together, a real couple.

The thing came up early on. She liked it and said they could learn how to do it properly, as if it was something that benefited from instruction. Their first attempts were, she said, like the "blind leading the blind" but they both managed to laugh about it. Most importantly, neither lost enthusiasm. Tom found it scary but had long since taken the decision to press forward and he did. Like farm hands across the globe, though, Louise had seen so many animals procreating that it was as natural to her as sweet creamery butter.

When summer arrived, they muscled Joe into lending him the use of one of Windsor's dinghies. They would take the skiff out to a lobster pot, tie up to the buoy and then skinny dip. If someone came along, as they sometimes did, they would wave, smile and keep moving, usually behind the boat. Just as Louise had said. They were seldom caught and even then, they just laughed about it. No big deal.

John Nicholas surfaced a couple of times. He seemed to have his hand in everything. Louise didn't gossip but she didn't consider it gossip if it was a fact. "He's always hustling," she said. "It almost doesn't matter what kind of hustle, either. He just loves the chase."

This was news to Tom who assumed a profession was a profession and a career was a career. He didn't believe that the way to make a living was to jump from one dicey deal to another like a mafioso or a trader in shares. A real job had to have substance, he thought, until he saw John Nicholas at the Founder's Day fandango. John had set up a little tent alongside other tents and he was selling miniature trucks that had a cup holder instead of a bed. When you wound them up, you could place a drink on top and send it across the table to your friend. He sold millions. Dozens, certainly. They were completely and utterly useless but he made $6.23 on every one. Tom tried to do the math in his head.

Joe had already explained the hustle to Tom but Tom hadn't understood. It just didn't seem real to him, the gypsy life. But when he saw John Nicholas, a credible, distinguished looking young man, he could see how it worked: You can pull off a lot of stunts if you look the part. Unlike a lot of what he learned, though, this lesson wasn't something Tom would ever use. It was for other people, not for him. It just settled among all of the other flotsam and jetsam that floated around in the back of his head.

THE BIG TIME

Senior year flew by. Joe had no time for himself. None. He whined and complained when Es scolded him. "You never call your brother," she said. "I don't think I've ever seen you write him a letter." And it was true. But then, Joe had his reasons.

Joe was really busy at Windsor's and really busy at school. He toiled away at his studies with the sole purpose of passing and finishing up. It was a sweat, too. In his mind, he had long since graduated and hated the time he spent either at school or doing school chores. The time he spent on homework was like a dream where the bus was driving slowly away and though he yelled at it and ran as fast as he could, he couldn't catch up. Every fibre in his being strained to get out of there but he had to trudge stubbornly forward as one day led slowly into the next.

Windsor relied on him more and more, too. Windsor was lazy. He could have interviewed others or (Perish the Thought!) hired someone to help but he didn't. He was perfectly happy to crank up the hours on Joe and then "forget" to add the overtime. By the end of the year, Joe had made a lot of money but he was beat.

The only pleasure he got from school was the occasional encounter with Mrs. Crisp. He liked a lot of the other girls, even going reluctantly on the occasional double date. He liked Donna Cossette a lot. She was cute, too and fun but she wasn't his crush--Angela. Yes, he had finally discovered Mrs. Crisp's first name. He had dug out one of the old yearbooks and there it was: Angela Crisp, Guidance Team.

When graduation arrived, it arrived suddenly. He was actually scheduled to work that day because Parler and Windsor had conveniently forgotten to look at the calendar. The date had been flagged for months. Parler groused that it would be "inconvenient" but waved over his shoulder dismissively and gave Joe the day off.

It wasn't much of a day. Cal and Es provided the ceremonial half gallon of Neapolitan ice cream, a Hood's Dairy staple, but Parler called and Joe had to go back that night for someone else's graduation gala supreme.

His skin was grey for lack of sunlight and bags were forming under his eyes. His youth wasn't so much slipping away as being beaten out of him.

Summers on the island arrive suddenly, too. Joe had no sooner slipped off his NHS robes than he was hauling boats, cleaning hulls, fetching laundry and shifting tables out back on the porch. "The Piaza". All that forced exercise had made him lean and he'd put on muscle, too. He was still an amazingly skinny guy, sliver thin, but his shoulders and back now boasted raw sinews of surprising strength.

Occasionally he saw Mrs. Crisp as she made what? A regular tour of the dock? She took the same walk nearly every day so he would catch glimpses of her from an upstairs room at the Inn. She had a white windbreaker that was easy to spot so he was able to pick her out. Very distinctive. By the end of June he knew both her route and her schedule.

One day, he made a plan. He would intercept her and say hi. One hot Wednesday morning, he did. There weren't a lot of other people around; the tourists were just starting to arrive and fishermen were off the pier no later than 7. By 6, most of them. She looked delighted to see him.

"Hello, Joseph," she said with a little smile. "Congratulations on your graduation." He nodded dumbly but she carried on anyway. "You're finally through!" Thinking that was a bit dismissive, she added, "You did well, too. Really well." He had even gotten a "B" in something, she thought.

"Yeah, well, I tried," he mumbled, looking for more praise.

"...And it paid off!" she said, a bit too grandly.

"Well, I was busy; that's for sure."

Mrs. Crisp didn't know how many hours he'd been working but it dawned on her that he had, in fact, been very busy. "That's right. You've been working down here all winter, right?"

"Yup. They couldn't run the place without me," he said, making a face.

"Well, I'm sure they count on you."

"I'm the General, the Captain and all five platoons, I guess," he said, rolling his eyes. It wasn't modesty, either. It was surrender. He simply accepted the drudgery knowing it was a lot better than unemployment and both were better than Viet Nam. Yes, he'd heard about that now, too. She laughed and they both looked down at A, B, C and D, tied up smartly on the dock.

"Ya wanna try your luck again in the skiffs some time?" And she did.

She really had enjoyed their little row last summer and she wanted to figure it out. She wasn't very strong but it all seemed about the rhythm. You used your abs. That, she knew.

"Yes, I do," she said firmly. "I'd love to try it. I'd like to try it myself."

So, just like that they sealed the deal. He had Thursdays and sometimes Mondays to himself. They always needed him on weekends. They settled on the following day, a Thursday, because it looked like a perfect day. No rain and little wind. "Should be fine," they agreed.

This time, she was better prepared. She had been caught with a dress and a sweater the last time out and then had no time. Errands at the house. This time, she had on shorts and a nice cotton blouse. She had taken the precaution of bringing her windbreaker but once they had gotten into the boat he stowed it with the anchor in the little cubby at the bow.

Getting out was no problem. He'd now had lots of practice and rowed like a zen master. Each stroke was precise and crisp. Each one plowed them four or five feet into the oncoming tide. She watched his wrists as his forearms swelled with every stroke. Strong veins stood out against the raw muscle underneath.

A comedy ensued when she tried to change places. He had taken them out to a depth of five feet in the cove, a safe depth, and then instructed her on the rotation necessary to switch seats. Once he had secured the oars in their locks, they would both rotate in the same direction, to their right. They would keep their weight down and avoid tipping. Even an eleven footer, hard chined as it was, could tip like a cork if every caution wasn't shown.

Quite naturally, she went to her left. They collided and he gripped her arm to steady her. She shot out a short, "PffffT!", ducked her head and circled back to her right. They both sat down heavily and he instructed her about taking the oars. "Thumbs below, four fingers on top." Made sense.

"When you get into a groove, you can knock the ends of the oars together at the end of each stroke," he said proudly. He could do it, too. It sounded like a simple thing but it's not. When done properly, a rower can develop a sound that reinforces his rhythm. When it's done wrong—as it is most of the time—the wrists never return properly to the same spot and all harmony is gone.

She had trouble setting the oars in the locks. She couldn't get the lengths right, at all. One oar dipped heavily into the water and the other stuck up in the air. They drifted toward shore. Joe leaned forward and yanked them together. He then sat down and coached. "Reach, dip and pull," he said. "Reach, dip and pull." He said it quietly, too, smiling encouragement but watching closely as they drifted toward the rocks.

Mrs. Crisp must have tried it before at some time because she did exactly that. She reached forward, dropped the oars almost simultaneously and then pulled them smartly back to her chest. But then she stopped, taking a little breath. An anxious breath. Exhaling loudly, it looked as if she was done.

"No, no," Joe said, staring over his shoulder. "Again. Again," he almost shouted.

Then she saw the problem. They were washing backwards on to the rocks. Biting her lip, she reached out again and dug in. She continued to reach and dig until she had pulled them out to the center of the cove.

"Boy, that was great," he said and she accepted his praise with a look of utter bliss.

"That was really great," he repeated, honestly impressed.

She didn't want to seem too cocky but she admitted, "I can do this, I think. I can do this."

She really had done wonderfully well and was duly proud. Looking over her shoulder, she tried again, this time more slowly, more rhythmically.

"Out and in," she thought. "Out and in." She caught a lot of crabs and doused El a dozen times, once spraying a bucketful of water in his face. He shrugged and simply wiped it off. It was warm and he dried up quickly.

When they got back to the dock, he took her arm firmly again and helped her up. She accepted his help and said brightly, "I want to do that again some time." They agreed on Monday and she was off.

"Pretty nice", he thought. "That was pretty nice." But what he really thought was raw emotion, the absolute opposite of thought. His thoughts were conventional; he'd taught someone a skill or at least started to teach someone a skill. His emotions had taught him something else, though. His excitement wasn't going away. If anything, it was worse than ever. It was out of control. He couldn't wait to get through the next three days.

Monday morning, she arrived at 9:30 sharp as they agreed, looking once again, full of game. She wore a smart green cotton blouse above a pair of Bermudas and he could sense that she was ready.

He took the skiff out past the rest of the dinghies but once they got to the end of the dock, he got up and they executed their switch again. This time, she managed without dunking them both. The wind was a little higher so she frowned with concentration as he repeated, "Reach, dip and pull", and hauled away with healthy strokes.

Smiling and full of accomplishment, she made for Wouldbe, a small island about a hundred yards offshore. You could walk to it at low tide but now the tide was full, making it something more special, a secret place. There was a small beach so Joe jumped out and pulled the skiff up on to the sand as she gripped the seat to steady herself.

Exploring the "desert isle", they both felt bold and adventuresome. Despite its modest size and the fact that it was within clear sight of land, it was a world apart, exciting and new. Or at least they felt that way when they scratched their way through all the weeds, scrub pine and tough little oaks. Everyone did. It was a real destination, if seldom used.

A narrow path led around to the right, so they pawed away the branches and made their way to the end of the little key. There was a small area there where they could sit and admire the vast oceanscape. The thick grass was covered with pine needles someone had trampled down, making a large mat, big enough for two. They plopped themselves down, Mrs. Crisp still breathing heavily from the row and the climb through the bracken. A half dozen Novie boats stood a mile out to the East, hauling traps. They settled down.

As they scanned the sky and the ocean, their thighs touched briefly, something they didn't expect. Joe shivered from that touch. And so did she. They were both breathing heavily now. Joe tried to distract her by pointing to a cargo ship on the horizon but she showed no interest. Instead, she stretched out heavily on the grass. She looked up at him and heard a low, soft voice issue from deep within her chest. "I want you to kiss me," it said. When Joe turned and looked down at her, he was overwhelmed by her beauty. Her arms, her hair, her lips, her tongue.

He rolled over slightly and their thighs touched again sending thrills to the base of their spines.

"I want you to kiss me." He heard it again and again even though she never parted her lips. She just looked him in the eye and he knew that's what she was saying. To him. To herself. To them both.

Slowly, with a gentleness he had never felt before, he bent and pressed his lips softly to hers. For a long moment he held them there, then pulled away. Her hand reached to the top button of her blouse and slowly slipped it out. Then another. He didn't know what to do at first but then did the same. Soon, his chest was pressed to hers and they could feel the heat. The rest of their clothes melted away as if they were smoke or mist or part of a dream.

When it was time, she raised her knees to her chest in the Happy Baby pose and guided his hips. Her body welcomed him. It opened up to him and as she held him gently, he entered the soft, warm folds of her down below. She pressed her knees to his sides, directing his energy and marshaling his strength. They rocked slowly and rhythmically until quite suddenly, the rapids shot him over the waterfall and he collapsed from the weight of the surge.

It was quick, that first time, but she consoled him when he tried to express his regrets. "Don't worry," she said, stroking his arm. "In a minute or two, we can try again." When he looked doubtful, she said softly, "You'll see."

Against all odds, Joe was turning a corner. He had been failing and learning, failing and learning and failing and failing all his life. Now, with her help, he was just learning. That summer, he learned a lot. He never had access to tools for this kind of education so he had to chart a whole new curriculum for himself.

If college or grad school is the pinnacle of learning, Joe was grinding his way slowly up from the primary grades to Junior High and he was climbing with a will. He was going from the little room full of crayons at one end of the hall straight up to the big room at the other end, chocked full of Thucydides and quantum mechanics.

GOSSIP

One legend has it that the word "gossip" is a conjunction of sorts, formed from the two words, "go" and "sip". Traders in the 17th Century would "gossip" about ships and cargo at a coffee house either in London or Boston or Philadelphia and then knock down their deals. "Gossip" was serious business, indeed.

Just how "gossip" became the lifeblood of whole communities is not known but many consider it one of the most important parts of their lives, even their raison d'etre. It's that important. It might more properly be termed an "Expose'" but "gossip" survives as the term applied. It often fulfills a need by allowing us to diminish others. It can make our miserable lives seem more worthwhile and can also bring down the big-headed people, the hypocrites and people who inspire contempt. If a bad thing happens and they are implicated, it's a joy to behold. The whole town can revel in their slow, painful decline.

Joe and Mrs. Crisp were, in many ways, immune from that contempt. Everyone knew them and liked them so when they were seen occasionally in a boat, people thought nothing of it. During the winter, when Joe was left alone to manage an empty inn, no one thought much of that, either. He hung out the Christmas lights, put up a menorah and took down Mrs. Crisp's knickers without a blink from anyone. He even put out cider and doughnuts for the Holiday walk that she served to the cheerful throng.

Tom and Louise got all the attention. You would have thought that a camel was breeding with a nanny goat; the pair was so extraordinary. It just wasn't natural, a Yankee boy from an old local family and a Greek girl from God Knows Where. Their children would look like she-wolves or Presbyterians!

None of this mattered to Tom and Louise, though. They were quite properly living in the moment. Neither felt encumbered by their heritage; if anything, they felt liberated by it. Tom didn't know a thing about his grandparents, let alone his family tree. He didn't know and he never asked. It was of absolutely no interest to him.

Louise thought for herself. She adored her family and everyone in it but she could see how firmly they were tethered to the past. Like most second or third generation people, she just wanted to have friends. Friends and a family and, of course, a career.

People gossiped and found fault. It gave them a sense of importance and a little glow. It felt great! "There she is!" they'd say but the conversation quickly palled. There really wasn't much to say. It was the oldest story in the land: Boy meets girl, everyone sees how wrong they are for each other and they get married anyway.

The whole "marriage" thing had been a gaff from the beginning. It was tradition speaking and not real people. Her family jumped to conclusions based upon customs that dated back aeons but had no relevance in the modern world.

Tom and Louise knew this: Marriage is a big deal. Going around together and having fun? Well, that's just fun. It took them a long time to come around to the idea of something serious, to commitment. They did finally come around to it but they did it in their own way, slowly and surely with real confidence.

Tom was learning to compartmentalize which, of course, can be dicey. It takes some maturity to do it properly and no one ever does. However, when it came to Louise, he was a natural. They were a natural. Like any successful couple, each had his/her own domain. He was the detail man and she saw the bigger picture. He took care of the widgets and the whatnots but she never took her eyes off Polaris, the Northern Star. Her smarts got it done. He tidied things up, cared for the little things. Not much got past the two of them, or so it seemed.

DX, RX OR EXIT?

Tom's transfer from Kleenex tissue to the dispensary might not have seemed like much. It was all about the bathroom, right? But it wasn't.

He had learned the basics of being a Medical Corpsman but that training had largely been associated with "the field", the battle zone. He could slap on a tourniquet and apply mouth to mouth.

Are you suffering from a sucking chest wound? Strictly routine. He'd stuff your guts back into your chest and call for help. That was it, though. Other guys'd haul you back to the field hospital if, perchance, you survived his ministrations.

Doling out drugs to patients was something else. It was a lot less stressful than the "field". Monday mornings were always busy and long weekends always meant there'd be a crush; that's all. For the most part, people received meds on a regular basis. Ten milligrams of Valium for Sergeant Wingood and forty for Corporal Blake.

Tom didn't have to actually diagnose anything; that, after all, was the hard part. If a guy was lying in a ditch screaming his brains out, you had to think fast. It could be his heart, his liver or a hole in the back of his head. Figuring it all out was a job for professionals, not for PFCs.

At the dispensary, all that work had been done for him. He just had to look at the script, then go out back and dive into the stock. They had tons of supplies from skids of Vaseline right up to the good stuff, amphetamines and opioids. Crates full of it, all marked "XXX" or "XXXX". If he'd been a grifter, he could have sold half of it but he didn't. It never occurred to him. He just wanted to serve his time and get back to Louise. He counted the days.

Sure, basic had been fun. And then Camp Drum with all its ice and snow and thundering emptiness. His first few months at Dix were great, too, with a change in uniform, a hike up to E4—along with the raise in pay—and now, a seat at the counter. He was a formally trained and certified Pharmaceutical Tech and his course was charted for at least the remainder of his hitch.

He didn't think he'd stay on, though, "re-up". His suddenly friendly Sergeant kept hinting at all of the benefits enjoyed by "lifers", the guys who did re-up. There might even be a bonus now that the draft had started and President Johnson was knocking heads out there in Viet Nam. Well, not President Johnson himself, mind you, but all of the guys he sent over there were sure knocking heads.

Every day they got a press release on the body count of black shirts we had slain. It was like the "catch of the day", scrawled on blackboards at the Coop back home. Each fisherman dumped his catch into a trough full of fish, slapping and gasping their last breath. The catch was then weighed out and he picked up a check. Now, of course, it wasn't haddock or cod, it was Viet Cong. Or, at least that's what he thought they were. Tom didn't really know. Good thing they were going to wipe them all out and come home soon!

He didn't want to wait, though. He wanted out. Louise had completed the first phase of her apprenticeship at the Oceanographic and they were already pitching jobs to her. Some of them meant travel and unless the travel was to Fort Dix, he wanted her to stay home. He was getting nervous. They were still too young to marry but they were hooked. It was going to happen; they just didn't know when. Pretty soon, maybe.

As it so often does, worry became a habit. He worried about his folks as they aged. They were now pretty much unencumbered with obligations so they were free. Free! Free for the first time in a long, long time. They started saying outrageous things about sex, "Oh, it's wonderful!" and religion: "I hope Reverend Walton doesn't retire soon. I want him to be the one to bury me." They stayed out late and went to restaurants on Friday nights.

Tom worried about his brother now, too. He was smoking grass; Tom was sure of it. He got it from the college kids; he knew that, too.

"That stuff is for hippies!" he'd shout at Joe. "It's for jazz quartets. It's for junkies." He paused for dramatic effect and then came down hard: "You'll be taking heroin next. Mark my words!" But that last bit even sounded phony to him. He'd picked it up from his parents who always told him to, "Mark my words!" be it a science project he'd ignored or his lifelong aversion to carrots and peas.

Without even knowing it, Tom was becoming conservative. It was a slow, slow process, this education, but he was learning. He liked order now more than any other time in his life. He hated a mess. If the guy on duty before him left his counter sloppy, he was ripped. If Louise was stuck and had to work late, he himself was a mess. He liked things "normal", something we all like but never encounter in real life.

As his tour wound down it looked more and more as if Louise would have to make a decision. She had lots of choices but if Tom was going to make his claim stick, he'd have to speak up soon. The clan had stayed unified but he saw cracks in the wall. They recognized him now and said hello. They'd tell him Louise was "over there" and point because they knew that's why he was there, be it the Elks Hall or the bank, the lighthouse or the beach. Everyone knew they were together.

John Nicholas appeared now and then and he sometimes saw the dragon Christina but he just got a wave from John and a glare from her. No one attacked. Maybe if he showed some promise, they would relent. This, again, proved the ultimate challenge. After White's and Feldstein's and now, after the Army, he still had to get a job. A real job.

At the same time, Joe was working himself sick at Windsor's. The old guy never lifted a finger and Joe was run off his feet. Monk had returned but his heart wasn't in it. His brain had stayed in "Dooblin" along with most of his money but he didn't care. "Oy!" Echoed through every corner of the town; no one ever knew why. Joe did the work and although he was grateful to "Maynard" for getting him his chance, Joe himself did the business. Monk just fooled around, a perennially fun loving, irresponsible and often superfluous employee.

Joe heard rumblings, too. Sure, the place was empty all winter but Windsor's kids saw potential. They wanted to expand, something that sounded no better to Joe than putting mittens on a snake or Drano in the fruit cocktail. The place was already a fright. The joke was that some people never came out. Once they'd entered the furthermost rooms of the Inn, they just melted away......or became part of the beef stew on Thursday night.

You couldn't add on to the building anywhere. There was nowhere to go but that didn't stop the kids. They, too, had been spared the necessity of developing a work ethic. Their sole motivation was simply to pump more money out of the inexhaustible fun site, Windsor's bodacious B&B. Hunter Windsor wanted a Jet Ski; his sister, a place of her own. These were their imperatives. They didn't even live on the island any more. They rented.

No one in the family stayed in the Inn, as it turned out. It was neither safe nor salubrious. The walls were so thin you could poke your nose right through them. And after the first couple of hours of, "Ohhhh! Ohhhh, Jimmy! More! Give me more!" you stopped laughing and just wanted a good night's sleep.

And the threesomes! The threesomes! They never stopped. On any given night, the sounds emanating from "Suite 14" could have served as the sound track for "BEHIND THE GREEN DOOR", the video portion being omitted, of course. The next morning, after you pounded on the wall all night, they'd be down in the breakfast room, munching on granola and sipping tea. "Bastids!" you thought and "Bastids" they were.

Mrs. Crisp was the one who finally figured it out. "You could set up for yourself," she said flatly. She was, after all, a leader of lost souls, the ultimate life coach, a professional Guidance Counselor.

Joe shook his head. What did she mean?

"Look: You've done everything at the Inn, right?" she asked. To which he nodded emphatically, "Yup!"

"So you've had to cook, right? And clean?" Yes, he had.

"You've also had to do some plumbing. You fixed that faucet in the basement. And you wired that light in the garage, too. Didn't you?" Again, Joe just nodded.

"You do the boats, you do the trailer and you can paint! You've been painting every day this year, I swear!" She was getting hot now, knowing that Joe had given better than he got. Windsor had been taking advantage of him from day one. He still only got $1.78 an hour, not enough to feed a cat.

"How about that window you replaced?," she started but he just held up his hand.

"Sure, sure," he said. "You're right." He thought a minute and then muttered, "....and I've replaced three of the gutters, too." The list was endless.

"Well, why not set up on your own?" she repeated. "Why not just quit and do odd jobs? Nobody does odd jobs any more." She waited for that to register, then added, "You could make a lot more money and have a lot more time to yourself, that's for sure."

The thought had never occurred to Joe. But then, why not? He could go downtown, see Mrs. Truscott and get some licenses. While he waited for those to arrive, he could paint and paper, beat rugs or walk your golden hind. He could freelance.

And unlike his more cautious older brother, the guy who wanted everything just so, Joe started really thinking about it. "I can get a truck," he thought, the extravagant first step of every contractor who ever walked the earth. "It would have my name on the side," he opined. "I'd be like a real grown up." And he would. Like many who simply blunder into a profession, the answer had been staring him in the face for four years now. He'd be his own boss! How about that!?!

He told Tom. For Tom, there couldn't have been anything more timely. He never listened to his hophead brother, but this time, he did. He'd get his ass up to the island, get a solid briefing from Joe and then go see old man Windsor. "Who else did he have?" he thought. "He'd be lucky to get me!" Things were falling into place. Little did they know how well.

SWAPPIN' OUT

"I'll give you two bucks an hour but that's it," warned Windsor. He was used to being pushed and he knew a bluff when he saw it.

"No, no," Joe said. "I'm not trying to squeeze money out of you, Mr. Windsor. Honest."

"All right. Two ten, then. But that's my final offer." Windsor stared down from his huge oak desk and clenched his jaw. "Thirty-two cents more an hour! The ingratitude! I've given this kid a great job and a great start in life and what does he do? He screws me!" Self pity comes easily to the self-absorbed; self-righteousness, too. "The little bastid!"

"Well, I appreciate that," Joe said, trying to remember the coaching session he'd had from Mrs. Crisp.

"He'll try to manipulate you," she said. "He'll try to be your friend and when that doesn't work, he'll try to bully you. It's classic narcissistic behavior." She let that bit of basic psychology drop, then added, "He will do anything to knock you off balance. Lie, cheat and steal."

"Gosh," thought Joe. "She's tough." But in the end, she was right. She knew bullies when she saw them; she had worked in education. She also knew cheapskates, one of the many iterations of narcissism. They were all basically hoarders; they just tried not to show it.

"Don't forget your ace in the hole, either," she counseled. "You can tell them that you've got a replacement. Your brother."

"That's true," thought Joe. He and Tom looked so much alike that a man with poor vision could hardly tell them apart. It would be almost as though he had aged a couple of years and suddenly acquired better posture.

So when Windsor played the guilt card, Joe was ready. "I'm not abandoning you, Mr. Windsor. I've already spoken to my brother and he would like to be my replacement."

This was unexpected. "I thought your brother was in the service."

"Yeah, yeah. He is. But he's getting out soon. He's had it. He wants to get back to the island." He let that sit, then said, "He's a good worker, too. I promise. I'll bring him down to see you in a couple of days. You should see him. He's very responsible."

".......and he'll work for less because he's new," thought Windsor. The thought of coming out of this discussion with a savings made his heart flutter just a bit. It felt like being kissed.

Joe told Tom on the phone that night. "You get down here this weekend and I'll set you up." Tom said he could make it and duly thanked his younger brother, the one whose head was in the clouds.

This was exciting! Joe's mind was buzzing. He'd get a truck. He'd always wanted a truck. And then he'd get one of those magnetic signs you stick on the side with your name on it. Pitiful, really, but the mind of the newly minted contractor always and invariably follows the same illogical steps. Pickup truck, sign with your name on it and debt. Last but certainly not least, the work.

Cal and Es had no influence over him at all. They told him what he'd have to gross if he wanted to make money and he shook them off. "I'll be fine," he said. They then tried to tell him what it would cost to buy a new truck but he shrugged that off, too. "I've got it covered." It was an impasse as it always is with children. It doesn't stop until they pass the true test of adulthood, the ability to laugh at their parents. Then and only then are they all grown up.

When Cal and Es finally accepted Joe's intransigence, Es took him aside and uttered the three words he had always hoped she'd say: "Ask Mrs. Crisp." It shocked him out of his boots. How did she know about Mrs. Crisp? And how well did she think he knew her? And did she know that he and Mrs. Crisp were making haylofts over there at the Inn? Had he left her underpants in the car or something? What!?!

But Es wasn't going to give anything away. She smiled sweetly and then changed the subject to the Baltics or the BoSox or Battalion command. He never knew what but that was the end of it. In those three little words she had given the couple her blessing, her acknowledgement. Maybe the old girl wasn't so daffy after all!

Tom showed up that weekend with fire in his eye. He had given Windsor's a lot of thought since Joe suggested the job. He was ready. He was learning now in a new way: He wasn't just learning and failing on his own; he was learning from Joe's failures, too. Joe had served Windsor's as a sort of indentured servant, being forced to run circles for the guy. Tom would put a stop to that, right quick.

He would learn the job, make himself indispensable and then put the hammer down. He'd call the shots, not the grasping and conniving boss.

He knew logistics and could organize vendors, assure better quality fish, meats and produce and then upgrade the place. For a price. He could do it in his sleep. Junior partner, here I come!

The first interview with Windsor got off to a shaky start. Like many who have fallen into the deep pockets of inherited wealth, Windsor was unable to see out of it. His view of the world was extremely limited but it was all he knew. He would have been surprised to know that some people don't receive dividends every month. Many don't even know what that means and can't tell the difference between a debenture and the deep blue sea.

Windsor had been schooled early in finance, though and had a solid grip on his investments. His broker told him so. His broker never spoke of the many times he had "adjusted" one of Windsor's impulsive decisions but it all worked out in the end. Windsor even developed a sense of infallibility. That's bad enough but he also took it one step further, as people do. He took a good long hard look at his wealth and elevated status and concluded that he knew everything else that needed to be known, as well. He was a kind of genius. He accepted this conclusion with quiet pride, as he should.

This led Windsor to make a lot of foolish, ill-considered decisions. Yes, he should have stuck to what he knew or, in his case, gotten others to figure things out for him. He didn't, of course. He made decisions and everyone cleaned up after him.

That was the only hitch in the switch. That was where things could go wrong. Windsor was such an insufferable snob and so thoroughly wrong-headed that he was almost certainly going to gum up the works. It made both Joe and Tom a little nervous.

But again, Tom had figured it out. He showed up in uniform. In uniform!

He looked as smart as a new coat of paint and twice as bright. Brass! Polish! The works! Windsor was prepared to talk down to the kid, just another undistinguished local kid, but he was impressed. The kid looked good. He looked together. "What's your name again?" he asked.

"Thomas, sir". And he knew right away that he had gotten the proprietor's full and complete attention. Those two words alone nearly sealed the deal.

Windsor started out by asking his experience and his strengths but he didn't seem to be listening. Instead, he was playing the angles. He was ignoring the simple process of application, examination and exchange of ideas. In this game, though, he was shooting pool with a broken stick. Tom had all the advantages because Joe had told him everything about Windsor and the Inn and he had told him in great detail. He also knew the guy needed someone who could do the job.

But first, an awkward probe or two: "I suppose it will feel good to be back home and out of uniform, eh?" tried Windsor.

"I don't know. I'm not sure. I have a chance to go abroad if I re-up... ..," Tom answered coolly, "...but my brother is leaving and asked me to talk to you. He thought you could change my mind."

"....and they pay probably don't pay much to a Corporal, I'll bet."

"Well, all my expenses are covered so I mostly send money home for my folks or just save it. I've done pretty well." Tom let that hang and then dropped the crusher: "The only thing I've missed is the opportunity to travel and now they're offering me a foreign post. I could live out my days in either…." Tom tried to think of some exotic places. "….in either Germany or….Brazil." He had forgotten that Brazil was one of the few places where the Army hadn't established a presence but no matter.

Windsor just nodded his head.

Finally, Windsor accepted the inevitable. Not with grace and not without a struggle but his survival mode kicked in and made the decision a fait accompli. "Well, we don't want you going to Brazil, do we?" he said with a strained smile. "Bastids!" he thought. He was stuck.

Joe had told them both his timeframe: It was flexible but could not be stretched too far. Tom told Windsor that he'd be free in three months but that he had a lot of accumulated time. He'd be home frequently. He could follow along with Joe, learn the ropes and then slide right into the job. This left the lazy and distracted proprietor with little choice. None, really.

Finally, he hired Tom and then got him to work out the details with Parler. Hours. Days. Months. He also got the two of them to see how closely they could match Tom's skills to the endless facets of the job. If Tom answered all their questions honestly, he would have said, "Zilch. Niente. Nada. No comprendo. I don't know boats and I don't know food. I haven't yet managed one complete trip through the Inn on my own and haven't driven a truck since I picked up eggs for Doc Matthew."

Instead, Tom nodded, "O' Course." "Sure." "All the time." It got so silly that when asked if he knew how to jibe a catamaran he remembered the James Dean line from REBEL WITHOUT A CAUSE. "It's all I ever do." Both Windsor and Billy Parler were nodding their heads. They agreed to a buck sixty an hour "because you're a veteran" and Tom was hired.

With Joe's help, Tom had cast a spell of gypsy magic around their heads.

They were enchanted with their new "boy", almost in love. They could both goof off more now. Parler had his eye on a Nine Ball tournament in Providence and now he'd have extra time to practice. A lot of money was at stake.

Windsor just stroked himself. He felt so smooth that it almost felt like the real thing, amour. When he closed his eyes he just saw dollar bills. Then, casinos. And after that, a thousand dancing girls. Girls who danced for him and loved those dollar bills. It got all mixed up but he loved it just the same. His face glowed with self importance; it was better than sex.

THE TRANSFER OF POWER

The boys joked about the ease with which they'd swapped places. They were duly solemn whenever on the job but when Tom realized how totally free of supervision Joe had been, he couldn't take it in. He was finishing three years of complete submission to his superiors and this was a big adjustment.

"You mean, you just do the job and they leave you alone?"

"That's pretty much it," Joe said. He never forgot either Windsor or Parler and quite rightly expected—really expected—them to be hiding behind every door, watching him. Observing him. Checking up on him. He found himself acting all the time, as if on camera. He never slipped up. On the few times when they had, actually, snuck up on him, he was doing his job, tending to stores, moving the boats.

Tom would have to go through a trial period just like his brother and adopted the same pantomimes. He felt like a teenaged girl who rolled her eyes at every parental shout. After a while, it was almost fun. He told Louise about "the grunt" he'd make when he hefted an anchor or hauled laundry out to the truck. If Windsor was around, he'd heave up the hood of the truck, squint a bit, shake his head and then make believe he was checking the fluids. He didn't know which dipstick was for oil and which for the windshield washer but he made a terrific show of it. He just took them out, frowned and put them back in again. It all looked very efficient, though.

They both made good use of the ten weeks at the end of Tom's hitch. Louise knew a guy who knew a guy, too. She tipped Joe off to a seven year old pickup that if not glamorous, ran as smoothly as a public official. Gas powered, too, not diesel, so it didn't stink.

Mrs. Crisp returned the favor by advising Tom on the layout. "These additions would never meet the current codes," she told him. "This construction is totally illegal. It's claustrophobic and it's confusing. What if you had a fire!?!" That got Tom thinking.

"Maybe I can put up some signs and diagrams," he said. "Tack'em on the back of the doors." Tom was learning and learning fast. His mind was working hard, imagining the order he'd impose on the place. Insurance adjusters from here to Omaha would be clapping their little hands.

Joe was learning, too. He sent away for some business cards. At first, he thought fifty would do but was talked into ordering more. He found a place that made magnetic signs, too. The door on his truck would carry his name proudly, "Joseph Bustle, General Contractor". He wasn't going to be a "general contractor" in the normal sense but he liked the martial sound of the title and insisted on it. He would be a big shot now, with his name splashed all over town. The guy talked him into a couple of lawn signs, too, at a "special rate". He'd stick them out front of a job site and people would see them as they drove by. Advertising. Wow!

So, as Tom headed toward the day when he rolled out his last box of tissues and left this man's Army, Joe tied up loose ends at the Inn. He caulked the dinghies and shellacked the oars. He even bought a new mailbox, the old one having rusted so badly that the door fell off. He bought it with his own money, too, just to show Windsor how appreciative he was.

"Always leave them laughing," Mrs. Crisp had said and she was right.

She had even introduced Joe to "business plans". It turned out that you became "established" and made friends at the bank if you did that. He couldn't imagine why he would ever need a loan but she got him to do it anyway. She typed out a plausible story and he signed on the dotted line. It said something about building up and knocking down; that's all he knew. "Repairs", too, he thought. He trusted her with the details and didn't care about them anyway.

Cal and Es were delighted because both boys would be home and under their roof again. Ah, the bliss!

For the first couple of years, things worked well. By 1968 the country was struggling but Joe had easily doubled his income and Tom had taken over the Inn. He ran it smoothly, too, as smooth as the heavy, dark Vermont maple syrup that covered his buttered buns. All this worked out fine until a sea change arrived that completely reconfigured the coast.

Tom and Louise were thinking of marriage but the Oceanograhic was making offers. Greenland. Ceylon. Every place but the Siberian Veldt. She was itching to go but she wanted Tom more. They had the "talk" and decided to do it. She went to the family and gutted it out.

"But you can't marry an American boy," said Mr. Papodopoulos. He frowned as only an elderly Greek can frown, with a sadness as deep as the Aegean sea. His eyes closed to stanch the flood and his chin dropped until it pressed down hard on his chest. His whole body sagged. It wasn't the tearful collapse of a teenager but sorrow put his whole body to work. He even got his knees to buckle, or so it seemed.

"You can't do it," said her mother with tears of her own, clearly showing the state of her despair. She looked away and shook her head dismissively, too, waving her off. Louise thought the wave was too much, reminding her of the Chinese man at White's who knew absolutely no English and was forced to confine his responses to nods, winks and brutal chops with the side of his hand. "No!"

Louise had a good plan, though. She picked a school holiday when Christina and John Nicholas and the whole Matsikas clan would be away.

It was actually a Jewish holiday, "Tu Bishvat" or something, a holiday that celebrated good works or horticulture; she never knew what. She did know that she could handle the folks but if she tried to face the clan, they would gang up on her. They were so dramatic, they'd overwhelm her. So, just before dinner and just after a small glass of retsina, she laid it all out. She and Tom were going to keep house.

They'd even located a cottage out in Surfside that nobody seemed to want. They could buy it cheap and fix it up. A perfect first home.

In the end, the energy fell out of their opposition. Each desperate surge of passion was answered with a shrug.

"You don't even know the boy!" This after six years.

"What about his parents?"

To which Louise answered coolly, if not tactfully, "We're going to live on our own. We're not going to live with them."

"What does he do?" they asked and she patiently explained about White's, the lemonade stands, the Army and now, management of Windsor's Fabulous Inn and Whatever.

They got under her skin when they asked about the Oceanographic but she winced a bit to herself and then answered as truthfully as she could.

"I will always have options with them. They like me and I love the place. I may ship out on assignments from time to time but Tom understands. He's fine with that. In the mean time, I'm on a long project that will take years to complete."

This was a perfect diversion because they both wanted to know what she was doing. "I'm doing local shellfish right now. Way cool. Stuff you eat. Ocean harvests and stuff like that." She even punched it up with a little arm waving of her own.

Eventually, she wore them down. They had Tom to dinner and he brought a military bearing to the table. He answered politely, "Yes, sir," and, "No, ma'ame" to everything and they liked that.

"Nobody shows the respect," Mr. Papodopoulos said later. When his wife gave him a hard look, he just shook it off.

"They must raise the children Greek," she said and by "Greek", she meant "in the church".

"Of course," said Mr. Papodopoulos, as if that didn't even bear discussion. His mind went to the nippers, though, and how he would teach the boys to dance and the girls to fish. Or vice versa. They'd have a big party and enjoy the true St. Nicholas Day, not the foolish one embraced by the Western church.

So it is written and so shall it be done. Louise apologized but it didn't matter to Tom anyway. "These Greeks are terrific planners," he thought.

"First we can or can't get married---and that's on our first date. Then they say how we raise the kids."

"It won't matter," Louise said matter-of-factly. "They'll probably be dead by the time kids come along anyway." The coldness of the remark caught Tom off guard but when he looked at her she was laughing and unbuttoning her blouse. Just for fun.

Things went differently with Joe and Mrs. Crisp. "I've told my husband," she said one morning. They were stretched out in the room Tom had reserved for them--Room 13, his lucky number--and were staring out the window at the thunderheads as they blew offshore. They both radiated a post-coital glow that was so warm they kicked the covers to the floor. She quietly stroked his arm.

Joe didn't know what to say. He looked closely for her pain. None showed or at least none seemed to show. She was still full of rapture from the morning's tryst. He looked down at her shoulders and her soft, white skin. She simply looked him in the eye. "He was surprised," she said, finally. "He's not very observant so he hadn't seen any telltale signs."

His mind raced. "What telltale signs?"

Again, she answered his thoughts with thoughts of her own. "There were no signs," she said. "We were always very respectful and very discreet." They had, too, Joe thought. They didn't want to embarrass the guy. Far from it.

"He took it quite well," she said finally. "We had one of the best talks we've had in years." She paused to let that sink in and then added, "He's closing in on sixty so he's focused on that. He's also more interested in his new MacGregor irons than he is in me."

Joe was insulted on her behalf. "What?"

"No, no," she said, holding up a hand. "It's all right. He only thinks about his stock portfolio and his bloody golf." Joe looked puzzled but long years with Mr. Crisp had given her deep insights into an essentially shallow man. "He'll be fine."

Again, Joe was out of his depth so she laid it all out for him. "I'm not going anywhere; that would just cause problems." He reluctantly agreed. "My mother can't be moved, either. She's getting really forgetful now so her next move will have to be to nursing care. In the mean time, I can't disturb her any more than I have to."

"Wow!" thought Joe. "This lady should be in charge of the U.S.A.! She really has figured it out!"

In the end, they all realized it was a matter of dramatically shifting sands. It was time for younger folk to take their place in the world and it was time for older folk to make room for them. Things would be different. Sure, the young were jubilant, excited even, but those older folks who were wise enough to understand knew it was time. It was time. They had exhausted themselves in an effort to stop the inevitable and now they had to let go.

KIDS

Windsor had two children, both of them special. Hunter played second fiddle to his older sister Alexandra but they were both special. Alex entered the challenging world of kindergarten at St. Luke's and Hunter wowed them two years later at Grace. From that moment on, they showed the world the meaning of "exceptional". They excelled at everything they tried, often making it embarrassing for the rest of the class, the ones who couldn't keep up.

Alex had her first work hung at the Whitney, the local grange hall, and each piece was a showstopper. Other works had been hung there, too, but they were mostly done by upperclassmen, the third and fourth graders, and were arguably more "advanced". Nonetheless, her work was then and is now, unique, another word for "special".

Hunter's art was performed either in, on or under the water. He was a terrific swimmer and took honorable mention and a bright new ribbon from every event. The headmaster himself told him without irony that he was "special". He went on to say that all of us, near and far, are special but Hunter didn't hear that; he was too happy being reminded again just how wonderful he was. He carried that glow right into adulthood, beaming confidence from every pore and through a beautiful set of bright, white teeth. He always had great ideas.

They both played golf because when Nantucket sent off its final whaler, the SPERM SEEKER, it had to reinvent itself. There was nothing else there but a few beaches and for most Americans it simply wasn't worth the trouble of going to an island for a swim. They needed other attractions, other hooks. Some of the more urbane habitues got together and suggested golf. You could mow down some fescue, dig out some bunkers, plunk some flags out there and just like that! Become a destination.

It was safe, too, much safer than real sports like basketball or football. It was even safer than tennis where, after all, you can turn your ankle. It wasn't "real life" where you risk far more than ankle sprains and it wasn't "real life" in the sense that you worked and then took your reward in the form of an 18 hole round. Life for special kids is recreation. All of it, from the fourth hole at Doral right up to the gala for charitable impulses.

At some point, though, even special kids realize their lives are empty and unproductive. They collect dividends and loan out money to themselves but they don't actually earn anything. Many, including Hunter, decide that they have to assert themselves. They've long been proven special so what could go wrong? Everything they touch turns into a lollipop! They always win and therefore must know best.

Hunter thought correctly, that Windsor's had potential. It was a gold mine; it just needed more aggressive management. His father was getting on in years and it was time for him to take over. Amazingly, his first suggestions were largely ignored. The senior Windsor swatted his ideas away like an earful of the famous island ticks.

This only served to confirm that it was time for Hunter to take over.

Clearly, the old man was no longer capable. "He wouldn't know a good idea from a bad champagne," he told Alex. She agreed, of course, and could also see dollar signs. It was time to give the old guy the push.

They didn't form a plan, exactly, but acted on intuition. Hunter started hanging around at the Inn, moving tables and switching the light bulbs on and off. Alex was busy but flew to the island on weekends and managed events. She stood by while Tom and Parler organized or catered affairs and corrected every phase.

"Those heaters should go over there," she said, pointing her crooked finger like a cartooned Disney witch. Her long nails had been painted orange, too, so the effect was wholly theatrical; more like a drag queen's naughty vamp.

"....And we'll have to have more shrimp." She didn't like cocktail sauce so she banned that as "too proley" and substituted a special concoction of her own, soy sauce in everything but name.

Soon she was having so much fun that she wanted in. Hunter was just a dumbhead, she thought, so he could take over the dock. She would handle the food and most importantly, the decorations. "God knows the place needs a do-over!"

Old man Windsor eventually felt the push. If he'd been self-made or even vaguely interested, there could have been trouble. But after all those years of cheating contractors, underpaying staff and fantabulous paydays, he was tired. He was! It finally dawned on him that he could still make money if the kids took over. He'd relinquish control slowly to insure that cash flow but otherwise, why not? He'd worked long enough and now it was time to enjoy the fruits of his labors. That, and his other family, the one off Barcelona on the island of Impetigo. God, how he loved that blue, blue water! His little chubby was doing flips.

At first, neither Tom nor Parler paid much attention to Hunter and Alex. The kids were in the way but Tom had established such a smooth routine that even though the kids interfered, they, too, were largely ignored and didn't do much harm. They got complaints from the staff, the hirelings without which there is no party and they got complaints from the "poonters" as Monk said but that was all. Nobody stormed off and they didn't lose much business. If anything, receipts were up due to some of the repairs Tom had done. Things were cooking along in spite of the kids.

Hunter actually helped at times. He wouldn't caulk or clean bottoms but otherwise managed the boats pretty well. No one was hurt, at least. Alexandra was a different story. She had an inspired design sense and kept abreast of the fashion scene. She was known to subscribe to at least a dozen slick magazines and kept in close touch with friends in "the biz". They said she knew Halston or had met him that time. No worries, she would turn a dozy, quaint hostel into the Savoy or at least an island version thereof. She couldn't wait!

She saw a lot of reasons to sideline the old man. He had started calling everyone "Arthur" for some reason, particularly the help. Not the women, of course; he called them all "Maisie". She thought she'd better stop that before someone was offended and filed suit against them.

The staff, of course, didn't care so long as they were paid. There was actually something quite delicious and zany about being called either "Arthur" or "Maisie". It brought back warm thoughts of slave days when all the servants were "Uncle" this or "Aunt" that. Nobody ever thanked old "Massa" Windsor; that would be too much. Instead, they showed their appreciation by thieving from him every chance they got. Hams and turkeys went South regularly, true to the spirit of those bygone days.

Alexandra didn't care for any of the established practices but as her father's clarity slowly faded, she saw a pathway to her own success. More a boulevard, actually, or a ten lane freeway like the ones you see out west. She was the heir apparent and presumptive—along with her thick-witted brother-- but now she would assert herself. She faux apologized to the staff for her father's growing incompetence, thereby earning not so much their warm regard as their suspicion. They could smell a rat and that odor was starting to permeate the place. "If she can give the old man the push, she won't worry about us; that's for sure."

Morale, then, just got worse. Hunter knew precious little about dock management and habitually offended staff or, more seriously, condescended to the "the poonters." . People stopped showing up. The regular flow of customers started to decline, be they people from the inn or just day-trippers. A very profitable hustle was producing no income at all.

Eventually, it would come to a head but nobody saw it coming when it did: Alexandra, her father and Hunter were going to clash. One always expects it to be something cataclysmic but in this case it came down to a can of worms.

Someone had rented a boat, taken it out fishing, hooked into a school of mackerel, dropped off the boat, gone excitedly home with his "catch" and failed to clean up the boat. "Staff" hadn't cleaned it either and the next morning it was unapproachable. The stench could have broken windows; it was that bad.

Hunter showed up, was horrified and called an "Arthur" to clean up the mess. The otherwise anonymous "Arthur" nodded his head thankfully, "Yes, boss," and disappeared. When another "Arthur" sidled down the gangway, he was summoned to do the work and he, too, said, "Yes, boss" and disappeared. Hunter was furious as much with the lack of respect as he was with the stinky boat and hurtled up the stairs in pursuit of an Arthur. None could be found. They had all disappeared. Vanished. Evaporated.

This left Hunter with no choice. He had to clean the boat himself. He dug out a pail and a pair of boots, some gloves and a hat that looked a bit like a beekeeper's dashing chapeau. It made for a fascinating but unfashionable ensemble and caught the attention of his sister, who stared down from the Inn, horrified.

Alexandra was having none of it. "That does it!" she thought heatedly and bolted down the stairs. She would lay him out like baccalat and he'd never cross her again!

Sparks flew out of her ears as she charged across the street. Alex and Hunter were both tall and skinny like their father but she was bad diet slim. Her shoulders were no wider than her hips and her bottom was narrow and flat, suited perfectly for the broom she was rumored to ride. Local gossip, that, but firmly established, too.

Hurtling down the ramp, she threw herself at her poor, befuddled brother. He was wearing not a beekeeper's veil, though, but a hat he'd been given in Australia to keep off the midgies. The broad brim was perforated with a dozen little holes and from each hole a cork had been strung making him look so not much like a beekeeper as a native Aussie on walkabout.

He was still down in the boat when she got there, his outfit splashed with fish guts, sand worms and that indescribable stench. "What the hell do you think you're doing?" she shrieked.

"I'm....."

But she gave him no more time to complete his explanation. Her eyes turned red—RED!---and snakes crawled out of her sleeves. Her crimson toenails looked suddenly like daggers and her knees flexed as if she was about to spring.

"What are you doing?" she screamed again, now bending at the waist, her arms akimbo.

"She will strike!" he thought. "She's going to hit me!" He instinctively covered himself and he did it just in time as she grabbed a boot from the dock and hurled it down at him. When he looked up at her, she was already firing the other boot at him. Then some waders and some pot buoys. More buoys followed but when she bent down to drop a pot on top of him, they heard another voice.

"Whoa down there, missy!" It was said quietly, but it cut through all the other noise. Both Alex and Hunter turned in the direction of the voice and saw Barry "Big Ears" Frazer, a local fisherman.

"That's my gear you're throwin' down there," he said. They could see a dark, dark frown beneath the whiskers, a dark, forbidding frown. A frown that spoke of death and daily acquaintance with death.

Like a lot of privileged people, Alex did not have the common touch. She didn't relate to people well, being exceptional. She also couldn't read the crowd. "Who do you think you're calling 'missy'?" she screamed, much to Hunter's relief. Suddenly, her rage was directed sideways, deflected from her brother and fired like an almighty glare at Frazer.

"Well, those boots are a hundred fifty a pair and the buoys are another twenty-five each plus the cost of the paint," he said quietly.

These facts did have some effect. They slowed her down. Someone will have to pay for them. It wasn't going to be her; that's for sure.

"Now, look what you've made me do!" she screamed, returning her fire back at Hunter. "You've made me throw that crap at you and you're going to pay for it."

Hunter looked first at one and then to the other of them. Then, he looked beyond them to the crowd of visitors standing on the dock.

Socks were falling down. Mouths stood open and one old man was laughing uproariously, displaying a large gap in his front teeth where the bridge had fallen out.

This was too much for Hunter and he lost his footing. He tried to recover but stumbled forward instead, throwing all of his weight to one side and capsizing the boat. The oars floated off, his tools went to the bottom and even his hat, buoyed by the corks, seemed to be seeking escape as it floated quickly beyond the rest of the boats and out to sea.

Hunter scrambled back to the dock where he was greeted not with welcoming arms but by the bright red toes of his sister's feet. One foot was stomping up and down in time with the hell fire she was raining down on top of him. He hauled himself out of the water and kneeled there in defeat.

Frazer had had enough. He walked up to the two of them and said simply, "I'll send the bill to the Inn," and walked up the ramp to the top of the dock. A dozen "poonters" stood at the top but they parted to make room for him, no one saying a word.

Alexandra stared down on her brother and let go. Hunter was not nor would he ever be anything but an idiot. He was incapable of doing anything productive and would never learn. He couldn't even do a decent job as dock boy. "A twelve year old……." and so forth.

Hunter stood there and took it or rather, kneeled there and took it.

He was still trying to catch his breath and was weak from the fear. She had caught him at an especially vulnerable moment and she took full advantage of it, rattling off one weakness, one failing after another.

A lifetime's worth of grievances spewed forth, ending in this: "I'm taking over this hotel and not you. You are going to have to find something else to do with yourself." And then, remembering a line from a really great movie she had seen at the Bijou, she dropped the bomb: "I can't work with you."

Alexandra stomped down the dock, up the ramp and away from the assembled spectators. What a pistarckle! They were already gossiping before she crossed the street. This was fantastic! A military coup in the making! Their tongues were wagging even as Hunter made his humble way up the ramp. They parted for him and looked away in silence but as he crossed the road he could hear the hum of their backchat like a hatful of cicadas. This was fantastic! "I can't wait to tell Gladys! She hates'em, the bastids!"

SUCCESSION

Tom learned about the battle when one of the Arthurs rushed down to the boats. Hunter had left the capsized dinghy right where it was and stuff was still floating away. Would they lose the anchor, too? And everything else in the cubby?

One of the kids rushed by Tom and yelled back that, "The shit has hit the fan!" Tom looked around and saw the bedraggled form of his boss's best and brightest coming his way.

"What happened, Hun?" Hunter just glared at him.

"Are you okay?" Still, the glare.

"Can I get you something?"

To which Hunter answered, "An axe. You can get me an axe so I can crush her bloody skull."

A tiny bit of Tom's brain said, "Yes. Get him the axe. He'll chop up the sister and you'll be in charge." But Cal and Es had raised him right so instead, he asked, "Let me get you a towel, okay?" And the glare returned.

"I'm gonna take off her mashed potato head," he screamed only, he didn't say "mashed potato". He used an epithet so rude, so insulting, so ethnic that he must have learned it from either The Rolling Stones or prison, hopefully the famous British singing group.

Tom was shocked at the language but he'd heard that kind of talk many times in the service of his country so it wasn't so much the vulgarity as the context that jarred him. He didn't stop, though. He was programmed to function under the most raw and desperate of situations. He reached out, took Hunter firmly by the arm and led him upstairs. Along the way, he grabbed an armful of towels and some disinfectant they used when the sewer backed up.

Hunter allowed himself to be led, surrendering totally to Tom's control, in fact. Tom slid open the shower door and turned on the flood. Hunter was soon under the flow and was hosed down like the daily catch that he'd become. Tom didn't even ask how it happened because every guy needs just that little bit of self-respect. Instead, he assumed something bad had happened and imagined the consequences.

Somebody would get in trouble; that was a given. He couldn't lose any staff so he'd have to cover for them. He quickly and neatly set out a handful of possible excuses for malfeasance on the part of an Arthur or a Maisie. He laid them out on a table in his brain:

1. Trouble at home.
2. He/she tripped.
3. A momentary lapse in judgement but overall, a good worker.
4. Faulty vision/ health problems.

All of these seemed reasonable so he fanned them out and then pondered each one. One excuse notable for its exclusion was the slightest possibility that Hunter had done something wrong. That explanation would only cause problems. Beyond that, the thought that his sister had erred in some way was beyond consideration. It was impossible. Special people simply don't foul up. We know that, he knew that and most importantly, Mr. Windsor and his kids knew that.

Finally, there was nothing to do but wait. Hunter said nothing when he emerged from the shower. Tom just smiled, handed him a couple of towels and said, "Well, yell if you need anything." The kid nodded and turned his face to the mirror above the sink. He was already thinking about his hair.

By the time he'd gotten downstairs, though, the staff was buzzing. A wonderfully theatrical event was now playing out, complete with hoots and guffaws and sincere wishes of a permanent injury. None came. In fact, when Hunter finally descended the stairs, he just looked bloated from all the crying and hysteria. Everyone found something to do and quickly disappeared. Windsor's was known for its labyrinths and now they were calling out to everyone. Every man jack of them just vanished, poof! They'd hear the details of the whole four act drama eventually and weren't going to hang around to become one of them.

Tom had to stay for the denoument. Years later, he'd say it was "an education".

BUSINESS AS USUAL

Joe seemed to have one hand on the phone and one hand on a deposit slip most of the time. Certainly, he did when he wasn't physically on a job. Just like his brother, he'd long since adopted the answer from REBEL WITHOUT A CAUSE and it had become his answer to everything: "That's all I ever do." It didn't matter if someone wanted a squirrel removed from the attic or a screen door put on a porch.

"Masonry?"

"Sure!" he'd say.

"Did you ever pave a driveway?"

"How about roofin'? 'Dja ever do a roof?"

His answer to everything was, "Yup!"

This led to some embarrassment but never to a change in reply. If you asked about any job short of open heart surgery, he could do it. He once did a roofing job that created a runway for squirrels and that led to repairs and a red face but it didn't slow him down.

Soon, he had to take on a kid, a kid just like him. A kid who knew absolutely nothing about hand tools and the willingness to prove it.

Sammy "Sam" Claveau would come to work, put on his tool belt and stand a little taller. He had the eagerness of a compulsive gambler. He wanted to learn, though, so Joe dragged him along. Jobs went faster and the kid really did get it after a while.

There's always a "however", of course. "However" this time was the war. It was now a hot war out there in Southeast Asia and Joe had read enough to know that it had nothing to do with the U.S.A. It had only to do with the Dulles brothers and the CIA and "the best laid plans" of an incompetent and arrogant cadre of old men who couldn't accept their own intelligence reports. Never mind apply common sense.

"They have to talk to Ho Chi Minh," said Mrs. Crisp with an irritation he rarely saw in her. She was worried; he knew that. Things were getting bad.

"I think you have to branch out," she said one day. The draft was also hotting up and Joe was a prime candidate without either a convenient college deferment or kids.

"You're gonna have to enter 'essential services'."

"What's that?" he asked.

"You're going to have to work at a job where you get an exemption. Like the aviation industry or something." When he nodded uncomprehendingly, she added, "I'm gonna look into it."

In the mean time, Joe saw increasingly chilling reports. Data streams meandered their way from Saigon to Pacific Command to the Pentagon and down through the hallways of officialdom. By the time the reports had been sliced and diced, filtered and sanitized, the USA was way ahead. The daily count of enemy who were "neutralized" was breathtaking.

"We must be winning," he told her. "Look at the numbers!"

But Mrs. Crisp wasn't fooled. She knew a bit about bureaucracies. No one took responsibility and nobody questioned the boss. It all came down to the boss, just like it did back home.

"I think I have an idea," she said one day. "I think I've got the perfect job for you."

When she told him about it, he only said, "It stinks." That is, her solution was elegant but the job itself did, in fact, stink.

Mrs. Crisp had gone to see some growers. Agriculture was going to be the path they took to "essential services". If you grew a product essential to the war effort, you got a pass or at the very least could argue eligibility for that pass. She even checked with a local attorney, a scrappy, almost scary guy in his fifties named Culver Michaels.

Michaels had been a champion hustler back in the day when golf and poker or pitching pennies meant big bucks. He possessed remarkable instincts and never lost his cool. It was often said of him: "He has the blood of a fish!"

Mrs. Crisp had known Michaels for a long time and had even served on a committee with him, an adjunct to the zoning commission. Both had been appointed by the Board of Selectmen and reluctantly inquired into the "feasibility" and "appropriate nature" of some renovation in the historic district. It was all nonsense—whether a vinyl insert could be used in a wooden window frame—but they tried to look serious and exchanged a lot of eye rolls.

She called him up and he remembered their service together. When she asked him about deferments, he had already had two cases, both of which resulted in a waiver.

"You can get out of the draft for essential services, yeah," he said.

"What about agriculture?" she asked.

"What're ya growin'?"

"Garlic. Garlic and onions," she said.

"Oh, yeah," he answered briskly. "I would think so. I mean, I'm not Italian but what is food without garlic and onions? You gotta have'em. You gotta. We gotta have garlic and everybody eats onions. It's in everything." He paused for a second to work up a full head of indignation, then rushed ahead, "Oh, yeah. You gotta have onions...and garlic, too, of course." His nose was already sniffing a fight.

So the next stop for Joe and Mrs. Crisp was the Irvings. Jack and Dahlia had had been cultivating the more aromatic of our vegetable friends for years. They explained their dilemma and the Irvings, who were against the war were either Socialists or Pacifists or both. Who cared? They were quickly on board.

"The thing is that we don't really need any help," Jack said.

"Yeah," Dahlia added. "They're root vegetables. You don't have to do much with them. After they're planted, you just watch'em grow."

"Well, there must be something...." said Mrs. Crisp, her determination showing by the furrows that suddenly formed across her forehead.

"We do need a shed for the tractor," Jack said. "...but that's about it."

Joe leapt at the chance and Mrs. Crisp filled in the blanks. "Okay, so I can get on a weekly payroll, right?" And they nodded their assent. "And I can build you a shed," he added.

"Well, why not go for a barn?" asked Mrs. Crisp.

The Irvings looked doubtful but when they projected it over a two year period, they started to come around. "That would actually be pretty cool," said Dahlia. "I could do my painting on the second floor. Sort of a studio or something." Jack and Dahlia were newlyweds so they were still deciding who made the decisions. He had learned the benefits of agreeing, though, so he just nodded his head. "Of course."

"The gypsies use it to ward off evil spirits, you know," Dahlia added as they went into the house. "Garlic, I mean."

That got Joe's attention. The vision of Johnny Ice raced back into his brain. The black hat, the black shirt and pants and, of course, the Cadillac Coup DeVille that was not only black but the size of a clipper ship. He saw them all. All of the romance, all of the danger returned and he heard, actually heard the clacking of castanets. Ole! From that day on, he wore a clove of garlic around his neck. To keep him safe.

Joe set up a whole new schedule. He had so much to do! He had a sink and toilet to install for one guy, a porch to wire for another. He'd have to get cracking and get Sam to rough out the jobs before he went in to finish them up. It meant more hours for his new assistant, too, so smiles all around. In the mean time, he had to sign all of the income tax forms, the withholding forms and all the insurance forms to show he was a full fledged, 100% authentic agriculturist. A farmer, through and through.

All this work didn't leave him much time for fun but he always made time for Mrs. Crisp. She continued at the school so they were both busy during the day but the rest of the time they just spliced their schedules together. As time went by, they began to realize how lucky they were. Or, as she said, "blessed". They never fought; they never seemed to disagree. He was so totally smitten that he was happy having coffee, so long as she was there. She was just happy that she made him so happy. They were great to be around and didn't once embarrass you by holding hands.

UNDER THE FLOOD LIGHTS

Alexandra was too savvy for her little brother. By the time he had taken his shower, recovered himself and gone to see his father, she had already set the stage. She had worked up some tears and run into his office exclaiming, "Oh, Daddy, daddy! He's just awful. He's just awful!"

Windsor had been absorbed in a recent copy of GOLF DIGEST and was in the middle of an imaginary round at Pinehurst #2. He could see himself just beyond the fairway trap on the seventh and he was preparing his approach.

"Who's 'awful', dear?" he asked, trying to appear as if it mattered.

"Hunter! Hunter!" she shouted, rubbing her eyes. "He's just impossible!"

"Well, what happened?"

So she told him the whole story: How Hunter had gone down to the dock to prep the boats and how he had made such a mess. About how he had "made her" throw stuff at him and how he had hurt and embarrassed her in front of "everyone". "It's all his fault!"

"Well, of course it is," said the old man, again trying to appear concerned.

"He's going to pay!" she screamed. "He has to pay!"

"Well, of course he does," he said, returning his gaze to the seventh green and the bunkers he'd have to negotiate. "Probably have to hit an extra club," he thought.

By the time Hunter arrived, his goose was cooked. His father had taken his feet off the desk at this point and was glaring at him. "Your sister says you threw stuff into the water and now we have to pay back that bastid Frazer!" He paused for a second and then through narrowed eyes asked, "Did he say we owe him a hundred bucks and I've got to pay him?"

Hunter was stunned and just mumbled, "Something like three or four hundred, I think."

"Well, that's crazy!," yelled the old man. "What were you thinking?"

Hunter was too scared to speak. He just stood there waving his arms, finally collapsing into a chair.

Alexandra made a little moue`, something she considered a more stylish form of gloating than either a fist pump or a moon. She took a position just behind her father and placed her hand on the narrow slope of his shoulder. It almost looked affectionate; it certainly looked supportive. They were a team, united in the one goal of bettering the Inn. They would stand together as one, partners. Even if it took an LLC to do it. She'd see to that.

The whole production had played out even better than she planned. She started patronizing her brother in a new, much more calculated way. She would ask her father questions like, "Do you think Hun can handle the trailer all on his own?", diminishing her brother each time with brilliant little jibes. Soon, he was no more than a cypher, barely distinguishable from one of the staff. Another "Arthur" but not an Arthur from the round table, more like Arthur from the dog house out there in the back.

Tom, Parler and Monk Phillips kept their mouths shut and did their jobs but once Alexandra had her hooks into the place, their days were numbered. Parler was the first to go because he was paid the most.

"No loss," she said when her father questioned the decision. He just shrugged his shoulders and the guy was gone.

Monk was next. He'd never really done anything but follow orders and was just another member of the staff, if an employee of longer tenure. Soon he, too, was made redundant. "A kick in the ass and the thanks of a grateful nation," said Tom, familiar as he was with the loyalty of superiors.

That left Tom to fend on his own and it was too much. When you run a small business by yourself, it's hard. There are challenges every day and you struggle just to keep up. When someone else is adding to those challenges, throwing a stick into every wheel, it's impossible. Soon, he was looking for another vehicle by which he could make his climb to the top. He had learned many things but most importantly, he had learned the great, good lesson that comes from being dumped: There are some who will find a way to fail despite every possible advantage. He wouldn't get caught in the middle like that again.

He had Louise to consider, too. He not only had to find a new job but that job had to be one that looked good to her folks. He didn't want them to find an out. They were going to get married and he didn't want problems, just a nice, smooth path to conjugal bliss.

John Nicholas had the way. He seemed to have a sixth sense when it came to disasters and sniffed out the difficulties at Windsor's with a remarkably keen nose. "They're gonna be dead without Parler, you know. And if you leave, they're goners. They don't know anything."

Tom always wondered about the Greek pipeline but it was high and wide and thoroughly uncanny. They seemed to know stuff the minute it happened. They knew stuff before it happened. "Maybe they're gypsies," he mused.

But, no. John Nicholas was no gypsy; he didn't have to be. A cousin of his friend was a "Maisie" at the Inn and he heard about Hunter's collapse and fall from grace that very day.

"If you leave, they're…..," and he turned thumbs down, "…..dead….."

Tom had to agree so he and Louise spent a night strategizing. What could he do? He could organize. He could make order out of chaos.

He knew logistics and most importantly, he learned. He learned when things went well and he learned when he fell on his face. The question before him was, "Can I take all those lessons and really make them work for me?"

John Nicholas had an idea, too. The Greek pipeline had provided him with some inside information that could prove useful to Tom. Janey's, the candy store in Hyannis, was going to open a shop on the island.

"Whaddaya know about candy?"

Tom had to think a minute and asked finally, "You mean like Milky Ways and Three Musketeers?"

John Nicholas flashed him a look of disbelief, then said simply, "Good. Then you won't interfere."

"Huh?" Tom asked.

John Nicholas bit his lower lip and launched into an explanation about candy manufacture. He seemed to know a lot about it but then he made it his business to know odd bits of things no one else would consider interesting. It paid to have an edge and he always had an edge.

"Basically, you start with your chocolatier or your sugar guy and go on from there. That's a real big deal. The cook is the guy because he's the key to the whole operation." Tom nodded. Makes sense.

"But the real business is sales." Tom snuck a peek at him because it sounded a lot like self love. "No, really. It takes a great cook to make a product but it takes us—sales guys---to get the product out there."

Tom hadn't really thought about that much. He just figured you bought that junk at the counter when you were there for something else. Every cash register he'd ever seen was always surrounded by junk— jerky, cigarettes, Chapstick or something for a goiter.

John Nicholas could read his thoughts. "I'm not talking about Clark bars or Almond Joys, you know. I'm talking about the real thing, local specialties like rock candy or salt water taffy but chocolates, too. Meltaways, truffles and raspberry creams." Tom wasn't even sure what a "meltaway" was but didn't want to admit it.

"People really want that stuff," he added. "and tourists are crazy for it."

Tom had seen that, all right. Every room he cleaned at the inn had a box or two of some kind of candy. Everyone seemed to like the salt water taffy and he'd seen lots of chocolates, too. The little kids gorged themselves on the rock candy but parents kept the good stuff out of reach.

"They're cheap souvenirs, too," said the ever excited John Nicholas. "People go on vacation and they want to bring something back home to either show off for the neighbors or give to the guy who fed their cat.

They want to feel good again about their week on the Cape. Candy is the perfect souvenir. You don't even have to store it after you're sick of it. You ate it all up!"

"Yeah, yeah," Tom replied, allowing the idea to sink it a little deeper.

"But where would I come in?"

"You move stuff, right?"

"Yeah."

"....and you handle supplies, right?"

"Yeah," Tom answered again.

"...and you can be nice to people when you need to be, right?"

"Of course."

"Well, they don't need a chocolatier. They need guys who can get this stuff in front of the public. They need sales guys and they need operations guys. They need a guy like you!" He poked Tom hard in the chest and laughed as if possessed.

"You got it made in the shade!" he smiled.

Tom wasn't so sure. He was going to have to think about it. He would have to learn about candy before he committed but it could happen. This was possible.

"What's the hours like?" he asked.

"It's not like a bakery; I know that. Pretty regular hours, I think."

That was a big relief, for sure. Tom had been bounced all over the place in the Army and at the Inn, even at Feldstein's. He wanted a little more stability in his schedule. That way, his hours would be more predictable and he could spend more of it with Louise. He'd have to learn a bit more about the product, though. Maybe take a taste.

If Tom had the good luck to see his situation from space, he would have seen that the whole drama at Windsor's was playing out very much along traditional lines:

Guy builds business, kids manage the business, grandchildren "improve" the business, business collapses and a new "Guy" comes along and picks it up cheap.

ISLAND FOLK

You can't hang back if you live on an island. You have to network and while that sounds as though it comes from the playbook at Yale or the Odd Fellows Hall, it's no joke. If you don't get the word out, you'll never get a problem solved. This doesn't come any more naturally to island folk than it does to normal people, either. Most of us learn early in life that other people are annoying, self-centered and not to be trusted. They certainly don't make us a priority.

This doesn't matter too much when you live in a city or are otherwise surrounded by lots of other people who, like you, are sure to be famous some day. They understand. If you need something, you ask for help and they find they're suddenly busy.

Island folk can't snub each other. It will always come back to haunt them. More importantly, we all need favors at times. If you alienate a guy and show him in no uncertain terms just how little you think of him, he'll remember. He may not even remember your name but he'll remember you for the perfect bastid that you are. He'll remember the time he asked you a simple question and you weren't even civil to him.

No: Island people are civilized because they have to be civilized. You have to share. You are stuck with each other and whether you "like" someone or not doesn't matter. You have to extend a helping hand because your hand will be reaching out the next time and no one will be there to take it. It's not complicated; it's not higher math. It's a fact of life.

If, however, you're a child of privilege and never had much contact with nor ever wanted to acknowledge your fellow man, you're going to be just fine until that moment comes when you're in a fix. When that happens, you will have no community, no peers from whom to seek advice. You may have friends and you may have colleagues but you are very likely not to have people who can fix things for you.

This is precisely the dilemma many rich folk find when they've been removed from the mainstream. They've lost the ability to cope and any skills they developed in their youth have withered away. They've relied instead on wealth to answer for all their problems.

"Why try to save three dollars when that three dollars doesn't mean anything?"

"Why fix a car when you can simply buy a new one, a better one?" and, of course,

"Why worry about an annoying employee when you can go right out and replace him/her anytime anyway?"

See? No brains. No navigation. Just money. It becomes the only solution to every problem, the only tool in a now teeny, tiny tool box.

These lessons are hard for all of us to learn but if you're special and above it all, these lessons can be impossible to learn. We need other people. That's it. So when Alexandra inserted herself into the business and gave her brother and then her father the push, she was in for a big surprise. Morale at the inn had sagged when she and her brother arrived but Tom and Parler had acted as a buffer. Monkey Phillips had provided the comic touch, too, a guy who could joke if not command.

Now, there was no buffer. Alexandra had built up no karma and any that her father had cultivated quickly evaporated when he left. Karma seldom survives a generational change and this was no exception. It all came down to bucks. If an Arthur didn't want to work on a Friday afternoon, he felt no obligation to come in. He'd suddenly develop a chest complaint and would be out for "a few days." If a wedding or a funeral or a retirement party flopped, well...... That's just too bad.

Worse yet, Alexandra had no roots in the community. She didn't know a guy who could fix a broken window or mend a fence. She didn't know any support people, come to that. She had also never developed the skills necessary to deal with new people, old people, women and minorities. She just treated them as anonymous "Arthurs" or "Maisies" fresh off the plantation. This led to problems.

Things might have gone better if Windsor himself had stayed on as a "consultant". It even made good sense from a tax standpoint but he had pulled up his anchor and made for more promising shores. He had retained a financial interest but no longer advised, guided or coached. He was out and he was out with a smile on his face. Sadly, this would lead to lessons none of them wanted to learn.

ONE FOOT ON THE BOAT AND ONE ON THE DOCK

Joe now had two jobs and Tom had none. He had a shot at the candy job but he hadn't stitched it up yet. Cal and Es were shaking their heads and making Sunday dinner a strain. Louise was still getting offers at the Oceanographic and fending them off was becoming harder and harder despite the wonderful news she reported to Mrs. and Mrs. Papodopoulos every day.

"We've got to make a plan," Louise said to Tom. She was serious, too; he could tell.

"I'm never happy without one," he confessed.

"We want to get married, right?" To which he turned a blank face.

"Of course," he said.

"Okay. Then why don't we lock it down."

That sounded great to Tom except for the job and the money and his entire future. Those were more concerning at the moment.

"I think I know how to do it," she said. He looked at her with a mixture of surprise and real fear.

"I think we present it as a fait accompli," she said, uncertain of his French.

"...And how do we do that?" he asked.

"First, we lock down the candy job." When he looked uncertain, she said, "They need a guy with local knowledge, somebody who knows the island.

That's you. And you need a job." He nodded hard at that.

"You can do it," she continued, confidently. "You can do it. I can get John Nicholas to help, too. He has all kinds of connections." That was certainly true. Yes.

"Then we buy that old house between Nobadeer and Surfside."

"You mean that one near the dunes?" he asked. They had seen it together and joked about it as a first home but it had been empty for years. An old "For Sale" sign bearing an off-island phone number had been stuck up in front for as long as they could remember.

"I can ask Michaels if anyone has shown an interest in it. Maybe the guy is asking too much and just maybe it's been neglected for so long that nobody asks any more. It might be perfect for us."

Tom's mind was racing. "So, we'll need a loan or something….."

"Don't worry. We've both got a bit put away and my folks can help if we need a hand. We just have to sort out the details." When he flashed her a hard, skeptical look, she added, "You'll see."

Her initial call to Michaels got her nowhere. He thought he knew the place but when she gave him the address he couldn't find it in the town records. "Maybe it doesn't exist," he said, attempting a joke.

Eventually, he found that it was originally part of a larger parcel and had been adjudicated by Land Court. If that was the case, it might have been recorded as registered land. Those deeds were harder for lay people to access and would have discouraged some developers. He'd see what he could find out.

Meanwhile, Tom sat down with the folks at Janey's. They seemed really uptown to him, a boy from the island. They had NDA's, background checks and asked him for references just like a real job. John Nicholas had smoothed the way, though, so once they got through the initial awkwardness he sat down with the boss. The chef really was the boss, the chocolatier.

Like many chefs, Marcel was a prima donna. Tom saw the neck kerchief, the goatee and earring for what they were, clear signs of a dilettante. Chef wanted nothing but the freedom to create his many truffles, meltaways and other magnificent confections; he didn't want to deal with the public. "They're idiots," he said casually. "They buy salt water taffy the same way they buy my chocolates. My chocolates are the product of genius. Each one is a masterpiece. They leave the shop with one box of my chocolates and one box of taffy as if they are the same. Idiots."

"Yeah, great," thought Tom but he smiled back in a way that would become his default expression. He smiled and smiled as if looking at a love object. He smiled as if the chef was Jesus Christ. Sandy Koufax at the very least. He somehow managed to sustain that smile, too. It didn't crack and it didn't wilt. It just stayed there on his face as if glued there with a great whack of Elmer's glue, the household adhesive that seemed to solve every problem that ever befell the family home. He just smiled and smiled.

Chef saw that smile for what it wasn't: Adoration and sincere. It was a fraud but it was an agreeable fraud. He was, after all, the chef, the maestro, the brains and more importantly the palate of the business. He knew his chocolates and more people should wear that smile. More of his customers should show him the respect, the love that Tom showed him.

"I think I've found my man," he opined. "I've got to hire him. He's got a great looking ass, too." That last thought was by the way but first impressions count so Tom was killin' it. Marcel knew what he wanted and what he wanted was Thomas Bustle. He nearly hired him on the spot. A glow began to warm his chest and the muscles in his face relaxed. "Now, I can create my treats. Now, I can create perfection." He even envisioned the ultimate delight, the one that would get him into the Michelin, the perfect combination of caramel, dark chocolate and....... pecans. Yes, yes, pecans!

Tom stepped away from Windsor's gracefully. People from small islands learn very early not to burn their bridges. And even though his final week overlapped with his first week at Janey's, he found time nights to oversee and smooth the transition. Alexandra had a problem with his lack of "loyalty" but was confident that she could do his job. It meant a savings, too. Smaller payrolls meant greater profits, right? It's simple math.

Down below, on the docks, it was a different story. Boat people will tell you that boat maintenance is a constant struggle against the elements but you don't believe it until the weather hits. Everything goes wrong.

Boats leak and sink. They get swamped and sink. Their caulking gives way and the wood starts to rot. Then, dry rot sets in. Then, the oars need shellacking again and again and again. The maintenance never stops until it's time to haul them for the season. That's when the real fun begins because the water is ice cold and you're constantly soaked to the skin. Your hands are so cold that you lose all feeling in them and then bash them with an anchor or cut them to pieces on a stay.

Hunter wasn't used to physical labor; he was used to fun. The dock was no fun and he came to realize the contributions made in the past by the staff. It wasn't all profit for him now; it was work. It was a hard and sobering realization. He was humbled. Not A.A. humbled but humbled.

When he got a weekend off "to do some stuff", he took time to reflect. He was going to have to learn how to work with others. He was the boss, sure, but he needed to learn.

When he went back to work, he went up to the first Arthur he saw and asked him about teak. He asked the next guy about motors. He even asked them about bait for the pots they fished off Wouldbe Island. Pots were a big hit with the poonters who screamed like teenagers when they hauled them up, found a crab or a couple of shorts. If they dragged up a keeper, it was served to them that night. Or at least, a lobster was served to them that looked like the one they'd hauled. Whatever.

Over time---a couple of summers---he became almost competent on the dock. He learned his trade and saw the day when he rose to the level of a bona fide dock master. There were so many facets to the job, he thought. So much to learn. And as he got better at the job, his confidence grew. Better still, he no longer had "Arthurs" working for him, just regular people. He even liked a couple of them and although he was the boss, they started to like him back. He would sometimes even receive the ultimate compliment: "He's an okay boss." Not exceptional and not "special". Just okay.

Hunter also noticed things he'd never noticed before at Windsor's. The staff hated his sister. She was a bully and a snob. He learned that, too. He even learned from Monk who had picked up this little witticism: "If ya're good for nothin' else, ya can always serve as a bad example." He realized with some regret just how that applied to Alexandra. She'd never change, either. Her attitude had become her destiny. It wouldn't happen to him, he thought. "It might have happened but I was thrown out and I get it." Forty days and forty nights in the wilderness had led to some real insights. He'd be a better man for it. How about that!?!

CALCULATIONS

We can either cling to one another and quite possibly survive our trials or we can make our own way, a separate way. The boys were learning that lesson and they were learning it fast. They put their heads together and devised another scheme that would benefit them both. Michaels had dug through the Registry and called the Boston number that was posted on the cottage out at Nobadeer. Tom and Louise had done a lot of window peeking, too. It needed insulation; it was just a summer place. It needed plumbing and its electric was knob and tube. They could see the hand pump at the kitchen sink and smell the propane that leaked from the rusty tank out back.

None of this discouraged them, quite the contrary. Tourists seemed not only more abundant these days, they seemed more affluent, too. They wanted upscale accommodations like the kind envisioned but not yet realized by Alexandra. They had no interest in a fixer upper. And Nobadeer was nothing if not a fixer upper. It needed everything but then, Joe really had learned a lot about the building trades. He got along well with the licensed guys, too, and traded favors all the time.

When Tom and Louise presented their vision to her tearful parents, they faced some resistance. "You can't. You can't!" declared Mrs. Papodopoulos who showed her misery by seizing her apron and clutching it to her eyes. The tears still flowed, though. "You can't."

Louise calmly asked, "'Can't' what?"

"You can't get married and you can't buy a house. You're too young and you're not established. You have no children."

Tom and Louise let the pot boil over until there was nothing left in it. They held hands, something they rarely did now that they were tumbling on a regular basis. When the flow finally stopped and Mr. Papodopoulos had raised a wise and powerful hand, Tom said, "We're not kids any more." This, of course, wasn't true but they had to respect the sweetness of his naivite.

"We're not kids and we think it's time to put our plans into action."

This set Mrs. Papodopoulos on another round of weeping punctuated with cries and shrieks and the production of more expressions of sorrow than Tom had ever seen before. She seemed capable of expressing the fears, the pain and the astonishment of an entire chorus all at once. It was a masterful performance but it wasn't a performance at all: It was the real thing, the product of a rich and resourceful culture.

Mr. Papodopoulos was the problem solver, though, the practical one. He'd negotiate.

"So, you have no job and no money and you want to get married and buy a house?" Stated that way, it didn't look so good. He sat back a little, sure that he'd stitched them up. He'd be no match for Louise, though.

"We have a plan. There are a number of steps along the way." The old folks nodded glumly. They both thought the same thing: "So this will take some time."

"Tom is looking good at Janey's," Louise said with assurance. "... And we've already done our research on the house." Again, that was partly true but too many facts would only confuse the old folks so she kept moving.

"I'm stationed here for the foreseeable future......."

"True, true....," thought Mr. and Mrs. Papodopoulos.

"....and we want to start a family."

"Family" was the showstopper. That meant kids, little boys and girls who would adore their grandparents so much that they would want to stay overnight with them and stuff themselves with grape leaves and olives and moussaka and learn to dance and be named 'John Louis' and 'Dikka' and....and....." And they kept on thinking, humming along, spinning out the future to the end of their days. Yes, yes, yes!

Both Louise and Tom saw their eyes glaze over and their backs become suddenly erect. It was magical. A miracle! A complete transformation! The old folks had suddenly grown younger. A playful sparkle had come into their eyes. Now, they, too, were holding hands. They were still hopelessly overweight and they still suffered from poor vision and each had a bulging disc but now they were renewed. Revivified in a way that they never could have possibly expected. They had hope!

When Mr. Papodopoulos finally opened his mouth, it was unexpected. "How much you need?"

Louise had always known and Tom was learning that even when you bet with an empty hand a quick shuffle can change the odds. It can make you unbeatable. As they walked away from the house that night, Tom's palms weren't sweating any more. He'd lost that green, froglike tinge around his gills, too.

"You're the best," was all he could say. He was afraid he might cry.

"No, you're the best," she replied, setting up their standing joke.

"No, you're the best," he said, and it went on from there until the two of them were laughing too hard not to kiss.

"This is going to work," she said firmly. "This will work."

And she was right. The next day, Tom took an early ferry to Hyannis.

He wanted to be there when Marcel showed up for work. If he showed how keen he was, he just might get the job. He didn't have to wait long either because he could see Marcel's tall, slender form approaching. He always wore his small, round chef's hat and tight, white jacket to fend off burns. His sharp, crooked nose led him toward the building but when he saw Tom his stride slowed and he passed him a flirt. "Well, fancy meeting you here…."

It wasn't much of a pickup line but Tom just smiled. "I wanted to talk to you about the job….". Surprisingly, the chef was one step ahead.

"Come with me. I'll show you how we set up." More encouragement followed and Tom soon gathered that he'd been hired. Nothing was formally stated; it was just understood. This, it seemed, was the way the chef always did business. He assumed others knew what he was thinking and was shocked when they didn't.

Tom walked into the chocolate factory as if into another world. Everywhere he looked people were whisking and folding, melting and tasting. Pots were quietly bubbling and an ancient stirring contraption kept things whirling. Every worker wore coveralls and snoods, making them look more like nurses for the critically ill than purveyors of priceless pralines. It wasn't a factory at all. It was an alien environment ruled over by a mighty, persnickety hand.

He wasn't even allowed on the floor. He had to "observe" from a sort of balcony. When he was handed a puffy cap, he reluctantly put it on. It looked like his mother's shower cap and he was heartily ashamed. "If my friends could see me now….." But he wore it anyway, an official acknowledgement that he was on board.

After they finished their tour chef directed him to his office manager. He never even shook his hand. He was too busy. The manager came directly to the point, though. "All he wants is total commitment," she said, her eyes boring into the back of his head. "C. Hibberd" it said on her desk. Tom just smiled and signed on the dotted line.

That afternoon Ms. Hibberd laid it all out for him. It turned out she was more an operations manager than an office manager although she seemed to do the work of both.

"We make the candy here and ship it to you," she said briskly. "You got here just in time. We're setting up the island shop now." That accorded nicely with Tom's plans. He could watch while they set up and not only learn their layout but maybe make changes if something didn't look right. He had, after all, shifted one hell of a lot of toilet paper over the years. Not to mention eggs and cabbages and Feldstein's bloody Monopoly pieces. In a short life he had done a lot of shipping.

Louise was predictably pleased and wasted no time telling the folks. She then got back to Michaels. He'd been busy with what he called his "real job" but had tried the owner of the Nobadeer house again without much luck. No matter, Louise would track the guy down. In the mean time, Tom started to dig into the candy business. That meant learning at least a little bit about candy but it also meant he'd have to hustle. How do you do that? How do you make people buy stuff?

"Look for the little things," John Nicholas advised him. Tom felt almost Greek now and was accepted as such. Part of the clan. "When you're selling stuff you have to push and the way to do that is to notice things. Little things. Things that get your product in front of people." He told Tom about the displays he'd set up at fairs and outdoor markets. "Sure, people don't always buy but you can make them curious so the next time they see you they buy." The whole thing, "Marketing" seemed like a gaff but it got Tom thinking.

The island shop was taking shape quickly. Tom fussed over the loading dock and they agreed to extend it a couple of feet on both sides but the layout indoors looked solid as it was. Marcel and Company seemed to know retail. Display cases lined the walls to allow for maximum floor space but they had set up three islands in the middle of the floor that could serve multiple purposes. They could showcase new products or specials or set up a spot for seasonal favorites. It all made sense.

Tom officially came on board the first of the month but he made sure he was there every day before that. He would be ready when duty called.

Any free time he had was used looking around town for "the little things" that John Nicholas had mentioned. What could they be? What could they be?

It took a while but once he had one idea, more followed and soon he had a whole hatful of ideas to promote their stuff. He barely saw Louise. Between the Oceanographic and the Nobadeer property, her time was taken. A full week had passed before she announced, "I found the guy." Who?

"I found the guy," she repeated excitedly.

"Who?"

"The guy who owns Nobadeer."

"Wow!"

"Yeah. Michaels had gotten a hold of his friend, another attorney named Barger. I guess he's an old school friend or something."

Tom nodded for her to go on.

"Yeah. And he knew all about it. I guess the family had always meant to go back and update the place but now they've got other priorities." She didn't know what that meant but, "….They'll sell if the price is right."

"Well, what are they asking?"

"Barger didn't know but he's going to find out. I sent Michaels a description and Joe made out a list of improvements. He even made estimates for the work to show that the work would likely discourage other buyers."

"So…..it's really happening," Tom said, uncomprehendingly.

"Well, it's a start," she said. "It's a start."

Joe had drawn up a laundry list of repairs, updates, and mandatory steps that would have to be taken to bring the property up to code. They went on and on. Both Michaels and Barger had advised them of a recent development in the Massachusetts Consumer Protection laws, too. It said, basically, that once a seller knew of deficiencies with a property, he/she had to divulge those deficiencies to subsequent buyers. Once Tom and Louise had reported the many problems to the owners, they had to report all those problems to any subsequent prospects. That meant that a "green" prospect couldn't outbid them. Even the green prospects would be told how much work was needed.

They couldn't believe their good luck. There was no fooling around, either. If you knew of a problem and someone bought your property, the seller and his realtor could be subject to as much as treble damages for deceit. "Consumer Protection" they called it. How about that!?!

Once again, they huddled up. Michaels' approach was, "They're stuck!"

Barger's approach was, "They're sort of stuck." They decided on the softer approach. They went to Michaels' office and called the buyers from there. Their name was Ascenso, maybe Portuguese. It was hard to say but likely fishing people.

"Michelle here," they heard at the end of the line. Louise started to explain holding the phone far enough from her ear so Tom could hear. The voice said, "Oh! You want to talk to my father. I'll go get him. He's in the other room."

When Mr. Ascenso came to the phone he was obviously annoyed. "I'm right in the middle of my programs," he said. "What do you want?"

"I wanted to talk to you about the house out in Nantucket," said Louise, biting her lip. Tom just froze, waiting to hear the reply.

"Oh, that thing," said the voice. "What do you want?" He then asked hurriedly, "It didn't burn down, did it?"

That gave Louise a lead. "No, no. It didn't burn down but I did smell some propane out there the last time I stopped by."

"Those damned gas guys. There's nobody there and they still insist on filling the tank."

"Well, yeah, they do," she answered, casting a puzzled look at Tom.

"Can you ask them to stop?" he asked.

"Well, no, I can't. I actually called for another reason."

"What's that?"

"I've been by there quite a few times and I wanted to know if it was still for sale."

"'For sale', You say? Yeah, it's for sale. What makes you think it's not for sale? Do you know something?"

Again, Louise was puzzled but pressed on. "Well, my husband and I live on the island and would love to make it our first home."

"You can't live there," the old man shouted. "It's got no water, no electric, no insulation and the roof is no good." Louise looked at Tom. They didn't know about the roof. The roof too?

"No. Nobody can live there. It's a summer place. Maybe good for three, four months a year."

"Well, we would fix it up," she said. This caught Mr. Ascenso somehow as a completely novel and unexpected use for the property.

"....and live there?" he asked.

"Yes. We'd fix it up and live there." Tom was making circles around his ear with his index finger: Cuckoo!

"You mean, you would fix it up and live there year round?"

"Yes. That's what we were thinking." Remembering John Nicholas and his gift for patter, she quickly added, "We're newlyweds."

"Oh, that explains a lot," said the old man. "Sure, sure. That explains a lot." In other words, only newlyweds would ever think of a stupid, stupid idea like that. They'll freeze to death. He was sure of it.

"So, what do you say?" Louise asked finally. Push was coming to shove.

"Okay, okay. I haven't thought about it for a while. I'm gonna have to think it over. Gimme your number." She gave him her home number and got off the phone. Her first objective had been accomplished, contacting the owner. Now, she had to wait. She would also do more homework, maybe look at some comps. "Sixteen?" she wondered. "Eighteen, maybe?"

As it turned out, she wasn't far off. Most cottages had been going for something over twenty but most were closer to town where another human being might occasionally be seen. Most were in better shape, too.

Still, there was something about Nobadeer. Tom and Louise had each loved it since they were kids. The salt sea dunes rolled their languid, almost sensual way to the water where the North Atlantic thundered down the shore. The sound of waves rang constantly in the air. It was the sound of water and of life. It was a reminder of the thin line between the living and all eternity. Dolphins, even whales washed up on the beach. Not often, but they did wash up. Other, lesser forms of marine life washed up, too. It never stopped. Every day, every hour was different from all that came before. "Eternal", yes but "monotonous", no: Once you lived by the sea you could never live anywhere else.

"Look, you've got to come up with comps that are light but plausible," Barger told them. "Don't listen to Michaels. He's too combative. You ask him for a figure and he'll say something ridiculous. Eleven or something. You'll offend the old guy."

That made perfect sense. Treat a guy fairly and he'll treat you good, too. It had even started out as the American way and worked for a long time until people got greedy. That's what Tom and Louise would do: They'd do their homework, make sure their figures were right but also that they were fair. If they owned the property for fifty years, a thousand dollars would only be twenty dollars a year, after all.

The comps took some work but they checked them with Chris Cowden, a local realtor and she assured them they were on the right track. Sixteen to eighteen was the right ball park. If they took the four or five thousand they had saved, they could swing it. They could swing it if they could get the mortgage, of course.

"Trus" Sheridan was not named "Trus" because he wore a device to ease the discomfort of a hernia or because he was the President of the local Trust. "Trus" was short for "Truscott" because he, too, was one of the Truscott clan by way of the Sheridans, a famously raucous and athletic family long established in the town. Tom and Louise made a time to meet and then sat down anxiously with him. Worry had replaced all reason and they both felt, "We're so near… We're so close….but bad things happen."

Trus stared across his desk and seemed as big as a house. Ominously quiet, he let them lay out their case and then asked them what they thought of the brand new baseball he had on his desk. It was signed by a dozen Red Sox with a huge, "Yaz" emblazoned across the seam. A national treasure!

"Boy, that's great!" said Tom enthusiastically. Wow! Sheridan glowed and glowed. He had been a Sox fan his whole life and would have slept with his fielder's mitt under his pillow if his wife would let him. He loved the smell of leather and Neat's Foot oil. It was in his blood.

Louise was more focused. She had brought their bank books, their latest pay slips and as much bluff as she could carry. She smiled at the baseball and also, "Wow!ed" but then moved quickly on to the mortgage.

Taken out of his reverie, Trus was a little bit defensive. "Well, we like to loan to local people……," he started, "...but we have to protect our depositors….." The usual bank guy chatter.

"You say you've got a property in mind already?"

Louise had taken a few snapshots and even secured a local map so she could lay it all out for him.

"You've certainly done your homework," said Trus. He was clearly getting into professional mode. He rubbed his chin, put his glasses back on and took a good, hard look.

"It's gonna need a lot of work, you know," he said. "These old cottages were thrown up like stables back in the day." But he was interested and now he wasn't just treating them like kids. "They're okay", he thought. "They seem like good kids."

Finally, he told them he would have to think about it but he asked them to keep him posted. If it looked like the old guy was going to sell, he'd be happy to talk to them. They shook hands and Tom and Louise made their slow, gleeful, dignified way out of the bank. They stayed that way, too, until they got to the car when Tom let out a Whoop! and Louise threw her arms around him. They were learning about banks and loans and promissory notes and titles and things were looking good.

SEMPER FIDELES

Joe was keeping under the radar. He enjoyed his time with Jack and Dahlia and often finished his day there, having one last cup of coffee before heading home at night. He had framed out the barn with Sam but left his assistant to do most of the rough work. Once the concrete had been poured, the studs went up and then the roof. That took about two months, part time. They then closed it up with plywood and it was safe to work inside. They'd be able to continue during the winter and have a lot of the carpentry done by the following summer.

Sometimes he'd take Mrs. Crisp by the place. "I see my own house going up just like this," he'd say. She would nod and smile but they both knew she'd never be sharing that house with him. It was a heartache for them both but it was part of their real life, different from the one they had created in their dreams or after a skirmish on a lazy afternoon.

When Joe learned that Tom might buy that cottage out in Nobadeer, he fantasized about sharing the lot with him. They'd be together but apart, each having his own household and privacy but knowing his brother was just footsteps away. They had gone their separate ways but their fraternal bonds had strengthened, surprising them both. Louise and Mrs. Crisp had developed a close friendship, too, neither challenging the other, both respecting the razor sharp intellect of the other.

Reality arrived on their doorstep every morning, though, in the form of the Daily Eagle. News of the war. Nixon, who had promised an exit strategy was instead pounding the Bejesus out of the infernal Vietnamese who, it turned out, were a whole lot more resilient than they had thought or reported. Students had even started demonstrating, many in their fatigue jackets like a second front. This served only to infuriate the President who ordered that measures be taken to snuff them out. They were horrified to find that those measures led to the suppression of protesters or worse, their death.

The more they read, the more the Seventies unfolded, the more they were determined to stay out of the war. They just had to wait it out. They had always taken their loyalty, their love of country and their citizenship for granted but now they asked themselves a lot of questions, the main one being: How can I support a country, even if it's my own country, when it's absolutely dead wrong? The answer was always the same. You can't. You simply can't.

Instead, it was necessary to support the students and their sympathizers, all of whom would happily carry the flag on Memorial Day but could never carry a rifle in Viet Nam. Joe and Tom would support each other, too. Semper Fideles: Always faithful.

The boys still didn't hang out together much; they were too busy, but when they talked there was a mutual respect that they surely hadn't known as kids. Almost a special language, like twins. Joe might run out of the house when he'd heard TEEN ANGEL one too many times and Tom had had it with flamenco but that was it. On those rare occasions when they were home and weren't driving each other out with their music, they were fine. True compadres, but very, very different.

Mr. Ascenso did finally call, too. All four of them had been creating castles in the air and they knew it. Their now well-developed plans were hanging by a slim, slim cord, the telephone line.

"I can't make up my mind," confessed Mr. Ascenso. Was that a ploy?

"On the one hand, I would be getting rid of a headache." He paused and then continued, "But on the other hand, the house has been in the family......." and his voice tailed off.

Louise was ready for that. "Of course you're reluctant to part with it but I can promise you that we would treat it right. We don't want to change it in any way. We just want to winterize it and bring it up to date. You can come by a year from now to see. It will always look the same."

"Yes, of course," replied Mr. Ascenso. "I'm sure you're nice people but I just don't know."

Tom pointed to the comps, suggesting a different tack.

"We've done a lot of homework," said Louise. "We really love the house and we've really tried to find a solution."

"I'm sure, I'm sure."

"So, just for the fun of it, I'm going to tell you what we found."

"Okay, okay," he replied guardedly.

She gave him the addresses and specs of several homes in the general area and told him how and why they were either similar or different from Nobadeer. He seemed to be listening and mumbled to show he was still on the phone.

"If we take the two cottages that sold last year near S'conset, that would give you an idea. They both went for about twenty." She let that hang until he grunted his acknowledgement.

"They both needed some work but not as much as your house. I can send you quotes from our builder and you'll see......"

The old man was weakening, tiring, actually. He wanted to get off the phone but he didn't want to be rude. That's where Louise had him. She just kept talking. She talked about the electric and the knob and tube.

She talked about the well and the rabbit she thought had fallen to the bottom. She talked about the rusty propane tank and the quaint but now obsolete hand pump in the kitchen. Water! Water needed to be plumbed throughout the entire place!

Finally, the old man stopped her flow. "Okay, how much you wanna pay?

I'm not sayin' I'll sell, but you say: How much you wanna pay?"

Louise was planning on offering sixteen but at the last minute she panicked. Instead, she said, "Look: I'm not going to beat around the bush. We've gone to the bank. We've shown them our bank books.

We have to budget money for all the work but figure we can offer you Seventeen Five. That's it. That's all we can do. That's the truth."

This pathetic proposal struck the old man in a very peculiar way. Something about the heavy breathing and raw display of emotion struck a chord with him. He'd been young and foolish and afraid when he was a kid and he could sympathize. He paused for a second, took a deep breath and blurted out, "Okay. Okay. That's okay. We can do it. It's a stretch but it's okay. It's okay." He kept repeating himself almost as though he needed confirmation somehow. He was going to do it and he had to accept it himself.

Tom was over the moon. He started to saw his finger across his throat in an effort to get Louise to, "Cut!" "Cut!" but she was too focused and too tough to quit there. Instead, she calmly and carefully told him all the stuff they'd have to do to effect the sale.

The old man had been out of the real estate market for a long time and a handshake didn't seal the deal any more. There would be paper work, something everyone hated and he surely would hate. He stayed on the line, though, until she had detailed the process to him. Lawyers, offers to purchase, Purchase and Sales agreements. Deposits. Crap like that. Crap they both hated but, unfortunately, necessary crap. He seemed to accept it in much the same way a penitent mounts the steps of an ancient cathedral. Silently and on his knees. When she got to municipal lien certificates and smoke detectors, though, he'd had enough.

"Okay, okay," he said. I'll have my son take care of it. He's an engineer with GE." As if that explained everything.

When she rung off, the couple was delirious. When they told their folks, the folks were delirious. And when they told Joe and Mrs. Crisp, it was the Fourth of July. Red, white and blue stars filled the sky that night. Great, wonderful harbingers of good fortune. Never seen before and there they were, the real thing. Impossible but true. Now, of course, they'd have to hurry up and get married.

GREETINGS

Joe recognized the envelope the minute he saw it. Cal and Es did, too. He opened it with trembling fingers and a weakened heart. The envelope gave him some trouble at first so he finally ripped it apart. He found himself unable to breathe as he read the first line. "Greetings…..", it said. He didn't have to read the rest of it; he knew what it meant. Skipping the sales pitch, his eyes went directly to the bottom of the page where he was given the time: October 3rd, 9:00. Hyannis Induction Center.

Joe's blood ran cold. He'd always had problems with his circulation but now his hands were clammy and his mouth was cactus dry. If a stethoscope had been pressed to his chest, the only sound it would have registered was the rattle of castanets.

He didn't waste any time, though. He was prepared for the letter. He got on the phone asap with Culver Michaels, the amped up, almost maniacal attorney recommended by Mrs. Crisp. When Michaels called him back, Joe gave him the necessary information and they rang off.

"Look," he said, "We went through this before. You're employed in an essential service." He paused for a moment to check. "You're still doing that, right? The whole garlic thing?"

Joe quickly confirmed. "Yeah, as you said, I'm occupied full time in an essential service, food production. Agriculture. We got lots of garlic."

He paused for a second to punch it up a bit, "…and onions, of course. We got onions, too."

"So that's why they call you 'Stinky', is it?" joked Michaels.

"Yeah, yeah. If I gotta stink to avoid this whole Viet Nam thing, they can call me 'Buttboy'. I don't care."

"Okay, okay. I'm gonna prepare an appeal based upon our agreed strategy: We did this right, laying out the groundwork beforehand." For one brief moment, Joe relaxed, knowing he'd done all he could do but that moment quickly passed. He was worried now. When he hung up, he could feel his nerves jangling as if a thousand volts had been shot through his spleen. He tried a call to Angela.

"It's a worry," she said, "...but everyone your age is in the same fix. You've done what you can do. I really feel you're going to be okay."

Mrs. Crisp was a comfort but she was equally concerned. She did what she could to distract him but even working around the clock Joe found his mind returning to the letter. If he turned on the TV or picked up a paper, he'd see the latest body counts. Ten of ours, twenty of theirs. Thirty of ours, a hundred of theirs. The U.S. was winning or so they were told. Each week there were more and more U.S. casualties, though; they were running out of medics and even Tom was nervous. He had done his hitch—all three years of it--but could he be recalled?

Fortunately, Joe and Mrs. Crisp made a good team. They managed to reassure one another and boost each other's spirits. If one's sagged, the other was there to jolly them up. This allowed them to function if not well then at least they got through the day. They hung their hat on reason. They had signed on with Jack and Dahlia. They had taken weekly pay checks. They had done the business.

Joe had filed his annual income tax returns too, showing agriculture as his main source of income. He had also observed the independent contractor's time honored custom of accepting payments in cash. Sixty to seventy percent of his income was under the table. He would stand in a queue at the bank every Friday with all the other small contractors as they cashed check after check from countless small jobs. The Fed and the MASS Department of Revenue were never the wiser. The humble role of "independent contractor" had given him an unexpected edge.

Now, it was up to Michaels to take all that evidence and make the Selective Service un-select Joe. Mrs. Crisp accompanied him to their meeting and the ever feisty Michaels was ready. He had a flair for the dramatic, too, asking not for one or two pay stubs from Jack and Dahlia but for as many as they could find. He would slap those down on the table and make a real show of it. He would then slap down the income tax returns that showed how very little people made in agriculture but how very, very important they were.

"Without them, we starve to death," he vowed, shaking a finger at a now bemused Mrs. Crisp.

When the time came for them to go to Hyannis, Joe asked her to stay home. He'd go alone with Michaels. She had tears in her eyes when he told her but she understood. No man wants to be seen blubbering in front of his girl friend. It's unmanly and he would never be her hero again.

On the ferry to Hyannis, Joe sat inside. They weren't sightseeing. They managed to find a free table and did a review. Neither looked out at the water. They focused on the story instead. They went over the details, the big picture, the little picture and back again. About half way across, in the middle of a healthy chop, Joe reached into the chest pocket of the overalls Michaels had made him wear. He dipped down with his long index finger and dragged out a locket with a thin, gold chain. He held it up, looked Michaels in the eye and didn't speak. When Budlong grew impatient, Joe said, "It's garlic. I want you to wear this at the hearing."

Advantage, no matter how small, is an electromagnet to the warrior breed. Michaels seized it in his fist and quickly slipped it over his head. He didn't say a thing. His face went hard but it wasn't obstinance, it was resolve. He was through talking. He just said, "Let's take these bastids!"

The road leading up to the Draft Board was lined with people speaking their minds. One side wanted to cover them with filth and the other side wanted to cover them with blood. The noise was shocking. Some held signs saying, "Your country: Love it or leave it!" Some held signs saying, "Hell no! We won't go!"

Everyone was yelling and gesticulating. He remembered later thinking that if there were any pacifists out there, they must have been a very violent form of pacifist. Legions of cops were holding the two groups apart. By the time he got inside, he was numb, dazed. He sleepwalked through the review. He entered the dreary room with its green walls the color of dog sick, saw the gummint issue green metal chairs and simply took his seat.

The three officers conducting the interview looked strangely similar: Each was white haired, overweight, tall and red in the face. They all looked like Saturday poonters from the pier, sunburned and exhausted from too much beer. Their demeanor varied, though.

The guy on the left sat forward and toyed with an elastic band, totally absorbed. He never looked up. The guy in the center folded his arms across the dome of his belly and stared directly at Joe the whole time. The guy on the right seemed nervous as if he might miss a flight or something. He never paid attention to anything but his watch.

Michaels was focused, though, sharply focused. When they turned on the tape, you could feel the voltage in the air. The guy in the middle started the show:

"This is case number B1313, appellant Bustle, Joseph D. Social Security number 005-29-4737. He appears today on an appeal from an initial request to appear received by this office...." and it went on and on.

"Officialdom," thought Joe. The great broom that was sweeping across the nation, sweeping thousands and thousands of boys just like him west. West across the Mississippi, west across California, west across the sea. Sweeping them west until they were covered with insect repellent, black eye shadow and the sweat that you could never, ever wash away. West into the jungles of unrelenting fear and instant death.

The roundeyes had swept across North America virtually wiping out the native population but they hadn't stopped in California. Now they were sweeping even further west with the single-minded purpose of wiping out an entirely new people on an entirely new continent. Their blood lust was unquenchable and horrifying to every thinking person on earth but for the champions of the sweep. They blew kisses to each other each time a new tally of kills came down from Pacific command.

His mind wandered and his ears buzzed as if filled with wasps. He could see the disinterest and smug contentment of the board but he couldn't hear their bureaucratic, disembodied replies. He could hear Michaels, though, even when he was briefly silent. Michaels was on fire. He was furious that a son of their small neighboring island should be treated like a common criminal. Guys like Joe were saving this country and feeding the troops. He was a hero as much as anyone who worked at Sikorsky or Boeing or Colt. He was on line every day, growing and producing so that this man's Army could stay well fed, healthy and on its feet!

The change was slow. The board was used to challenges but not the kind of frontal enfilade now being fired at their position. Michaels was not physically imposing, either. He was slender and no more than 5'10" but he was filled with rage, that and the self-righteous fury of an angry god. When he slammed the pay stubs down on the desk and then did the same with Joe's tax returns, his eyes turned crimson, the blood red of sacred hate.

The guy on the left flinched just that little bit and looked at the moderator. The guy on the right adjusted himself in his seat. The guy in the center spoke first. He coughed into a closed fist and then said, "We'll take this matter under advisement."

That would mean another delay but Joe didn't mind. He was so relieved to be out of the room that he had to stop himself from running down the street. Outside, Michaels just laughed and laughed. Sure, he wanted Joe to win but even more than that, he wanted to beat the system.

Something, some deep pain at the very bottom of his soul, made him want to physically thrash the whole panel. He could do it, too, he thought. He'd take all three of them on! His mind raced happily along: He'd kick the guy on the left in the balls with his left foot, then let the moderator have it with his right. By the time the third guy got into it, he'd have squared off and would be pounding him with uppercuts. Bastids!

Joe was in a state of shock. He had envisioned the panel and he had even guessed how dreary the room would look but he hadn't expected them to be so detached, so disinterested in his fate. Or the fate of the other boys who went before them. It would have been great if he, too, had been detached about the result but he couldn't have been more involved. His life hung in the balance; he knew that all too well.

They kept as silent as friars on the ferry back. All of their energy had been left in that room. It was even a bit awkward. Neither wanted to speak but felt the social obligation to chat, to do something other than simply sit and stare out the windows. Still, they were spent. When they got to town, they each waved quickly and stalked off. It wasn't until he got back home and called Mrs. Crisp that Joe started to feel normal again.

"It went pretty well," he told her, knowing she would be suspicious of too much enthusiasm. "I think Michaels did a pretty good job."

He didn't really want to say more but she wanted details. Surprisingly, he found himself portraying the scene just as he saw it despite the fog he'd felt at the interview itself. He told her about the three guys, Tweedle Dee, Tweedle Dum and Twiddle Dee Dee. He told her about their indifference and their casual disregard for the simplest of courtesies. "They were bored stiff," he told her.

Mrs. Crisp just shook her head and punctuated his story with, "Sure," and "Of course." "I can see that," she said repeatedly as he painted a thorough and complete picture of the review.

"It was something I never want to do again," he confessed, as close as he would come to admitting the depth of his fear and the bruise it would leave on his heart.

Decisions took between "four to six weeks" so they just carried on. There was a sadness that hung in the air, though, a realization that their days together might be numbered. They both felt it but left it unexpressed. Instead, they simply pushed everything else aside and spent as much time together as they could.

His gentleness amazed her and her clarity never failed to surprise. There was no question: He wanted so much to be with her that he barely took his eyes off her, even in a crowd. She had never felt the kind of devotion he showed and it moved her deeply. It would never be betrayed. Yes, Tom and Joe were always faithful to each other but as time went on, Mrs. Crisp entered that circle. She would always be faithful to them and to Louise, too. Louise, too.

CANDYLAND

Tom took to candy like a frog to still water. He jumped right in. He had always liked candy but now he loved candy. There might be the odd worry that his skin would break out but he tore into chocolates like a man possessed. He was going to school and the subjects covered at Janey's were an education anyone could understand.

"Just how exactly do they get the walnuts to stick out of the corners of the turtles so they actually look like turtles?"

"Do they inject the raspberry cream like a jelly doughnut or do they dunk the centers into a big pot of hot chocolate?"

And most importantly, "How much money can I make on each box?"

These questions and many more were all answered in due course. In the meantime, just like at Feldstein's, Tom would be learning on the job. The one thing he didn't have to learn was how to ship. Moving stuff was his metier; he knew about trucks.

Tom had taken John Nicholas's advice to heart, too. He had been looking for the "little things" that got his product out there. Even the phrase "little things" shook ideas out of his head. When he added those ideas to the networking lessons he'd already learned, he was ready to roll.

He went to Marcel and floated a big idea. "How about we go around and give folks a taste? Samples." Chef wasn't crazy about giving money away so he stuck up his hand. Tom continued, nonetheless.

"We will be meeting people, potential customers, and introducing them to the candy. Combining public relations with product exposure." Tom was even impressing himself. Where had he learned that baloney?

In the end, he managed to talk the Chef into a limited trial. His buddy Monk was still looking for work so he gave him a blue and white apron with matching cap and put him on the street. First, he'd go from shop to shop, treating up the staff. Then, he'd lie in wait for the "poonters". He'd chat them up with Janey's patented patter and then offer them a pick from the box. On a hot day it would be messy, but think of the exposure! You could feel the love!

At the same time, Tom would do more serious marketing. He would revisit White's and talk sales with Doc Matthew. He was such a kindhearted soul that Tom was sure he'd make space for him. After that, it would be Feldstein's where he might not unload a lot of chocolate but he just might reel them in with peanut brittle and taffy. Little treats that they could chew during the day. Fun stuff. And he could duplicate the circulation system of the Daily Eagle. Instead of a paper route, though, he'd set Monk out on a candy route. Soon, there wouldn't be a dentist for miles who wasn't cursing him as a threat to public health.

It all went as smooth as a pot full of hot caramel. He'd use his already extensive network and then go on from there. One thing led to another: John Nicholas knew the guy at Nantucket's little airport so when Tom showed up the guy pointed to an unused display case. "You can stick the stuff in there, if you like," he was told. "We can take the usual twenty percent and pay you at the end of the month." Wow!

The guy at the airport sent him to the gift shop in S'conset where every tourist ended up. You had to leave Nantucket with a sweatshirt from S'conset or there was no point in going. Even the patrolmen who biked up and down the island all day were hot prospects. Every one of them, without exception chewed Juicy Fruit for ten or twelve hours a day and were grateful for a change. Ka Ching!

The shop itself was a breeze. Chef Marcel may have been snobby and a terrible flirt but he knew his trade. He knew it down to the ground. He knew which chocs to put on top and which to put on the side. He knew all there was about displays and he carefully calculated the rollout of each seasonal favorite. What a guy! This meant that Tom's job had two basic parts: He would follow Chef's instructions to the letter inside the shop but he would have a free hand on outside sales. He would own distribution. He'd be looking at some sweet, sweet pay checks, for sure.

Louise had her pencil out, too. She was calculating, preparing and planning on a new and exciting scale. They had four thousand between them and needed fourteen to cover the rest of the cost and expenses. Her father had another thousand, reducing the loan, if they could get it, to thirteen. She went to see Sheridan again.

This time the guy wasn't so friendly. At first, it seemed as though he didn't recognize her. When she placed a neat three ringed binder on the table and started to show him photographs and cost projections, he seemed on firmer ground.

"I think you've done your homework but I'll still have to take it up with the committee", he said. This would allow him to deflect her rage when he turned her down, too, a common banking ploy.

"I gotta verify incomes. And I should take a drive by and see the property." All of that. Louise was frustrated but left him with a box of meltaways, one of the endless uses for those delicious treats.

Tom just kept grinding. Soon, he not only had the gift shop at S'conset but two tourist information centers, too. He took a deep breath and called Alexandra at the Inn but she had turned haughty in the intervening months. She all but slammed the phone on his ear because her takeover hadn't gone as smoothly as she expected and now, in the time honored tradition of complainers all over the world, she was blaming the prior administration: Tom. It was his fault that….. and it was his fault that….Well, just everything was his fault.

"We were on the right track until you and your brother came along," she observed correctly, failing at the same time to mention that once they had left things really got bad.

They'd lost a lot of business because their catering was verkakta. Each caterer has "his little ways" and Alex didn't get it. The caterer is the show and not the property owner but she just didn't get it. She wanted complete control and when she didn't get it she, "….just can't work with them." It was getting so she couldn't get a booking.

As if that wasn't enough, the rooms were down, too. They had always had at least a passable breakfast to offer, "Continental style", which is to say, "You pick up a muffin and a coffee and that's it." Now, people expected more. They wanted an egg or something. French toast. But if you can't keep your kitchen happy, you're not even going to put out a decent omelette. There was trouble on every front. As it turned out, the only component that ran smoothly was the dock. Who'da guessed?

Hunter had gone clean and sober. Well, if not entirely sober, he had certainly dedicated himself to the dock. It ran as smooth as the little brown tummy of his beagle pup. He had people stacked up to use not only the skiffs but three small sail boats, Day Sailers, that he'd picked up from a guy in Boston. They'd run aground, of course, or need a tow but he did that, too.

"They take out the boats, run aground or capsize and we call it, 'sailing lessons'" he joked. He had nearly doubled their gross and was looking to expand. When Alex saw people walking right past the Inn to get to the dock concession, her eyes would narrow like a cobra ready for lunch.

Fortunately, they had both fully understood the papers she'd drawn and that their father had signed. Hunter had been cut out of everything but the dock. Now, the dock was the only part of the business showing a profit. Even Alex understood that if she cut more employees the place would fail. Quite naturally, she turned her venom on Tom. Quite unnaturally, he shook it right off. "So it goes," he thought. So it goes. She wouldn't buy his candy; that was her revenge.

Tom kept his head down and when the store opened he put out balloons, samples, street signs and just for fun, dressed Monk up in a cupcake suit and had him walk around in front of the store. They didn't actually sell cupcakes but it was the only costume he could find so they sent him out in that. Everybody loved it. They all thought the costume was a goof and it got to be a weekly thing.

Every Saturday when the ferry arrived the visitors would be greeted by a different eye-popping sensation. One week it was Sir Galahad and the next it was Papa Smurf. No matter, just so long as the buzz kept going. They even tore a patch off Feldstein's by dressing the poor guy up as a gigantic silver thimble with little dimples, fresh off the assembly line.

"We're not a 'Monopoly'," Monk would say, "...but we ought to be." He would then hand a sample to a bewildered tourist. That poonter would go home with a story and often with a box of chocolates too.

Chef Marcel was impressed when the first numbers came out. He would have to restructure their relationship, ie, reduce commissions, but even then Tom would be happy. Chef was sure he could keep Tom happy, too, because he, himself was happy. He was more than happy; he was fat and happy. The money kept pouring in.

When Sheridan finally did get back to Louise there was little doubt that they could swing the deal. He started to fuss with the interest rate because they were "new loan customers" but when Mr. Papodopoulos called him up to remind him of their long and very happy association, he backed off. They got the standard rate and could go ahead in a couple of weeks.

All that candy was leading to a sweet future for Tom and Louise. Now, they were faced with two big jobs, the marriage and the house. They'd gotten Tom into a good thing and now they had to tie up the deal. They had to get married and keep the ball rolling.

The first part was easier than the second. They got Cal and Esther to a Greek dance and although they were sweaty and hot and left early, they saw Louise not just as a good fiancee but as part of a vibrant, even exciting culture. One they'd never known much about. They were happy about the wedding and as Cal observed, "…..if they had be Greek for a week, that was okay, too."

The house had problems, though. After securing Mr. Ascenso's permission to enter the place, they found stuff they couldn't believe. Voles had taken up residence and would have to leave. There are no skunks on the island as there are on the Vineyard but that was small comfort. The voles would have to go. The insect and spider population had taken over, too. They were so firmly established that the cobwebs had become a huge ball of cotton candy, one they'd have to battle whenever they entered the house.

Joe had developed a pretty good nose for dry rot, too, and he had to tell them that most of the window sills needed work. "You just can't let these old places sit," he said. Even his short experience had taught him the necessity of maintenance. "Pay me now or pay me much more later," was his sorry refrain, one his customers always found hard to swallow.

Tom and Louise were organized, though, and set up deadlines for the onslaught of paper work they'd encounter at the bank. They had wisely selected Barger as their attorney because, as Joe had said, "I think Michaels is a bit psychotic. I think he would have physically assaulted that board if he had half the chance." He would have been shocked if he knew just how right he was. Lloyd Barger was more temperate. He had both Tom's love of detail and Joe's easy manner so he got on well with people. He didn't scare them anyway, so he was the obvious choice.

Barger kept the thing rolling and before they knew it they were at the table. They'd be signing a promissory note, a mortgage, an insurance affidavit, the list went on and on. It was just a blur after a while as it is for all of us. Finally, about an hour later, they were done. They had no idea what they'd signed but Barger tipped up his glasses, nodded briskly and they all went home.

They were ready, too. They had already cleared out one room, the bedroom. They had swept it and dusted it and even washed the walls. It didn't sparkle but the windows had been cleaned and bright rays of sunlight lit up the room. When they opened the windows, a lovely breeze swept across the room. The bed was covered with one of Nana Bustle's lovely blue and white quilts and was, for all intents and purposes, open for business.

They had already promised themselves that they would honor the prior owners by making love in every room of the house and they did their level best to do just that. Their horizontal best, to be accurate. They never got out of the bedroom but they tackled the job with a will.

Two out of three: The job was working and the house was working and now they had to tie the knot. Tom stepped aside as was only fitting and Louise and the family took over. His ears could not take in the chatter. There would be food and dance, of course. There would be a ceremony that honored established tradition and custom, both of which were as foreign to Tom as Czechoslovakia. Almost exactly as foreign to Tom as Czechoslovakia, in fact.

When the day came, he put on a good suit and plumped up his nerve in front of the mirror. He could hear Joe getting ready too, but he needed a moment to give himself a pep talk. The ceremony was intimidating, not Louise or the family. They were great. The ceremony, though, was too complicated. Part of it was in Greek, too. You even had to wear a sort of hoop over your head that was connected to another hoop and little kids circled you....... He was really lost. Lost and confused.

Bucking up, he told himself the same thing most guys tell themselves at this most desperate hour in their lives: "Things will be different when this bullshit is over. When it's all over, I'll be the boss. I'll never have to do stupid things like this again." He said it with finality, too, not suspecting for a minute that it could work otherwise.

When they had completed the ceremony and had a piece of cake and everyone had danced their last dance, he sat with Louise and looked out over the ocean. The moon and the stars cast a grey pall over the sea. Both were exhausted but his mind had one last burst of inspiration. It said, "The job, the house, Louise? They're all candy. My whole life is candy. I'm living in Candyland." And he gave her one last peck on the cheek.

MARGINAL CHARACTERS

Joe was happy to see his brother doing so well and he wasn't prone to envy but he couldn't help hoping that his own "situation" would settle down. He was sick of playing at "agriculture" and he was sick of skulking around at work. He wanted the freedom that he felt was his right and privilege without fearing any minute he'd be shipped off to Da Nang. He wanted adjudication and he wanted it now.

His envelope did finally arrive and when he tore it open it gave him back his life. Well, part of his life. Very, very grudgingly, the board had come to the conclusion that his commitment to agriculture qualified as an "essential service". He'd be exempt for the foreseeable future, at least one year. That would get him into 1973, he reckoned, and maybe the war would wind down by then. Maybe. He had hoped for more, of course, but he was happy to keep that status for the time being. He didn't like garlic; he loved it.

Like so many of his peers across the great continent of North America, his status was in limbo. He'd never really be able to relax, just rest briefly until the next big ideas from officialdom. He'd try to ignore it and get on with his life but it would always be there, a heavy weight on his heart, his mind and his future. It would hold him back in a hundred ways, ways he would never suspect. It was a special form of purgatory only a gassed up DOD could possibly have contrived.

Fortunately, Mrs. Crisp was there to ease the pain. She was remarkably unlike his first, second and third impressions of her. She was sexy, sure, but she had a wonderful sense of humor and humility, too. She helped him in so many ways that he couldn't begin to count them all. He did have one worry: He was worried about the husband. The fact that they went home at night and slept under the same roof hurt Joe at times but he did what he could to push that aside. He trusted her, too. He didn't ask questions and she didn't offer any explanations until after Tom's wedding. When it came, It came at some cost to her so he listened quietly as she explained her thoughts.

She had long felt that her relationship with her husband was unusual but now she sensed the truth. "Not all golfers are gay", she said drily, but she felt sure that her husband was. He was attracted to long drives and long putts but he seemed to be attracted to Ernie Jenkins, too. They spent a lot of time together, often into the wee hours. They both drank a lot but it was more than that. They laughed to each other in a way he never laughed with her. They even giggled on the phone sometimes. He never did that with her. They were truly happy together and, she thought, only when they were together.

"What do you know about Ernie Jenkins?" Joe asked finally.

She shrugged her shoulders. "He likes fires. That's all I know."

Joe didn't know any homosexuals, or so he thought. He had read stuff about them in Argosy magazine, the men's magazine that always graced his father's night stand. Right next to ads for pump guns and ammo, they talked about gay people and how they had special bars and clubs. Like the Masons or the Elks. Argosy always had something about extraterrestrials, too, so Joe was a little skeptical. He knew there was no life on Mars so he didn't know if they were a reliable source on gay people. Maybe not.

Joe was more worried about his exemption. He'd have to continue in agriculture for the time being but he was still in limbo. Anything could happen. He'd have to gut it out. His phone was still ringing for odd jobs so he and Sam kept knocking them out. As soon as Tom and Louise closed on the Ascenso place, he went over to help there, too. That was where the idea came for a house of his own.

Joe had completed a large shed for a guy in Miacomet and while he was working on it he asked himself an important question. "What the heck is the difference between this shed and a house?" he wondered. "Why can't I take a barn like the Irving barn and make a house out of it?" For a minute or two, he just glowed silently to himself. Money then stuck its head up and waved a hairy finger in his face.

"You're an idiot. You've got no money, no moolah, nothing. How are you going to build a house?" It's true. He hadn't saved a bean.

But this didn't bother the ever flexible Joseph. He didn't freeze in a fight; he finessed. He could get materials; he knew that. And he could build the house. He knew that, too. He just needed a place to build it. When he saw Tom's place, he had the place. But: What would Tom and Louise think about that?

Seen from a distance, their house looked as if it had dropped there from the moon. It was surrounded by low, sculpted sand dunes that rolled down leisurely to the sea. It was also surrounded by the genius of modern man in the form of beach grass, the long, slender grasses that lacerated every finger or toe that touched it.

Beach grass was miserable stuff but it was placed there by loving hands in the solemn belief that its deep roots would help keep the sand in place. An ever-rising sea would make short work of these safeguards but that wouldn't be until the future arrived, way out there in the clouds. Tides crept higher and further every year but that meant nothing to the conservationists who planted those grasses. They'd set out their little shoots and it would stave off the flow for at least a decade. Maybe two.

The Ascenso house had been plunked down in the middle of those dunes and was completely isolated. The plot had been clipped off a large parcel in much the same way you clip the nail off a pinkie toe. It had been owned by a once grand family that ruled over a big chunk of southern Nantucket long miles from the town itself. The land was barren and windswept and no longer boasted arable soil. When a builder came along and asked to buy that little toenail, the owner gladly sold. Clip, snip and off it came.

Ascenso came to own the little parcel but no one followed his lead. His lonely cottage stood out there as grey and solitary as a churchyard grave. At least, it looked that way to most people. It never looked that way to Tom and Louise. They loved the peace and quiet. They loved the serenity that was deep and profound but for the pounding of the waves.

They loved them too, though, and would plunge into them bollocky bare assed all summer long. For them, it was perfect. Why would they ever want Joe there?

"Because I'm broke," was Joe's answer. "Because I can help with your house and I can build my own." That answer gave Tom and Louise a lot to think about. They could swing the mortgage now but improvements could take years. How could they live in an uninsulated house? How would they make it through the winter? Would they burn the place down with the crazy electric? Reality was dawning on them, too. Maybe Joe's solution could work.

Joe and Tom went to separate corners. They weighed the pros and cons and took the advice of Cal and Es, Louise and Mrs. Crisp. Older heads cautioned against it, particularly in the early years of marriage. The younger heads did, too.

"It would be like living together and you boys have been trying to get out on your own since you were fourteen," said Es with a clarity that rang in their ears.

Their answer came from an unexpected source. One day when he was passing out chocolates, Monkey Phillips saw Tom. He had chosen a long, red silk dress with accompanying handbag and shoes and looked a treat.

He had found a glorious blonde wig, too, the tresses of which reached halfway down his back. If you ignored the black stubble, he looked even more delicious than his boxful of raspberry cremes.

Smiling with his famously splayed front teeth, he went up to his boss. "Fawk it!" he shouted. "Jost do it!" He paused to let this sink in and then grabbed Tom by the shoulders. "He's yore brother, for fawk's sake!" Apparently, his Irish spirit had returned.

Tom was shaken with that, really shaken. He had failed a lot during his life but he had learned, too. Maybe he shouldn't go through life by the numbers. Maybe there were other things to consider. He knew one thing: As annoying and headstrong and foolish as Joe might be, he was still his brother. And Tom and had never failed him. He had been furious at times, frustrated, too, but always faithful in every way. Monk had turned him around. He'd do it. He'd do it.

As it turned out, Louise had arrived at the same conclusion. Sure, Joe had put them on the spot but that's families, right? They're always right up there, right in your face. Still, you tried your best to help whenever you could. This was one of those times. Nobody had to explain fidelity to a Greek; they had practically invented it.

Their timing for once, was favorable, too. They sought and then secured an okay from the building commission whose only demand, unbelievably, was that Joe's new structure should be fifteen feet from the neighbor's right of way. This restriction was for the purpose of insuring fire safety. It didn't matter that there were no other buildings within a thousand yards; he still had to have a fifteen foot setback to allow room for a ladder to be placed against the house. "Those are the rules," said a very, very proud Mrs. Truscott. She was thrilled at the opportunity to assert herself and beamed gleefully at their blank, uncomprehending faces.

Cal and Es stepped in at this point. They had put aside over three thousand dollars for the boys so they made them each out a check for half. Both boys would now have at least a running start on costs. It would take some time before they realized their good fortune but they were sincerely and genuinely happy with that cash. Now, they could proceed. Joe even joked that he was saving steps. He could bring his truck down loaded with stuff for two jobs at the same time. Think of the savings!

They were doubly fortunate, as it turned out. The war was finally winding down and the boys were coming home. The bad news was that the war machine would close down and the river of money that had been flooding the economy would slow to a trickle. Guys were thrown out of work, jobs were being cut and to make matters worse, interest rates were going through the roof. It wasn't funny and it didn't take long to impact the island.

Joe's phone stopped ringing. People were either doing without or doing it themselves, often much the same thing. Tourists weren't coming to town, either, so Tom's display cases stayed full. There was even some talk of shutting down the store. Guys who had existed on the fringes like Monk were hanging by their toes. Sam got a little work from Joe but was effectively laid off.

There was some good news: the draft was no longer a threat. Joe could go back to a regular job and stop playing farmer at the Irvings. American boys were no longer coming home with chronic injuries and PTSD, either. That was a relief. No one mentioned the boys who didn't come back; no one outside the family, of course.

The boys who did get back were unemployed; the economy had tanked. It would clearly take a long time before things returned to normal. They might not recognize normal when it finally came, either. It had been too long since they had lived in a world of balance and contentment, a few years maybe before the Peloponnesian War.

Peacetime, then, meant an excruciating grind for Tom and Joe. It was harder on Tom because he had pushed all of his chips into the candy jackpot. If it failed he'd be back on the street again. He was already out on the street anyway, he thought ruefully, having to don Monk's monkey suit on weekends to draw in the few poonters who did visit the island.

Tom's other sidelines added a bit to the pot, too. It meant a step backward but Doc Matthew had needed a man of all works for a while. He was finally giving in to his age so hiring Tom to fill in "now and then" meant ten or twenty hours a week. He'd also caught on at St. Paul's, oddly enough, because none of the regular parishioners wanted to be Sexton. That meant a couple times a week he set up or knocked down chairs for A.A., Bible Study and their shameless a capella group, the Off Tones.

Joe would always be busy, if not actually making a buck. He had two houses to work on now, Tom's renovations and his own. He was learning from Mrs. Crisp about the benefits of organization, too. With her help he had laid out an "offensive" much like his counterparts in the military.

He tried to explain it to her in as professional a manner as possible. "The house will first start with a cinder block foundation, one I can put up mostly on my own. Sand shifts, a'course, so I'll plant stabilizing rods to minimize that shift." That meant trips for supplies. Lots of trips. When he could swap off favors with a dump truck guy, he grabbed the chance. Their goal was to plunk down the foundation and then get a good run at the frame before cold weather set in.

Their goal for Tom's house was just that much more advanced. The rough exterior had been lived in for years. Now, they had to update the electric and close in the walls. Sam could do the wall board but an electrician, a real electrician would have to certify that job. At the same time, they'd try to get some plumbing indoors, too. No more privies, no more jokes from the neighboring kids. They'd have real indoor plumbing with a toilet sink and tub just like in America. Good stuff.

Joe was working around the clock with nothing but equity to show for it. He was paying Tom for a share of his land by renovating the old cottage and he was paying himself by putting up a cottage of his own. It was a wearying business but every time he had to say, "No", to a treat he tried to remember the long term benefits he'd enjoy. It wasn't his nature. He liked to live in the here and now, smoke a little weed and relax. Listen to a little flamenco. Maybe take out the fiddle and practice but he had precious little time for that.

Other guys were completely unemployed, after all. At least he was making an investment, another disturbing change in his universe. "Investments" were for rich folk, not for him. He had to force himself to think of each two by four, each nail as being an investment in his future. Every time he swung a paint brush he was doing it for himself. Some time, way in the future—that fairy land---his house would be worth twice the twelve thousand it was going to cost him to build the place. Maybe more.

UPSTREAM

Alexandra was now the queen of an empire in decline. She'd been smart enough not to get deeply in debt but improvements meant money. As she looked around the place she could see how much better it looked but she also congratulated herself for good judgement, forgetting the advisers who had urged her not to max out on her loans. She had stayed within reasonable limits but was still struggling. Taking on water.

She knew down to the fraction of a guest how many rooms she had to fill to keep the place afloat. The numbers said she was 18% off that figure but she couldn't look them in the eye. She looked elsewhere, to her father and kid brother. They had taken the easy way out. Her father lived off his savings and the delicious fruiti di mare from the waters off his home on Impetigo. Hunter had limited his exposure by maintaining a small concession, the boats. His earnings seemed to be modest but surprisingly consistent, the bastid.

Alex was stuck with a huge ark of a place and that ark was not filling two by two with Croatians, Indians, Germans and Turks. It was empty most of the time and sinking fast. She was sneaky smart, though. She had seen how Tom and Monk had teamed up for the Janey's launch so she cooked up some promotions. She started to offer three for two deals and knockdown rates for midweek. The place filled up again.

Unfortunately, lowered rates and knockdown deals are like chum to the schools of undergraduates who constantly seem to swim around resorts. She hadn't foreseen that. They swept in and packed the place with rowdy, drunken and often half-naked partygoers who would race nightly through the place. They didn't need a band, either. Someone always had a guitar, a drum or a penny whistle. That was enough to attract the crowds.

The back deck, formerly home to elegant Christenings and even more elegant funerals was now home base for what seemed like thousands of half-crazed kids. It was a good night when no windows were broken and the police didn't break up a fight. Nantucket had officially arrived on the kids' radar like the homing instinct of a great white shark. They chewed the place up, leaving nothing in their wake but wet T-shirts, blood and bits of bone.

Alexandra was now not only on a sinking ship but more importantly, one that was unattractive, almost unfashionable. Her heart ached each night as one wave of kids succeeded another. The kids were happy; they could party and the lucky ones shacked up. They snuck enough booze into the place to avoid a big bar tab, too. Especially the kids who were under age. When it all played out and she got her mind around the risk and the liability, her already cold blood turned cryogenically cold. She'd have to find a solution or the unthinkable would happen: She would fail. And even though her natural impulse was to look elsewhere for the source of her defeat, deep, deep in her heart she knew she was sinking the ship. She and she alone would not only catch the blame but she'd signed personally for the loans, as well.

So, what do desperate people do? She had already tried blaming others but her brother was still making money, getting high with the rest of the slackers and so far as the dock was concerned, running a pretty tight ship. People might walk right by the inn but they'd stop to gawk at the dock and talk to Hunter or one of the summer kids he had working there. Sometimes they'd even hire a boat. Ka Ching!

No: she couldn't blame Hunter now. She might even need him. It would do no good to blame her father, either. He was four thousand miles away. She was stuck. She could only blame the lawyers and the bankers and that could backfire on her, too. She would have to be very creative if she wanted to blame someone else.

People without either shame or self-doubt often plunge blindly into foolish ventures and the only imagination they show is in their selection of victims. They either see themselves as victims (67%*) or find some other poor guy who can fill that role (33%*). *These are current stats, too, from the Department of Hard Labor and Broken Promises.

The seeds for her failure had obviously been sown by Tom and Joe, the prior managers. If it hadn't been for their feckless waste of money and resources, the Inn would still be prospering, way in the black. They were the ones to blame. So when she went to the bank and saw Trus Sheridan for additional funds, she told him in no uncertain terms that the Bustles were to blame. She had the unenviable task of repairing the harm they'd done and that would mean more money.

At first, Trus Sheridan was doubtful. He'd seen how much had been accomplished by the boys with the small loan he had provided to Tom and Louise. And he had seen how the Inn had declined. It was no longer the place you brought the wife on Friday night. It had become Spring Week for college kids for the entire summer. He served on the volunteer fire department and they had special drills, assuming a fire could break out any time.

The Truscotts were a little inbred, though. Not Cocker Spaniel inbred but a little inbred. Their minds didn't always follow either conventional or sensible paths. When their minds tried to crank out clear thoughts there was often a broken spoke that caused that thinking to crash. They seemed to get by on good luck and a prayer, mostly the former.

Trus reasoned that the Inn had been there a long time (Check), and it had always made money (Check). Now, just a short time after Tom had left, it wasn't doing well. Therefore, it must have been Tom's fault.

Why, Alexandra was standing there saying that and stamping her foot, too. It must be so. Poor Alexandra. Poor kid. And after her father had entrusted her with the family business and all…….

So, Trus just shook his head at her plight and told her he'd "..see what I can do." This meant that he'd have to check with the board but the board was composed of similarly disadvantaged Truscotts and the loan was a sure thing. In the mean time, he'd be very careful indeed, about lending money to Tom or Joe. Those guys were trouble!

DOWNSTREAM

As winter approached, Joe found himself wishing earnestly that he had another hand. He could have scratched his nose once in a while instead of having to stop everything he was doing, remove a glove and satisfy an itch. All together, he might have saved six minutes a week. He was just that busy.

Joe was stuck in the most accursed place a man can find himself. No matter how hard he worked he fell more and more behind. His dreams never stopped; they just repeated themselves. Dreams of chasing after a bus or a train that sped away, just out of reach. He couldn't catch up.

He had long since finished up at the Irvings and they had given him a garland of their finest garlic "for luck". That was spooky but he took it anyway because only a very lucky guy was going to complete all the work he had lined up. Every day he set Sam to closing in the walls at Tom's house but the plumber never showed up on time and they waited and waited for their electrician.

When Sam stalled out at Tom's house, Joe put him to work framing up at his own place. It would be a very simple design, barely more than the barn he had done for Jack and Dahlia. They were both familiar with the layout so when Tom had a few minutes they put him to work on that, too. It was all hands on deck. They were squeezing every penny out of the money they'd gotten from Cal and Es but it would still never be enough. Sooner or later, they'd have to find additional funds. Probably from the bank.

By early October, they were just waiting for the electric. The plumber had set up a toilet—a red letter day-- and was expecting the shipment of a bathtub "soon". When they caught up with Buzz Fazzone, they were alarmed. Would he ever finish? He was a quiet man, not given to conversation, but was really good and very reliable. He didn't even seem to be that busy but he still wasn't showing up. What was the problem?

Louise went to the source. She stopped by the Fazzone house and asked Nancy if she was still planning to attend the village fete.

They had always turned out scones and butter cakes and would she be doing that again this year? Nancy invited her inside and Louise sniffed out the problem. She had forgotten that Nancy, too, was one of the redoubtable Truscotts. A picture of the family took up the whole front of the refrigerator. Had something happened at the bank?

As they sat and sipped their coffee, Louise told her about their dilemma.

They had to finish the electric or they couldn't move into the house. It was that simple. Nancy was clearly uncomfortable but she plucked up her nerve and said, "Well, lots of people aren't able to pay Buzz now. They need work done but they don't have any money to pay for it."

Louise could smell dead badger: "Wow! That's really tough. I'm sorry to hear that people are having a bad time. I'm glad we've got the money saved for the job; that's for sure." Nancy blinked but didn't reply.

"I bet that's tough for Buzz", Louise added. "I'd hate it if I did a job for someone and then got stiffed." Nancy nodded this time. "I guarantee you that that would never happen with us. I guarantee."

Eventually, Nancy confessed to hearing a rumor. She hastened to say that she "..never believed a word of it..." but people were saying that the Bustles were broke and did nothing but foul up. Everything they touched turned to bullpuckie! The guys at the bank said so.

Louise quickly set her straight and went one step further, too. "You get an estimate from Buzz and we'll pay him up front. He doesn't have to worry about us." Rumors! Gossip! Their whole future was being delayed by the townies and their incessant backchat.

Now, they had a shot at it. Now, they had a chance to get Tom's house up and running. It gave everybody a boost. When Buzz showed up the next morning, he put his hand up. "You don't have to give me anything right now. Don't worry about it. I didn't believe the rumors either but…..."

"Nope. That's not the deal. You're not walking out of here today without a check for four hundred dollars," Tom said firmly. "We need this done and we need you motivated to do it." And that was the end of that.

In two weeks, the electric was done and the walls closed in. Outlets were spaced out evenly around the walls so you could plug in the TV and the toaster at the same time without exploding the place.

Fortunately, the plumber was Doc Matthew's brother, Dil. He never listened to gossip and remembered all those years the boys had worked over at White's. They were good kids and he wasn't worried. He had put in the boiler and run the piping out to the radiators at least two months before. They tested it on one of the hottest days in August and when they cranked it up the heat drove them out of the house. All winter long that new boiler and those big, pink pads of insulation would keep them as warm as a new litter of pups. They could feel the love.

The dam broke at Joe's house, too. They banged away furiously at the sheets of plywood that had been stacked up all summer. They whacked them up against the studs and the framework and before long you could see where the windows would go. They completely forgot an opening for a staircase so they had to improvise in early November but by that time they were well and truly inside. They'd have a first floor window in the wrong place; you'd see Joe's bottom as he ascended the stairs but that didn't matter a bit. Joe still lived at home but he could see the time very soon---in six months or so---when his house would stand complete, out there on the dunes next to Tom's, a sort of cockeyed twin.

Still, someone had poisoned the well. Joe shrugged it off as nonsense but Tom knew better. He called attorney Barger and asked him what he thought. Barger had an idea and would call him later in the day. "Well, this is interesting," he said that afternoon. "It turns out that Alexandra just took out a big second against the Inn." Their noses both picked up the scent.

Tom went to see Trus Sheridan the next morning. If anybody knew anything, it would be Trus. He didn't waste any time. "Trus? How long have we known each other?" That question always gave Trus some trouble. People were always asking him that, hoping to trade on their long association and not on their current insolvency. He was a good hearted soul but as sheltered as a Rolls Royce convertible. However, he hadn't risen to Bank President by ignoring reality completely.

"Why, I remember you pitching on the Mustard Seeds, let's say, ….Oh, ….Twenty years ago."

"...And have I ever been anything but honest with you?" Trus frowned, looking the perfect twin of his cousin, Whiskey Bob. It stopped Tom for a second, that resemblance. Pudgy face, red cheeks, perspiration: Uncanny. But Tom couldn't be sidetracked. He had to go on.

"I've been hearing rumors lately that me and Joe are broke. And worse'n'at, we're unreliable. 'We don't fix stuff; we mess it up.'"

"Gosh, I don't think they heard that from me," Trus said, shaking his head. "No. I never said anything like that."

"Well, I know you to be an honorable man, Trus, but that doesn't mean everyone else is as straight as you."

"I suppose not, although I think we're all pretty good," he answered, a little defensively. "We have a good team here, ya know."

"Well, I want to say two things here," said Tom, sticking out his chin. "Both Joe and I have been running very successful businesses here for the last few years and our bank statements can prove it." Trus nodded. That was true.

"And the only failure on your books is the Inn right now." How'd he know that?

"Their latest mortgage is on record at the Registry, you know." Of course, the Registry.

"And we were all making a lot of money when we were there." Trus nodded again. Yes, they were.

"And Hunter is still making money, am I right?"

"Well, you know about confidentiality……." Trus said, trying to protect the remainder of his aplomb.

"Oh, come on. Hunter is cruising. He's making tons!"

Trus just nodded. It was common knowledge that the dock concession continued to be the goose that laid a formidable pile of golden eggs.

"Anyway, if I'm right, Alexandra has been blaming us for problems at the Inn." He waited to see Trus's reaction but Trus was scared now. His face was immobile, a pose he hoped would convey a form of inner strength but instead just made his fear that much more apparent.

"I can't comment....." he said quietly.

"Okay, okay. I understand. But for the love of Cheese, let's get the story straight. She's the one who sunk the Inn and I warn you: More money won't fix it." This really had Trus worried because it was almost certainly true. Against all reason, against all odds and against his better judgement he had probably made a very, very bad loan. Now he felt both queasy and afraid.

Tom's feeling of satisfaction was short-lived. The very next day he was brought up short. He had the "economy" to worry about but back home, he worried about Janey's. Would it survive now that money was tight? He called Marcel and asked to see him. Chef loved the attention but grew cranky when it cut into his day.

"Okay, okay," he said. "How about you come in tomorrow at 8?" Tom would be there, no problem. It meant getting up early but he'd set the alarm. He was now sleeping at the house and the smell of wood shavings was the greatest sleep aid he'd ever found. It seemed to act as an aphrodisiac, too. Imagine!

"Don't forget to ask him about Monk," Louise reminded him. "He's a good kid and we want to keep him as long as we can." So generous. So thoughtful. He gave her an affectionate pat on the bum to say he would.

Tom caught the early ferry and was at Janey's door at 7:30. He strolled around the parking lot for a minute and then went out back to take a peek at the business end, the shipping platform. Where he had formerly seen all sorts of action, only two trucks sat there, the drivers drinking their coffee.

"What's goin' on?" he asked.

Rodrigo was a tall, burly Dominican guy and spoke in a slow, dignified drawl. "Nothink. 'S'all good."

When he looked in the back of the truck, though, there was only half the usual sugar stacked inside. The big fifty pound bags of sugar and the huge jugs of corn syrup that magically became taffy were usually stacked to the ceiling but now they didn't even reach the warning line, the red line about four feet up that circled the inside of the truck.

"This isn't good," Tom thought. "Not good at all."

That little bit of information helped him when he got inside, though. Marcel was flustered but it wasn't because he was overworked; he was flustered because he had no orders. Some people can accept a slow down with some grace but Marcel was not one of the enlightened or flexible ones. He was all stirred up.

"I geev and I geev and I geev," he shouted, piteously. "I geev and I geev and I keep geeving! I geev them everything," meaning, Tom supposed, that he gave everything to his craft. Yeah, probably that.

"...And what do I get? Returns!" He was screaming now, waving his arms and shouting dramatically to the skies. "Returns!"

He had tried to send out extra product in an effort to max out each outlet but when they didn't sell, he got back the boxes. They'd all been time stamped as required by the FDA and once they had exceeded their shelf life they were destroyed. He got back the empty boxes as proof of that destruction the same way the Daily Eagle got back its front pages as proof of non-sale. He was understandably distraught.

Tom couldn't have arrived at a worse moment. Karma had caught up with him. He'd been lucky so many times before: He got the house on luck. He got his mortgage on luck. He was more than lucky with Louise and now his luck had run out. Marcel was putting the numbers together and the numbers were very bad, indeed.

Chef was still breathing heavy when he gave Tom the hard, cold facts.

"We're stuck with the lease we've got on the island but the shop we have to close. You can open on weekends if you want but otherwise, no. It's got to close." Tom waited for more.

"Then, we've got to take you off salary and put you on commission." Piece work again. Piece work! Tom could feel the sands slipping away under his feet, quicksands. Bloody piece work! Because like it or not, commissions was piece work, plain and simple.

"We keep shipping to you but you have to keep a tight thing…..a tight control. We don't want no more bloody returns!"

It really wasn't Marcel's fault; Tom knew that. It wasn't his fault, either. It was the "economy", not having the slightest idea what that meant. Sure, the "economy" now had to absorb a million vets who wanted to work but the real kicker was the loss of jobs. Millions, probably, were getting laid off because they were no longer making instruments of death. The war machine was on holiday. You almost wanted it back. Almost, if not quite.

No one had money for travel and nobody had money for treats. And no matter how much you love candy, it's still a treat. It's "Candy", not your daily bread.

They bounced it back and forth for an hour or so and Tom came away with one victory. He could keep Monk on the payroll as an adjunct to his concession. Tom would get what amounted to a franchise, a strange beast no one seemed to understand. He'd pay Monk a modest hourly wage and then give him bumps when he helped move the product. He wouldn't get the boot. It was a small triumph but at least he could tell Louise that he'd had some success. Never mind the hit he was taking himself.

The most persuasive element in their new agreement was that there was no investment. Tom simply continued pushing chocolates. He'd do it under different licensing terms but he was still in sales. Most emphatically, in sales. He just wouldn't have to go to the bank, thanks be to God.

THE LONG WALK

Joe's mind was in trouble. It floated from sector A to sector B like so much space junk. He simply couldn't stay on top of it all. He was crazy for Mrs. Crisp but between the mother---the one who hated him---and the husband who was in love with his buddy, he felt adrift. Add the ceaseless work schedule and it was easy to understand why he was down.

Over time, he'd become very close to Monk. He didn't think Monk was the right guy to talk to but he was always positive and not, after all, a family member. Family always seemed to think a confidence justified followup questions and Joe definitely couldn't do followup. He needed to vent, though, and soon.

One day, as they sat on a pair of saw horses, he spit it out. "I don't know how long I can go on like this," he said, surprising himself. His friend looked up at him and nodded. He put on his most serious face, too, even though he had no idea what Joe was talking about.

"I think I'm buggin' out," Joe said, his voice tight and strained.

"Well, we all bug out from time to.....," Monk replied.

"Naw, I don't mean just like that," Joe said, cutting him off. "I mean really buggin' out. Like *really, really* buggin' out."

"Yah, I know whatcha mean," Monk replied and nodded darkly, looking away. He didn't want to meet Joe's eye. When Joe failed to reply, though, he added, "I t'awt about suicide once, ya know."

"What?" Joe asked, astonished.

"Oh, yah. No job, no money. No home, really, udder than a little bolt hole at de backa de Inn."

"Jeez, I'm sorry," Joe said, still taken aback. For once, he gave Monk a careful, close look. This was serious.

"Oh yeah. I went down ta da bridge, ya know," he continued. "I looked around and thought about a jump."

"What happened?"

"Well, ya see, day installed these nets so if I jumped I'd get caught in the nets and I'd look a proper eedjit!" He had succeeded in frightening Joe who was clearly astonished. When Joe fell silent, he added, "Day'd hafta get a crew and fish me out, ya know?"

"Yeah, you'd have to bring a knife." Monk didn't get it so Joe repeated himself. "You'd have to bring a knife to cut through the nets, ya know?"

"Are you kiddin'? Do ya know how t'ick dem ropes are in dose nets?"

"Uh, yeah, a'course. Sure."

"...And I coulda cut myself on the bleedin' knife when I fell, ya know?"

"A'course." Joe waited respectfully, then asked, "So, wha'd ya do then?"

"Well, I t'awt I'd better write a note but I couldn't even find a bloody pencil and paper."

"A'course."

"So I decided to top myself and fugget the note. I'd just get a gun and KaBoom! It's over." Joe's eyes opened when he heard that: Jumpin' Jesus!

"But there's no crime on Nantucket. Why'd'ja have a gun? For 'self protection'? Don't make me laugh. Nobody needs'em. If a guy is stupid enough to break inta yer house all day gotta do is go down to the ferry and pick him up when he tries to leave." Joe nodded uncertainly. "Dare's nowhere to go! It's a bloody island!"

"So you couldn't find a gun?"

"Well, I found a twenty-two my cousin used for rabbits but a twenty-two is useless when ya wanna do da business. It's pitiful. Ya want sommat that's got a real kick, ya know? A pump gun, maybe."

"A'course."

"Ya need a twelve gauge, sixteen at the least. Even a four ten is no good unless you're a bleedin' squirrel." Sticking out his hands in a plea of utter frustration, he asked, "And didja ever hear of a squirrel blowin' its fawkin' head off!?!"

"A'course."

"So, just when I thought I had run outta idears I remembered rat poison. I could make a meal out of it and Bob's your uncle!" he said proudly. He was clearly enjoying this opportunity to unburden himself, one he'd never had before.

"...But have you ever tasted that shit?" he asked. "Have you ever tasted that shit?" Joe shook his head as much in bewilderment as in rejection of the idea.

"It's horrible! It really tastes like shit!" Monk yelled, making a face. "I took one mouthful and spit it out." He stuck out his tongue and closed his eyes, miming a man in the throws of a power flash. "I couldn't hold it down. It's just bloody terrible!" He shook his head, sadly. "It just don't work."

He shook his head slowly back and forth, clearly saddened by the memory.

"I didn't even get a headache."

"And so now, you're gonna live and that's it, right?" Joe asked hopefully.

"Oh, yah. The whole thing was too much trouble." Just for a minute, Monk looked embarrassed. "It took too much time, too. I mean, ya gotta be in the mood." Joe nodded at that. "After a while, I wasn't in the mood. Trootfully, I just wasn't interested any more."

"A'course."

"If ya're not in the mood its just another job. Anudder t'ing ya gotta check off for de day: 'Mow da lawn, clean da chimney, top yerself.' All da fun is gone clear out of it. It's just another bloody chore."

"Well, I can see…."

"Yeah, it's just too much trouble. I had t'accept dat. I went out and got a haircut instead. I needed one for a long time and…....." He paused as if he'd just thought of something: "Have you ever been to that new guy downtown?"

When Joe said he hadn't, Monk added his assessment: "He's really good. He took just enough off the sides and left the front as it is." He posed theatrically for Joe, showing the sweep of the wave in front. It was truly distinctive. Part Elvis, part Rita Hayworth.

"You forgot about hangin'," said Joe, finally. "You coulda just thrown a rope over one of the......" But Monk was done.

"Get on witchyuz! Fawkin' asshole!" he said with a wave of the hand.

"But I'm tryin' to helpya."

After that, Joe didn't feel so bad. He had learned another lesson. Not only do other people have it worse than you do, you don't want their problems. If anything, their problems are often more embarrassing than your own. He had learned something else, too: When he asked Monk all those questions it was just like he was a member of the family. Monk had actually--and without any one noticing—become part of the family.

When he took the time to think about it, he knew that a big part of his angst had to do with Mrs. Crisp. They had been managing to steal time together but it had been hard. Once his own house was done, though, it would be easier. They had no neighbors to snoop and Tom and Louise were completely on board. They joked about it.

On a couple of occasions when Tom joined her at the Oceanographic, Louise had "left the keys under the mat" and whole weekends had been spent in the peace and quiet of Tom's new house, forgetting the hole in the floor and the bathtub that always seemed to be on the back of someone's truck out there in America. They had coped, though: They had rigged up a sun shower, a simple plastic bag full of water heated by "solar" energy and suspended it from the roof, facing south to catch the sun. If the occasional scalloper passed by, well that's just too bad. He should be fishing instead of gawking at the neighbors, anyway.

It didn't take much to get Joe stirred up about Mrs. Crisp and the thought of that sun shower warmed his cheeks. It also motivated him in a big way. At the end of the day he could look at his work with pride. He'd gotten a lot done. His house wouldn't be ready as soon as Tom's; he had too much to do. But he could definitely occupy it come Christmas. They'd need a few quilts and he had picked up some surplus Army blankets. Those would serve. Again, every time he raised a hammer or slapped on some paint he was getting closer to the finish. Maybe even get the hearth done so he could get a fire going.

THE INERTIA OF INERT OBJECTS

Things happen and then other things happen and before you know it, you've reached the end of your days. If you're foolish enough to make up a list of Pros and Cons, you will be looking for that rope Tom suggested to Monk. We all make mistakes and for some reason, those mistakes weigh so heavily on our souls that the good works we've done can never offset them. We lose every time.

No matter how positive you are when you start that exercise, bad thoughts will always weigh you down. Anyone doing an inventory will tell you the same thing: Don't do it unless you've developed a taste for self abuse. You'll always weigh your sins so heavily that they will sink any little skiff full of good deeds that you've hoped will keep you afloat.

Mrs. Crisp had made some mistakes; she knew that. Her first encounter with Joe on Wouldbe Island had been a mistake so far as convention is concerned but she remembered it as one of the sweetest moments of her life. She could hear the bible thumping in the back of her brain but that noise was still not enough to reduce the heavenly glow she felt each and every day. She had experienced happiness—and a very rare form of happiness—on that little island. She could not feel badly about it; she only felt joy.

Had she been selfish? Or worse, predatory? Had she done Joe a harm so great that he would never heal?

Or, had she been generous, generous to a fault? He said so. He said so often. He said he'd never get over her but he clearly wasn't thinking of an injury. Far from it.

Or, had she simply acted in a natural way, defying custom certainly, but acting in the most natural way possible. Loving someone and accepting love in return? She had given him a gift that he could never fully repay, the gift of everything.

Few have the courage to make such a gift; few have the courage to trust fully and completely. Even fewer have the strength it takes to live with a decision that, after all, was impulsive. Rash, even.

Fortunately, Mrs. Crisp wasn't given to second guessing or at least wasn't overly given to second guessing. When a dark shadow crossed her path she might start and catch her breath but she always tried to keep her focus on the horizon. The future, the infinite was where the truth lay, not in a dark place just two or three steps away.

The time finally came when her mother needed full time care. Mrs. Crisp had managed on her own until the previous year but then she had to get help. Help came in the form of an older woman named Barbara (Babba) Sails who had grown up black in racially hostile Florida and who knew what she was about. She watched Ida's every move and put her back on track.

After that first year though, Babba couldn't keep up. Ida was in rapid decline. She couldn't remember the difference between Sweet Jesus and sweet potato pie and was constantly getting lost. Babba told Mrs. Crisp and that was that. Ida was off to Hollyhocks, a rest home for the aged with cognitive deficits. She'd get a nice room in the Sunset Wing where they put all the forgetful folks.

This left Mrs. Crisp home alone with Mr. Crisp. They never realized how much of a buffer Ida had been. She had always been an irritant but now there was nothing but a void. The two of them traveled in different, silent orbits like asteroids. When they did occasionally collide it surprised them both. They had traveled so many miles alone and they had traveled such different paths that they had nothing in common but that brief moment when they met in the kitchen or the garage. They would then politely withdraw to separate rooms and resume their solitary journeys through interstellar space.

Sooner or later, though, they'd have to address their "situation". Each would first have to be clear on what he/she wanted and then would have to accept the expectations of the other. This meant listening, of course, something rarely done by partners, let alone asteroids.

Mrs. Crisp wanted a peaceful life; she knew that. She would also like to continue with her job, one she found enormously satisfying. She knew that her life with Joe would be limited but she wanted to enjoy it as long as she could. What did her husband want? And would he be able to articulate it? Those questions had to be resolved before their future could ever be clear.

One Saturday morning, just after walking the hellacious dog and before her morning coffee, she decided to ask. Just what did he want? What did he want now and what did he want for the future?

Mr. Crisp obliged by rising shortly after she did and came down just as the coffee was ready. They exchanged terse greetings and she poured a cup for him. She asked if he wanted sugar, then asked him how he was doing.

"I'm fine. Yeah, fine," he said, clearly unwilling to say more.

"Well, we haven't talked much in a long time and now that Mom is gone I think we should think about the future." Mr. Crisp (Donald) just stirred the coffee and looked out the window.

"Seriously, Don, I hope you're okay but you don't elaborate."

"I bin busy, ya know," he lied.

"Well, I don't want to pester you. And I don't want to irritate you. I just want to have a talk some time." He nodded and picked up the paper, ending the discussion.

A few days went by and she tried again. He usually had a couple of beers before dinner and that might loosen him up. That day, he was home when she got out of work. It had rained since eight in the morning so he was stuck there. No golf. When she showed up, he headed to the fridge for a beer.

Mrs. Crisp sat primly on the couch but, she hoped, not too primly. She asked him to join her and, unusual for her, asked him to bring her a beer, as well. They made a mock show of a toast and then she turned serious.

"Where do you see yourself in ten years?" she asked.

He was ready for that. "Florida," he said. "Or Myrtle Beach."

She smiled and asked why. He seemed surprised. "I just like it there. Nice guys and no snow. I can play golf all year and just relax. Have a good time." He had clearly thought it all out.

"That sounds great," she said.

"Yeah. I'll bet ninety percent of the guys at the club are planning the same thing."

"Why don't they do it now?" she asked.

"Well, they've gotta work, I suppose," he replied, then added, "You know, they've got kids in school, jobs, obligations…. You know."

"Okay," she said, trying to understand.

"Yeah, I see guys disappearing over the hill all the time. I'd love to do it myself but I've got work so I've got to wait, too."

What work? she wondered, but knew not to ask.

She was a planner, though, so she asked. "What does it cost to buy a place down there?"

"Oh, I don't know…..," he said. "Not too much, I don't think." He wrestled with that thought for a minute and said, "But I wouldn't want to own two places at the same time, anyway."

Again, she wondered, Why? But that led her mind down a little cul de sac, one she hadn't considered before.

"Why not rent for a month or so during the winter and see how you like it?"

"Yeah, that's what Ernie did. He rented a place for one month two years ago and then last year he took one for two months. He loves it. He's definitely gonna settle there when he retires."

Don hadn't given a lot of thought to his wife. She never seemed much of a consideration. It was his dream, unclouded and uncomplicated by others. His golf buddies were part of his dream but nobody else.

"Well, now that Mom has gone to Hollyhocks, we don't have to see to her daily care," she said. "…And we don't have kids….." She let that drop, too.

"….So what's preventing you from doing it?" This really jolted him. He had been dreaming for a long time but reality? That was something else. That presented a whole new series of "ifs" and "maybes".

"Well, I've got obligations….", he mumbled.

"Of course," she answered. And let it drop. The beer was over and the conversation was, too. Still, she had planted a seed. Maybe, anyway.

Later, she wondered why he never asked about her. He wasn't a completely selfish person, after all. Still, selfishness comes in many forms. He didn't take a chicken wing out of her hand and eat it himself. He didn't buy a Mercedes and leave her by the side of the road to walk home, either. He just didn't think about her.

He'd been wrapped up in a dream and she had jogged him awake.

He could actually do it. He could "work" from Florida as easily as he "worked" on the island. Maybe easier. He just had to talk to a broker now and then. That was about it. He managed his property; that's all. Why not Florida? Why not Timbuktu?

Two days later he got home all excited. She had just gotten off work and would have liked to take a bath but he was all worked up.

"I told Ernie about your idea and guess what?" She had seldom seen him this excited before. She shook her head, unable to "guess what".

"He's invited me to stay with him this winter." He looked at her, expecting her face to glow just as brightly as his own. At first, it didn't; she was completely unprepared.

Then, as the idea sunk in, she did start to smile. And once her smile had started, it was hard to stop. Soon, it covered her whole face, her back, her bottom, her knees and all the way down to her toes. "Delight" was what she called it later, such delight that she strained not to let it show.

"Well, that's really amazing," she said, in much the same way as a teenager says something is "interesting". The subject was beyond all ken, past knowing in a way that defied the slightest comprehension.

"Yeah," he went on. "It's funny. He said it's something he'd been thinking about a lot but had just never had the nerve to 'pop the question'."

But Mrs. Crisp had recovered herself at this point, a point she said later was the furthest she had ever traveled from the fulcrum that kept her brain in proper balance.

"Well, that is really quite a coincidence, isn't it?" she said. "Why, just the other day we talked about...."

But Mr. Crisp was too excited. He couldn't even let her finish. "That's right!" he exclaimed. "Amazing! He did it the winter of '73, '74 and he's full speed ahead this winter, too. How about that!?!"

Her mind did flip flops trying to see the thing from his perspective. What could she ask him? Did she dare ask when? Finally, she just tried to keep him talking. Smiling warmly, she asked, "How did this all come up?"

"Well, we were sitting on the ninth tee and I was thinking..." She nodded and he went on. "...If I picked up a birdie on nine, we'd be even." She frowned now: This was serious.

"We had to wait, though, because the guys in front of us had lost a ball or something." And he did an eye roll to show how thoughtless our fellow man can be.

"Out of nowhere, Ernie started talking about going south and how he had to pack and get everything ready. Stop the paper and get a guy in to check the fridge. That sort of thing." He paused again out of sheer excitement. He couldn't wait to tell his story. "So I told him that you and I had talked about that just the other day and he sprung it on me! Just like that. Can you believe it?"

"Wow!" was all she said and all she thought, too. Now, her enthusiasm was rising with his. They had not only collided but were traveling the vast distances of interstellar space together. For the first time in a long, long time, they wanted exactly and precisely the same thing. For different reasons, maybe, but exactly the same thing. Even the same direction: Due South.

It turned out that Ernie was leaving the following week for two months with an option on two more. He was already thinking of taking at least one of those months. He would get the place ready and Mr. Crisp was welcome to come any time after that.

The questions that filled her mind were like those we ask at the moment before death:

"Are your affairs in order?'

"Have you chosen the clothes you'd like to wear?"

"Why were you born in the first place?" She decided not to ask.

But Mr. Crisp's mind had been racing, as well. "I'd love to go but I'm going to have to talk to the guy at Smith Barney."

"Well", she thought, "...that would take about fifteen minutes....... Twenty tops."

"…..And I'm going to have to go to the bank….." He turned and headed for the door.

As an afterthought, he shouted over his shoulder, "You can take care of most of the other stuff, right?" The innocence of the question, the total lack of comprehension struck her with such force that it knocked her right off their asteroid and back on to her own. Their orbits would surely never meet again.

"Of course," she said and then thought how little her life would change.

She would continue to pay the bills, take in the paper and see to the occasional household disaster. She'd walk the infernal dog. She'd get the driveway shoveled, take in the mail and go to the library now and then. Otherwise, she'd work and see to her private life. Her very private life. That would be the biggest change, that and the smile that never left her lips.

NIXON'S REVENGE

Nixon had been chased out of office and the economy was blown to bits. His V.P., Gerald Ford, had taken over the reins of government but after all of Nixon's follies, Ford would not survive the election in '76, the bicentennial year. Interest rates were higher than they'd been in decades, inflation was running wild and banks that had money to lend could not bring themselves to lend it. It was tough all over. When the lease ran out for Janey's island store, they closed the outlet altogether. The shop in Hyannis would still crank out candy but now Tom had nothing more than a chance to sell and distribute.

Monk worked for Joe now part time whenever Joe could find a job. They made enough to keep them alive but not enough to enjoy that life. Jobs were spotty, at best. Tom still kept candy moving on the island but it was more of a sideline now. Something they came to call a "cottage industry" like soaps or candles. The stuff you second gift.

The only bright spot anywhere seemed to be the dock. Hunter's simple little concession continued to show a profit and to the astonishment of everyone, he didn't blow the money. Instead, he bought more boats. He picked up a couple of skiffs and cleaned them up so they looked just fine. Then, he picked up a couple of small sailboats--lake boats--a sunfish and a laser. You could feel very daring indeed when you sailed out of the harbor and into the rip. You got plenty wet whether you suffered a knockdown or not. All this meant that there was room for Monk when he asked for some hours. Hunter couldn't do it all. He just couldn't.

The Inn itself didn't fare as well. Alexandra had managed to screw some money out of the bank but when faced with the decision about how to spend it, her sophisticated sense, her downtown self called the shots. She would have a place that looked okay—maybe Yankee magazine would pick it up—but she wouldn't dive beneath the surface.

The antiquated electric and plumbing would have to wait. She had to rope in the multitude first. Her bet would have disastrous results as we shall see.

The problem was nightly rates. If she put the rates too high, they were empty. If she put them too low, the kids showed up as if there was an underground pipeline of some sort. The minute her rates dropped, kids would come out of nowhere. It absolutely bedeviled her.

Soon, the wear and tear of heavy traffic began to show. If the Inn had been a little old-fashioned or tatty during her father's reign, it now took on a new kind of look: Early Alpha Omega Kappa. Or, Sunday morning Alpha Omega Kappa. The smell of beer could never be removed entirely from the carpets and the smell of kids permeated the place like a youth hostel in rural Slovenia. The background odors of chlorine and Tide provided the only relief from adolescent pong. Cheap but down and out; that's all it was. As overnight accommodation, it made a night's stay in one of Hunter's dinghies look good by comparison. He'd actually found a couple of kids doing just that, having pulled a tarp over themselves to keep out the damp.

You could still hear through the walls, too. She had done nothing to mitigate the "Oooohs and Aaaahs" emanating from the rooms. She hadn't even hung up a quilt or two. The sounds of sex in the raw echoed constantly up and down the narrow halls. They were living DEEP THROAT, not just reading about it in their favorite magazines. You yearned for the peace and quiet of a monastery or at the very least, a tenement next to the "T".

The little guy had ended war in Indochina. Ho Chi Minh was a little guy; he told you that, even though it wasn't true. But he didn't end the war himself anyway. Peasants ended it, peasants and protesters. Down on the ground, peasants had made the conquest of a native people impossible. They had dug in and dug down. They'd created a network of tunnels that frustrated every assault. At night, those simple peasants reconfigured the landscape and thwarted the military industrial complex that laid siege to it. Simple, humble but determined peasants. No one could beat them.

Back home, protesters kept up their campaigns. Endless campaigns that took endless, imaginative forms. Their faces were on TV from one end of the day to the other. Every one of them was sick of the incessant marches but they kept it up anyway. Young people wanted out and older, more staid people couldn't understand. "Why did these kids protest the clearly stated policies of their government?" My country, right or wrong!

This benighted view passed from Nixon to his henchmen to his military command and down to all of the Moms and Pops who had so nobly served during WWII. All those poor souls backed him to the hilt and looked with disfavor upon all of the punks and slackers who just wanted to chase girls and get high. "College kids!" Whoever listened to college kids!?!

In the end, the "college kids" prevailed but at a terrible cost. Their protests had saved thousands and thousands of lives but the country was divided in a way it had never been divided before. A father and a son stood not at arms length but at a continental divide. They couldn't hear each other and even though the son was right—The war had been a huge, unforgivable mistake—the father wouldn't hear of it. "Kids!" was all he could think, indignantly. "I changed his diapers until three years ago!" Completely irrelevant but embraced with all his heart.

The kids would have to pay for being right, though. They'd sunk Nixon but now Nixon was sinking them. His buddies had all survived; many had become fat and happy but those were the few and the fortunate, the wealthy and cynical, the profiteers. As for everyone else? There were no jobs.

The economy kept shrinking and shrinking along with rampant inflation and Nixon's master stroke: A devaluation of the currency by ten percent! Forget your savings! He just took ten percent away! Just like that! Just like magic. He waved his arms, said he wasn't a crook and nibbled away at pay checks until they were substantially less than bite sized.

Tom and Joe had been struggling but holding it together. Now, they were on the ropes. They'd been careful with expenses and their houses were largely done but they were struggling to pull them all together.

They had made the most of the dollars they had but they'd exhausted their funds. Their slim, slim margin was gone.

They had bowed their heads once too often, too. Both parents had kicked in what they could to fund the houses but were all tapped out.

They had to look out for themselves. The kids couldn't ask again, either. They just couldn't. If they were ever going to reach adulthood they'd have to solve their problems for themselves. Like a crime family under siege, they went to the mattresses.

Tom and Louise sat down with a stiff drink and a plate of orange parfaits and worried through two solid hours of possibilities. Joe did, too. He and Mrs. Crisp curled up under a quilt and lit a couple of candles. As the wax poured down the sides they kept cranking out ideas. What to do? What to do?

At the end of the night they had each come to the same conclusion. The little guy had ended the war and now the little guy would have to end the peace—or at least, make the peace. They'd have to rely on themselves for answers, not anyone else. Everyone else was struggling, anyway. Everyone else was in the same boat as they were, fighting a strong, strong tide.

The germ of a solution came to Joe just before going to bed. Mrs. Crisp declined but Joe rolled one little doobie and then enjoyed a couple of puffs. It made him relax. He closed his eyes and allowed the pictures to float across his mind. He saw Johnny Ice, tall and straight but he saw garlic, too. He was Johnny Ice but garlic had been his charm, his good luck, his talisman.

Then, he saw a bus. "Why a bus?" he wondered but let it go. Johnny Ice was boarding the bus. The bus was full of chocolates. Boxes and boxes of chocolates. As he grew sleepier and sleepier, he reflected on his favorite treats from Janey's boxes: He loved solid milk chocolate and considered himself a purist but beyond that, he loved the way a white chocolate felt on the tongue. It had all of the smoothness of milk chocolate but it had just that little extra sniff of something else. He couldn't quite put his finger on it but.......

His mind trailed off as sleep overcame his waking dream. The next morning he awoke feeling totally refreshed. Wide awake and aware. Somewhere in that smoke lay the secret to his future, to his true North and to his success. He didn't know what it was but the image of Johnny Ice followed him throughout the day. Monk asked him why he was so quiet but he couldn't say. All he knew was that he knew. He knew how to conquer the almighty troubles that surrounded him. He knew; he just had to figure out what he knew.

Tom had come up blank. Louise told him not to worry. He told himself not to worry, too, but worrying had become a habit. Almost a default mind set. He had to worry. Why? Because if he didn't worry, nobody else would worry and he was on the job full time.

꩜

Worry is a habit, after all. We're not born with it; we're born without it.

We make everybody else worry as we cry about wetting ourselves and then cry because we're hungry or we cry just because we want some love. We want some sugar. We want some attention. We want lots of stuff and it's all provided so why worry?

No: Worry happens when we pass from infancy to toddlerhood. We get yelled at when we steal our friend's shovel from the sandbox so we worry that we'll get yelled at when we take his pail, as well. Sure enough, we catch holy hell. Soon, we catch hell every time we act up. It's awful. And it's hard to adapt. No wonder little kids have that frightened look on their faces. "I'm supposed to be the king and now you tell me I'm not." Of course they worry.

꩜

They'd have to go to the bank, both of them. Tom and Louise looked to be okay because she had a steady job and could point to consistent earnings over a dozen years. Joe could not. Joe found himself in the same bind as freebooters everywhere: He had made good money when the rest of the world was working but he hadn't declared any of it. He couldn't slap a stack of pay stubs on the desk and claim the higher ground. According to the IRS, he was a farmer and not a very high earning farmer, at that. Garlic was turning against him.

Both boys were learning the true meaning of the word "economy". They had always known it was "out there", something that influenced industry and big business. They'd never thought of it as a butter and eggs issue.

Nixon had somehow gummed up the works by dumping the gold standard: What was that? Maybe they should have paid more attention in history class.....

The real answer, if the world was a balanced or sensible place, would have been for Joe to resume management of the Inn. He then would have had a regular income and the Inn would have a chance to recover from Alexandra. Instead, Joe would have to raise money somehow. If he wanted to complete his house and permanently get out from under his parents' roof, he'd have to do one of two things, get work or go to the bank.

Trus Sheridan was a good man. Encumbered as he was by a townie mentality and weighed down as he was by banking practices, he lacked a dynamic vision. He lacked imagination. He was a good man but not a problem solver. In fact, the very last thing he wanted to encounter in any given day was a problem. Just like his cousin Whiskey Bob and just like the three little piggies, he could not look out his window without seeing a big, bad wolf at every door.

Married couples have an advantage when they see the bank. They're more stable and more reliable than their single, unattached friends. They're more accountable. This is the accepted wisdom of bankers far and wide. It gave Tom and Louise just the advantage they needed when they went to apply for a "construction loan", something they'd never even heard of before.

Tom and Louise didn't need much, after all. A couple of thousand dollars would serve them straight through to completion. They were on pretty solid ground. Not so, brother Joseph. His status at the bank was similar to that of Sandy Saddler, a black featherweight who tore through legions of white guys deployed to take him down in the forties and fifties. Saddler was eminently quotable. When asked his chances against the best and the brightest, he said, "I have to knock out a white guy twice to get a draw." Joe took a look at his savings book and gave himself just those kinds of chances.

Trus looked at Tom and Louise and saw two nice kids. He wouldn't favor them with a loan perhaps, but they were nice kids. They put all their cards on the table, smiled a lot and left. He'd have to talk to the committee.

Trus looked at Joe a different way. He struggled not to ask, "Just what are you doing here?" He didn't dislike the kid; he just couldn't understand how on earth he thought he'd qualify for a loan. No: He'd be polite but not encouraging. He didn't want to have that scene occur that had happened last year, the time the guy dropped to his knees and started head-butting his desk. That wasn't good. He thought he'd have a heart attack. Too much raw emotion. Too much drama and excitement. Too much of everything.

So when Joe left the bank he was hopeful. He, too, would have to wait for the "committee" but he thought he might have a chance. Just maybe. When the letter arrived only four days later, he was shocked back into reality.

"Despite your many references and your favorable credit history, we are forced to respectfully decline.......", etc., etc. The old jigsaw pieces fell into their familiar pattern: If you didn't need the money, it was yours for the asking. If you actually needed some cash because you were in the middle of a big project and couldn't pay for materials, there was no hope for you. Thumbs down.

Now, although Joe could help Tom realize his dream and finish in time for the holidays, he wouldn't get there himself. Mrs. Crisp had offered to help but he was too proud to accept. Old age would beat the pride out of him but it hadn't happened yet. He thanked her but turned her down. He was back at the Bustle house with his folks for at least the foreseeable future. He felt like a kid again but not youthful, just kid-like, a perennial adolescent straining to grow up. If he could have taken anything positive from this experience it would have been a better way to handle frustration. He didn't.

THE FALL AND THEN THE FALL

Alexandra sat and stewed. She simply couldn't figure a way out of her dilemma. She was stuck between two intractable forces--rates and clientele. She loved the money but she hated the kids. What, exactly, could she do to attract better patrons and discourage the kids?

She had already tried everything she knew. She'd sent out mailers and notified prior visitors of their "new pricing policy" but word had gotten out: If the kids were there, their older, more well-to-do clients would stay home. They weren't coming back until some level of peace was restored to the place.

It never occurred to her to seek help or advice; she was too hard-headed for that. Instead, she went from week to week without guidance and without a resolution. Rudderless.

Her brother was still raking it in. He worked hard and the operation ran smoothly. It was, after all, fairly uncomplicated. They had boats. If you wanted to rent one, you either booked a boat or caught one when one was free. Pretty easy. He had help keeping the boats fit and trim, too. He'd hire a couple of college kids in season; they always pulled their friends, too. The mainstays, though, were Monk and Sam who alternated between carpentry with Joe and boat haulin' with Hunter. Their heads, at least, stayed above water.

The bank's first timid notices were dumped in the trash. Their next, somewhat more ardent pleas met the same fate. When a month had passed, then two months, the bank went to registered letters. These were refused at the door. She was behind and getting behinder. She would soon default and the bank's otherwise oblivious committee was making noises. Trus would have to get her on the phone.

Trus loved his job. He loved the big desk and the fan he'd placed just inside the window. It blew a cool breeze on his face all summer and was easily stored during the cooler months. He had no need for air conditioning and thought the expense outrageous. He was true to the island in every way. It was blessed with salt sea air, a soothing balm for the most sensitive skin. He slept like a baby all year long and his face was free of the wrinkles seen on his American counterparts.

However, even with all the amenities, there was a down side to his job as there are with all jobs. Sometimes, he had to get tough. Sometimes, he had to put the hammer down. People defaulted. They did it rarely, thanks be to God, but they did fail and he did foreclose. That was the hardest part of the job. He hated it.

Trus really was a good guy. He would have done well in other professions, too. He could have sold ice cream and seen smiling faces all day long. Or potato chips. He could have played the clarinet and again, seen people laugh and dance. But Trus learned early that if he wanted to make money he'd have to choose a different, less self-indulgent career.

He chose banking and it was a good choice but for that one day in a hundred when he'd actually have to work for his pay. This was it.

By his count, he called the Inn at least six times before he got through to her. She was dodging him. When she finally got her on the phone, she answered each question with one syllable, a grunt.

"We see that you've gotten behind, Alex," he started.

"Mmmmm".

"...And we are afraid you're not catching up...".

"Mmmmm".

"....And we don't want you to fall behind...."

"Yuh."

"We want you to succeed." This was hard for him to say because even though he was obliged to speak these words, even Trus had his limits.

She wasn't listening and he knew it. She stayed on the phone because she was stuck. She wasn't going to apologize or offer a solution. She'd ditch as soon as she could. No question. He'd have to lay it out for her, after all.

"We don't want to......" Trus choked. He didn't even want to say the word but managed finally to finish the sentence, "...to....foreclose."

That one word, a very rude word, indeed, shocked her back to her real self. She started screaming and railed against Trus and the bank and the bloody college kids and her brother and her father and...... She only stopped to catch her breath. Trus waited for more but she ran out of gas.

"We have to talk," he said, using the cant phrase he'd once seen that scary guy DeNiro use in a Godfather movie. It made him warm all over, the power of that phrase.

She dodged him again but finally ran out of reasons to avoid the meeting. They set a date and he would see her there, at the Inn.

When the day for the meeting arrived, Trus wondered how long it had been since he'd set foot inside the Inn. Quite a while, he guessed. He took the back entry, through the porch and everything looked pretty good but when he got inside he was shocked. The reception area was cluttered and the furniture was all beat up. The whole place looked tired, right down to the curtains and the terrible "stylish" décor.

Alex had chosen to increase the seating so it was cramped. She had also decided to go with dark colors, something she'd seen in Vogue. Those colors worked when they graced the walls of well lit ateliers on Park Avenue but they were positively scary at the Inn. The low ceilings and worn carpeting made it look spooky instead of stylish, fussy instead of fashionable.

It got worse, too. Trus's eye fell on appointments in the main dining room. The table cloths had been neglected and now looked tacky and threadbare. She had concentrated on the reception area but she had ignored the dining area, the place where people actually spent their time. When he looked overhead at the lighting, it had simply been ignored. He saw cobwebs and black light bulbs that had surely been there for a long, long time.

They sat at one of the tables. She seemed more comfortable there than in her office. As he started to probe her finances she simply tightened up. Her grunts were sometimes alternated with a single syllable but he got no real explanation from her. She had withdrawn all of the money available on her line of credit and her receipts were not enough to pay back any of it. Even a "restructure", the kindest word he could produce, was not indicated. She was sinking fast.

In one brief moment of clarity, she pled her belly as if faced with transportation to Australia. She would do anything to avoid the inevitable—They'd call the note. Given no choice, she groped for an answer. Fumbling awkwardly, she finally asked in desperation what she might do. She asked for suggestions.

"Well, I might have an interested buyer…..", he started, thinking how he could make some calls and then rake in a referral fee.

Her eyes bulged out. "No!" she screamed. And then a little less stridently, "No!" She was frightened now and nervously pulled on the cuffs of her blouse. Her right eye started to twitch, as if being tweaked by an angry nerve. "No," she said finally. "If I could just get a little bit more…..."

But even she knew that wasn't going to happen. Trus leaned back in his chair and made sympathetic noises. "I know it's been difficult….."

"There must be another way," she said finally, fighting off the tears that were now welling up behind her eyes.

"Well, I could maybe get you a month or two if you could start making money but….." They both knew that would be hard, if not impossible.

"There must be another way," she repeated. Perhaps she was given to magical thinking or, being special, she thought her charm and sheer irresistibility would turn the tide. What about her superior finger painting and what about that time when she tapped her little heart out and got a special bouquet?

They talked about it a little longer and he really did try to help. He asked about the operation and he asked about the management. Then, he got to the staff. When she answered that they'd all been let go, he sat back again and said quietly, "Well, right there may be your problem".

"I'm gonna go out on a limb here now...," he said, "....and guess that the main problem with kids is that they're unmanageable." She remained silent so he asked, "Am I right?"

"Well, yes, but they're dirty and sloppy and they drink too much. They even bring their own booze......"

Trus put up his hand. "I think I can help you," he said. "I think I know how to make money, keep a roof over your head and...." He wanted to say, "I can get my money back." Instead, he said, ".....and you can get yourself out of this pickle."

For the first time since they'd started their conversation, she paid attention. She looked up at him like a young nun at the communion rail and murmured, "How?"

"You're not going to like this......", he said, hoping she'd ask him to go on. When she was silent but continued to look intently in his direction, he said, "Bouncers."

"Oh, I can't hire more people," she said. He nodded. He could see that her solution to everything was to cut costs, not to invest. This situation would not improve without an investment. Any banker could have told her that and any fisherman worth his salt would also have told her the ultimate truth: Sometimes you have to dive down into the depths in order to free yourself. Only then can you bob up to the surface and breathe the Almighty's sweet, sweet air.

Her leg was wrapped tightly around an anchor chain and she was held fast below the surface. She'd have to steel herself, dive down and get free before she'd ever see the surface again. As anyone who's been in that position can tell you, it's a frightening, frightening moment.

She didn't get it but she didn't bolt, either. "What?" she asked. Then, "Who?" Her lungs were crying for that air but she was still trying to find a better way.

"I don't know who to suggest but you might have a chance to save the place if you can control the kids. Make'em pay but keep them out of trouble. Their parents will love you for it, not to mention the local police."

Her face showed that she was working on that idea, so he asked her about Hunter. "Oh, no...no," she said, not wanting him involved.

"You know, it's not all about muscle," Trus explained. "It's about control." He had three wild kids so he knew what he was talking about. You can keep ahead of them but first you must outsmart them.

"They're scary," she admitted, finally letting down her guard. Trus just nodded his assent. Yes, yes, they are.

"They don't listen," she added.

"Well, you just got to find the right guy, somebody who can deal with them without necessarily breaking any skulls." She shook her head back and forth as if to indicate that breaking skulls wasn't entirely off the table. She hadn't established any kind of network on the island, either. She'd always felt too good for island folk and didn't encourage local associations.

"Who was the manager before you took over?" Right there, he put his finger on it. Right there was her answer. Right there was the place she didn't want to go.

"Bustle," she said. "Joseph. No, Thomas. Bustle."

He paused for a moment to let the idea sink in, then put it to her: "You still on good terms with them?" She looked at her fingernails and then pressed them to her lips. She hadn't even let Tom sell candy there.

"Not exactly," she answered finally.

"Well, I'd give that one a good think," said Trus. "Those guys could help you out, you know."

She would not go crawling back to the Tom or Joe. They had abandoned her to those college kids. Bastids! She wouldn't go down on her hands and knees....... She wouldn't lower herself....... She just wouldn't.

But Trus could read her thoughts. "Look, we have lots of ups and downs in business. Don't let a bad history dictate the future." When she didn't reply, he said, "Think about it."

As he left, he tried one last time to make it all clear to her. "Look, you can swallow your pride and maybe save the place or you can continue as you are. It's up to you." From a banker, it was a surprisingly paternal thing to say but that is, after all, the island way. Island folks are stuck with each other. They have to offer a helping hand or word will get out.

"He's a schmuck!" And that is very bad for business.

SINK OR SWIM

When Alexandra finally called Tom, a couple of days later, she had run out of options. She actually reconsidered asking her brother but he was happy. Happy! He was making enough money to satisfy his needs and was surrounded by gangs of kids. Mostly slackers, yes, but a few serious sailors, too. He was easy going, friendly and very content. No: She needed someone who was hungry. All roads led in the same direction.

Tom didn't know what to say, at first. She muddied the waters, too. She was going to expand. She was thinking of buying the property next door. Maybe another Windsor's Inn on Martha's Vineyard. But Tom knew that wasn't happening. He had learned something she hadn't: People aren't as dumb as you think.

When he discussed it with Louise, he saw just how focused she could be. She heard about the call, the possible expansions and took it all in. When he had finished, she said simply, "Okay. I get it. I'm going to check with John Nicholas but I think the truth is very clear here. She's desperate. She is stuck and I'll bet she's run totally out of options. She's going down."

It took a couple of tries but when she caught up to John Nicholas, he just laughed. "We've got a stop watch on the closing date. They are in a heap of trouble." He went on to explain about the two mortgages and the many consistent reports he'd heard of wild parties and the rapid decline of the place. "I guarantee: they're gonna close her down."

Sales people have a tribal world as much as lawyers do, or doctors. They recognize each other and buddy up. Tom had met a couple of the liquor distributors and they told him how their necks were on the block.

"We gave her credit and she owes everybody."

"She doesn't pay her bills.'

"I tried to cut her some slack. My boss wants to kill me!"

When they asked Joe and Mrs. Crisp over to talk it out, it didn't take long to decide what to do. They had to get past, "The Hell with her!" and "She got what she deserves." And they thought the same thing about the bank. "I got no sympathy for them, either".

Then they thought about how they could turn the whole thing to their advantage. They combined their skills: Tom was the details guy and Joe was more of a people person. Louise and Mrs. Crisp knew how big operations functioned but most importantly, they knew about kids.

"You have to scare them," said Louise.

"...And you have to establish strict rules and enforce those rules," added Mrs. Crisp, shifting to Gestapo mode.

".....We could ask for large deposits.....", Tom suggested. "Then they'd have something to lose when they trashed the place."

Joe was more mellow about everything. "I think we can do this," he said.

"I think we can do this."

"So the important thing will be the terms," said Mrs. Crisp.

"Yeah. This is a tough time for all of us but it's no time to let her off the hook," Tom exclaimed angrily. "She has to be neutralized or she'll just get in the way." The scars went deeper than he thought.

Louise raised her hand. "Well, two things then: We need to be paid a lot of money," she paused while everyone nodded. ".....And we need to have complete control of the place."

That pretty much said it all. All four were normally kind, thoughtful people. They were good neighbors and felt a certain pride in their positive attitudes. This was different. They had to be tough. That meant Tom would have to lay it all out clearly right from the start. If she balked at it, he'd walk away. If she agreed, which was unlikely, then he and Joe would step in and take over. At a price, of course. At a price.

Tom met Alex on the porch. It looked like rain but she had now become self-conscious about the place and didn't want him to see its condition.

They didn't exchange pleasantries. Tom asked her immediately what she wanted from him. At first, she struck a pose as if waiting for someone to fill her glass but then admitted, "We've had some problems."

Tom nodded but then just sat back and let her finish. She had suddenly become an expert on the economy. "This recession has kicked us in the pants just like everyone else," she started. "...And we're barely making it." Tom knew they weren't "making it" but let it slide.

"We're thinking of trying something different," she added and looked to Tom for encouragement.

"I think I know how things stand….," he started and he saw her wince.

"I think you're in trouble." He eyes darted toward the kitchen. This was going to hurt. Her most vicious demons were coming back to haunt her. She'd been able to suppress them but now could see their blood red eyes and slashing talons. Coming for her. Coming for her hard.

Tom laid it all out, just as he, Joe, Louise and Mrs. Crisp had agreed. It was tough but it had to be done. Every protection, every artifice had to be torn away and the wound exposed. He had to lay out the treatment, too. That would be at least as painful as the bandage pull. It would take a lot longer, too. And the killer? It might not work. She might still go down.

Alex summoned all her self-control and smiled. It took all her strength to do it. Her demons were shrieking in her ears. "What will people think?" And more importantly, "What will the haute monde think of me?" Like an adolescent, she just wanted to be popular, one of the cool kids. She couldn't just let a bunch of townies take over the place! She'd be a failure, shunned! People would look away as she walked down the street instead of gazing in admiration at each and every one of her impressive steps.

She thanked him and managed to say, "Well, let me think about that and get back to you," but she didn't say the words as much as hear them coming out of a mouth that was being worked up and down by the invisible strings of a puppeteer, Trus Sheridan. Her mouth felt strange, in fact, as she uttered these very polished and well-worn words. Inside, she was stricken with a fear that she'd never felt before. There was no other way out. She couldn't hide any longer. This—this plan of Tom's and the bank—this might have to happen. It was too much. She just smoothed her way out of the discussion before she was legendarily sick.

~

A word about pride here. Pride rests on many pillars. Some of them are made of experience and some on a wish. The ones that are based on experience can be based upon long experience like dribbling a basketball. It's no big deal but it is a skill. You can do it any time you like.

Other experiences are more recent and more complicated, like driving a car or running a business. That's where your pride can be questioned because that's where your pride may rest more on a wish than on cold, hard fact. That's where your pride can lead you very badly astray because we know that we're wishing but we don't want to acknowledge it. Those pillars, the ones made largely from a wish, can tremble and fall. When they fall, though, they bring down all of the good stuff, too. The whole catastrophe collapses and we're left with nothing but wreckage and humiliation.

Now, this may work great at Alcoholics Anonymous because those guys really do need a do-over. But starting from scratch is harder for those of us who can't and won't surrender to the inevitable. We lie to ourselves. We obfuscate. We tell ourselves firmly and defiantly that we're just fine. Everything is going to be okay and we've just had a bad day. Or week.

Or life. We're okay.

"I just wish everyone would leave me alone!"

There are no statistics available as to gender, either. There are no predictors. Just because you were born a man or a woman doesn't mean that your sex is proof against self-deception. It can happen to anyone.

Foolishness is distributed pretty evenly throughout our population. We all deny it and we all try to wish it away. It's only when politics is involved that we abandon pretense and embrace our foolish ways with all our strength.

⤸

Alex walked away from the table clutching at her throat. She was going to heave; no doubt about it. Gag. Blortch. Blow.

The next day, she called the bank and told Mr. Sheridan that she couldn't do it. She'd find a way but she…. He cut her off. He had been reviewing her accounts and he'd been too soft on her. She was going down and that was that. Slowly and as patiently as he could, he took her through unpaid vendors, COD mandates, unpaid utility bills, unpaid taxes and then, of course, the precise amount she needed to hold off the bank. She was way behind. Way behind.

"I don't like to do this, but….." He was turning the file over to the lawyers. Maybe this week.

Alex was now in full panic mode. She gripped the phone and her fingers went white with the pressure. She heard a "Thank you" come out of her mouth and she hung up. Now, she really was sick. All over the waste paper basket and all over her desk.

THE ASCENSCION

The hand of God swept down low across the water and up over the dunes, gently lifting Tom and Joe and carrying them to a higher place. Well, it wasn't that much higher; it was the booking desk at Windsor's where they laid out their strategy to Alexandra. She would, in effect, have to surrender the keys to them for the next eight or ten months. At that point, they'd review things. She could stand by, observe and make suggestions but they would run the place.

They gave her an idea of the cost and she visibly shrank as if the life force had been sucked out of her body. Still, she sat there and took it. She would be on an allowance, essentially, and they would take the profits but they would keep clean books. No fiddlin'.

There would be expenses simply because they needed staff but they wouldn't pay staff for the first two weeks so they had a small cushion with which to work. All this was too much detail for her and she glazed over. She just wanted to hear the word "money" at the end of their seminar, not the word "foreclosure".

They would not answer many questions. They weren't going to give her all their ideas and then have her back out of the deal. Instead, they had Barger draw up a simple agreement that left her as a "consultant" without specific duties and no supervisory role. They would do the business, no questions asked, like in Monopoly. She nodded and reluctantly signed.

Right off the bat, they began spending money. They saw security as their main issue, so Joe got some very realistic looking CCTV monitors and nailed them up all over the place. They weren't connected to anything but the kids would never know that. He then placed four very stern signs at the front desk, the entry, the parking lot and the back porch.

The signs were the work of Louise and Mrs. Crisp, both of whom had taken a silk screening course at New Christ Church, the local church for liberals and people who secretly grew marijuana. First, they warned of CCTV and the penalties to be suffered if any rules were violated, the rules being related to BYOB, property damage, excessive drinking and noise. At the bottom of each notice the kids were warned that, "These premises are monitored by ACE SECURITY SYSTEMS". That warning was accompanied by the company's logo, a creation of Mrs. Crisp's, a little Ace of Spades. The whole thing had run them fifty bucks.

Tom and Joe alternated at the bar. Nobody had his hand in the till at any time but the boys. They were sure that they could double or triple profits immediately just by enforcing the rule that stated, "No Liquor may be brought on to the premises." The kids had been buying cheap beer and wine, even dragging coolers up to their rooms. No more.

They then cast Monk in his most challenging role. He would be Johnny Ice. He would wear the black boots, black pants and shirt and he would don the black shades and Stetson that Joe had remembered from the A&P all those many years ago.

Monk was a little short for the part and a little plump but he captured the attitude perfectly. He thought "Menace" and he thought "Danger" and then like any practitioner of "the method", he grew into the role. He would speak to no one. Ever. His sole job was to instill fear. He would just glide around the fringes of the place looking for victims. His hands would never leave his pockets, either. He would nod his head and the perp was toast. When he suggested putting a garlic wreath in every room, they all cracked up.

They had long since decided to take deposits for possible breakage and now they took big deposits either by credit card or in cash. No one under the age of fifty could get a room without that deposit. They'd never have to absorb all those damages again.

Alex had her reservations but decided to sit and watch. The first weekend was a total success. Monk caught a half dozen kids with coolers that were quickly confiscated. And that was just in the parking lot. The boys watched for bottles and cans that didn't belong and kept an especially keen eye out for spirits. They picked up a dozen on Friday night alone. The kids weren't very smart about it, either. It had always been so easy before.

It turns out that Alex had developed the habit of dipping into the till herself. She seemed to think of it as her personal piggy bank. Whenever she needed the odd hundred bucks, she just peeled off the bills and stuck them into the backseat pocket of her skinny jeans.

                                               ⌐

A quick word about embezzlement here: It's fun, it's fast and you feel great. Forget about taxes: You're just going to skip all that and keep it simple. "One for you, one for me. Two for you, two for me...."

It always starts off the same way, too. A guy is a buck short for his morning coffee so he takes out a dollar, closes the register, crosses the street and brings back his coffee. He almost always promises himself that he'll repay the till the following day. He doesn't.

Instead, he lets it ride. He dips into the register the second day for two bucks, the whole cost of his coffee. He swears again that he'll repay the two bucks along with the first dollar but now his resolve is weakening. He tells himself that he's going to repay but he knows he won't; he just tells himself he will. He even feels a little guilty about it because the boss is a good guy and he knows he shouldn't take the money but he does it anyway. Weak is getting weaker.

The course is simple and straightforward and the path is unimaginably clear: One day it's a coffee and the next it's a vacation home.

                                               ⌐

"Ya lorn so motch about a poreson when ya've gotchore hand in their register, don'tcha?" Monk observed early one morning. The kids were sleeping like the hypersexed postadolescents that they were and Monk was just sitting around having his morning coffee. "They're sotch arseholes!" he said, summing up all their thoughts.

Tom and Joe couldn't believe the difference in the liquor receipts. Their profits would exceed their wildest dreams. In two short months they had gone from "marginally employed" to one of Sheridan's best customers. They were killin' it with no downside in sight. They had no shame: They began charging each room an extra ten bucks but leaving a box of Janey's chocolates on the bed "as a gift". Profits to Tom, of course.

It even looked as if the kids were backing away a bit. Older tourists were returning. They came back slowly but when they did they were pleased to find more gracious accommodations throughout. Much of the old, beat up furniture had simply been hauled away and Joe was systematically running through the rooms, updating them. He painted and varnished where necessary and put Sam to work on the bathrooms, making them acceptable if not a salle de bains in Gay Paree.

It wasn't that hard to figure out. It didn't take a guy from the Cornell School of Hotel Management to see how badly the place was run. They started up a program of referrals that was modeled after the system used by pimps to steer prospective clients. Both Louise and Mrs. Crisp were reading the exciting and instructive autobiography of Malcolm X and had benefited by his experience. If you sent the Inn a good customer you'd get a bump. Not a big bump, but a "Thank you." It could be anything but mostly it was chocolates. Soon, they truly were humming along like a well-oiled machine and money was pouring out of the top.

Wasting no time, they prioritized creditors. He'd been stiffed a hundred times so Joe knew what to do: Communicate. Call them up and tell them that they'll get their money. They'll just have to wait to get it all. Partial payments would resume as soon as possible.

They then got the bank first and then their taxes on track. They went to see Trus Sheridan and laid out a schedule that would get them caught up inside of a year. He wouldn't have to foreclose, just charge them a reasonable late fee. There would be no restructuring. If they did that, Alex would just blow it again. She'd think, "Problem solved" and go right back to cheating the bank out of its hard earned cash. They could save her from herself if she paid attention. The problem was solved for the time being; she'd just have to stay on track. They figured it was even odds that she'd do it.

In the mean time, the boys were sticking money in the bank, splendid spondoolix they would need in the future but were way, way, way too busy now to spend. Some of the finishing touches on Tom's house would have to wait and Joe would still have to look at the weather reports before staying the night at his house but all in all, they were surging forward. Once again, they were learning and learning. They weren't failing this time, either. They were plowing ahead through rough seas and making headway by the hour.

THE BIG IDEA

Great ideas can come from humble sources. That's why they're so often ignored. You have to have a keen eye for them, like an antiques dealer at a rummage sale. People in positions of prominence can come up with a good idea and Hey, Presto! It's adopted. But regular folks have great ideas too; they just don't get much attention.

Monk was a guy you could easily overlook so when he told Tom that he had an idea, Tom told him he was busy. He told him that three times until Monk wore him down. "You can have theme weekends." That was it. That little idea sat on a shelf in Tom's brain until later that day when he passed it on to Joe. Joe really was more of a visual guy and was much better suited to fleshing out the bare bones of Monk's suggestion.

When they went back to him, Monk elaborated. "Look: Why not advertise special weekends for special things. A bridge tournament—although they'll just drink coffee—or a Red Sox weekend?"

The boys nodded to each other and a whole new hustle was born. They talked it up at home and one idea rapidly led to another. It could work. A couple of days later, they thanked Monk. He'd really put them on to something. "So, what do you see as our first theme?" they asked him.

Would it be a Disney theme? Or something from history, a whaling theme? Monk just shook his head.

"Proid," he said. When their faces displayed their lack of comprehension, he repeated the word. "Proid." They still didn't get it.

"You guys've bin to Provincetown, roit?" The boys both chuckled and said they had. Stories started and then more chuckles followed.

"Well, ever since th' Stonewall Riots in New York, they bin holdin' 'Proid Weeks'."

"And you want to do that here?" Tom asked, astonished.

"Shore. It's an islin', innit? Let'em take over th' islin'."

"But….." The boys were both silent for a moment, sneaking glances at each other.

"'Bawt' nothin'!" exclaimed Monk. "It's brilliant, that is!"

"We're gonna have to think about that one," Tom said finally. "I mean, who'd come?"

"Yeah," said Joe. "We don't even know any gay people."

"Oh, no?" asked Monk. "How about me?" The boys both shot him a look of complete incredulity.

"Yer jokin', right?" asked Joe.

"Oy'm not jokin'," Monk said, thrusting out his chin. And the boys began peppering him with questions. How long had he been gay? Did he have a boy friend? Who else was gay? And finally, why had he not told them that before? They couldn't get their mind around it. Monk was so….. so….. normal. A bit goofy sometimes but otherwise just like them.

Monk listened patiently but with a little glint in his eye. "Shore. We bin mates a long time but ya know, dat stoff is private."

"But Monk….," Joe implored, "….You're like family to us."

Monk blushed at that and said only, "I know. I know. But people don't get it: Gay people are ostracized! Day get the shit kicked out of'em." Now, it was the boys' turn to look ashamed. Yes, yes. It was true. To be gay was to be at risk. Period.

"Boy, I don't know," Tom said finally. "I don't know. The Inn could be in a lot of trouble."

"Well, ya don't own the Inn," Monk said. "Try it. It will work, I promise ya." He stood there rock steady. He certainly was sure of it. Maybe it could work. That was the hook he needed to get them. Joe was always the idea guy. He went for a new idea the way stripers go for a school of pogies. Cut his belly open and there'd be a dozen there at any given time, half digested.

"Okay: Then how would we promote it?" Joe asked. "You advertise and the whole town will be up in arms."

"Ya don't hafta!" Monk replied. "Ya just get the word out, ya know?"

When neither of the boys responded, he leaned forward and closed the deal. "Oy kin do it for fifty bawks."

They had nothing to lose by hearing more so they told Monk to go home, draw up his plan and they'd talk about it. In the mean time, they went home and told Louise and Mrs. Crisp about Monk's "unbelievable" idea.

"That's fantastic!" said Mrs. Crisp. But she didn't mean "fantastic" as in "idiotic". She meant it as a really great idea. Her politics and her thinking were a little more progressive than Joe had thought, it seemed. But then, in guidance you become educated yourself. You meet a lot of people and discover things about their private lives that are completely and utterly foreign to you. After a few years of that, you're just happy when people are decent and thoughtful. You don't care about their sex lives. You just want them to be kind. Bias is just foolishness.

Louise said the same thing. She worked with guys, very buff guys, divers most of them, who were as gay as a party hat and they were great.

"I'll tell them," she said, "...They'll love it." Without trying, then, the thing was already on the wire. They really didn't have to advertise. One guy would tell another guy and he'd tell two other guys….. It could work. No, it definitely could work.

"It's October we're talkin' about, ya know," Joe reminded Tom. They had anticipated a slowdown. "If this works, we could rope guys in every October. Why leave the rooms empty when you can fill'em and turn a buck?" Neither of the boys was phobic or had biases against the gay world, either. They had simply never known much about it. Subtract the silly gossip they had read years before in their father's mens' magazines and they knew next to nothing. It could work.

They still had three months to go on their agreement with Alexandra.

They had banked a surprising amount of money and gotten bills under control. Not paid but under control. They could project a time when the creditors were up to date and they were square with the bank. A year was still very realistic. Sheridan was purring now, no longer the vulture he'd been just four months before.

But the new plan was awkward for them. Neither Tom nor Joe had much experience with the demimonde; they had troubles enough with Alex and the haute monde. They had more than they could handle with everyday life on the island. How could they even think of innovation? The economy was in the crapper!

Was there really an alternate universe out there? Would they risk trying for it? Louise and Mrs. Crisp were all in. Did they know something that the boys didn't? It would take some courage to find out. Or, as Joe finally thought, maybe it just took a different attitude. They had nothing to lose....sort of. Maybe you just had to ask yourself the question that Whiskey Bob would ask: "Who gives a Hell?"

Finally, they firmed up the date. Columbus weekend. It would be a three day holiday and even though it was a weekend designed to celebrate the achievement of a singular sailor, it was more than that. It was also a weekend that celebrated the star-crossed, the benighted, the screwballs who wander the earth.

Columbus had an idea, just that far removed from a wish: "I can sail off, far from sight of land and just keep going. I can talk a lot of very reluctant, superstitious and dangerous people to go with me. And when they riot and threaten to cut my throat, I can tell them what Andrew Carnegie said when asked about his enormous wealth: 'I just want a little bit more'."

Columbus needed time and he needed a crazy crew, guys who could believe without the faintest reason that they'd meet success at the end of their voyage. Crazy guys. Stupid guys. Ignorant and suspicious guys. He did it and he hit land. Maybe the boys would hit land, too. They'd soon find out. They pulled up anchor and set sail, informing everyone that the weekend was booked. The Inn was closed for a "private function".

At first, reservations trickled in. A friend of Monk's took a room for two. Then another. A guy from the Oceanographic called. He'd be coming and bringing a friend. One of the town's guardians, a bicycle patrolman stopped to ask hesitantly whether, "...town residents could attend." Before long, they were getting calls from Cleveland, from Detroit, from San Francisco Bay.

Chef called from Janey's. "I will bring taffy for a taffy pull," he said emphatically. "It's a good ice breaker." Oh: And he'd want a room.

Before long, they realized that they'd need more help. They went to Hunter and asked about guys he might know. They checked with Louise and Mrs. Crisp for suggestions. Both of them instantly volunteered. This party was going to be completely off the hook and they wanted in. They told a pair of women friends from their Book Club who were married in all but name. "We're goin'!" was all they got from them.

Amazingly, Monk spent less than fifty bucks on advertising. When it looked like it really might work, the boys agreed to spend a little more. They gave Monk a budget and told him to "Pride Up" the place. Two or three phone calls later and he had his plan. The whole place would be turned into one gigantic rainbow. Maybe with swans. He wasn't sure quite yet.

Alexandra nearly snapped her cap when she heard about it. She went searching for the boys but couldn't find them. They'd left to pick up some new bedding in Hyannis. This gave her the opportunity to sniff around a bit. Everywhere she looked she saw a new and improved Inn and she liked what she saw. She didn't want this new crowd but she was stuck. The boys had a free hand. She chose to complain about it instead.

She had kept in touch with her friends in New York and now got one on the phone. "I can't believe......, " she started but her friend quickly set her straight. It was not only acceptable but chic to support Pride Weeks. Alex was going to be ahead of the curve, a pacesetter. Trendsetting in their little corner of Paradise. She went to the bar, poured herself a couple of ounces of The Glenlivet and rolled them over her tongue.

She waited until the ringing stopped in her ears and then slammed the empty glass down on the bar. "Fawk it," she told herself. "Let's do it."

She was on her way. She was out of trouble and quite remarkably, a leader of her generation. What the Hell did she need the boys for any more? She could walk this one into the net without any further assistance. As soon as she could, she'd dump the boys and take over the place again. Piece of cake. Or, in this case, piece of cheesecake.

She was en fuego!

RISE OR FALL

The boys were anxious but Monk reassured them. "Thay'll all be happy ta be here. Believe me, it'll be a roit rave." The boys were still nervous. It would take more than Monk's assurances to calm them down. The weekend would mean ordering stuff, lots of stuff but they worried about perishables. How many quarts of strawberries could they get and how much champagne? The champers they could always salvage but strawberries? They didn't want to be stuck with a dumpster full of rotten strawberries; that's for sure.

What do gay people eat? They wondered. And what do they drink? They were so new to "Proid" that they panicked and went as deeply into cliches as they could possibly go. They bought pink everything: Pink lemonade. Pink champagne. Pink bud roses just for show. Desserts would be pink too: Pink cupcakes, pink trifle, even their Key Lime Pie would be pink, starkly defying standing tradition.

The bookings kept pouring in, though. Pretty soon, they were "wait listing" people. They sent a few to B&Bs nearby and put others on a call list for the following year. No doubt about it: They had hit on something, something big. But then other worries crept in, as they always will: What if they're too rowdy? What do we do then? These guys weren't a bunch of pansies. Look at Stonewall! They had faced down legions of seasoned New York City cops, whole precincts of them.

For once, they thought through the problem. They figured if they could get to leaders in the community they'd be able to get the word out and avoid confrontations. Monk suggested talking to Marcel for starters and he "knew a couple of guys", too. It felt like dealing with the mob but they did it. Marcel immediately calmed their fears.

"Don't you ladies worry," he said, flouncing a bit. He was showing off now, having fun at their expense. "My people are smart and nothing if not discreet. They want this to work just as much as you do. After all, the holiday is named after one of our principal heroes, Christopher Humungous. He was named that because of the impressive dimensions of his perpendicular. It was said—seriously—that his foreskin could upholster a barcalounger."

Tom held up his hand but it failed to stop the flow. Marcel explained, "It was said to be a thing of great beauty and the real reason why Ferdinand and Isabella admired him so much. He's basically the patron saint of gay people." He paused to allow them to close their mouths and then said, "Did you know he barred all women from the boat? It was men only as, of course, it should be. Under the circumstances."

They were now both worried and confused. The worry never left them but now they began to understand that like the Army, they had to learn another entirely new language: Fantaspeak. You couldn't just develop an ear for it, either, like "Southrun". You had to imagine it and that could challenge your brain.

Joe and Tom were out of their depth but Louise and Mrs. Crisp were swimming with the flow. When given the job of decorating the dining area, they nixed crepe and went for silk. Long, gossamer swatches of red and purple hung from the old, tawdry lighting fixtures and more was draped over the curtains giving the room the appearance of a Turkish bordello circa 1820. You could almost smell the rich petroleum odor of latakia tobacco, the acidic black tea from a samovar.

Outside, the whole place was awash in light, rainbow light. Perfectly sober and staid during the day, the shabby facade became a liquid dreamscape at night. Monk had arranged for a friend to light the place using nothing more high tech than floor lights from the local casino. These lights used slowly rotating discs that cast a dozen vivid colors across the building. Again, he made due with low budget. Something less than forty dollars had been spent on lighting, that along with a free glass of champagne and a ticket for admittance. His friend was keen to go.

Were there vibrations of envy coming from Key West or Provincetown?

They'd never know. They booked guys from both places, though, so any animus couldn't have been too bad. As the day approached, you could almost feel the tension. Tom fussed over everything. He was afraid and getting afraider. Joe was holding it together and would half-heartedly joke about there being "...nothing to worry about..." but he was feeling the pinch just as much as Tom. Mrs. Crisp had done the calculations and if she was right, they could both earn enough to pay for the entire balance of their respective improvements that weekend. That, or go into a deep, deep hole. One or the other.

Certainly, the Inn would do okay. Unless the place was completely trashed, they'd been booked for weeks and it was all cash on the barrel head. Ka Ching! Sheridan would be happy and the creditors would be out of their heads.

Their main concern was the kitchen but at the last minute Louise asked a half dozen of her aunts to pitch in. Each one was a professional in everything but name. They had worked in kitchens since they were old enough to reach the pots and if anything, would breeze through dinners there. No problem. The menu might turn a little Greek but then, who doesn't like eggplant and lamb? Are you nuts? Pass the olive oil!

〜

A word about journeys: Surprisingly, the best parts of every journey are the surprises. We plan and plan, taking every conceivable detail into consideration and when we return from a trip we tell our friends about things we never, ever could have anticipated. We talk only about the things that we remember and we remember most vividly the little things that we've encountered along the way. Little things we could never have foreseen and yet they knock us off our feet.

There's a little bit of God in those surprises. A hardware store in Rome. An infant in Pompei. Never mind the kid who asks you to play tennis with him in a depressing suburb of London. The secrets you uncover and the sweet souls you meet are yours forever, courtesy of the Almighty. They become the real reason you left home and braved the bump and hustle of the air. A sleepless night in a miserable seat on a cramped airplane fades to nothing when you see a child proudly carrying her fourth grade science project, a little volcano, in a church yard on Capri. That's what you remember and that's what you'll see to your dying day.

So it was with Proid Weekend. So it is with many of our most bold and outrageous ideas. Forget the ones that fail. Remember the ones that lit up the night!

⤿

Friday evening, as the stars began to appear and the sun set slowly over America, the first lodgers came out of their rooms. Each guy looked a little apprehensive as if someone might shove a camera in his face. Soon, a dozen or more were out on the deck. The scene that greeted them was a confection that could only have been inspired by divine lunacy.

Marcel had created the ultimate taffy pull. He had shipped over a large, round working station which had been broken down into eight individual sections. Each section contained a deep bowl. You put on gloves, reached into one of the bowls and pulled out a handful of taffy. You could pull out strawberry or lime or root beer. Watermelon, blueberry, orange or grape. It was your choice. You then had to pat it, pull it and then roll it out. That roll would be about six inches long and an inch thick. You then placed it on the chopping block to be sliced into five or six delicious little segments. Little squares of wax paper were available for each piece.

Guys approached the taffy a bit tentatively but when they saw the many uses to which the six by one inch cylinder could be put, they saw why Marcel had hosted the event. Slices were exchanged. That was a start.

Slices were put aside "for later" and that was a start, too. When someone took strawberry ripple and formed it into a six inch candy rod, the reason for the candy was apparent. When someone wrapped it in a Myone condom, it was all too apparent. Marcel had said it was the ultimate ice breaker and he was right.

Soon, the buzz outdoors attracted others downstairs. Even the shy ones couldn't resist: What was all the noise about? What was going on?

Before they knew it, though, even the shy guys had three or four chunks of taffy in their pockets. Each one was a promise if not of true love or a taste of true love then of bonhommie and well being. Of belonging.

The bar kept busy all night and nobody even thought of cheating the place. There were no suspect bottles of hootch and no coolers. There were just happy revelers who listened to music by a Wellfleet group called simply THE ORIGIN, a couple of old math teachers who were closet rockers if not closet gays.

Dinner plates were filled at the buffet and nobody got a bad leaf of spinach or rotten tomato. The stock of pink champagne went down slowly but not as quickly as the real champagne or the high end spirits. Malt whiskey evaporated and to their surprise, so did the Aqvavit. Were they all Swedes?

The next morning, the place was clean and neat courtesy of Monk and his friends. It looked like nothing had happened the night before. The place had never looked better. Would they be ready for another whole day of hell raising?

Guys got up, had their coffee and croissant and then headed either across the street to one of Hunter's boats or down to Jetties beach. It looked like they were all health nuts, not the degenerates the boys expected. They were learning a lot and they were surprised with what they learned. It had been a lot of work so they'd have to square things with the crew.

Louise's aunts laid down the law late that night: They would stay and help on Sunday night under two conditions: 1) the Inn made a big contribution to the church and, 2) The next Greek dance would be held at the Inn free of charge. Tom nodded quietly without even asking "When?" He was too busy with the money in his head.

If anything, Saturday night was practice for Greek Night. The aunties turned out tray after tray of Moussaka and Greek Salad with black olives and a particularly pungent feta cheese. The aroma of roasted lamb permeated every corner of the place. Grape leaves and olives stuffed with cheese and garlic and a kind of prosciutto were stacked up like cannon balls. The breads! The breads! Your mouth watered as you walked by the room. It wasn't a success; it was a triumph.

Guys streamed into the kitchen to praise the food or ask for recipes or just simply to stand there and watch it being prepared. The kitchen became an extension of the dining area. Joe finally just stuck a wedge in the door to keep it open. Applause greeted every dish and at the end of the meal the aunties were called out into the dining room to a rousing round of, "For she's a jolly good fellow!"

By Sunday night, they were exhausted. By Monday noon, they were numb. It had been a real gamble but it worked. It had worked so well that they were an instant legend all around town. Doc Matthew, who almost never left his store, delivered the eggs himself on Tuesday morning. When Tom stuck his bleary-eyed face around the corner to greet him, Doc said, "Okay, boy. Now you know what you did right there, don't you?" Tom didn't know.

"You started something." Doc nodded to himself and stuck a finger in Tom's face. "You started something and I'm gonna finish it." Again, Tom had no idea what he was talking about.

"I'm gonna book this place for *my* people," leaning hard on the word "my". "I'm gonna cook up some black eyed peas, some ham hocks and some collard greens and show this town how to have a good time."

Tom still didn't know what...... "I'm gonna take over this place and play some down home music, some real music. R&B. Soul! That's what I'm gonna do."

Recovering a bit, Tom said, "I think that's great, Doc. I'd love to do that. You let me know what you'd like to....."

"You white folks are pitiful. Pitiful! It takes a bunch of guys to do a Pride Week here to liven the place up. Well, you listen to me and I'll show you the meaning of 'liven things up'".

Tom still looked confused so Doc frowned and exclaimed, "You ever been to church, boy?"

THE ONE THING YOU CAN ALWAYS FIND WHENEVER YOU LOOK FOR IT

Alexandra had taken it all in and she knew she'd seen something special. Dollar bills were coming out of her ears and she could taste the gold. When she closed her eyes, her tongue rolled over the smooth, cool surface of an imaginary Krugerrand, savoring its heft. No kiss had ever been this sweet.

She knew she'd have to wait a couple more months but the place was back on its feet. She knew it. The boys had said as much. That meant that the temporary period of what she termed her "reorganization" would soon come to an end. She had suffered mightily, been kept on starvation rations, but that would soon end. She'd be the queen again in large measure due to the queens who had streamed through Windsor's for Proid Week. In fact, they continued to come; they liked the place so much.

The boys just went to the bank. Trus Sheridan was all smiles, now. He'd been wrong and although he never apologized to them for slamming the door in their face, he was far more gracious to them now. Their deposits alone would cover the cost of home improvements so he assured both of them that loan applications would be favorably received.

The final months ran smoothly and when the bank saw how profitable they'd been they had no problem approving Alexandra's resumption of control. The limited takeover—the "interruption"--had been completely successful and the condemnation forestalled. Everyone got a clap on the back. Pretty smart, they thought.

Most of us learn when we fail. We fail and learn. It's as natural as a baby's pratfall or letting a wet dog into the house. We pick ourselves up, towel off the house and go back to the mean streets and daily grind. Not so, Alexandra. She had made a lot of egregious, unforced errors, been saved from the brink and now set about doing the same thing.

She had no sooner left the bank than she was planning changes at the Inn. She had more bookings now than she had during her first time at the helm and she had some amazing events planned, hoodoos that were sure to make a buck. But she hadn't learned anything more about operations. Instead, she'd sat by the sidelines and watched while Tom and Joe dealt with the staff, fought off the bank, massaged the vendors and schmoozed the "poonters".

Neither her skill set nor her sense of self had changed. She was still wiser than them all. She was still very, very special. She hadn't even learned the most simple lesson of them all: The one thing you can always find whenever you look for it is Trouble.

The one area where Alexandra excelled was laying off staff. Suddenly, Hunter didn't see the guys around he'd seen all fall. Thomas and Joseph were gone, sure, but where was Monk? And where was everyone else? The place had a skeleton staff most of the time. Jobs continued to be scarce so Alex believed she could call up help whenever she needed it. In the mean time, she could cut staff and still get everything done. Think of the savings!

↫

Life is a lot like golf. You can see what another player is doing wrong but you never see your own mistakes, no matter how obvious. Your friend is flailing away, topping every shot. His weight is on his back foot so he can never properly finish a swing. His shorts are too long and his shirt is too short. Everything about the guy is painful to watch and yet he radiates confidence. He does eighteen holes in five long hours, hacks away and hacks away and never once corrects himself. Why is that?

There are two basic reasons why he'll never improve and they form the two basic components of denial. (1) He wants to believe that he's right and (2) he doesn't want to admit that he's wrong.

Nobody wants to believe that they're wrong, ever. Everyone, regardless of age, really and truly wants to believe he's right. It's impossible to be right all of the time and yet we all insist that we are. It's arrogant but it's unreasonable, too. It's really quite astonishing!

We know we can't be right all the time but each and every time we consider whether or not we can be wrong we conclude that we're not. We're right, goddammit! This can only lead to the same result. We'll never change unless forced to change. Something will really have to hurt. Really, really have to hurt. As we all know, pain is the ultimate convincer but how much pain can we take?

∽

Alex watched the calendar to make sure she wouldn't miss a big date. The place was always packed for Mother's Day and Easter was always good for them, too. She was ready for those days and things went pretty well. Things also went well during most weekdays when the volume was low. Her regular staff was small but doing okay.

She didn't watch the weather, though. Or the signs of an improving economy in America. When Spring arrived, it was surprisingly warm. The seas weren't cantankerous, either. Sailors were popping their boats into the water much earlier than usual. They were also renting earlier than usual. Hunter's business was jumping. When tourists started arriving, the Inn wasn't ready. Soon, she had problems.

The hotel and restaurant businesses are tough businesses. They almost have to be in your blood. If you're doing well, you'll have something to show for it at the end of the year. If you're not filling the rooms or putting out meals, you won't. Regardless of that, though, you will find that every hour is filled. You put the place to bed at one a.m. and you're in the kitchen the next morning at eight. In a very real sense, you're married to the business as if you're a Franciscan monk, wed to the cross. You'd better believe in it.

For Alex, it was just a way to make money and, of course, to shine.

She hadn't even been tactful when she let the boys go or the "extra staff". She just let them go. And she had ignored the details that made the whole Proid Week work. Monk had not only come up with the idea but had delivered on the lighting outside, as well. The kitchen only worked because Louise got the aunties in gear, something they weren't going to do as a regular thing. They did it that time for Louise but they weren't going to do it again.

A good manager would have protected what they had and then maybe, just maybe, expanded into other areas. Doc Matthew was ready to take the place but he wasn't sure how to deal with Alex. He knew the boys but he didn't know her. When she was running things, she owed him money. He'd been lucky to get it and he was pretty sure he only got paid because Tom got him the money.

Alex had cut so much staff that she'd have to be the one to do the dirty work, too. She'd have to be the one to rehire staff and get the place ready for early bookings. When she started to recall people, she thought they'd be grateful. Instead, they told her tactfully—in most cases—that they'd moved on. They were working at the Post office or at White's. A couple were down at the marina making good money. Two got picked up by the Steamship Authority and were working regular hours outdoors. Why would they go back inside?

She worked her way down the list pretty quickly but came up empty. She hadn't noticed the connections islanders have with one another. She hadn't understood about loyalty and its flip side, betrayal. She hadn't appreciated the importance of associations and relationships, never mind personalities. She had always thought of staff as hirelings, modern day sharecroppers dependent upon this year's cotton. She couldn't recruit people; they just weren't interested.

Soon, there were problems. The staff she'd retained were overworked and morale had bottomed out. Any good karma built up during Tom's reign had now sadly melted away. No one felt any fondness for her and even fewer any obligation. If they needed time off, they just took it.

Simple routines like room prep and cleaning were barely covered. The kitchen looked unclean and she needed a new dishwasher; the Board of Health could shut them at any time. It was getting bad.

Tom and Joe knew almost nothing of her state. When they left the Inn Tom kept up the candy concession and Joe worked odd jobs. They were doing a little better than they were the previous year but not thriving. Neither was making enough but the profit they'd made from their stint at the Inn was enough to finish the two houses so they kept banging away at them.

One day, while they were painting Joe's living room, Mrs. Crisp asked, "I wonder how they're doing at the Inn." Joe hadn't heard much so he spoke to Tom.

Tom had heard some stories but he'd soured on the place and didn't really listen. "It sounds like she hasn't changed."

"Sorry, but she'll never change." Joe paused for a second and said, "Look at how Hunter's been doin'. He's doin' great. If she could only learn from him..... Never mind learning from us!"

"Well, she had her chance," Tom said with a shrug. It really wasn't any of his business. He was still struggling with the candy business. Times were getting better and he was starting to make more sales but the glory days were over. Now, it just gave him a little something to do.

Basically, Tom was still stuck with the problem of finding a real job. If he didn't find something soon, he'd be struggling. Louise was still doing well at the Oceanographic but she would have to ship out soon. She couldn't stall them forever. If he didn't find something soon, he'd be home alone with nothing to do. He'd crack up!

People liked Tom, though. Sure, he wasn't as much of a raver as Joe but he was steady and reliable. Doc Matthew had liked him since he was a kid so when he saw him mooching around town he could see that he needed something to do. One day, he tackled him. Kindly souls will do that sometimes. They'll think of someone beside themselves.

"So, Tom: You doin' anything this weekend?"

"Naw, I'm just getting the house finished." He paused briefly, then added, "You know. There's always something….."

"Well, I could use a hand with something if you think you've got a little time."

Tom couldn't refuse Doc; he had always been a terrific guy and a wonderful mentor. He was a little too easy on Tom but that was because he was soft-hearted. "Sure, I always got time for you, Doc."

"Well, we're gonna have a barbecue….." It turned out that Doc was having no luck with Alex and the Inn and was going to do up a big feed on his own. He had friends and family coming from all over the place and he needed an extra pair of hands. To Tom, it was another skill. He'd cooked a little before but nothing on this scale. This would be big. Doc had signed up some of the volunteer firemen who put on a good barbecue but his was going to be special. Doc's fry up would be authentic in every way and he was very, very serious about it.

In the mean time, Alex was getting desperate. She had lowered herself a dozen times, first trying to reach people she'd recently let go and then people she'd dumped a long time ago. No luck. She was running out of network even though she had booked a lot of rooms and was expecting a lot of guests. She had no one around to help. She even tried Monk "because we always got along, sort of" but he wasn't interested. He just didn't like her. He'd rather hang out with Joe and Mrs. Crisp, smoke a little weed and paint a room or two.

The weekend broke down into two separate and completely different scenarios. People couldn't even get into the Inn. They were all backed up at reception because Alex was the only one there. Each reservation took time and she was constantly interrupted by kitchen staff who were afraid to make any decisions on their own. "Should we use the regular menu or the holiday menu?" "What about lunches?"

"The beer guy is here." "The wine guy is here." "The laundry guy is here." It never stopped and even though she had only a passing knowledge of any of it, she insisted on making all the decisions herself.

At White's, tables and tents had been set up out back in a large grassy area where the staff had always played whiffle ball. It was big enough for a hundred people, more if they ate with a plate on their knees. Tom had never seen Doc so serious. This was food, by God, and when it came to a fish fry or grilled chicken, Doc brooked no mischief. Even the grandchildren had to stay away until he gave the go ahead.

Everyone showed up at 9 sharp and listened hard as Doc explained each and every step of their fry. He had half barrels from the firemen, enough for a six or eight cooks. He had apple wood and cherry wood that burned as hot as bituminous coal but damped down good on demand. He showed them how to batter the fish. Double battered in corn meal, hot fry mix from New Orleans and a dash of Romano cheese to help them brown. Each piece would be as crisp as a brand new five dollar bill.

The guys already knew chicken but they were amazed when they saw how Doc had marinated it. He had soaked half a 55 gallon drum full of wings and legs in cooking oil and rotgut wine along with a dozen of his "special" spices. He had taken a dozen bulbs of garlic from Jack and Dahlia, crushed them, thrown them into the pot and put a lid on it. The aroma could knock down a horse.

By ten they had fired up the barrels and by 11 they were ready to fry.

The whole place hissed as whole trays of chicken hit the grille and baskets of fish filets were slapped on top of a griddle. Steam and smoke enveloped the place. They had to towel off just to see. The smell of that fry raced through town like an ugly rumor. A breeze from the South blew it down the road and up the noses of everyone north of White's.

Most everyone was seated when the service began at noon. There was no shoving and no kicking but there were a lot of anxious glances. "Will I be served now or ....?" "Am I in the right seat here?"

But because Doc had cultivated friends across the island for many, many years, he had all kinds of help. At least three servers stood at the elbow of each cook and each server had his own table assigned. The whole operation ran as smooth as a salt lick at the dairy farm. Nobody panted and pawed the ground. Everyone was served with remarkable efficiency.

Corn bread. Honey and Molasses. Lemonade. Iced tea with just a pinch of mint. It was all there and it was all served up family style. You just reached across the table and took you some. After first tipping your cap, of course.

Doc stood back and smiled and smiled. He couldn't eat, of course; he was too excited. But he could still take it all in with a satisfaction that bordered on the ethereal. No beer in the world could make him feel this good.

Back at the Inn, things weren't going as well. In a moment of desperation she would later regret, Alex dragooned two of Hunter's compatriots. Hangers on, really. She saw they weren't doing anything so she crossed the street, dragged them into the kitchen and put aprons on them. "You're serving!" was basically all she said.

The new "waiters" had toked up moments before they were hauled off by the ear and stood giggling in the back of the dining room. They had no idea what to do, so they folded their hands behind their backs as if at parade rest and nervously awaited instruction. A couple of real wait staff yelled at them but it took a lot of coaxing to get them to the tables where they handed out menus and made believe they knew something about the dishes.

"Oh, I'd recommend that highly," Steve replied when asked about the hollandaise sauce.

"Yes, yes, fresh today," Jeff said, nodding his head to add that little bit of finality to his approval.

They even committed the sin of all sycophants and praised the choices of each diner. "That's a wonderful choice, ma'ame. Yes. The fruit cup is one of my favorites." Steve was having a lot of fun. Jeff covered his mouth to avoid laughing. They weren't fooling anyone.

"It's fruit cup, for Christ's sake," yelled Mr. Sturtevant. "It's fawkin' fruit cup! It's not the eighth wonder of the fawkin' world!"

"Oh, Harold, he's just trying to be nice," said Mrs. Sturtevant, patting his hand.

Mr. Sturtevant erupted. "What kind of assholes does he take us for?" Mrs. Sturtevant just blushed.

They were lucky to get anything at all, as it turned out. The kitchen was frantically trying to keep up but the salad guy was off missing and the sous chef had a cold. He snuffled and wheezed over every dish until chef sent him home. Now, it was all hands on deck.

Jeff was yanked off the floor and put on salads. He chopped the tomatoes and carrots with incredible care, afraid to cut himself. He got behind on the romaine too, and just tore it apart, heaving in the dark green ends and discarding the sweet, juicy lighter base. A simple, traditional salad was clearly beyond his skills.

This left Steve alone on the floor with two experienced servers, both women. They were older and seasoned staff and briefly tried to coddle him but he was hopeless. He couldn't seem to remember anything. He actually succeeded in serving Mrs. Sturtevant's fruit cup to a bewildered woman at a neighboring table, then stood back and asked her if it met with expectations. Up was down and down was up.

Alex now faced two uncomfortable realities. Local folks soon got wind of her staffing problems and stayed away. People looking for a week in Paradise quickly learned that Windsor's was not the place to find it. She had been pushed off shore in a perfectly serviceable vessel but she'd punched a hole in the bottom and was sinking fast.

Across town, at White's people were stopping at the store just to ask if Doc would have another hoedown. They'd heard about the fish and beans and the chicken and corn bread and they wanted in. What a summer he would have! What a triumph for King Cholesterol!

BATTER UP!

Tom had held his own at the cookout while he was under Doc's close supervision but he knew he was a rookie. His appetite had been whetted, though, so he set out to learn more. First, he checked with Doc to make sure his sources were one hundred percent authentic, then he set up a miniature version of Doc's operation out behind the house.

His mind was racing as it does when you're excited but a little overwhelmed. He had carefully noted the ingredients in Doc's fish fry and he'd watched how to double batter. As anyone will tell you, it's tricky but he was determined to master the technique.

Chicken was the real challenge. He'd marinate that with lots of garlic and then let it flame out. That's what gave it the smoky, irresistible kick. He'd try battering up the chicken, too, he decided. He ticked off the steps again and felt pretty good. He'd blunder along with it for a while, learning the right egg wash and batter combinations until he got it just right. Glory Hallelujah!

What he didn't do was learn more about grilles. He knew he didn't want the trouble of charcoal so he opted for propane. If you got the flame just right, everything came off just as tasty as charcoal but a whole lot easier.

One day, while he was prepping the chicken, he turned the gas on. He then rushed into the house for some chili, leaving the cover down. He forgot to see if the spark had taken. A minute or two went by while he fussed a bit more with the egg wash and then returned to the grille. Nothing happened so he hit the ignition switch. He didn't remember much after that.

Joe had been setting out some concrete paving blocks about fifty feet away when he heard a gigantic Whoof! Just like that: Whoof! He said later that it sounded like an enormous St. Bernard but he made that up.

At the time, it sounded like rage of an angry god. It was so loud it that it blocked his ears. He may have heard "Whoof!" but the real sound was more like "HOOOOFF!", the sound a ton of napalm makes when it lands on top of your hootch. Not the Whoof of a great big brown and white puppy dog.

Joe rushed over to Tom and threw the chicken out of the way. Tom was screaming obscenities and shouting something like "belt…...belt!" Somehow, Joe realized that he meant tourniquet and quickly slipped off his belt. He gripped it hard between his teeth and then wrapped it tightly around Tom's calf, just below the knee. He then ran for the phone and called the fire house. A couple of guys were sitting around playing Setback. They reluctantly answered the phone but once they got the message they were off in a flash.

The pump truck was way too big to navigate Nobadeer so they took the chief's Range Rover. They argued about it later but it took them less than ten minutes to get to Tom. Some said as little as seven.

Joe had covered Tom, spoken calmly to him and given him some water. He was breathing okay but he was definitely in a state of shock. The firemen quickly put him on a litter and threw him into the back of the truck. They bumped along the old dirt road but got him to cottage hospital in remarkably good order. Doctor Walendziewicz was waiting for them.

"Doctor Wally" was not a specialist in traumas like this one but she knew the basics. She ordered up some bloods and got him prepped at once. The firemen had already administered some morphine so by the time she was stitching up, Tom was as peaceful as a monk. Joe and the firemen just looked away and tried not to gag.

Doctor Wally cleaned and cleared the wound, wincing just that little bit as she tore away the fabric. It was a neat separation if there is such a thing, perhaps because it had happened so fast. She cleaned it and started cauterizing the vessels almost at once. It had been a slow day and but it hadn't stayed that way. This was tough.

"He'll live," was all she said but she said it with a gratitude they'd never understand. It had scared her right out of her usual well-check mode and straight into the world of combat trauma. No matter how ready you think you'll be and no matter how well you prepare, the real thing is terrifying. You'll remember it as vividly as the first time you made love. You'll be just as grateful when it turns out well, too. And just as anxious the next time if it doesn't.

Louise, everyone was in tears. Tom came out of it well and seemed okay when they started talking prostheses. He joked about getting a couple of other new parts too, but nobody laughed. The whole thing was likely to take a year during which time he'd have to cope with the misery of crutches, a wheelchair and frequent visits for "observations" and "fittings". He wasn't going to do much physical work.

But misery seldom comes in isolated, clearly identifiable moments. Misery comes in clusters. There's always more. Louise learned that her tour at home was over. If she wanted to stay with the Oceanographic— and she did--- she'd have to choose either Greenland or Iceland. No place warm. She'd missed her chance for the Galapagos and St. John, U.S.V.I. was taken the minute she passed.

No: She was going to have to ship out. She talked about it for days with Tom and he was entirely sympathetic. She would ship out but she could get leave fairly often and he could come to visit, too. There just wasn't a spot for him to stay with her on any long term basis. He'd have to batch it at home for weeks at a time. It was like the Army in reverse: She was the one who had to serve and he was the one who'd be keeping house. He'd have a lot of time on his hands.

SWINGIN' FOR THE SEATS

Alex enjoyed a spasm of sheer pleasure when she heard of Tom's misfortune but it was short-lived. When we're in trouble, it's fun to see others suffer but it's no cure. She would fail if she didn't solve her staffing problems. She had burned most of her bridges, too. Without the HR department that strokes its employees and makes them feel important even while pushing their heads under water, Alex was left with few resources. She had reached the point where good looks and money were not enough.

She decided one last time to see the bank. Trus greeted her with just the slightest bit of reserve when he opened the door and without his usual glow. She laid out her difficulties and then rather astutely, pointed to staffing shortages. Bookings were up but there simply weren't enough hands on deck. If she didn't solve that problem, the bookings would dry up and the ship would sink.

"Pay'em more," Trus said suddenly. When she stared back blankly, he repeated himself. "Just pay'em more."

Now, we make a lot of fun of bankers, the way they swan around and charm the poonters but they really know a lot more than we think. Often times, they've been involved in a wide variety of businesses. It pays to listen to them. You don't always have to agree but you should hear them out. Most customers respond in much the same way as the family dog that wags its tail and waits for the magic word: Food! Most customers simply smile and wait to hear the magic word: Yes! They don't listen to much else.

Trus wasn't going to waste their time by explaining. He'd make his position clear in those three words: "Pay'em more."

All that wisdom wasn't going to get far with Alex, though. She had only one solution to every problem: Cut costs. Strangely, she never applied this same solution to her own expenses; she spent what she pleased.

But when it came to employees, when it came to maintenance, when it came to anything related to the business, she was a one-trick pony.

Cut costs.

She wandered out of the meeting absorbed in thought, nearly walking straight across the street into oncoming traffic. "How can I cut costs and still get more people on board?" These mutually exclusive goals quickly put her in a spin. How could she do it? How can anyone do it?

The window for her decision was closing, though, as the days lengthened and summer approached. Spring visitors were up and traffic increasing. More and more people were taking their cars on the ferry, too, so they weren't confined to pleasant little walks in the village. They could rent a cottage in S'conset, pick up some groceries and cook for themselves. They didn't need the Inn. If she failed, people would go elsewhere and the Inn could close forever. Jet black cormorants massed ominously on the roof like so many harbingers of doom. More and more were coming all the time.

The final crash came on Memorial Day, a day when resort people normally rub their hands with glee. It means the beginning of the season, a time when they go from first to second gear, a time when a well oiled machine can turn out a Christing amount of cash.

She just wasn't ready. She'd already been embarrassed by Hunter's friends and their hysterics. That wouldn't happen again. Staff would have to have experience but again, she found them very thin on the ground. At the last minute, she managed to persuade a couple of old hands to help, people who'd found berths with the Harbormaster. College kids could take their spots in slack time but would not be able to handle a holiday crowd.

At first, things looked okay. Wait staff showed up in black trousers and white shirts or blouses, neat and trim. They all took instruction in the same way they always did, huddling up in the back of the dining room.

They were brought up to date on the menu, the chef's specialties and, of course, the booze. The cost of drinks had been bumped up when Alex panicked about expenses and old timers would likely raise a stink.

Indeed, the first salads came out fine and the entrees seemed to be coming out well, too. Alex relaxed and congratulated herself. She'd been right all along. Desserts were slow and she later realized that they—the desserts—were her problem. The second seating had been planned too tightly and now the back porch and the foyer were filling up.

Their attitude was growing increasingly hostile, too. When they were suddenly—and quite unexpectedly---hit with a ferocious squall, it was pandemonium.

Ten minutes later, there wasn't a diner in sight. Some had gone back to their rooms to change but others had just vanished, never to return.

When the first seating had safely departed, the dining room was empty but for two couples who had just wandered by. They sat painfully apart, emphasizing the emptiness of the room.

The third seating suffered cancellations but even the hearty souls who braved the mud and broken limbs had lost their appetites. When they saw the price of drinks, they suddenly lost their thirst, as well. The whole thing had been a disaster due, of course, to the desserts and the goddammed squall.

The rest of the weekend was slow torture as first one and then another mischief fell across her path. The dishwasher finally did crash leaving the back of the restaurant shrieking angrily at itself. One of her new old hires quit on the spot and her buddy left shortly thereafter. They said something about roaches but to be fair to Windsor's, no one else saw any. There were too many spiders to allow much of an infestation.

No matter what she did, there were tears. Alex would later say quite bravely that she didn't know how she had found the strength....... but she survived right through to Tuesday morning. She'd be lucky to survive her meeting that morning at the bank. It had become painfully clear to everyone but Alex that hostelry was not the business for her.

Trus tried to be polite but his job was tightly circumscribed by what he called "rules".

Banks, it seems, are not like other businesses. They are "regulated". There are some awfully good reasons for that, too. In the early days of the century, anyone with a couple of bucks could open a bank. If you had a gift for backslapping and a taste for the cowboy life, you could rent a nice storefront, move in a vault and declare the place a lending institution. It was fun; it was dangerous and it was thick with thieves. Basically, your certificate of occupation was a license to steal.

In those hurly burly days of early banking, you could take in deposits, lend them to your cousin Eddie and then go bankrupt the very next day. You'd leave town, move across the state and do the same thing all over again. What a delicious, delicious scam! It was great! No wonder people loved Dillinger. The bad guys had been stealing their money so when Dillinger robbed all those banks, he was a hero.

Trus was stuck. He'd have to call the note. He'd have to tattoo a notice of condemnation on her door and worse yet, he'd have to tell her face to face. When she walked into his office she had a plan. She'd first ask for time and then she'd ask to restructure, to stretch out payments.

She'd get back on her feet. She'd recruit help from America and put them up at the Inn or if not at the Inn then nearby where they could live together in a kind of youth hostel like they have over in France and Switzerland. Like that.

Trus heard her out but even his legendary patience had its limitations. When she finally looked to be tiring, he broke in. "I'm sorry," he said but was then interrupted himself.

"You're not sorry!" she exclaimed. "You're all the same....." and so forth.

Trus had that odd moment when he could sit back, and dispassionately look at a phenomenon--at an applicant. He pressed his fingers together and brought them to his lips as if he was listening carefully to every word but his mind was miles away. "She'll soon stop. She has to," he thought. "But she doesn't get it." He continued to ponder, trying to gain a benefit for himself from her folly.

"She could have succeeded by making a few simple changes." This worried him because, of course, that's true for all of us, even him.

But then he realized, "She can't change. She's not capable of it."

His mind drifted further. "Look at Hunter. The kid is a complete doofus but he discovered his faults and he figured out his strengths. He also learned his limitations. He's doing just fine. He'll never be rich but he's certainly happy. He gets up each morning, works a little bit and has some fun."

"....so if I have a little more time or, if you think it's wise, we can simply stretch out the payments a little. That could work."

A little cruel or maybe humorous streak in Trus urged him suddenly just to hold up his fist and turn thumbs down. It would have made a wonderful story the next time he had a couple of beers in him. "So I just stared at her blankly and gave her a thumbs down! How about that!?!"

What fun!

Instead, he just shook his head quietly and stared down at the desk. Experience had taught him to frown convincingly so he did that, too. When he saw his ceremonial pen protruding from its base, he briefly worried she might stab him with it so he took it out and stuck it into the top of his desk. "Better safe than sorry....."

She had almost bought into the reluctant refusal and the frown but that didn't stop her from clawing at him one last time. "You people! You people! You island people stick together like leeches. You're all the same." And she tore out of the office, her dignity, if not her solvency, restored.

Trus breathed one final breath, a long exhale that seemed to last a full minute. "Boy, am I glad she's out of my hair," he thought. And that was that. The lawyers would do the rest of the dirty work. He didn't envy them but that's what they signed up for, he decided. He remembered that she would have to pay his attorney's fees so his smile returned.

THE FIRST GRAVE

Tom was really mad at himself for blowing off his leg. There was no one else to blame, either. He'd slipped up and paid a terrible price. It left him angry and with no way to blow off steam so, like all of us, he just got depressed. The more he thought about it, the more depressed he got.

Joe stopped by as did Monk and Mrs. Crisp but all they could do was offer some help. There was no way they could earn a living for him or kick a can. He'd have to figure that out for himself. It was always a pleasant distraction when people stopped and he appreciated it but when Louise shipped out to Iceland he was alone a lot. She said Iceland was going to be "interesting" so he blamed the whole island for being "interesting". Bastids!

And people are funny: When they suffer misfortune, people do extraordinary things. Most people stuff it down and make believe it didn't happen but some few of us—and this included Tom---want to be reminded of their follies. Those poor souls want either to torment themselves or, if they're idealistic, remind themselves to do better.

To strive and overcome adversity. To be a better person and inspire others to become better people.

Tom fell into the former category. He wanted to remind himself daily; he wanted to remind himself over and over that he had been so stupid that he not only didn't improve on Doc's chicken recipe, he had blown his leg off. He was wallowing in self pity, waist deep and sinking so the best way he could find to feel better was to lacerate himself daily with reminders of his unbelievable foolishness. "How many guys blow off their own legs?" he asked himself a hundred times a day.

Oftentimes, people see themselves in the mirror at 6 a.m. in the morning and think, "How many guys......foul up the way I did yesterday?" and they're satisfied. They get mad at themselves all over again, shave, shower and go to work. Eventually, they stop beating themselves up. But Tom wasn't going off to work. He was stuck with that mirror a dozen times a day and the mirror kept answering him, "You! You're the dumb shit who blew his leg off!" It didn't help much.

Finally, he stumbled on the solution. Literally. He had been fitted with a prosthesis and while it was cranky at first, it was remarkably well made. It just took some getting used to. Each day he'd walk down the road and mark the spot on the pavement where he turned back. Each day he tried to walk a little further than he'd walked the day before. One day, as he crested a small hill, he nearly tripped over the carcass of a herring gull.

Tom had seen a lot of dead gulls over the years but this one struck him differently for some reason. He felt a little sad about it. Its only purpose now would be as snack food for the crows. It deserved better than that. He walked back to the house, got a sack and threw the gull into the sack.

For some reason, that gull triggered other thoughts, too. He called up the firehouse and asked about his leg. What had happened to it? Was there anything left of it? Where is it now?

Once again, the guys had been deeply absorbed in Setback but they folded up the cards, went to the roster sheet and reported back. "It was sent to the lab," they said vaguely. "The lab" could mean anything but Tom decided Dr. Wally would know so he called her office, too.

"Yep", her secretary said, after checking his file. "It's up at the morgue. I think we gotta check it out before it goes to the dump or whatever." This seemed wrong to Tom. It wasn't lobster bait; it was his leg, one to which he'd become attached over many years of close association.

"Can I get it?" he asked. The secretary didn't have that kind of authority but she said she'd put a note in the file. When Dr. Wally called him later that day, she was a little confused.

"You say you want it?" she asked. When he said he did, she asked, "What are you going to do with it?"

"Well, I guess I'm going to bury it," he said.

"Well, sure, I can see that," she said. But just when she was about to ask for details, she was called away. Another emergency. Another big mess.

Tom called a couple more times but couldn't reach the Doc. She was out straight so he got on to the secretary again. "Look, I'm gonna bury the leg. Can I come down and pick it up?" he asked.

The secretary/office staff was now confused but when she pulled the chart, Dr. Wally had placed a check mark under the box labeled "Inter" so it must be okay to release. She was tired of talking to Tom every fifteen minutes so she told him to come down and pick it up. She'd have an order for him when he got to the desk.

He grabbed Joe and one hour later had picked up the order with its impressive "Cottage Hospital" stamp. They then brought it downstairs and worked their way through the basement until they found the room labeled "Morgue". The attendant had just started his shift and quickly released the "subject body part". He wanted to get a coffee and was hoping the cafe was still open. Locking the door behind him, he never thought of it again.

Tom had a plan in mind. He outlined it to Joe on the drive home and his brother just nodded. That's really all you can do with crazy people.

Louise was away—in Iceland, for God's sake—so Tom stuck the leg in the fridge until he could execute his plan. Joe tried not to look. The next day, the two of them went out and dug a small hole in the back of the property. It had to be at least three or four feet deep to keep out the dogs so Joe got down into the hole and banged away until he was down waist deep. They then dumped the remaining bits of bone into the hole and covered it up. They threw in the dead gull, too, for luck.

As soon as possible, they would put a stone there to memorialize the leg. "Rest in peace," they mumbled, attempting vainly to simulate a prayer. They had both been away from the church too long to remember anything vaguely traditional so they just made it up. It made them feel a little better. Joe muttered, "Bone Voyage!"

THE SECOND GRAVE

The years went by. Tom kept up the small candy concession he had with Janey's and paid the bills. Louise came home about every ninety days and Tom managed a couple of visits to Iceland but it was hard for them. Joe's business picked up when the economy improved and Mrs. Crisp looked for a way to early retirement. Their lives had settled into that slow glide path of middle age that leads back down to where they started in the first place.

Mr. and Mrs. Bustle had done well until age seventy-five. They were then stricken by a shocking run of bad luck. Es couldn't see and Cal couldn't walk. Their world shrank back to the house and the yard. They rarely went out except when one of the kids took them for a treat. No grandchildren seemed in sight so they kept the old, faded pictures of Tom and Joe taped to the fridge. When they went into decline they assured both boys that they were fine. They knew their time would come soon and they weren't afraid. When they did go, it was no surprise to them but a big surprise to the boys.

Certainly, they had learned a lot from their folks but they took all that for granted. It was only after the service and they were walking away from the church that Joe reflected.

"I never liked her meat loaf, ya know?"

"Too much….what was it? Ketchup?"

Joe nodded quietly. "Yeah, ketchup."

Tom tried to honor them the best he knew how. "I did like the shepherd's pie, though. That was pretty good." Somehow, their memories seemed linked to food. "Remember the ice cream? 'Neapolitan'? What the hell was that?"

"I don't remember them ever fighting," said Joe. "...Why is that?"

"Who knows? They just got along, I guess." Neither gave it much thought at that time but when they did, they realized how right they were. Both folks were kind, agreeable sorts who just wanted a safe and peaceful life. It was a little late in their lives to be learning big truths but they did learn that: You can be happy with less of one thing if you've got more of something else. In their case, it was peace. They had plenty of that, even with the boys.

Mrs. Crisp was always a source of comfort to the boys, too. Joe especially, of course. Over time, she'd come to respect Tom's sense of propriety and honor. He always tried to hold up his end of a bargain. But she had fallen in love with Joe and the magic that always seemed a part of his life.

Maybe it was the garlic; maybe it was the flamenco and maybe it was just serendipity but his whimsical self was in perfect accord with her deeper sense of the absurd, of the outrageous fact of our existence.

Whatever it was, they, too, never seemed to quarrel or, for that matter, disagree. She looked to him for madness and he looked to her as the solid bridge between daft abandon and dry land.

Life did play tricks on them, though. When her own mother had died, it was a relief. Ida had long since forgotten her daughter's existence and only remembered Rodney, her old Rottweiler and some chickens she had raised as a kid. Whenever Mrs. Crisp paid her a visit, she thanked her for coming and asked if she had seen the dog. How was he? And would she bring him sometime?

Mr. Crisp had died in a state of complete and utter bliss. He had moved to Florida with his friend, companion and paramour Ernie Jenkins and rarely returned to an island that held little attraction for him. What assets he had he left to Mrs. Crisp but for funds that had been discreetly set aside for his beloved golf partner. Each would have enough to be comfortable but not enough to become silly or arrogant.

When Mrs. Crisp herself got sick, it surprised them all. "It can't be nothin'," they decided and were shocked when it was. Some congenital anomaly had been planted among her organs long ago and its time had come to bloom. Her pulse went down, her b. p. went up, and her breathing went up and down, depending. She seemed okay at first, just a little tired. That soon changed.

Joe was frantic. He wouldn't admit it but he was more frightened than he had ever been in his life. Nothing calmed him down. Not Monk, not Tom, not weed, nothing. When he tried to calm her down, he just upset them both. He took no comfort from her assurances, either. Like a frightened child on the TiltOWhirl, he just wanted it to end and be happy again.

Mrs. Crisp was philosophical. She wasn't in any real pain, just a little tired. Instead of making a soap opera out of it, she looked to the doctors. Then the oncologists. Then hospice. Four months after her primary had detected "something we want to look into", she was leaving for parts unknown. She wasn't afraid, either, at least not for herself.

She thought only of Joe. Her path was certain; his was not.

Louise got leave and helped to pull Joe together. She knew she couldn't reason with him so she sympathized. He didn't hear a word she said but he appreciated her presence. Tom just stood by and went for coffees as the vigil went on and on.

When the doctor finally emerged from Mrs. Crisp's room, she was walking slowly. There was no longer a need to hurry. She seemed to be rationing her steps as she approached them and she was. She was trying to think how, exactly, to tell them. That was her job. But she didn't need to say a word. They knew by her gait and her posture that a new chapter was about to unfold. It only needed her official declaration.

When it came, they didn't hear that, either. It was just so much noise.

The ultimate truth had been told when she walked through the door.

More official declarations followed, though, that made things complicated in the short term. Who was in charge? How to proceed? Should they call a church? A funeral director? What?

But Mrs. Crisp had made plans. She had prepaid funeral expenses and the firm of Crutchley, Crutchley and Kravetz arrived at the hospital to take possession of her physical self. She had left clear instructions to cremate and that Joe be given the urn. She had even selected the urn, a Grecian Urn, perhaps to honor her friendship with Louise. Its black paint had been etched with figures at play and, of course, a couple about to kiss.

A short service was held at St. Anthony's, a church they chose because of Joe's Little League association. Team pictures were hung in the downstairs hallway and if you looked closely you could see little Joe proudly clutching his Louisville Slugger and smiling for the camera.

A somewhat formal portrait of Mrs. Crisp had surfaced so they put that on a table in front of the altar next to the urn. A dozen or so mourners showed up and paid their respects. For someone who had taught and guided for so many years it was a modest turnout but then she had always kept to herself and to a small circle of friends.

Once the service was over and the kindly priest thanked, Joe swept away the photograph and the urn and plunked them into the back seat of the car. He, Tom and Louise drove back to the house in silence. Louise wasn't entirely in agreement but she chose not to say anything when Joe went out to the back of the property, shucked his jacket and began digging a hole next to the one for Tom's leg.

"She was pretty smart," Tom said as Joe stomped down hard on his spade. "She must have known that you couldn't bury a body out here but I guess you can bury an urn, right?"

Joe just nodded and kept digging. Louise brought them out some lemonade and then fetched a couple of red and white beach chairs. She sat down with Tom and sipped her lemonade as Joe banged away at the cold, dark sand. He stopped digging when he got waist deep, then stuck the spade down, carved out a little hole in the bottom and reached up for the urn.

The urn was surprisingly heavy. It seemed to emphasize Mrs. Crisp's determination to stay in one place. She didn't want her ashes scattered to the winds; she didn't want them floating on the sea. She wanted to stay with Joe, right there next to his little house. She'd always be there and she'd always give him strength.

It took them a while but within six months or so, they had secured two tombstones for both Tom's leg and for Mrs. Crisp. They had gone to Hyannis and requested two small grey tombstones like the ones they had seen on old burial hill in Boston. The stones were small, only three inches thick and fourteen inches wide. They'd stand about two feet above the ground. Unlike the newer, more ostentatious stones, these stones were traditional. There was room for dates of birth and death and, if appropriate, a thoughtful word for passersby.

Perhaps: "Be kind to others" or "Love your neighbor"

The message on the stone for Tom's leg read, "I never learned to dance."

Mrs. Crisp's read, "Try anything. Just try!"

A VOICE FROM BEYOND

The trips to Hyannis became incessant. Tom had to deal with Janey's chocolates and Joe had to sort out paper work on Mrs. Crisp's estate. Sometimes they went together and sometimes they went by themselves. The ferry always seemed cold, the water and the wind colder still. They had, in fact, very few happy associations with the ferry. Even candy let them down. Tom wasn't selling much chocolate; the market stayed flat.

Joe had to suit up and go to Barger's office for all of the malarkey related to her estate. Why? He kept asking himself, "Why? She's dead and none of this bullshit will bring her back." It all came down to property, something neither he nor Mrs. Crisp had considered as important as a quiet night in front of the fire.

She did have some assets, though, and she had been pretty definite about her wishes. Her will provided a gift of $20,000 to Joe and the rest to a number of charities. The Eighties had torn through the gay community like a demon from Hell so she gave to an AIDS foundation. She also gave to an animal shelter out of deference to her mother and the rest went to the United Negro College Fund. That was it. Why did it take so long? What was the problem?

Barger explained about court procedures and notice and statutory time requirements but Joe just glazed over. He felt the same way as he had as a kid, listening for that slight pause when he could break in and excuse himself. He was so bored he finally just said, "That's great, thanks. Where do I sign?"

On the drive back to the ferry, he was just angry. Such a waste of time. It woke him up. He wanted her back! That made him angrier still. He sat up in the seat and stared at the back of the big yellow school bus in front of him. Kids were giving him the finger out the back window and he just waved and smiled. But they were stuck. Something was holding them up. He stopped waving and smiling and the kids stopped flipping him the bird. Everyone stretched his neck to see but they were just stuck in traffic. Not going anywhere.

As he tapped impatiently on the steering wheel and craned his neck, his eyes darted first across the street and then into his rear view mirror. No luck: They weren't going anywhere. His mind ran through the usual possibilities—accident, paving crew, fire, etc.--and settled on accident.

He hadn't seen any crews at work on his way to Barger's, after all.

When he sat back in his seat, he slumped resignedly and stared straight ahead. A couple of kids wanted to insult him again but their friends had lost interest and gone back to their seats. He was bored again, his attention directed solely at the back of the bus. He stared first at the big windows and the lights, then at the bumper. "Hyannis Public Schools" was painted in neat black letters across the back with their uplifting motto below: REACH FOR THE STARS.

Joe wondered how many of the kids who had ridden that bus over the years had actually reached for the stars. Most had likely reached for the first thing that would assure them a job and been happy with that. The motto had been forgotten and they had lived out their lives. He also wondered if he had ever reached for he stars. And if there were stars out there, which ones had he reached for?

The traffic refused to budge and Joe sank down deeper and deeper into his seat. He heard a couple of horns blasting but he was lost in thought. His days weren't over yet. He could still reach for the stars if he didn't give up or become cynical. Why not? There were still worlds to conquer, still tricks to play.

His mind then traveled back to Mrs. Crisp as it often did each day. Her last message, the one on her tombstone, was "Try!" "Try" what? He wondered. "Try reaching for the stars," he thought. Why not? Why not? He had no obligations. He had no encumbrances. There wasn't even a child to embarrass. Louise and Tom were his only family and they didn't care if he succeeded or failed no matter what he did. They loved him. They just wanted him to be happy and content. Why not "Try"? "Try" what, though? "Try" what?

Joe just made the ferry but by the time he reached the island his engines were all fired up. It had taken a school bus to put him on track. What track? Well, he'd have to figure that out. He didn't even know where to start but he knew he was right. Mrs. Crisp had been right. The Hyannis School system had been right and he'd be wrong if he didn't listen.

After dinner he sat out back as he often did. He had a little smoke and then just watched the clouds as the sun set over America. There was a little purple and a little blue but it was mostly pink. His mind drifted towards the sky. What made those colors? He wondered and then tried to explain the science. Purple came from the passing clouds and pink seemed to occur at the fringes where the light wasn't entirely absorbed by the denser accumulations of moisture.

All that made sense but why was it so enthralling? Why did it captivate and cause an almost universal feeling of well-being? Why was it so beautiful and what is "beauty" anyway?

Joe wasn't given to deep thinking but he had always had an instinct that attracted him to the unknown. He was never satisfied with simple solutions. Even his trade as handyman had taught him to question the obvious. A bad window sill often meant that rot had crept below the sill and then established itself beneath. A superficial view of that window would not have shown that; you had to have an eye for it and know that in all likelihood there was trouble down below.

Joe was also given to fancy. Maybe it was the weed and maybe he had always been that way. It was probably a bit of both. He wouldn't have described himself as cynical but certainly would have agreed that he and Mrs. Crisp doubted the natural order of things. They joked about it all the time. This freed them up to think beyond the obvious and conventional. Their sense of the ridiculous informed every part of the day and led to the creation of a whole new universe of their own. A parallel universe. A universe of infinite hilarity.

He and Tom had managed to get by over the years but they had only worked at something to make a buck. They hadn't had a vision or at least hadn't made any vision the central focus of their lives. Tom had probably become indifferent to candy by this time. It was nothing more than a way to pay the bills. And Joe wasn't really a fix-it guy. He fell into it. He was facing an end just as certainly as Cal and Es had done and perhaps as suddenly as Mrs. Crisp. What would his tombstone read?

"I've never met a gutter that I couldn't clean"?

No. As he sat there in the waning light, he could see a little glow over Hyannis. He could see Venus and Mars as they emerged from the gloom.

A screen door slammed behind him and he heard Tom's halting steps come up behind him.

"'Tcha doin'?" he asked, sitting down heavily in an old Adirondack chair.

"Nuthin'. Just lookin' at the sky."

"Gorgeous, huh?"

"Yeah." And they remained silent for a while.

"I bin' thinkin'," Joe said quietly. "I wanna do something." Tom nodded as if he understood but didn't comment.

"I got twenty years or so and I wanna do somethin'."

"That sounds great. Whattaya thinkin' of doin'?"

"I don't know. Somethin'."

"Well, all we need is another guy and we'd have the three wise men here," said Tom. "Maybe we should call up Monk. He's fulla ideas."

"Yeah, well maybe it's a pilgrimage I'm thinkin'a doin'," said Joe, seriously. "Maybe not to Mecca but somewhere. Cleveland, maybe. That's what you'd like. Go to the Rock and Roll Hall of Fame."

"Or Seville," Tom said, rising to the taunt. "You could hear some of that Flamenco music and maybe meet someone nice who could teach you all about love and castanets."

"Yeah. A gypsy woman," Joe agreed. "A gypsy queen."

They sat there for a while, saying nothing while the stars broke out of the dark. When he went to bed, though, Joe was sure he'd soon know what to do. He'd just have to pay attention. He'd learned that much; if he listened, he could hear things. That night, he slept better than he had for months.

PHANTOMS

Another trip to Barger's office, another logjam. It was a sewer pipe the last time but it looked like a phone line now. Joe thought he could see a cherry picker up ahead with a guy on top, the usual sign of a messed up line. In any event, he had to poke along slowly taking in the scene. At the last minute he'd agreed to take Monk along so Monk could see Marcel and catch up. They'd become good friends since Proid Week and they both loved the craic.

Monk and Marcel hated Alexandra so it was a lot of fun talking about the demise of the Inn. She had failed spectacularly, leaving vendors and employees unpaid, Trus and the bank without recourse. Once that bit of business had been addressed, they brought each other up to date on flirtations, real and imagined. Each had a new "possibility" and that kept the pot boiling. Monk got back just in time to meet Joe at Barger's and to make the ferry back to the island.

"Oy'm t'inkin' ya'd bettore stop for some gazz," Monk said, pointing to the gauge.

"Cheeses, thanks," Joe said, a little embarrassed. They had just heard of someone who'd run out of gas while on the ferry and it had held up the cars for an hour. "Mama mia!"

"Dare's a place," Monk said, pointing to a Gulf station just ahead.

"Okay, yeah," Joe said. "I'll pop in there." He looked at his watch and they were still early, even with the holdup.

Fortunately, there was no delay at the station. Joe jumped out to pump the gas and Monk got out to look around. He had meant to go to the Men's but when he turned the corner of the building he came upon a real surprise: a small school bus. Unlike its larger brothers and sisters, this bus was only half as long, the runt of the litter. It was inscribed "TOWN OF HYANNIS" just like its more favored siblings but a special notation had been made on the side. ADULT EDUCATION. That meant basically, the oldsters.

"Day've got a boss out dare for the geezers, ya know," Monk exclaimed when he got back into El's truck.

"A what?"

"Day've got da cutest little boss over dare," Monk said, pointing.

Joe could see the front and the front looked like any other bus but he was curious. The bus spoke to him somehow. "What is it about buses these days?" he asked himself. Most people would have thought nothing of it and just driven off. But something was happening; he was sure of it.

Joe got out again and walked around the side of the garage to take a better look. "Stumpy," was all he thought. It was funny looking, an abbreviated conveyance. It made him laugh just to see it. He had to get inside, he thought. He had to take a look.

"Izzat your bus?" he asked a mechanic who was standing in front of one of the bays, wiping his hands on a dirty rag.

"Yeah, I own all the school buses around here," the guy said, smiling broadly. "They call me 'busboy'."

"No, no, really. Who owns the buses?"

"Oh, that's a sorta tycoon. Name's LoConte. 'The Count'. He leases them to the schools around here. Good guy."

"I really like it," Joe declared. He stood there beaming as he took it all in, slowly walking around the side, stopping at the back. It's a beauty, he thought. A real beauty!

"Wanna look inside?" the guy asked.

"Izzat okay?"

"Yeah, he don't mind. If he don't mind kids ridin' in'em, messin'em up and droppin' shit all over the place, he won't mind you lookin' at it." He pointed at the door. "It ain't even locked."

Joe pushed at the door and it folded up to let him inside. He ducked his head a little self-consciously and stepped up the three stairs to the floor of the bus. The driver's seat was a well upholstered lounge chair capable of accommodating a healthy backside but the seats were like all bus seats, hard, green and stiff-looking. He counted the rows (8) and figured two kids could sit on either side of the aisle. At the back, there was one solid bench seat that ran the length of the back of the bus. That seat was the one that allowed the kids to stand up, clown around and moon the cars behind them. Maybe forty kids could fit inside. Pretty cool!

"He buys'em from some yard in Connecticut," said the mechanic from the door. "He gets'em used, he fixes'em up and I guess he makes good money off'em." Joe just nodded. His eyes were wide open, though. He gazed around the bus unblinkingly, like a sea bass and yes: He'd been hooked.

Something about the bus had caught him in the chest and held on tight.

Something was happening. Inch by inch, he stalked the inside of the bus. It wasn't too beat up. There were a couple of torn seats but a stitch here and there would make them right. It needed paint but if Joe knew anything, he knew how to paint.

"Whaddaya think he'd take for it?" he asked, still captivated and still gaping around the interior.

"Oh, it's not for sale, sorry. I didn't mean to say that…..".

"Oh, no. You didn't say that. I just wondered," Joe said.

The guy pointed to the front of the bus and said, "It's here for a new manifold. I gotta replace the gasket and….. I prob'ly gotta put on a new muffler, too."

He could see Joe's disappointment so he said, "You could call'im, ya know. What's he gonna say? 'Drop dead'? Who cares?"

"Yeah, yeah. I might do that." Spotting the glove compartment, he asked, "Mind if I look in here?" The mechanic shrugged and shook his head.

"Help yourself. Just don't take nuthin'."

Joe reached into the glove box and took out a small folder. Dusting off the registration, it was registered to LoConte's company, Grumpy Don's Transportation, Inc. "Okay," he thought, I'll check it out. In the mean time, he got LoConte's phone number and stuck it into his wallet for safekeeping. He would call when he got home but in the mean time he had to figure out what he was going to do with it. Something, for sure.

He and Monk joked about it on the way home. "Maybe sell chocolates door to door," he said.

"Or maybe make a deli out of it. Sell borgers'n'at."

"I could start my own school, actually," joked Joe. "...Teach kids a bit about hard work and fixin' things themselves...."

"...Put yerself outta work, right?" laughed Monk. "No, ya better not do da'."

"I love the bus, though," said Joe. He really wanted it. There was something so completely unutilitarian about it. It was not really much good for bussin'; it was just a goof.

"Stumpy! Stumpy! That's whatcha gotta call it. Stumpy!" Monk shouted. Joe had thought the very same thing. The ugly, ungainly, unnecessary bus had found a name. Could he find the owner? And what would he tell him? And just what, exactly, would he do with it?

Joe had learned a few things: Wishes are inspirations. Wishes are compelling but they're also unsubstantial. You couldn't put one up against a heavyweight. You had to let them live their own lives, too. They needed time to grow because they often led to surprising results. He knew that they're terribly fragile but they can have the power to change your life. He'd proceed slowly but he'd take that next step.

Joe had a wish. It wasn't even a well-formed wish but he knew about imperatives. Something—Someone?--was directing his hand. He almost felt he should look over his shoulder because that force, whatever it was, was breathing down his neck. He had never thought about a bus before, let alone thought of buying one. What was giving him the push?

The next day, he called LoConte. He was "tied up" of course, but would call back later. When he did call, Joe asked him if the bus was for sale.

"Geez, no," answered LoConte. "I been using it as a shuttle for the, you know, for the bingo'n'at." He paused for a second to think of its other uses and then added, "…..They got movies on Wednesday afternoons, too, I think…." He had kind of forgotten. He wasn't really involved in operations any more; his kids did that. He was more into acquisitions than the daily deployments.

"Well, I'd love to buy it if you want to sell," Joe said hopefully. He then listened hard to LoConte at the other end of the line.

"Sure, sure. Um….. I'll ask one of the kids. They know more about this stuff than I do. I'm gettin' old myself, for cryin' out loud," smiling into the phone. He still had a lot of charm and he loved nothing better than makin' a deal.

When Joe spoke to Tom later in the day, Tom was completely fuddled. What, exactly, did his brother think he could do with half a bus? With any kind of bus? Joe was in a fragile state, too, something Tom always kept in mind. Tom picked up where Joe and Monk had left it earlier in the day.

"You could take out the seats and make it into a kind of mobile fix-it shop," he suggested. Joe nodded his head but wasn't convinced.

Tom tried another tack. "You could donate it to charity," an idea inspired perhaps by Mrs. Crisp.

"Charity already owns it," Joe said abruptly. "No, I have this gut feeling that there's something I'm meant to do with it."

Tom was leery of Joe's gut feelings but he didn't discourage him further.

He just let it go. "Well, it's probably not for sale anyway so the question is pretty much moot." Again, Joe nodded but couldn't get the bus out of his head. It had been driving from ear to ear the whole time since he first saw it.

Joe may have been a dreamer but he knew an impulse from solid fact. He was startled the next morning, then, when LoConte called him up and said they might be able to do business. He couldn't sell him the one at the garage but his kids had another one, one that was being "decommissioned", ie, "scrapped". If he wanted to take a look at that one, he was free to do so. It was currently in Provincetown but it was being towed south in a week or two.

Joe wasted no time. He dragged Monk with him to Provincetown the very next day. He'd gotten the address of the shop where the bus was being stored and pulled up front at nine o'clock sharp. The stubby little bus was positioned like its twin in Hyannis, up against the side of the garage. First impressions were not hopeful.

"Well, it's got dat flat toyer dare," Monk said, pointing to the right front tire. The whole bus sagged to one side, making it look a little sad. The bumpers were rusty with neglect along with much of the outside. It hadn't been loved or even noticed in a long time.

As they walked around the bus they tried peeking in the windows. The usual graffiti covered the ceiling and the seats were faded and torn. They saw the word "fuck" a lot. It seemed to be the predominant theme for the interior and it struck Joe how much nicer it would have been if the kids had chosen a wider variety of expression.

"There's a whole world of possibilities. Why limit yourself to 'fuck'? If it was me, I'd do a Beatles thing and make it the 'Magical Mystery Tour'," he told Monk.

"A'course," agreed Monk. He had been thinking how badly Joe missed Mrs. Crisp and he just wanted his friend to hold it together. Joe had always been a lot of fun and now he'd been wounded. He wasn't the same.

They had the guy crank it up. It seemed to run okay but Joe would have Bartlett's take a look at it. They couldn't put it on the road so he left it there. When he called LoConte later and asked about price, he mentioned the condition. Any sale would be dependent upon its performance.

"Sure, sure," said the owner. "Listen, I'll have it tuned up, get the tire replaced and meet you there on Thursday. If we don't make some sort of deal, I'll just ship it out like I said before." Deal.

On Thursday, when they met LoConte, they met a guy with a lot of teeth. He smiled broadly in the tradition of insurance salesmen or wealth managers but he seemed to have the honesty and humility of his breed, the used car salesmen who try harder and just want to be loved.

"Listen to that thing hum," he said. He even cupped his hand behind his ear to show his deep approval. "This thing'll run forever," he said, forgetting for a moment that "forever" is indeed, a very long time.

Mike had left Greg in charge at Bartlett's garage and made the trip with Joe. He took his time under the hood and then slid his wheelie under the chassis for a look at the undercarriage. He didn't say much but after looking it over, he gave a solemn nod. Should be okay.

When they took it for a shakedown cruise, it was a complete goof. People watched out for you; they all seemed heartily afraid of school buses, regardless of size. They showed a lot of respect and waved them through traffic. When Joe got behind the wheel it felt like he was in a space ship, the visibility was so startling. The front window ran from his belly to a foot above his head, giving him a sense of flying through outer space. Wow! He was gonna buy it.

"What's the best you can do?" he asked.

"Well, I still got something left on the note, so...... I prob'ly gotta get fifteen. That's prob'ly about as good as I can do."

"It needs a lot of work,....." Joe pushed back. LoConte nodded his head. It was an eyesore to be exact.

"I can do twelve," Joe said firmly. "Remember that this bus will be put into community service again." He didn't really know what he was saying but he smiled confidently. It kept the talk from going cold.

They settled on thirteen six.

Joe had still not answered the question, "What are you going to do with it?" Some hand, some voice was guiding his actions. When he reached inside and took out the owner's manual, he knew whose hand it was.

Dusting off the tattered manual, he made out the name of the original owner: Raoul Espenshade. "A gypsy!?!" he thought. "A gypsy!?!"

WISHFUL THINKING

Your life unfolds one day at a time but your destiny unfolds sporadically, one phase at a time. You can often see a new phase coming, either a new plateau or a deep crevasse that you will never, ever be able to cross.

Joe didn't know yet what he was facing, whether his path would lead him to heights unknown or to the bottom of the deep blue sea. He just knew that he had a beginning. He had taken the idea of a bus and turned it into a real bus. Now what?

There were times when, late at night or early in the morning, he felt the presence of his great love. He felt it keenly. He talked to himself naturally and he talked out loud but now he included her in the conversation. He'd often ask himself questions like, "Well, what do you think? Should I put in some more beach roses or just let them be?" In time, he found himself asking her, "What do you think? Do you think a rhodie could make it here?" He'd be relaxed, calmly assessing a corner of the property and he would simply ask her out loud what she thought. It was entirely unselfconscious and felt completely natural.

Did she answer back? Did he hear her voice? He would claim not, even when Tom or Monk asked him quite seriously, "You talk to her?" He would just joke about it. He felt neither shame nor crazed. On the contrary, it felt great. After a while, they ignored him.

Eventually, though, Joe heard something because he was discovering a use for the bus. He saw it clearly: He would paint it white and instead of calling it "Stumpy" like its brother, he would call it "Moby Dick". It was certainly chunky like a whale; it just lacked a tail. Tom said he should drive it onaconna he only had one leg like Ahab. He could wear one of those high hats like Abraham Lincoln or Gregory Peck in the old movie. And Monk wanted to drive it because he had found it, sort of.

Anyone who sat behind the wheel wanted to drive it. There was a little madness in it. When you sat there, you were the commander on the bridge of a freeway going frigate. The visibility, so unlike that of a normal sedan, was panoramic. You could do anything and go anywhere. At least, it felt like that.

So Joe rolled it up behind their houses and left it there. He still didn't quite know what he would do with it but he did know rough carpentry so he built a garage for it. He felt a responsibility to it, a need to protect it. He felt Mrs. Crisp's heart beating under the floorboards. In a way, he was protecting her.

He also painted it white. There was no rush about it but he knew the temperature would be falling soon so he took out the seats, stacked them up and let go. He painted the outside white as he had first intended, then set about cleaning up the inside, too. He thought black for the inside of a belly would be too depressing so he chose a glossy turquoise: Caribbean waters.

On a typical day Joe opened a can of paint, started stirring it and spoke aloud. "Moby," he'd say, "What are we going to do today?" It might be ten minutes before he broke the silence again but then he'd ask, "Wanna take a trip downtown?"

One Sunday morning when Louise was home for a visit, Joe was left on his own. He felt a little blue and thought a ride downtown would be a bit of fun. He deserved a break. In a way, he was proud of Moby and wanted to show her off. He'd been nervous about painting her name across the stern but went ahead and did it anyway. It came out great. "Moby Dick" was scrawled across the back of the bus in turquoise outlined in black. When he stepped back for the effect, it had just the right amount of sassy dash. After a bit, he took out the paint again and cartooned a stylized tail that swept across the back.

It was nearly ten so he thought a ride past the docks would be fun. Look in on Hunter. See who else was around. When he got to the dock, though, two couples were standing there with their hands in their pockets. Nobody else was there. There was no sign of Hunter or one of his crew and sadly, the Inn across the street looked shuttered.

One of the men waved a hand to Joe so he pulled up and rolled down the window. "Where is everybody?" he asked. "We wanted to rent a sail boat. It was all set for this morning."

Joe didn't know why Hunter would be missing at that hour but didn't want to lose him any business. "Should be here any time, I would think." And for additional encouragement added, "He's very reliable. Always on time."

He looked down at the two couples, obviously tourists out for a day, and felt a little pang. They weren't having much fun; that's for sure. All four of them alternately stared at each other and then out to the cove. A couple of buffleheads stuck their heads up for a moment and then dove below the surface again. There wasn't much going on.

"'Zis your bus?" asked the man. Joe nodded yes, that it was.

"'Zit go anywhere?"

"Oh, I was just giving it a little shakedown run." Joe felt he should explain further so he added, "...No traffic today so......"

"Well, how about a ride?" The other three looked surprised and the two women looked especially doubtful.

"Naw, naw, she's just......," Joe said, "....she's just... I'm still workin' on'er."

"Well, how about to S'Conset and back," the man said. "I'll giveya twenty bucks."

And that's how the whole thing started. Well, to be fair, it started with Joe's wish, with Monk's encouragement and then with a hand from the unknown. Something had made Joe buy the bus and something had made him paint it with glossy white paint, the color of the inside of a marshmallow. But now, its destiny was clear. Why not a tour bus? Or a shuttle? No, no: a tour bus. Definitely a tour bus.

Joe laughed at first but the daytrippers were ready to go. They pushed open the door and Joe held his hand up. "I took the seats out so I could paint it," he said a little defensively.

"No worries. We'll sit in back." The bench seat hadn't been disturbed so Joe got up, toweled off the dust and with a sweep of his hand, invited them to take a seat. In less than a minute, they were off.

The old bus bumped along the road and the "poonters" just smiled and smiled. Something was finally happening. They were seeing the island not, as they had planned from off shore but on a bus. It was fun.

Joe instinctively gave them a tour. He told them about St. Paul's, the local Episcopal church, and about the town information center. When they passed White's he beeped the horn to see if Doc Matthew was around but saw only a couple of puzzled faces peeking through the glass.

There's not much to see. An airport with a bright orange wind sock. A couple of old wrecks. Cottages many of which had seen better days.

When they got to S'conset Joe had pretty much exhausted all the information he had. When he told them there was a gift shop next to the library annex, they were less than enthralled. They were good sports, though and asked for fifteen minutes or so to walk around.

Then, he could take them back to the dock. Maybe Hunter would be back by then.

That left Joe time to think. He had so many things to do before the bus was ready to put out on the road. The odor of fresh paint was a distraction, too. Still, the bus was shaping up. Why not give tours?

Why not try weekends? Pull the bus up to the dock, stick out a sign and see if people would go for it. He wasn't much for math but he figured that he could probably do a one hour tour three times a day. Multiply that by twenty tourists at five bucks a head and it was...... Three hundred bucks! Three hundred bucks!

As promised, the four tourists returned and Joe drove them back to the dock. Hunter had wandered back and was his usual charming, relaxed self. He apologized and offered them half off for their inconvenience. They accepted and the world was once again safe from Communism. Joe turned the bus around and headed back to the house. He had a lot of thinking to do.

DIVINE INTERVENTION

The boys had failed and learned, failed and learned and failed and failed again. Now, they were going to take all they'd learned and apply it to an uncertain future. Their youth had faded and old age was dead ahead. Neither one had managed to save much so they would not be retiring to an oceanfront condo in Florida. No, they would be staying put, doing what they'd always done: getting by.

Tom had lost his leg, of course, but he had other health problems, too.

He had to watch his salt and avoided the doctor who nagged him about his heart. Joe still had both legs but years of working outdoors in all kinds of weather had turned his hands to hard, sensitive claws that ached in the cold.

A couple of nights after he'd given those tourists a ride on the bus, Joe got together with Tom and Monk. He had an idea and wanted to see what they thought of it. He'd made out a profit and loss statement to please Tom and he had a couple words of madness that would appeal to Monk. It could be fun and it could be money but he'd need their help.

"We run a tour bus," he said when they'd all settled down. "We sell tickets and run the bus around the island giving tours." When neither Tom nor Monk showed any interest, he laid it all out for them.

"Look: We've got a lot of people who come to the island for the day. They can't see the south shore or get to S'Conset without a lot of hassle. Ferry space for cars is limited and you have to book in advance. Tourists want to see the whole place but they got no way to get around."

Monk looked at Tom and then back to Joe. "Dat's true," he said.

"So we take'em on a tour. They do it all over the world, ya know."

"Sure, but what about guys who have taxis? What about them?" Tom asked. He was sensitive about being undermined; it had formed a consistent thread throughout his life.

"Nah, nah, we're not competition. We're not takin' any jobs away," answered Joe.

"Yeah, and why not?" asked Monk. Some of his best friends made their living shuttling people endlessly around the little island.

"Because we're not really going to do a tour." They were baffled now.

Was this one of Joe's wonderful fantasies? Were they living in a comic book? They were getting a bit old to waste their time…..

"We're not going to give a real tour," Joe continued excitedly. "We're going to give them a good time. We're going to go sightseeing but we're going to see new and different things. All kinds of things."

"What's dat mean, den?" asked Monk. "You bin communin' wi'da fairies again haveya?" He smiled wickedly at Joe, then pulled at his nose and snorted to suppress a laugh.

"Yeah. It's the fairies," Joe answered. "The little people".

"I don't get it," Tom interjected. "What are you trying to do?"

"I took this group of tourists out to S'conset the other day," Joe started, then went on to explain the route and the visit. "They paid me twenty bucks but it was unbelievably boring." Monk and Tom nodded almost involuntarily. They didn't want anyone to insult their island but yeah: it was a little boring.

"I showed them the Information Center and St. Paul's and a couple of other things…….the airport….. but that was about all there was to show." He stopped for a second then went on, "…It's a great island but it's just a little planetary accident, really."

Tom flashed them both a look of serious apprehension. "There's a diorama at the Information Center that shows the island will be gone in two thousand years. Washed away. Didja know that?" They both nodded, yes. They'd seen it a hundred times and it hurt each and every time they saw it. They did not want to be reminded of it.

"Yeah, and so will we." Joe said finally and he was in a position to know.

"We'll be gone before you know it. Gone. In the blink of an eye. Gone."

Both Monk and Tom looked at him to see if he was getting depressed and were a little nervous when instead of sadness, they saw a glint of crazy in his eyes. Had his string become unstrung again?

"No. We're going to give our own tour of the island....." But Monk cut him off.

"Okay, I see. We kin show dem some sand dunes and the beach, maybe walk'em down ta da Men's shop, royt?"

"No, no. That's not what I mean. I mean, we make the whole thing up."

Now, they were really puzzled. Maybe he really had jumped the tracks.

"I've made up a list of stops on the tour bus. It starts with downtown where we pick them up. We tell them about whaling and then as we work our way out of town we tell them about the whorehouses that used to stand on every block." Tom and Monk opened their eyes as wide as they could to make sure they were awake and not dreaming all this.

"....like the Gonorrhea Tavern where the firehouse now stands. The guys will get a kick out of it. Run by Gonorrhea Ida in honor of Angela's hellacious walleyed mother. We can tell how she could see two excited prospects at the same time coming from different directions." He paused for a minute, then added, "I want to get that friggin' dog into it, too. Maybe tell how he jumped on guys with whiskers or something."

They both laughed but they still couldn't believe what they were hearing.

"Then we go leisurely down to the Inn where we can really have some fun. That's the former site of a looney bin. Thank heavens the building is being put to better use now...."

That got a chuckle, too.

"Then we go to the beach where we sweep an instructive hand across the horizon and talk about the Battle of the Falklands and the fierce fights waged just offshore. How Prince Edward and all his friends fired bottle rockets at a bunch of thoroughly bewildered Argentinian cattlemen."

Soon, Tom and Monk were chiming in.

"I t'ink dot Churchill and Stalin met just offshore here, too, at the Yalta conference," said Monk.

"No, that was the Gadsden Purchase. I remember that from history class. Mr. French was very insistent that we know as much as possible about the Gadsden Purchase," said Tom.

"You're both wrong," said Joe firmly. "Roosevelt and Churchill met to sign the Potsdam Agreement with Stalin but he never showed up. He was out here vacationing with a young Navy lad. They took a room at the Inn and no one saw them for days. It was a huge scandal at the time."

"Well, he shoulda kept his hands to himself and done his job," Monk said, reminding them of the standard of propriety that should be observed at international peace conferences.

Tom looked concerned. "Shouldn't we get our facts straight before we make fools of ourselves? If it wasn't the Gadsden Purchase, then how did we end up with Louisiana? Nobody gave it to us; that's for sure."

Joe frowned too, as he tried to remember his history. "Well, we took it, sort of. The Mexicans and Pancho Villa came here for a little vacation and when they weren't looking we took the whole thing. That's why they were so mad at us."

"Yeah, Yeah. I t'ink day held the ferry up, too. Day couldn't even get back to Hyannis," said Monk. "Fawkin' ferries, what?" he added, disgusted.

"Okay, okay," said Joe, breaking in. "You get the idea. So let me tell you what I think about the money." He unrolled his P&L sheet and laid it on the table. For him, it was a master work. Keeping it simple, he made what he hoped would be a conservative guess at the number of riders he could lure on to the bus and then estimated the number of days each month they were likely to run. "Remember, rain is not a real consideration. It might even help, ya know?"

When he multiplied the number of rides against a modest figure like five bucks, he came up with a truly astonishing figure. He'd have to deduct for the bus and expenses but even when those costs were stated conservatively, they still ended up with a ridiculous profit. Huge!

"Well, you got the town to think about," said Tom who, after all, had dealt with the Truscotts and the Board of Health and who knew the resistance they'd face.

"What can they say?" asked Joe and let the question hang.

"Then there's the whole licensing issue," Tom went on. "We'd need the Chamber of Commerce.......\"

"We just need insurance," Joe answered and someone, something (One of his "voices"?) had made him contact the company. He rolled out the rates and they weren't that bad. Surprisingly affordable, actually. They'd need liability coverage for a "conveyance" but the bus maxxed out at forty passengers so it wasn't all that bad. The tour would probably cover all of a dozen miles and last an hour. Hour and a half, tops.

"D'jew ever see dose guys in Boston?" Monk asked. "Day give dis tour and all dat shit and den day stand at the bottom of the stairs w'dare hand out for a tip. Bastids!"

"Yup. More money," answered Joe with a broad smile. "Mo' money, Mo' money," he repeated in a nod to Spike Lee.

"Let's do it!" Tom exclaimed suddenly. "Let's do it. It's just crazy enough to work. I like it."

When he got home that night and put his head on the pillow, Joe couldn't help smiling to himself. A voice (His own?) said out loud, "I told you so. I told you. I said it would work and it's gonna work."

LEGAL CHALLENGES

Bureaucracies were created a long time ago by the Greek City State. Apparently, people needed direction. They needed to be herded and who better than the Greeks to herd their fellow man? They were born to it. It was part of growing up. You had to learn how to tend the flock or you lost your place in the family or worse yet, your spot at the dinner table.

So the Greeks got together and cast lots. The "leader" would be the guy who won. It didn't work out. Sometimes, Charlie Hustle would win and sometimes it was the guy who couldn't remember his name. Sometimes there were fights. Eventually, they decided on what we have come to know as "the vote". Leaders were elected.

Unfortunately, leaders soon learned that they couldn't do everything themselves so they put their friends on the job. That didn't work either because their friends were invariably the less fortunate, the less gifted, the cranks and nuts who couldn't get jobs and who couldn't do anything else but work for the city.

This led to something we now call "hiring practices". That meant no favoritism and no baggage. You had to qualify, fair and square. The result was a system that was a tribute to fairness, honesty and most of all, competence. Its spirit if not its success has informed every hamlet and village since those early days of hesitance and uncertainty. Rules were put on the books and they were observed with something like religious fealty.

That's what we've got today: We have "bureaucrats" and we have rules. The whole idea of serving a wayward and muddled community has been lost but bureaucrats have survived and rules have survived. It often feels as if these rules will only change when the last civil servant has died and the rules forgotten. That will likely never be. Until that time, though, we are stuck with the Truscotts of the world and the Bureaus of

This and the Departments of That. All are designed to frustrate; none are designed to help. Their sole purpose is to perpetuate themselves and ultimately provide a job for the next unfavored son of the last town functionary. They no longer learn to herd; they learn only to obstruct.

How would Joe get around the rules? How would he secure approval of a plan that would confound the earth-tethered minds of the town fathers? That could take some doing.

That's where Michaels came in, the scrappy lawyer who had helped him with his draft board status. If Michaels had been a middleweight, he would have been known for a three punch attack. A quick jab would be followed by two even quicker jabs that would stun most opponents. He'd then finish them off with uppercuts, never stopping until they hit the deck. He was a canny fighter, too, sizing up each opponent with meticulous care.

"These guys are tough because they don't move," he said to Joe when Joe went to see him. "It doesn't matter if they're men or women, either. They all use townie thinking which is composed in equal parts of self-satisfaction, herd mentality and resistance to change."

Joe shook his head. Maybe the whole idea would never work, after all.

"They're stagnant, too. Unimaginative. They think of time spent 'at work' as 'working' when actually all they're doing is gossiping or looking at the paper. The only guys in town who work are the garbage men." Joe could see this wasn't the first time Michaels had been frustrated by town officials.

"You're going to be facing the whole Truscott wall, too, a wall of willful ignorance."

"Wow! He didn't like them much," Joe thought. "So what do I do?"

Michaels was wearing a baseball cap in the office for and pulled it down over his eyes. "You've got to baffle'em with bullshit. You've got to sound more official, more traditional, more technical than they do." He paused for a second and then said dismissively, "I'll work something up and get back to you."

Joe left the office afraid that his fears would play out. He'd be handcuffed by the old-timers and his application for a "public conveyance" stopped before it even got started. He winced when he thought of the numbers. He'd already sunk most of his money into the bus; he didn't want it to end up as the neighborhood chicken coop.

That night, Joe had a visit from Mrs. Crisp. He wasn't sure later whether it was a dream or the wishful moment just before he fell asleep but he remembered it as clearly as if it actually happened. She smiled her tender smile and said simply, "Don't worry. It's all going to work out fine." The bus, she meant. At least he hoped she meant the bus.

A couple days later he returned to Michaels's office and scanned the business plan he'd composed for the bus. Michaels watched him as he muttered a, "Whaaaaat?" here and an "Are you kidding?" there, voicing his amazement at each paragraph.

First of all, a broad statement of intent declared the many benefits such a conveyance would bestow on the community. People could get around. Businesses would thrive. Christ would return to planet earth.

It then went on to tell about the pride Joe and his family had always felt in their little island. Joe loved it. Then, and quite suddenly, it veered into a paean to education and to the importance that each and every tourist, "...nay, every citizen of this storied isle...." should be acquainted with its place in history. It couldn't have been better if Mrs. Crisp had penned it herself.

"What a lot of magnificent bullshit!" Joe said in amazement. "It's terrific!" Michaels just smiled, graciously accepting the praise.

"But will they believe it?" Joe asked. "They won't believe all this baloney, will they?"

"You haven't read the end of it. There are two parts. The first one they won't read. It's all about the tour being "'fantastic'."

Joe nodded his head, listening hard. "Well, that covers a lot of territory."

"If you notice, I've sprinkled stuff like 'fantastic trip' and 'not to be believed' throughout whole piece." Again, Joe nodded gravely. "Those phrases are usually what we call 'puffing' or 'exaggeration' but in this case they are meant to be taken literally. The tour is definitely 'not to be believed.'" Joe was catching on.

"Then, you'll see how you've praised all of the town officials and their tireless efforts to elevate and promote the place. If I wasn't so sure that it works, I'd be ashamed of myself." Michaels sat back, crossed his arms across his chest and glowed with satisfaction.

Joe skipped to the end and it read like a eulogy. Or, "Home, Home on the Range". Not a discouraging word, not one negative. It just heaped praise upon kudo, kudo upon accolade. Perfect, perfect crap.

"Wow!" he said, finally. "Phew!"

"I always wanted to write fiction...," confessed Michaels, "...and this is as close as I'll ever get. Good though, huh?"

"Wow!" was all Joe could say. Just, "Wow!"

Michaels leaned forward again and picked up the document. "Now, you've got to append this statement to your application so they get to see it before the actual board session. Otherwise, they won't read it or they'll just skim it. If they read this all the way to the bottom and they see how great they are, you've got a pretty good chance."

So Joe brought multiple copies to town hall and got his date. When he went for approval, he faced the three members of the board, seated at a long, four by eight table, much like a panel discussion. He faced them alone, the feeble supplicant. His mind veered off toward thoughts of Richard III and the likelihood that he'd end up in the tower to await execution. Somehow, he managed to smile.

Two of the board members were Truscotts and the third was new to the island meaning that she was only second or third generation. She wanted to please the Truscotts so, yeah: she'd do what they said.

Steve Truscott Blake pushed back his glasses and stared down at Joe as if he had brought a dead haddock to the table instead of an application. After taking a long, long minute, he leaned forward and asked imperiously, "Will you have a fire extinguisher on board?" They let him ride on the back of the hook and ladder now and then so it was a big priority for him. When El nodded that one was placed within easy reach of the driver, the commissioner sat back satisfied he'd done his job.

Harold T. (For "Truscott") Barber wanted to know if it would pass by his house ("No!") and if it would be parked anywhere near the post office. "People need those spaces," he said with real force. He always seemed full of rage and this was no exception. Joe would give no offense.

Barber was quickly assured that the bus would only be parked at Nobadeer and then briefly, of course, at each of its stops. Joe pointed to several big blue stars on a large map of the island and quickly dismissed any possible threat to parking or Mr. Barber's privacy. He was talking but his mind still wandered as it did every time he saw a map of the island: Isn't it funny how much it looks like a boomerang?

Both sat back, content in the knowledge that they'd done their job.

Miss Cataldo, the third member, couldn't stop worrying whether or not she'd fed her cat and just wanted to go home. She had to say something, so she said noncommittally, "Well, you've certainly done your homework." And left it at that.

Three days later, Joe had his approval. Once again, to show they'd actually done something, they granted him a license for public conveyance with two conditions, ".....that the aforesaid applicant shall operate the vehicle within the hours of 9:00 a.m. and 6:00 p.m., and that the vehicle shall be properly insured." They failed to say anything about the tour itself or the information provided to its patrons. It proved to be a loophole they could literally drive a bus straight through.

CAPTAIN AHAB AND THE BATTLESHIP POTEMKIN

"I think we have to mention the Sicilian Fraternal Organization, the Society of the Triple Crown," said Tom, hoisting a glass of iced tea.

"Nah, too ethnic," Monk put in and then immediately contradicted himself. "Mebbe 'The Hibernian Gladiators'. That'd be better. Caesar never got to Oyrlin', ya know."

"...And don't forget Captain Blood," Joe said, coming out of his chair. "Who's gonna look after his legacy if we don't?"

They had a lot of ideas. Too many ideas. Louise had come home for a visit and was dazzled as one inspiration tumbled over another. So far, they had agreed on only one thing: They had to script the trip. They had between six and ten stops to make along the way and had timed it at an hour. Add the patter and it was an hour and a half.

"We gotta plan on three trips a day, I think," Joe had said. He had the clearest vision of the tour but the others were getting excited, too. Monk was on fire and Tom was quietly percolating along, tossing out ideas of his own.

Louise finally chipped in: "Just make up your own," she said. "This tour doesn't have to be the same each time. It doesn't even have to be the same each day. You can do what you want."

That pretty much said it. They just nodded and smiled, their minds alive to the anarchy of it all. Monk could give his tour; Joe could give his own tour and Tom could do what he wanted to do, too. Once they had sorted that out, they just threw ideas into the box. Nothing was discarded; it was all kept for future looks.

They set the box aside for additional ideas, then addressed promotion, scheduling and work assignments. Monk rose later than the rest of them so he could take the later rides while Tom and Joe would split up the early ones. Tom even suggested that Janey's taffy be available for purchase at a dollar off or something. They were already headed into merchandising.

They'd try a weekday for their initial run. Joe could take the bus out with Tom and Monk riding along as observers. He was pretty excited but he was anxious about it, too so he tried to relax and visualize the tour. He even looked for advice. Rolling up a little smoke, he sat outside the night before and talked to Mrs. Crisp. "Maybe it won't work," he said. "Maybe this is really stupid and I'm just going to fail the same way I've failed at everything else." She assured him that he wouldn't or at least he thought she did. Maybe it just helped to speak his fears out loud.

Tom had suggested using crib sheets so he dipped into the box of ideas and pulled out a handful. As he read through the notes he was surprised at the range of suggestions. Inspired lunacy, he thought. "It just might work."

The next day was a beautiful Thursday, full of fall colors and fresh air.

The sun's angle was low, too, adding an extra sparkle to the sea. You felt good just walking around in your pants.

Joe pulled the bus up next to the ramp where the ferry would disgorge its passengers and cars and waited for the 2:00 ferry to show. Tom and Monk were mostly silent, sitting on a bench but Joe was nervous. He walked around the bus a dozen times admiring the stunning paint job and the newish or newly repaired seats. The bus had been given a thorough cleaning. All of the dents and rust had been repaired and painted. Even the bumpers had been sandblasted, primed and repainted. Bartlett's had given its final approval to the drive train. Moby Dick was ready to accept the hordes.

At first, only a few tourists came off the ferry. A dozen locals came out quickly, too. As the cars began to exit, though, more and more tourists piled out along with the locals. The bus caught their eye. Some, had business to do but others were curious and gave it a good hard look. A family of five, looking dazed, asked if he had a bathroom on board. He didn't.

Three couples finally stopped. They were visiting from Wisconsin, they told him proudly, "..The Cheese State...". They asked him about the tour and while Joe was explaining it a very large man approached followed by a very heavy, very dowdy middle-aged woman. "Is this tour in German?" he asked. It made Joe wonder just what he'd gotten himself into.

"No, I'm sorry," Joe said sadly.

"It's only that my wife does not have very good English." Joe frowned and shook his head: Nope.

"Perhaps I can translate for her," the man continued and helped his wife up the steps. That seemed to be all the cheeseheads needed and they, too, climbed aboard.

Soon, three other couples approached them along with four children ranging from seven to fourteen. They gave the bus a once over and asked about the tour. Joe had a map handy and showed how it would first go to Jettie's Beach and then make a circuit of the island, stopping at points of interest. They huddled up and then they, too, climbed on board. Joe was losing track but he had almost twenty people already. Holy Mackerel!

Tom and Monk went inside and assisted the paying customers while Joe waited for any stragglers who might wander by. Sure enough, four kids, college kids, hopped on board just for a goof. They went directly to the back of the bus where they could all sit together and raise Hell. Joe's mind was reeling. Even with a couple of bucks off for the kids, he'd be pulling in a cool hundred bucks. This could work!

After a few more minutes, Joe jumped behind the wheel and read a disclaimer notice to the passengers. Michaels had insisted that he do so to prevent problems in the future. Basically, they were warned against everything. They were allowed to pray to God for a blessing on their eternal souls but that was it.

"You can not touch anything. You cannot say anything. If you are injured in a traffic accident you can not sue without first posting a bond.

If you fall in a hole you are on your own and the conveyancer (ie, Moby Dick) and its employees are not responsible."

Everything was covered unless, of course, Joe physically assaulted someone. Even then, if he had a good reason to do it, simple assault was still covered under the waiver. No one paid attention; they just stared out the windows.

Having started well, Joe launched into a brief discussion of the dock.

Creeping slowly out of his parking spot, Joe declared that, "Countless feet have trod these narrow streets in search of vast riches, new lands and, of course the great white whale." He glanced in the rear view mirror and everyone was settling in. The German was muttering to his wife. The college kids were pantomiming oral sex to a group of other kids, who seized their groins and shouted obscenities in return.

"The first whalers came from this area, New Bedford, Fall River and surrounding towns. They were tough men, given to strong language and even stronger ales." He checked again and the men were nodding appreciatively. "Imagine yourself here those many years ago. There were terrible risks at sea but there were rewards, too. Treasure beyond imagining and glorious adventures awaited you."

The kids were now punching each other and their parents were looking anxious. "A boy shipped out at eleven back in those days and served the crew as cabin boy. They were worked hard and beaten often. If they didn't satisfy the crew and the captain, they'd be thrown overboard or cast adrift on a desert island." The younger kids became a bit more quiet. One or two were getting nervous and looked for signs of comfort from their folks.

"Some of the cabin boys rose to become captains but the ones who were cast adrift were forced to live out their lives on filthy, rat-infested islands where the only thing to eat was sea weed and slugs." The kids were all looking a little green now, and a lot less restless.

By this time, he had reached Jettie's beach and the usual flock of sea gulls had settled on the fence. Dozens of late season bathers were still venturing into the water but it was turning cold and no one went in too deep.

"Captain Blood was one famous eighteenth century captain who made his home directly across the street there, next to the old Inn. It was said that for many years the Inn was a brothel. Captain Blood got both his first taste of romance and his first dose of penicillin right there. He was fourteen." Confusion from the kids and suppressed laughter from the adults.

"Yes, Captain Blood was a murderous brute of a man who refused to tolerate even the slightest impropriety. He terrorized the crew. He once threw a man overboard for leaving the bathroom door open while he was taking a pee." They all looked aghast, the boys particularly.

"And it didn't stop there. He would throw you into the brig and put you on bread and water for the slightest offense. If you left the table without saying, 'Excuse me!', he'd slap you in irons and leave you to rot in the hold. He was merciless but he had the best behaved crew to ever roam the seven seas." Mothers, particularly, smiled their approval. "People in distant lands sometimes invited them to their homes just because his crew members possessed such wonderful manners."

Monk had been sitting directly behind Joe, taking it in. Each of Joe's assertions was seconded with muffled approval or a nod. Upon hearing of Captain Blood's fondness for pea soup, Monk muttered, "Oh yah. He was a great one for da pea soup; dat's for shore. Dat and pig's brains, ya know. He lawved nothin' better dan dat pea soup and some pig's brains on the side over dare."

By this time they had pulled away from the beach and were headed west toward Madaket. Along the way, Joe told them of some more recent events that had formed a part of the island's history.

"Few people know that Nantucket was a key port for rum running during prohibition. It's always enjoyed a reputation as a vacation spot but during the twenties it was home to millions of gangsters who shipped vast amounts of illegal Courvoisier and Johnny Walker Black to every city in the country. Miami! New York! Wichita!"

The German was doubtful. "How ken they ship to Wichita?" he asked.

"I am a professor of geography from the University of Dusseldorf and I know that Wichita is not on the Atlantic Ocean. It's not on any ocean so far as I know."

"Of course, you're right," Joe agreed. "It's nowhere near the ocean. But these rumrunners transferred their booze to container trucks and drove them out there on the interstate."

Everyone but the German nodded their heads. Amazing!

"No. No. Nein!" exclaimed the German loudly. "There was not a system of interstate highways in America until the fifties."

"Right again," Joe smiled. "I'm talking about the secret interstate. The one run by the midwestern people, the quiet and humble people from the midwest. People from Ohio and Nebraska. Most of them Native Americans."

Monk nodded his head. "No tolls, either," he said. "No tolls".

Joe broke in, saying, "Yeah. That's really not well known and right here, right near Madaket was where it all happened." Everyone craned his neck hoping that a mobster would appear among the dunes clutching either a tommy gun or a case of Bacardi.

When they made the turn at Madaket and headed east toward Nobadeer, Joe slowed down to show off his handiwork. He was proud of both houses and planned to make them a feature on the tour.

"These two homes were once one home, owned by two sisters but the two sisters could not get along. They fought all the time. Over the years they grew further and further apart. They hated each other so much that they constantly threw insults back and forth.

"'I was always Mom's favorite,' Eva would say and Leila would throw a towel at her. 'No you weren't. I was always Mom's favorite.'"

That went on for thirty years until they grew very old and very gray. By that time, they couldn't walk so they were stuck together all day in the same two rooms, the TV room and the cabana. Finally, they couldn't stand it any more and split the house in two. They put one half on logs and rolled it as you see, some thirty feet from the other half. They never spoke to each other again." The poonters Ooohed and Aaahed.

Joe paused for effect and added, "You can see their two graves in the back there. Two sisters who couldn't get along. Sad story. Sad story."

No one noticed that Joe's window was open and that he was smoking a kind of home made cigarette.

As he passed the dunes back to town he made another revelation. "It is commonly thought that the Wright brothers' first flight was down south in Kitty Hawk…..." Heads nodded knowingly. "….But their first flight was actually over here on the right." He paused to allow them time to gaze appreciatively out the window at the endless rolling hills of sand. He explained the rationale behind this deception. "….That was for security reasons. They didn't want anyone to know their secrets." Wow!

By the time the little bus reached S'conset, the party was gravely silent.

They listened carefully to every word, discovering the truth about the island, much of which they'd never suspected before. When they learned that the Potsdam conference had been held aboard a Chris Craft named the "Potsdam" and not in Potsdam itself, their jaws dropped. That little boat, with sleeping accommodations for four, had been moored just off S'conset and it had been a bumpy meeting in more ways than one.

"Yes, Churchill and Stalin had spoken through clenched teeth but that was because neither one could stand the pitching and rolling of that little boat. They stared at each other, bilious, refusing to spew until the other got up and left. Truman had looked on in disbelief; his granddaughter was less prone to seasickness than those two, supposedly two of the world's great leaders."

But that was just the beginning at S'conset. More was to come. The small cottage at the end of Truscott Lane looked undistinguished but three hundred years earlier it was the birthplace of Thomas Jefferson, the fourth or fifth president of the United States. Yes, his historic mansion Monticello was in Virginia but his roots were in S'conset.

"T. J." (as he was known to his friends) had learned to fish and spent many happy hours digging for clams just offshore. "He did it with his toes." The name "Monticello" was actually a contraction of two words, "Mountain" and "Jello", his favorite dessert. "He'd eat "Mountains" of it and, as you might know, Jello was discovered right here in Nantucket. It's made out of the goo you get when you boil down a barrel of fish bones."

As they made the long trip back to town from S'conset, Joe looked in the rear view mirror and saw a very subdued audience. They could have been star gazers staring into the sun. He lifted his left foot off the floor and placing it jauntily against the dash, launched into his final revelation of the day.

"The ancient and revered sport of Sumo wrestling actually got its start here at Wauwinet. Two very large men were out for a walk when they came upon a flounder that had washed up on the beach. Each claimed it as his own. A fight ensued but only after they agreed they would remove their shirts. They fought for nearly an hour until the smaller, younger man prevailed." Eyes widened in the mirror, unable to believe this remarkable tale. "The phrase 'Keep your shirt on!' actually comes from that encounter. If you took your shirt off, it was a challenge because no one in those straitened times would risk soiling much less damaging a shirt."

When a few of the older kids looked doubtful, Joe continued, "The Japanese were the first ones to wrestle without trousers. Why they decided to do that is unknown but as you know, they didn't adopt Western dress until the fifties."

By the time that first group of riders was dropped back at the dock, their heads were reeling. Some were astonished, some were bewildered and the rest were heartily ashamed of themselves. To think that they'd spent all that time in school and learned nothing. Not one of them had known of Frank Nitti's grip on the island during Prohibition and they were shocked to hear how many of his rivals were now "sleeping with the fishes" just offshore.

They all thanked Joe as they disembarked and some of them even stuck a few bucks in his hand. At the end of the day he reached into his pocket and was amazed to find twenty dollars there. Someone had even slipped him a five!

Both Tom and Monk congratulated Joe. Their maiden voyage had been an unqualified success. Their minds were buzzing, though. Just what would they do when it was their turn? Monk already had a dress in mind, something bright and red, studded with peach colored sequins that would reflect the light. He couldn't wait. He had a pair of crimson pumps to complete the ensemble, too. Stunning!

Tom had an idea, as well. He would stick to nautical themes. He was a big Civil War buff so he was carefully framing his account of the engagement between the Kearsarge and the blockade running Alabama.

History had long held that the Kearsarge called out the Alabama from its berth in Cherbourg but locals knew the real story and he would make it his job to inform the rest of the world.

He was also looking forward to a lively rendering of the battles of Midway and the Coral Sea. Those men had been outfitted at the Nantucket Naval Yard now, sadly, defunct. A factory stood where the Yard had launched so many American vessels and those halcyon days were gone. The factory that took its place made pieces for Monopoly boards—little hats and thimbles that were a staple in every household from here to Guadalcanal. He'd take them by Feldstein's and give them a look.

DICK

Americans will not be happy until they've reduced every possible noun to one syllable. Everything gets a nickname. No one knows why but this compulsion pervades every corner of the land. If your favorite beer is Budweiser, you order a "Bud". If you prefer soft drinks, it's a "Coke". If your name is "Reginald B. Stringcheese", it will be reduced to "Reg" or "String". So it is with everything we own, with everything we touch. And so it was with the bus.

"Dick" became the bus's nickname and "Dick" was on everyone's lips. It didn't take a week before people were lining up, waiting for the bus to arrive. The boys learned to go with the seasons, too. They'd do a tour with a Halloween theme at the end of the month and during Proid Week they'd dress up like financial planners. They spoke with touching affection of the warm bond they shared with their sister island, too, the Isle of Lesbos out there in the Aegean Sea. Or the Caspian Sea. No one bothered to look it up.

Word got out fast about the "small print" on the brochure and the disclaimer. When they said it was a "fantastic trip", that's exactly what they meant. It was entertainment, something made up out of sea foam and sewage. It wasn't real; it was a fantasy tour. When people took offense at having their home described as "a prominent part of the old red light district", they were shown the fine print. It was fantastic; that's all. If an anxious stranger mistakenly thought that one of the homes was still part of the old district, he should be shooed away and told to go home.

Three tours a day were not enough. By the time they had cleared all of the candy corn and Kit Kats from Halloween, they were booming. November was no longer the end of the season. They were booking four tours daily straight through Thanksgiving and beyond. Take a break for a couple of months and then start right up again.

"But they can't do this!" they heard over and over again. The old heads, particularly, were shaking with rage. "This island is sacred ground and they're defiling it." There was so much uproar that the licensing board was forced to reconvene. They listened to complaints and then turned to the boys. This was outrageous. It can't go on.

The boys felt they were on solid ground but as anyone knows who has dealt with committees, it's better to adopt Louise's age old wisdom: "Wave, smile and keep moving." Tom and Monk were afraid they'd mess up so Joe was designated to reply.

"Our tours are just meant to entertain. They're not meant to be history lessons and they're not meant to give much information about the island. They're meant to be fun. You have only to talk to our visitors and they will tell you. They all love Dick. They adore it. They can't get enough of it. Dick is terrific. And, I might add, we would all do a lot better if we got more Dick." Miss Cataldo nodded solemnly, secretly hoping she'd get some, too.

"If you close us down you'll have to close down Disney Land and Dolly World." No one would even think of doing that, ever. Both Disney and Dolly Parton were beloved. Beloved!

Dick was an attraction; there was no arguing that. People now called ahead and came to the island just for the tour. They would then grab something to eat, shop for Christmas and maybe even book a night's stay. Retailers were rising in support of Dick. Dick was good for business. Even some of the locals tried the tour. They'd usually sniff a little disapprovingly at first but then soften as the familiar ride over their little island unfolded. Everyone had fun; everyone got in on the joke.

Soon, they hooked up with retail outlets like White's. Doc Matthew was totally on board. He took pride in owning an historic establishment that was known one day as a stop on the Underground Railroad and on the next as the point of departure for Shackleton's assault on Antarctica. If they wanted to park while the passengers picked up some beach plum jelly or a box of chocolates, that was okay, too.

The boys had failed and learned. They had failed and failed again. But they had learned a lot along the way. They learned that even if you fail, the important thing was that you try. They learned that early on from Doc Matthew. They also learned that you could make a lot of money selling things that were completely useless. You just had to sell a lot of them. They learned that from John Nicholas.

They would never be rich; far from it. But all three would enjoy themselves and make enough money to ease the pressures of their later years. They had seen what happened when you overreach yourself and they had seen what happened when you underreach yourself. All three now felt confident that they were on the right track. They'd have fun and still pay the bills. All that, they learned slowly. They were fortunate, though, to have finally, finally figured it out: life.

They still had to keep an ear to the ground. They had to keep on learning. If they stuck with one idea or refused to acknowledge a blunder, they were doomed. They learned that from Alexandra Windsor who had left their enchanted isle for the big city—Nome—where she convinced herself she'd always been destined to thrive. She set up a boutique selling silky lingerie and quickly went under again. Fashion, it seems, is less important than function in the northern climes.

Hunter had taught them something, too, albeit accidentally. He was a natural at goofing off, at just being himself. He truly liked nothing better than messin' around in boats. He never really got to be much of a sailor; he just liked banging around in them. He even enjoyed the endless maintenance, oiling the teak and checking the lines. His sails were always in perfect trim because he inspected them weekly for loose threads or the occasional tear. It was a small world but even the days full of drudgery held special moments for him, moments of pure joy.

And finally, the boys learned about communing with the spirit world. They knew that few of their ideas had originated on earth. Earthbound folks think earthbound thoughts. People have too many burdens to think of something new. They're too busy dealing with the all-too-familiar problems of making a living and paying the bills. Getting the kids through school and out of their hair.

They'd been coached, too, by their better angels. Sometimes it had been obvious and sometimes they only realized it later. Tom, Joe and Monk had all been touched from beyond the veil at some point, Joe most of all. He felt the presence of his parents daily. They would invade his thoughts and often nudge him gently back on track.

Mostly, he thought of Mrs. Crisp. His feelings for her had never changed. Ever since the time he was attacked by her dog, thrown to the ground and then invited inside, she had been his crush. His heart was warmed whenever she came to mind. She was still a big help, too. She led him away from constant errors and foolishness; she still cared for him and watched over his every move. And he knew that soon, very soon, they would get together and have a good laugh about Dick. It had all been her idea, all of it.

THE END

AFTERWORD

I hope the good people of Nantucket will forgive me for any errors I might have made about the island. Our family loves every inch of it and I wouldn't want to be disrespectful in any way. Nearly everything in the book is pure invention. I saw the story in my mind's eye when I was there in the nineties and then took a few decades to write it down.

I also hope no one takes offense at the names I've chosen. Most were just for fun. I used the names of friends for most of them. The avenging angel "Michaels" is both a friend and the name of one of our kids. "Doc" Mathew is the slightly altered name of a friend who has always been an avid swimmer. "White's" was a general store near D.C. where he grew up.

The whole idea of the book was to be, as Graham Greene has famously said, an "entertainment". Serious themes pop up once in a while but are there for the purpose of adding a little meat to the story. They're not there to promote a political or ideological agenda. The book is just a try at having some fun, something that's been in short supply for the past two years, the years of the Covid Pandemic.

Sterling E. Rowe
Marblehead
November 2021

THANKS

Over the years I've asked a number of folks, both professionals and friends, to take a crack at one of my drafts. It's always a lot to ask and I appreciate it their help. In the case of THE BUSTLES, I asked my childhood friend Bob Alberico from Glastonbury, Ct. to do a run through. He dragged Paul Pappalardo into the read and together they came up with some great changes. Their thoughts have improved the book and I hope have made it more enjoyable. I've always counted on Bob to tell me the plain, unvarnished truth even when I didn't like it and he delivered in spades. Grazie molto!

My wife Jane agreed completely with Bob and Paul so I reluctantly changed some names and they were right. Still failing and learning...

OTHER WORKS BY THE AUTHOR

NON-FICTION

<u>A CADDY'S LIFE</u>—Life as a caddy during the 1950's when boys were employed as caddies both by club members and by professionals who toured the country competing in local P.G.A. tournaments.

ESSAYS

<u>ANSWERS TO EVERYTHING</u>—The way to enchantment, enlightenment and the end. A helpful guide to life on earth and elsewhere.

<u>NEWS FROM THE LITTLE WORLD</u>—We often encounter extraordinary people and events but we overlook them. These essays celebrate the little world, the one we neglect, the one that provides the richness in our lives.

Made in the USA
Middletown, DE
13 February 2022